THE SUMMER
FLETCHER GREEL
LOVED ME

A Novel

Suzanne Kingsbury

SCRIBNER
New York   London   Toronto   Sydney   Singapore

SCRIBNER
1230 Avenue of the Americas
New York, NY 10020

SCRIBNER and design are trademarks of Macmillan Library Reference USA, Inc., used under license by Simon & Schuster, the publisher of this work. For information regarding special discounts for bulk purchases, please contact Simon & Schuster Special Sales at 1-800-456-6798 or *business@simonandschuster.com*

DESIGNED BY KYOKO WATANABE
Set in Bembo

Manufactured in the United States of America

1 3 5 7 9 10 8 6 4 2

Library of Congress Cataloging-in-Publication Data
Kingsbury, Suzanne.
The summer Fletcher Greel loved me : a novel / Suzanne Kingsbury.
p. cm.
1. Teenage girls—Fiction. 2. Mississippi—Fiction. I. Title.

PS3611.I63 S86 2002
813'.6—dc21   2001049775

ISBN 0-7432-2303-9

For my Uncle Tee
and
for Karen, his living memory

THE SUMMER
FLETCHER GREEL
LOVED ME

1

HALEY

Sometimes you can't say no to someone. I sit upright in bed in the middle of the night thinking this. It must have been a dream that made me do it, and when I lie back down I have to work to steady my breath. Outside there's the dull thud of an oak branch beating against the house in breeze. Thick, fogged light comes through my window, and if I squint, it looks like the leaves are floating ghosts. My digital reads 4:15.

The thought of Bo Dickens wakes me up like this some nights. During the day he is on my mind all the time, when I am driving to school or standing at Elsa's store with Daddy, eating lunch with Gwyneth or riding Daisy through the backwoods.

Before I was born, when Bo was just eighteen, he beat another man so bad his head swelled to the size of a pumpkin and he was left a vegetable the rest of his days. That man had raped a girl Bo once loved. Bo served jail time for it. I always think of that girl and wonder where she is now and what she must have felt like to know a man like Bo was that crazy for her. Who wouldn't want to be loved like that?

Bo is tan as a saddle, with gray-blue eyes that won't quit looking at you as if you are naked in front of him and he loves what he sees. He tells the funniest stories of any man at Elsa's store and is one of Daddy's very best friends. He has been named the finest horse trainer in Fresh County, maybe in the whole of Mississippi. And he is in love with me.

He wants me so bad, he says he can't help himself with what he does when he can't have me.

The first time he touched me was this past March, just three days after my sixteenth birthday, the night we buried the black man in our woods while Daddy lay passed out on the den couch.

After we did the burying, I was going up the porch steps and Bo reached for my waist, took two steps toward me and put his mouth on my neck. He kissed it long, like a last thing you do before you die that you don't ever want to forget. His breath was hot. Mine went still inside me.

You did a good thing tonight, little lady, he said into my ear. Your daddy won't remember a lot of it, that guy hit him good in the noggin. We're not going to bother your daddy about it, either. Let's let bygones be bygones, there's no use sweating something you can't change. I'll tell him I've taken care of it, and if you need a person to talk to, you talk to me.

He touched my bottom. Now go on up, he said. Get some sleep before your daddy wakes up.

From behind the screen door, I watched his taillights retreat down the street and take a left onto Highway 12. The yard was misted with the hazy light of first dawn.

In the den, Bo had cleaned up the blood and pulled the rug toward the rocker so it hid the place where the black man had been. Daddy was sprawled across the couch with his arms slung in back of his head and his mouth open. His forehead was growing a knot the size of a pecan. I put my hand on his heart. It beat steady against my palm. Even though Daddy didn't move, I could tell by how hard his heart pounded that he was going to be all right.

Pouring blood and torn fists and swelled eyes, pistol shots and knife fights and whiskey brawls are normal as breathing to Daddy and his friends. But this was the first time I'd been privy to it and that night a kind of patient thrill entered me. It was a feeling I had finally arrived.

The next day Bo came to me while I was in the back tack room. He stood next to me and asked me how school was and would I like to ride his new stud. He didn't say word one about the night before. I shook while I hung the saddles and tried to keep my voice steady when I answered his questions. And then he touched me. It was just a small touch on my elbow. When I turned, his mouth was on mine. He kissed me like he was hungry. All of me went watery with it. He said, Shh, Haley. And then I was kissing him back and my hands were in his hair. I was being held by a man, not a fumbling boy, and he was saying, Haley Ellyson, sweet Jesus, I want you. I can't stop. Don't make me stop.

I didn't.

You couldn't have stopped it better than lightning finding metal in a field. It was the steam off Daisy's body and the smell of hay and the sound of bats flapping in the rafters and the quiet of the stables, Bo's black hair, and the way he said my name. It was the secret we had of the body in the woods and the way he'd trusted me with it.

After that I waited anxious for those moments when I could see Bo, when we would catch eyes in the dust and work of the stables and the air would go wiry between us. An untamed pulling passed through me every time. Life took on a kind of heightened feeling in want for his attention. What I don't understand is why he comes to me sometimes and not others. I hate the waiting and the wondering when he will decide to find me in the stables and ask me into the private of his truck cab or to some other place he knows of where we can be alone.

Before Bo touched me I was going out with boys who were cigarette-smoking, whiskey-drinking replicas of their daddies. They told me they loved me and some were fixing to marry me after school. All those boys ever do is fish on Saturdays and skip church on Sundays. They love only their mammas' cooking, talk bad on blacks and dirty on women, and think being free is having their own pickups and getting drunk on Old Charter Road. Their whole world is Houser Banks, Mississippi. More than one of them has been chased off our land by Daddy's shotgun firing in the air because they took me in later than curfew or tried to kiss me on the front porch while he was watching from the window. They are as afraid of my daddy as I am of winding up married to one of them.

I don't want to go back to those boys, but lately I have come to feel like Bo isn't a choice for me, he is a shaking need. It is a feeling people must have who crave liquor or cigarettes.

My sheets are damp with sweat, and I pull them back and get out, wrap the top sheet around me and kneel at my closet. I keep a chest in there I bought from a dead lady's house when her family had a tag sale. When I feel lonesome, I get it out and touch the things in it. It is like finding another Haley sitting in a lone, secret place. In it I have put the words of songs I wrote down because they were beautiful enough to make me cry and butterfly wings and bird feathers and scraps of notes people threw away that I picked up so I could copy the handwriting. There's a stack of letters Mamma has sent me over the years and the sapphire she gave me before she left, which is the first thing I'll save if the house ever burns in fire. On the bottom is Frey Little's photo album Gypsy let me have when he died. I believe he and I would have been wild in love if I had been born in his time. Sometimes I study his pictures and speak to him in my mind.

When I have looked long enough, I hide the chest under clothes and blankets on my closet floor and get up to dress by the first coming of dawn light. My door makes a whining sound as I open it. Every time Gwyneth stays here, she sleeps to Crystal Gale singing *Don't It Make My Brown Eyes Blue* over and again on the forty-five record player Daddy has set up in his room for her. It sounds faintly when I pass his door. I go slow on my way down the stairs because they creak if you step too heavily.

Under the sink in the kitchen, we keep a big flashlight in case the electricity quits. I go out the back sliders with it and circle the house until I come to the old mess of cypress roots. Then I follow a faint animal trail to the east of the house. The woods are alive with tree frogs and insects and the hollow, quick sound of woodpeckers. Dew covers everything, and moist May heat films my body. The sky is a faint pink and the moon's fading to the texture of cloud. I only turn the flashlight on when the day's light is hidden by straps of kudzu and the shadows of catalpa trees grown huge.

Once I lose the way and then find it again by the stumped live oak, just north of the river, where saplings and cedars grow along the sloped bank. On that crest of hill I see the freshly placed pile of dirt and leaves, built there as a hidden grave.

When Bo did the burying, he told me, Next hunting season won't find this, all of it'll be grown over. Anyway, hounds want new meat, not the bones of some old body. He was breathing hard and cording string, shoving the body from its metal carrier and dumping it on the ground.

I get on my knees and look at the copper-colored rocks and the thrusting of pebbles, the round, knotted branches and rotted twigs. Layers of leaves and sticks and red mud are wet from night.

That man's body is buried under four feet of mud and wood scrapings, so the smell is only a faint, rancid one of clumped and dirty clothes laying around too long.

A black man's buried there and the only two people who know about it in this whole world are me and Bo.

The dizziness comes quick as storm, and my mouth goes dry. I try to spit twice and breathe as deep as I can. When I stand up and back away, the leaves and twigs swirl before me and black outlines everything like it will when you walk inside from a strong sun. In that half blindness I think I can see the short stub of his arm straight out from his grave like a limbed weapon.

Turning quickly, I head back to the path, swallowing gulps of air while I go. Crawling vines and Virginia creeper threaten to trip me. I am running too fast to keep an eye out for coiled snakes. My legs feel like pieces of rubber and my chest can't keep my breath, so a choking, hoarse sound comes out me. I like the scared, though; it's the reason I want to visit this place. The going makes me feel like the secret is part mine, to fool with however I want to.

By the time I get back to my house the sky is opening up to purple morning, and the sun is just putting its nose over the woods. I wait inside the sliders until my breath calms, then climb the stairs quiet as I can. After passing Daddy's door, I step across the hall so I can look at myself in the medicine cabinet mirror.

My face looks different nowadays. I can't tell if it's my eyes or my mouth or what, but mostly it is something you couldn't ever name. A kind of mystery. Bo is right, it is the things that happen to you that no one else knows about that make you important in life. When you hold secrets, people can somehow sense it, and they respect you more because of it.

I turn off the light and go into my room. White streaks of early morning lie across the bedcovers. Climbing onto my bed, I let the tired burn my eyelids and leak out my body.

Before I fall asleep, I think of how the house smells different now. It is deeper than sweat. Daddy may never say if he smelled such a thing and Gwyn probably wouldn't notice. But I know what the house is doing. It is holding the memory of death, and since it can't speak, it will tell in some other way.

2

FLETCHER

Pops drives the Lincoln six hours south from Connecticut to Virginia through blasted rock, tollbooths and wheat-colored highway brush. I sleep and try to kill the ugly hangover hitting me behind my eyes. When I'm awake, I keep my eyes closed to escape that awkward quiet between us.

At four in the afternoon, we stop at a roadside diner with brown paneling, gum-ball machines and a veloured picture of Elvis on the wall. The waitress's name tag says *Sue* on it. She bites the eraser on her pencil and taps it against her thigh faster than a two-beat time.

Pops puts his finger on the picture of the ham platter. What's in this jamboree?

Sue pulls a piece of her straw-colored hair through her mouth and recites the ingredients.

I'll have the roast beef, Pops says.

I tell her to make that two.

She goes away with a hip shaking and both of us trying not to look.

There's a guy a table away from us eating a pancake-and-sausage breakfast. He's bald as a waxed baseball. When he catches me looking at him, he stills his knife and fork. I look away.

Pops pulls his shirtsleeves up half an inch. Not so bad a place, is it? He looks at the bald man and then quickly back at me.

No sir, I tell him.

He picks up his fork and fingers it. You feel any different? he asks.

No sir, I tell him. Not yet.

Yes, well. It takes time.

He puts the fork down and straightens the knife beside it. We sit in silence.

Sue flips a dishrag at the cook and tells him, Henry, you say that one more time I'm gonna bust you with a hot spatula, leave you sterile as a baby boy.

The cook laughs. One gold tooth shines in the overhead lights.

Pops shifts in his seat and says, I thought your class speaker was very good. She had a strong voice.

Yes, she did, I tell him.

On my right wrist there's an imprint from the cuff links Pops bought me. I try to rub it smooth. Above us a fluorescent lamp mashes down its sick light and makes Pops's face look yellow. On one side of his mouth he's got a twitch that won't quit.

Ten minutes later, Sue puts down two plates of roast beef the color of tree bark and mashed potatoes sauced in butter and string beans well done to almost burnt. Pops stares at the food for quite some time, puts his napkin on his lap and picks up his fork. What's Francie Hall doing this summer? he asks me.

Going down to Cape May.

You think you'll see her? He wipes his mouth with his napkin before he starts eating. She's welcome in Houser Banks, if you want a visitor.

The beef is tough. I have to saw through it with the dull knife. No sir, I say, I probably won't see her, now that I'm all done. She's got a year left.

He watches me. Yes, he says, well . . . Then he forkfills a bunch of potatoes and commences eating them.

After we eat, I drive and Pops sleeps slumped over in the passenger's seat with his mouth rubbery against the window. He leaves spitted streak marks down it. I wait until he is asleep enough not to wake up, and then I put the radio on old rock stations he wouldn't care about listening to and drive ninety miles per hour to the Stones' *I Can't Get No Satisfaction* and Led Zeppelin's extended version of *Stairway to Heaven*. I glance at Pops. He looks sad and a little sick, slumped like that. It makes me think of him as an unremembering old man, and I try not to look again. Once in a while he shakes his head awake, then falls back to sleep.

At about seven that night, he comes all the way awake. His hair is matted on one side. He looks through the rearview mirror like we have a chase going on. I ease my foot from the accelerator. Police out this way, he tells me. He wipes his mouth with two fingers and says, I'm sure of it.

Yes sir, I nod, I been watching.

You want to stop for the night at the Cedar Inn, or you want to keep going? It's your call, son. He looks at his fingernails.

I stare at the road, remembering all the times we stayed at that inn. It has a wraparound porch and a leather-bound reservation book. As soon as we'd get there, my mom would pick up the silver spoon in the bowl of mints and offer me some. She always took her after-dinner cognac on the front porch. I don't think I could stand to be there without her.

I think I'd like to drive straight through, I tell him.

And so we do. It's moist heat once we get south past Virginia and into North Carolina. By the middle of the night we mostly share the road with truckers, wailing down the hills high on speed, mouthing off to their CBs.

When Pops drives, he sings *Sweet Georgia Brown* aloud to himself and opens his window wide so as not to fall asleep.

It isn't until six the next morning, after a bunch of convenience-mart urinals smelling of piss and puke, that we hit Alabama and turn into a filling station. A red-haired guy holds the pump with one hand and shades his eyes from the sun with the other. When I get out to stretch, he says, It's gonna be a hot one.

I know it, I tell him.

You been drivin long? he asks me.

Came straight down from Connecticut.

Shit, he says. That your old man?

I nod.

I could never drive that long with my old man, we'd wind up shootin each other. He's ornery. He thinks he's the only one in this whole world knows how to drive.

I gesture to Pops. He's real quiet, I tell him. We both are.

The guy smiles. He's got a chip on his front tooth. I ain't, he says. I'll talk your ears off, you let me. The gas gauge clicks and he pumps twice more. Twenty even, he tells me.

You want me to drive, I say to Pops when I get in, you just let me know.

You must be plenty tired, he tells me. You go on rest awhile, I'll be fine. He leans forward and switches on the radio. *Afternoon Delight* comes on. We start to pull out.

That gas attendant looked a little like Chuck Skelly, he says.

I tell him I thought the same thing.

I didn't see the Skellys at the ceremony Pops says.

He didn't graduate, I tell him.

My father checks the rearview mirror and looks back at the road. How's that? he asks. A red Mazda RX7 passes on our left and Pops inches onto the shoulder, frowning at the back of it.

He didn't make the grades.

Pops studies the side of my face with his hand on the top of the wheel. Didn't you start out in a lower grade than him?

Yes sir, I tell him.

He wipes the speedometer clean. What's Mr. Skelly do, is he in banking?

He's a VP at Chase.

Manhattan or—

New Haven.

Shaking his head, Pops says, He must be pretty mad.

On the right side of the highway, a blond girl is sitting on a fallen-down telephone pole in a yellow bathing suit, holding a cat. When we go by, she looks up at me and in that instant I can tell she's been crying. I crane my neck to look back at her. She's still watching. I look until we're too far away to meet eyes anymore.

I remember when you brought Chuck down to Houser Banks, Pops says. Quick as a whip. I thought he'd make a good attorney, way his mind works. Great sense of humor, too. Your mother got a real kick out of him.

He glances over at me. Resting his left elbow on the bottom of the driver's-side window, he rubs an inch on his forehead back and forth many times.

I close my eyes and try not to think about my mother. Instead I picture all those Saturdays I sat on the English building's roof with Chuck Skelly, smoking homegrown and trying to avoid the bird shit. From up there we had a plane's view of the campus. When it got dark, we'd sneak off in his Mustang and go to townie keg parties where the public school kids snorted cocaine off someone's mamma's coffee table and made out with drunk girls. I fall asleep thinking about the roof of that building we used to go to. I dream of falling and falling without ever landing.

When I wake up, we're turning onto Highway 12, and Pops is slowing down to fifty. A sign reads, *Welcome to Fresh County, Mississippi!* and then below it, *Houser Banks: 15 miles. Alfred: 30 miles.* We stop half a mile from the sign at a gas station next to a Winn-Dixie. When we come out of the car, the air is dense with heat and gas fumes.

Inside the store it's half cool. There's a cranky old air conditioner sitting in the window behind the cash, roaring like a broke motor. In front of it a blond woman presses a pointer finger to her tongue and shifts the pages of a magazine.

Hey there, she calls.

Ma'am, I say. I stare at the cooler of sodas against the far wall.

She licks her bottom lip and watches me. There's a door connecting the store to a garage that smells of grease and gasoline and oil. A jackhammer sounds out there, and the place rattles. The lady puts a hand on her hip, rolls her eyes and says, Can you kick that door shut, sugar? Those guys are making some racket in there.

I close it. She reaches up and gets a pack of Salems from the cigarette shelf above her, starts whacking the box on her palm. Where you boys fixin to go with your car full up with suitcases like that? she asks.

I finger an orange soda pop bottle on the metal rack. I'm home from boarding school, I tell her. Just graduated.

She puts the stem of a cigarette in her mouth, raises her eyebrows, flicks a lighter and inhales. Her fingernails are the same color as my soda. Well congratulations! she says. She pulls the word out like it is fourteen syllables. Class of '87, she says. I was the class of '77. Party hardy, rock and roll, drink a keg, smoke a bowl, sex is great, feels like heaven, cause we're the class of '77. She smiles wide. That your daddy? she asks, gesturing her cigarette toward Pops, who's walking across the parking lot. His shoulders are squared and his gold monogrammed belt buckle shines off the sun.

Yes ma'am, I say. I take the Sunkist from the refrigerator shelf and keep the door open for the cool coming out of it.

She watches my father, smokes her Salem. The air conditioner blows a triangle of her blouse collar and shows me the slope of her breast. She turns to look at me before I can look away and smiles with her eyes blinking slow. I look back at the freezer. I'm half hard and my face is hot.

Pops comes in. At the same time the door connected to the garage opens. The man standing there has brown curly hair that looks like a windstorm got it and tore it up and put it back on top of his scalp.

I fiddle with the top of the Sunkist and walk toward the register.

Sandy, you done closed this door on me again? he yells to her. He's got the small, mean eyes of a defensive animal.

Sandy glances around first at me and then at Pops, who clears his throat and takes out his billfold.

The man opens the door wider. Did you? he asks, wiping his hands with a rag. He points an oily finger at her. You do as I say, he tells her. This door stays open.

Sandy stamps her foot and says, But Max—

Don't say it! He makes a sucking sound with his saliva and looks back at the door as if he were mad at it. Then he goes through it. The jackhammer sound continues.

Ain't he a bastard? She leans on one hip. Her cigarette ash is long enough to catch on a spoon. Pops glances at it, then at the garage door. He passes her his credit card. When she picks it up, a smile breaks on her face. Hey, she says, you Judge Greel from Fresh County?

My father looks at the card and then at her. I am, he says.

A car starts in the garage.

Well I'll be goddamned, she says. She opens her mouth wide, the ash drops beside her and her tongue licks one of her front teeth. She puts the card through the machine and hands it back, smiling at him. You got my sister's ex-husband slammed for negligence of a child, she tells Pops. She leans over the counter. You know what he used to do? she asks. She smells like candy left out too long. Her blouse falls again, and I see the black lace of her bra. I lean in while my father bends over to sign the slip. She whispers, He'd take that little girl, ride her around and get stony drunk on Jackie Daniel's.

Pops pushes the receipt over and works his credit card into the pocket of his wallet.

He used to get into honky-tonks, she tells us, and leave her out in his car for hours. My sister Allie would just be looking and looking, frantic like for that little girl. She leans away from us, crosses her arms in front of her and looks at Pops. But you done it for her, she tells him.

He puts the wallet in his back pocket, pushes his graying sideburns down with two fingers and says, Well . . .

You're a regular hero, says Sandy. She nods toward the garage door, tilts her head to one side and says, You think you could do something for me?

Pops smiles and turns to go. He puts a hand on the door, looks out the window and says, I suppose you're brighter than sitting around until it gets that bad. Have a nice day, ma'am.

The woman purses her lips and shakes cigarette ash on the floor. She looks at the open door between the shop and the garage and says, Bye now. Hey honey, she calls out to me, congratulations!

In the parking lot, the sun glares at us. Buckle up, Pops tells me when we get in the car. We roll to a stop at the entrance of the station to wait for traffic to pass. He says, She looks the damn spitting image of her.

Who's that? I ask.

That girl at the register, Pops tells me, she looks just like her sister. Her sister defended the daylights out of that man in court. Almost had him acquitted.

When we get to Elm Drive, it is familiar as when I left it, with kudzu burying all the trees on the left side and the manicured lawns of the neighborhood on the right.

It's going to be a hot summer, Pops says. On his left shirt collar is a smudge of dirt, just below his chin.

Yes sir, I heard that.

Shelby's standing in our yard hanging sheets over the outside clothesline. She rushes over when our car pulls up, puts both hands to her chest and watches me come out my door.

My, my, Mr. Fletcher, she says. You come over here and give me a hug. Ooh, you so tall I don't know how to kiss you cept on my tippy toes. Judge, she tells my father, I need to thank you for bringin this boy home to his mammy Shelby.

When I hug her, she smells of done wash and my growing-up days.

Pops leans across the car with his hands clasped over the top of it. His eyes are red rimmed and he needs a shave. You do okay here Shelby? he asks her.

Shelby's brown skin gleams with sweat, she smiles wide. I did more than okay, she tells him. I fixed you boys some supper. It's in the freezer. She grips my arms with both her hands and squints up at me. Tears come into her eyes. I breathe deep and watch Pops going in the house with a suitcase in each hand.

Your mother would have been mighty proud of you, she tells me.

I swallow and try to say, I know it, but I just nod.

She pushes her chin toward the clothesline. Your mamma loved her sheets air dried, Fletcher, you know she did. She looks back at me and studies my face, then lets me loose, pats me on the arm. You go on in now, she says. Wash up and rest up, you and I got plenty of time for chitter-chatter.

While I am walking away, Shelby calls after me, Mr. Fletcher, I sure am glad you're home. Your daddy's happy on it, couldn't anything make him happier.

I pick up a hand and wave to her and keep walking up the porch into that shell of a house, empty and clean like places that sit for a bunch of seasons waiting for someone to live in them.

Pops is in the kitchen putting ice cubes in a glass of Coke. He drops a cube on the floor when I come in, then bends on one knee to pick it up. He looks at me. How tall are you? he asks.

I lean against the doorjamb. Five-eleven, I say.

He stands up, throws the ice cube in the sink and takes a sip of his drink. You look taller than that, he tells me. He nods to the door frame. Your mamma used to measure you against that door frame, he says. Do you remember that?

Yes sir, I do.

He smiles, remembering. You want to start work day after tomorrow? He jiggles his drink around so the ice cubes clink together. Or you want to give yourself some time? he asks.

I shrug. I think the day after tomorrow would be fine.

He studies me a minute, then he says, I think you should give yourself the rest of the week, you just had a busy year, a little downtime might not be so bad.

All right.

He smiles. Good, I brought some bags into the front hall. You can start unpacking if you like.

Thanks, Pops, I tell him. And then I turn to go.

Son, he says to my back. I'm glad you're home. I was figuring it out the other night, you haven't spent a whole summer here since you were ten years old.

Yes sir, I say, too quickly. Then I go through the door and back down to the front hall, where my suitcases are standing next to each other.

I put my palms flat against the cool glass of the front window. Shelby has disappeared from the side yard. I close my eyes and against my will, the image of my mother comes to me, her face on that last night, when her eyes got suddenly clear and she'd told me, Keep your father well. Oh Fletcher, your father . . .

She didn't speak again for twelve hours. It was February and it had started to rain outside. The rain froze on the windowpane while one life found its way toward abandoning a father and a son.

I open my eyes. A black fly is buzzing around the windowsill looking for a way out. I can hear Pops clanging dishes in the kitchen. My feet are aching with tired and they punch the middle of the steps on my way up the stairs.

Losing memory isn't a simple thing. Somewhere I wish I had found a kind of instruction book on the way to do it.

3

HALEY

You been missing me? Hannaford asks. It's my last day of sophomore year and we're squooshed in Hy Belter's truck bed with seven other people. Hannaford's skin smells of wood smoke and whiskey and burned pork from the barbecue out at the old river dam.

Instead of answering him, I put my head back against the cab and watch the full moon chasing us down Battle Creek Road at eighty miles an hour. When I open my mouth to taste the air, all I get is fevered wind, smells like gasoline, and sounds like a muffler with bullet holes in it. At least it moves. The last four days of May have been ninety-five degrees and counting.

Hannaford palms my leg, draws a hard, straight line up my thigh with his pointer finger and says, Don't do this to me, baby. I never felt this way about a girl before. I'm in love with you. I was about ready to talk to your daddy on it once you got out of high school.

I look down at his hand. He's got a scarred birthmark on that tender place between the thumb and pointer. I touched it one night last October, when we lay in the middle of the Banks High football field on a blanket next to a Coke bottle full up with warm beer. I asked him about it, and he said he tried to shoot the birthmark with a BB gun when he was eleven because he felt like it was some kind of dumb defect. I'd rather have a bullet hole than a defect, he told me. He ran his fingers over it. I haven't told anyone that before, he said. Then he kissed me. Hannaford's got a strong tongue, and he uses it too much.

Now it's eight months later and he's whispering, You watching that moon? You see those stars?

When I don't answer, he tells me, If it would bring you back to me, Haley Ellyson, I'd make all those stars and the moon come out of that sky for you.

It might be the most romantic Hannaford has ever talked. He'll work hard at it when he's trying to get you and harder still when he wants to win you back. In between he isn't anything but fast rides and free beer and hard kisses pushed on you like a punishment. I lean over and plug my nose from his whiskey smell and say in a nasaled voice, I don't want those stars out of the sky, Han, I like them right where they are.

The truck slows at the intersection of Highway 12, and I stand up.

Hannaford grabs the bottom of my shorts. Where you going?

I pull away from him, step over the sleeping body of Frenchie Yule and hop out. There are two tupelo gum trees at the edge of the road and in between them a path starts to my house. I run toward it.

What in hell are you doing? He yells to me.

I'm going home, I yell back.

Russ leans over the truck side. You can't go in there alone at night, he calls.

Hannaford's standing up, holding on to the cab roof and trying not to sway.

It's real close, I tell them. I'll be just fine.

Haley, baby, come on, yells Hannaford.

Someone in back says, Well, hell boy, follow her.

I leap over the road ditch and start in on the path, knowing Hannaford is too scared to follow in the woods at midnight. Behind me someone says, Ah, let her go, there ain't nothin in those wood but ticks.

Right before the truck screeches away on bald tires I hear a girl telling them, Haley Ellyson's insane, she's always been crazy.

There's a living fern and moss smell in the woods. The moon makes shadows of trees stretch across the path. While I run, I sing aloud that song Daddy used to have on the record player when I was little. *I'm being followed by a moon shadow, moon shadow, moon shadow.*

The path I'm running on is to the south of our house, which is lucky since the body is buried in the east, so I would have to be able to find a crossways path if I wanted to go see it. There isn't a path like that, and I'm glad because I don't know if it's good to scare yourself too much when you are all alone at night.

It is strange how I always want to go see the body even though it makes me buckle up inside. It's like a compulsion. Daddy says there are men who love wicked women in that way. They keep going back to them, can't live without them. Kills them if they do, kills them if they don't, he says.

It takes me less than five minutes to get to the house. By the time I reach the back deck, I'm breathing hard and holding the stitch in my side. When I lean into the slider screen, I see Daddy and Gwyneth in the den. Old hurricane candles Daddy buys for storm are lit around the room. Gwyneth hunts them up out of our kitchen junk drawers. Candles make magic, she always tells me, they make women beautiful and men soft. The light from them flickers and shows the oval shadows of their heads against the far wall. I like to watch Gwyneth and Daddy together when they don't know I am here. Mamma left when I was six and Gwyn didn't come into our life until I was twelve years old. So for a long while it was just Daddy and his boys who raised me. They took me fishing for bream in the river out back and saved me from copperheads by shooting them in the path. They showed me best of all how to ride a horse so good I can teach anyone who wants to learn. I grew up with five fathers besides Daddy: Stony Davis, Archie Little, T. Fingerling, Billy Towle and Bo Dickens.

They were all I knew until four years ago Gwyneth arrived in Houser Banks like a storm does. The people of this town watched her coming with the childish excitement and pure terror of wild weather. Gwyneth Fox, childless and manless at thirty-two, with her blond corn-silk hair hanging down to her chin and her blue eyes wide around as quarters and her voice tender as mist. On her ears she wore diamond stud earrings too heavy for her little lobes and on her right pointer finger a chunk of diamond big enough around to touch the knuckle. Besides that she wore not a stitch of jewelry. She wore straight-legged jeans and plain white T-shirts and still she seemed overdressed here. She stood out and was noticed in Houser Banks, like you would notice warm air in January.

Tonight she is sitting on the rocker and Daddy is facing her on the footstool, saying, You're wanting to kill me with it, Gwyn. He picks up her white blouse and kisses her swollen belly.

Gwyneth runs a hand through Daddy's hair. Tonight, she says, of course I will stay.

He picks up her hands. Forever, he tells her. Jesus, Gwyn, I will love you right.

Sweat drips down my belly. The tree frogs sing like something electric on fire. Gwyneth leans her head back and smiles. Her hair falls away from her face and she looks down at him. You going to try to convince me again, cowboy?

If only I could convince you, Daddy says. He kisses her wrists.

She pushes a strand of hair from his forehead, Oh sweet man, we been talking on this for four years now. I just can't be that for you, wife and mother and all that. Love ruins itself if you try to put it in a house with names. I seen it.

Daddy takes her bare foot in his lap and strokes the arch while she leans over her ballooned belly and kisses his head. But tonight, she says, you could bring me upstairs and I could sing some lullabies. We got to practice for the baby. She watches him rub her foot. He stares out the window in back of her. A silence falls.

Mosquitoes buzz around my neck and I whack at them with my hands while trying to stay quiet so they can't hear me. Finally, Daddy places Gwyneth's foot on the floor, stands up and bends over her to pick her up. The way Daddy carries her to the stairs makes her look like a bride. I hear him say, Lullabies, huh?

And she giggles.

After they've gone to bed, I sneak in the sliders, sit in the rocking chair and rock back and forth gently. I think of that October Sunday when I was twelve and Daddy struggled home early as the sun rose. His truck screeched in the driveway until I thought he was going to hit the house with it. I waited on top of the stairs and watched him come in, rubbing his face with both hands, the lines of his neck dirt-creased and his left eyebrow blood-crusted. He started when he saw me, as if he'd been dead asleep and someone had rung a bell in his ear. He said my name in the form of a question and then he got gruff. Go on to bed, he told me.

Daddy, I been in bed, I said.

You have? He sighed and leaned against the stair railing. His laces were undone on one boot. I knew he'd been in a fight and I'd hear about it in school and at the stables where the men brushed the horses' sides, cleaned out hoofs, hauled saddles and paid no mind to who might be listening to the stories they told.

It was as if his feet were filled with steel for how heavy they fell on each step when he came up toward me. He stopped in the middle of the staircase.

You know a thing about love, sweetheart? He asked it tender.

I didn't answer, just tilted my head to him.

He took a hand off the railing and held his palm in front of him, inspecting it. He spoke slow and soft. I told myself after your mamma left I wouldn't ever fall in love again and I sure as hell wouldn't fight about it. But Gypsy's sister's just come to town. A fine lady, getting a bad rap already. I'm not going to stand for it.

I stood at the top of the stairs shivering in my nightgown and wondering at Daddy. He never talked about Mamma leaving or about love and women. I felt my blood pulse through me, quicken not so much with what he was saying as with what I was supposed to say when he was finished.

He rubbed the back of his neck. I've gone and done it, sweetheart. Love has hit Ire Ellyson in the goddamn noggin again and I haven't been able to think straight or drink a whiskey well since Wednesday.

Daddy had gone out the Wednesday night prior with few words and a pressed, bleached button-down shirt. His skin was soap smelling, his denims were clean and his boots were shined. He'd spent the afternoon cursing the trash in the Datsun two-door he never drove, working on its alternator, opening all its windows to get the smoke smell out and giving it a washing down. Then he showered for well over an hour. Afterward he'd walked the hall with toilet paper pieces on his razor cuts, his hands clumsily working an old tie he wore to weddings and funerals. I followed him around the house, amazed at the sight of him clean shaven and white wearing with his hair slicked. I asked him more than once where he was going. He said, To dinner with a sister of Gypsy's, Billy's mamma Doris is home. You know the number. Don't do anything dumb—Hetty's next door and she has the eye of an eagle and the tongue of a squirrel and the ear of a wolf, so she'll watch and tell in a heartbeat.

Then he went out and didn't come home until I was fast asleep.

Four days later, standing disreputable and cranky tempered on the stairs in front of me, Daddy patted his front pocket for his cigarettes, took one out with a bend in it and placed it between his lips, then patted himself again for a pack of matches. When he couldn't find one, he said, Screw it, and took the cigarette out of his lips. He looked at the unlit smoke as if it were a thing that had betrayed him. I'm going to make myself a sonofabitch fool again, he said quietly, and I can't stop it better than I could stop a moving train.

He shook his head and dropped the unsmoked Winston on the stair where he stood. Come here, Turnip, he said. He outstretched his arms so I could jump into them. When he caught me, I buried my face in his neck and straddled his belly with my legs. He brought me to my bed and laid me down and kissed my forehead and said for me to sleep long and well.

After that Gwyneth was in our lives. She didn't live with us, but she came from Gypsy's house near every day. She smelled of magnolia flower, laughed easily and treated me like a sister. At night she turned music on in the living room and danced the bump with me and Daddy, twirled us around and sang out loud. She brought dishes of candy and bunches of wildflowers. The house looked brighter with her in it. Falling to sleep at night, I could hear her wisp of a voice and it made me dream better.

Gwyneth has made Daddy into something I haven't ever seen before. He had always been a man breaking horses and lifting cars by their bumpers when they needed moving and playing cards until day dawned with tobacco in his cheek and whiskey in his belly. He carried a .45 and hunted deer and ran hound dogs out at Mr. Archer's and shot skeeters at the reservoir.

And then I saw him love Gwyneth, hold her with a tenderness that equals the way you would pick up a dragonfly wing if you wanted to keep it whole.

It has been four years since Gwyneth came to us. She's seven months pregnant with Daddy's baby and spending a whole lot of time at our house so that Daddy forgets about me for long stretches, forgets about a curfew or who I am running with or what boy is bothering up my attention. I am hoping with the baby coming, Gwyneth just might decide to move in. Then we could be a real live family. Daddy wouldn't ever have to be lonely again. And neither would I.

In the morning I find hardened waxed puddles of hurricane candles lying in saucers around the den. Gwyneth's sitting in that same rocking chair as if she hadn't moved, listening to Hank Williams on the radio and singing along to the words. I have a lullaby box in my hand. When you turn the crank, *Silent Night* plays.

What's that little whisper of a sound I hear? She leans back and turns off the radio. I hand her the music box. It rings out thin and tinkly when she turns the handle. Isn't it beautiful? she says, putting it to her ear like a seashell. She closes her eyes to the music and sets it on her belly. I sit cross-legged at her feet.

Where'd you get it, darlin? she asks me.

Mamma, I say. And then I tell her quick, But I want the baby to have it.

Gwyneth stops turning the crank and looks down at me. Oh Haley, she says, you should keep this if your mamma gave it to you.

Well I had a dream last night that I played it for the baby, I tell her, so I want to give it to you.

Gwyneth holds the box in her hand and looks down at it. She sighs. So you're dreaming about her, too? she asks.

In my dream it was a boy, I tell her.

This here's a little girl, Gwyneth says, patting her belly. The dream fairy is wanting to play with you if she showed you a boy.

How do you know?

Oh, I know. Women's intuition. Your daddy wants a complete surprise, but a woman knows. Some women say they don't, but they just shut out knowing. Gwyn rubs her belly up and down. Your daddy thinks it's hogwash.

Daddy's like that, I tell her.

Men never want to believe in the knowing of woman, honey. It scares them.

I bet he wants a boy, I tell her.

She raises her eyebrows and stops rubbing her belly. Why's that?

Because, I tell her, he uses up all his time being afraid a girl will go off and fall apart in some high school boy's hands who doesn't make your heart go faster than a slow motorcycle ride.

Oh, Gwyn says, patting her hand my way, you mean chasing your boys off the land with a shotgun and hunting you up after curfew? All daddies who got a lick of care in them about you will do that. What about his gifts, honey? No one gives a girl better gifts than your daddy.

That's true, I say, thinking of all the silver hand-mirrors from auctions and opera glasses in velvet-lined leather cases from secondhand shops, onyx necklaces with chips of diamonds that Daddy buys us and that a horseman's wage most likely can't afford. I save them all in my treasure box and will take them out when I'm a lady and someone's serving me champagne underneath a chandelier.

Well, I tell Gwyneth, I hope it's a girl because I'm going to move away from Houser Banks, and she can come stay with me whenever she wants to get out of this town. I'll let her do whatever she feels like. At night she can go out late and kiss boys and after she can crawl in bed with me and tell me all the things that happened that made her laugh. Or cry.

Gwyneth puts her head back and laughs. Oh sweetheart, she says, don't you worry about this baby getting out of Houser Banks, Mississippi.

I'm working on your daddy best I can to get his butt out to California, where the heat don't hunt you down and kill you six-tenths of the year. I got another sister out there wouldn't mind putting us all up.

Gwyneth sets her delicate feet flat on the ground and grips the sides of the chair as if to stand, then she slumps back down. You want to get me a little sweet tea from that pitcher in the fridge, honey? she asks me. I'm exhausted today. This heat.

When I come back out to the living room with the tea, Gwyneth's tucked her chin in and is looking down at her belly. She takes the drink and says, Maybe a woman wants a baby so bad because once you get one, men stop seeming so important. She twirls the ice cubes with her fingers. You want to help me bring some things to Gypsy today? she asks.

I pick dirt out my fingernails and tell her Daddy said she was supposed to rest, doctor's orders on account of early contractions.

She rocks her chair forward and lifts herself to standing so it looks like she might fall backward. I go to help, but she rights herself with the back of the armchair. That's the reason you're going to take me, she says. Go on and get dressed. We'll go in about an hour.

We go to Gypsy's in Gwyneth's convertible, which she lets me drive even though I am still shy of knowing stick shift so well. Her little MG is always going to sleep in the middle of intersections and grown men fall all over themselves trying to help her fix it. Usually it is only out of gas.

There's a pack of Marlboro Lights on the dash. Gwyn takes one out and pretends to smoke. She has quit with the baby in her belly, saying she won't start again until the baby is ten years old. She pesters Daddy to do the same, which he does when she's with him. Gwyn has these elegant fingers that always look like they're dancing, and I watch them while she flicks the unlit smoke around. She turns sideways and looks at me. Did you get your lingerie package? she asks.

Yes, and I love it.

She winks. Good. June's will be here soon.

When the June issue comes, Gwyneth will hand it to me on the sly and I am allowed to pick out one thing, which she orders for me. Then when it gets here, she leaves the package under my pillow. We've been doing that for a year now and I have a collection of silk bras with tiny pearls and satin lace-lined panties that hug my belly. All the colors are rich, even the whites are lush. My package came yesterday and so today, underneath my cotton dress, which is nothing fancy, I am wearing silk panties the color of red wine.

When we turn down Highway 12, Gwyneth says, Give it a little more gas, honey. So I press the accelerator and jump the clutch. Gwyneth closes her eyes and smiles up at the sky and says, Faster, until we are flying down the road quick enough for my stomach to turn over at the curves.

Once in town, I slow down some. Gwyneth keeps her eyes closed. When we go by Elsa's, I ask does she need anything.

Where we at, honey? She doesn't open her eyes.

We're passing the store, I tell her.

Oh, I don't need a damn thing, but when we get to Water Street, tell me. I'm sweating, and I need to mop down.

Water Street's a tiny road without a house on it and when we get there, Gwyneth raises her dress to her breasts and wipes a white handkerchief between them and all the way down her stomach. I chance a look at the knotted and wide belly button. At home when she mops down, Daddy gets real quiet. He watches her like a wild animal watches to see if something that moves in the wood will harm or feed it.

Damn, she says soft. I wish some of the old farts in this town could see me now.

Everything Gwyneth says sounds like a drag of perfume.

Gypsy and Spier's Beauty and Barber smells of hair tonic and bubble dryers. The shop is split down the middle. On the right side, Gypsy has a round tinted mirror hanging over a shining black dressing table that holds a lamp on it with tassels coming off it. The chair in front of it is covered by leopard skin. When you get your hair cut there, you sit in that chair and wear a black smock rimmed with gold at the collar and sleeves and bottom. Next to the chair there's a bright red love seat with cushions fluffed at the corners, where women wait their turn in it and smoke and talk to you and comment on your hair.

Across the room on Spier's side, a barber station is lit up by one hanging lightbulb. His customers wear white smocks and the men waiting sitting on metal folding chairs with newspapers and spittoons, talking about football and Saturday night poker games at Elsa's.

The shop is open every single day but Monday.

Gwyneth and I walk toward Gypsy's side, and the men flip their newspapers down to watch us. Hello! Spier calls. Spier is Gypsy's husband and Gwyn's brother-in-law. He's skinny and wears girly cologne. Gypsy must have been one lonely woman to marry him, Gwyneth has said to me. She says there's no other way to make love to him but with your eyes open so you can remember he's a gentleman.

I am piled high with grocery bags full up with books and clothes, and I try to say hello to Mr. Spier over the bag. Gwyneth says hi for the both of us. He's wearing a lab coat and black checkered pants, which he pulls up once a minute through the day like a nervous tic.

Hey girls, we been waitin on you, Gypsy says. She's smoked too many cigarettes in her life and yelled too many times, so her voice is raspy. Her nails are bright red and if she likes you, she lets you look at the little pictures in the middle of them.

Haley, baby, how you been? she asks me. I haven't seen you in weeks, my sweet. How tall are you, five-six? She takes a blue hair clip out of the lady's hair who's sitting in her chair and waves it at me. Look at her, Gwyn, Gypsy says. You aren't doing a thing for her. Doll her up, for Christ's sake.

Gwyneth eases into the red love seat. Her face gets pink with effort. I put the bags on the floor and sit on the arm of the couch.

Haley doesn't need to be dolled up, says Gwyneth. She reaches up to frisk my hair. She's got boys crawling the house like wood bees. Anyway, she doesn't want anything to do with all this beauty parlor stuff. She likes herself all messy like this, don't you, Hale?

Well I'll do it for her, says Gypsy. She doesn't have to do a damn thing. She points to my hair. Is that natural curl? she asks.

Gwyneth picks up my hair and says, It sure is, and not a split end far as the eye can see. She shows the hair to Gypsy, who walks over with her gold-sandaled heels clicking on the floor. She clucks her tongue.

She's got her daddy's eyes, too, says Gwyneth, touching my chin and turning my face toward Gypsy.

Gypsy nods. Green as Louisiana swamp, she says. Then she ducks her head at me. That's a compliment, sweetie. Gwyn, I'm afraid you won't be able to birth that baby being as small as you are. You need to eat more, girl. I thought you were confined to the bed. You go to the doctor again?

He says I'm doing just fine, Gwyn tells her. She looks toward the back of the shop. Oh Joy, she says. That is fabulous.

Joy Douglas comes twirling over from the back shampoo area with a cream-colored kimono on and her black hair down the back of it. Gold bracelets sing on her arms when she lifts them to show us the fabric. The men on Spier's side dip down their papers and clap and whistle. Joy bows and turns on her barefoot tippy toes.

Hole in the Wall Thrift Shop, Joy says. Ten bucks.

When she sees me, she stops twirling, opens her eyes wide and says, Haley Ellyson, well I'll be shocked silly. She walks over and rests the tips of her fingers on my chin.

Hi, Miss Joy, I say.

She presses her cheek against mine and then stands up and turns to Gypsy. She is growing up, ain't she? she says, nodding to me as if proud.

Yes, she is, says Gypsy. She wouldn't be hindered any by a little lipstick, though.

Joy touches my lips softly. Her eyes crease at the corner when she smiles; I remember how after Mamma left she used to come to sleep in Daddy's bed with him. Her husband worked trucking and she'd visit when he was away. She knew to come but not too often and to stay but not want too much. Daddy was still sad with grieving after Mamma first left. In the morning I always knew when Joy was there because the house smelled of full-on breakfast. She'd be dressed by the time I came down, wearing low-slung satin shirts and miniskirts, chattering away, slathering butter on our grits. She would hug me before I sat at the table, her mouth on my hair. Sit down, sleepy bones, she'd say. Eat up, darlin.

Where you been hidin her, Gwyn? asks Joy, still looking at me.

She teaches ridin at the stables. She's there near all the time, just like her daddy, Gwyn tells her.

What about you, sweetie? Joy asks, patting Gwyn's stomach. How's it going? When's it coming?

Feels like any day now, says Gwyneth. But I got about four and a half weeks.

Gypsy puts a bobby pin in her mouth and says around it, Joy's getting a divorce.

Gwyneth sits up in her seat. No you are not, Joy. That teddy bear of a man? Oh how sad! He's a sweet one, isn't he, Joy?

Joy's husband's as broad as an ox, with drinking lines running his nose like a road map. He's got small, unfriendly eyes. Gypsy makes a clucking noise with her tongue and shakes the Aqua Net.

Yeah, so sweet, Joy says, pulling a thread off the arm of her kimono, I hit the floor two weeks ago, passed out for dead. My mamma found me in the morning, blood coming out my ear.

Gwyneth gasps, Oh honey, I'm so sorry, I had no idea.

Joy sits down on the couch next to Gwyneth and lights a cigarette. That marriage was like a wounded bird flying around in circles, she says. You don't know whether to stomp on it or save it.

Well, says Gypsy, unwinding the cord of her blow-dryer, you got to get out of it quick or you could be six feet under. You hear about that guy in Taylor? He shot his wife at a fish fry last Saturday with a .25 in the back of the head. It was her birthday. They hadn't been married six months. Did it in pure public. Her birthday for crying out loud.

Joy smooths the lap of her kimono. Me and Sal were married seven years, and I been taking it for five.

Don't short us out, baby, Spier calls over. I'm putting on the razor.

Gypsy fluffs her customer's bangs. Sorry, honey, we gotta wait to blow it, she tells her.

He's in Roanoke now with his mamma and I hope he stays there, says Joy. I got an RO on him lasts me one year. I got bruises up and down my back should last me less than a month without him around to keep renewing them.

Oh Joy, I'm so glad you got out, says Gwyneth.

Leaning over Gwyneth's lap and patting my hand, Joy says to me, Honey, they aren't all like that.

Gypsy passes Joy an ashtray, then stands with her hair dryer on her hip and waits.

I went to that new lady sergeant, Joy tells us while she balances the ashtray on her lap. Not Sheriff Hill, he don't know his elbow from his patoot. But that new sergeant is supposed to be good. She looks like a man. You can't tell the difference unless you look at her boobies and listen to her voice. She said to me, Mrs. Douglas, you go down and get yourself a restraining order. And that's just what I did. Judge Johnny Greel passed it. He's a good one on that, bastard on other things, but a good one on that.

Shh, says Gypsy. She nods toward the door as the bell on it rings. Standing at the entrance, with his hands in his pockets and his golden hair covering one eye, is Judge Greel's son.

Joy puts her hand up to her mouth. Well, ain't that a coincidence? she says.

Gypsy leans into me and Gwyneth and whispers, That's Greel's boy right there.

Oh, says Gwyneth.

I don't say a thing.

Spier turns off the shaver, hikes up his pants and says, Fletcher! Well come on down, boy, there's one more seat, just for you. Haven't seen you since last summer. My God, you're still growin.

Fletcher Greel bites the side of his thumbnail and starts forward.

None of us know Judge Greel's son. He's been summer camped and prep schooled, but I've seen him around Christmases some and school breaks. He's two years older than I am and the kind of boy who looks like he could rope and ride a horse on his first try and has never tripped and fallen in his whole life. He has a shy way of walking and I imagine he speaks only if he has something real good to say. When he walks past us, he ducks his head, smiles and says, Good morning. He looks right at me when he says it.

Hi there, honey, says Gypsy.

Joy watches him walk over to Spier's side, then leans in and whispers, Oh jeez! That is Judge Greel's son. Christ, now I feel old.

Gwyn nudges me. He's a good-lookin one, she says.

I hear him ask, How are you, Mr. Spier?

When I turn to look, he's taking the last seat in the row.

Good, son, Spier says. How's your daddy doin?

He's fine, sir.

Joy gets up and starts twirling around in her kimono in front of me. I can't see the boy's side anymore.

Now I gotta get a job, she tells us. Gypsy, she says, maybe I could start cutting hair here or cleaning.

I need somebody to answer phones, says Gypsy. Gwyn, I do believe you should be resting, not out and about.

Oh my God, says Gwyneth, I'm doing plenty of resting.

You able to sleep with that baby in this heat? Joy asks her and takes a few steps forward. I look in back of her to watch the judge's son again and find him staring at me. We sit for some seconds looking at each other and then I smile. He smiles back slow and I tell myself to turn around in my seat. I will him to forget all shyness and keep looking over at the ladies' side, where I'm sitting. If he looks hard enough, he might be able to see through my clothes, where I have put that silky rich lingerie, resting tight against my body.

4

FLETCHER

There isn't a thing to do my first weekend home. Shelby has time off and Pops is in Tupelo meeting a guy there who wants to run for circuit court judge. I get my hair cut at Spier's Saturday morning and go back home. The heat is kicking my ass, so I stay inside and drink bottled Pepsi, look at the *Fresh County Times,* scan Pops's bookshelves for Faulkner books I've already read, and leaf through old piles of *National Geographic*s. Because I can, I drink milk out of the carton and masturbate on the living room couch. Then I wander into the garage, pick up the hood of the Honda Pops is letting me drive, and try to figure out the rattle sound on the left side. Nothing around the engine makes any sense to me.

Finally I leave Pops a note and drive into town for nothing else to do.

Outside the door of Elsa's store, two men are sitting on milk crates drinking out of paper-bagged bottles, talking to a lady in red who's as old as Pops and has hair the color of a tangelo. They stop talking when I come up. Hello, I say. The sidewalk in front of me is spotted with lopsided bubble gum pressed in and blackened.

Hidee, one man says and stares straight ahead at the cars passing.

Elsa's screen door bangs on broken hinges. Her store's dry as a sunburnt cardboard box and the floorboards are dusty. There's a fan blowing around the stacks of roped-up newspapers behind the counter. Elsa is filing her nails. When she sees me, she stops and smiles big. What do we have here? she says. Little Judge Greel back in Fresh County? I hope you'll be stayin with us awhile this time.

Good evening, Miss Elsa. Yes ma'am, back for the summer.

That's great, darlin. How's your daddy holdin on? she asks.

He's fine, thank you.

Hotter than a stove top, ain't it?

It is that, ma'am.

You go on help yourself, sweetie. She nods her head to the store and starts back with her filing.

The place smells of frozen meat and dish detergent. The shelves are crammed with anything you might need: bar, liquid and powdered soap, Spam and Slim Jims, bug kill and suntan lotion, canned iced tea, rat traps, bags of charcoal, linked smoked sausage and greeting cards. There are jarred pig feet and pickled eggs and pig snouts and boiled peanuts, bread, milk and fishing rods, caged crickets, lawn chairs and birdseed, stacks of notebooks and card sets for a buck.

The cold drinks are against the far wall in a glass freezer and a guy is standing before it with a back that looks like a slab of barbecue tanned to almost burnt. He's rapping his oil-stained fingers on the door handle, singing *Tangled Up in Blue* too loud with a bad voice. On his hips are denim cutoffs without a belt. He's barefoot, and his hair is a tangled mess of pony-tail, too long for any Mississippi man without a guitar on his back. I wait through a whole verse before I realize it's Riley White, best buddy of mine from grade school, who used to keep garden snakes in his desk and ride home early on the tail of his brothers' pickups. He and I would throw anything that stank on the end of a line and fish catfish, singing country songs to the river. Then we'd muddy ourselves with ride at the dirt bike track. He always could repair anything with a broken branch and some spit. I don't know if he will recognize me and I'm too shy to say his name, so before he can start in on the second verse, I say, Hey there, excuse me.

Oh, sorry, he says and pulls aside, holding the door handle so it swings open. I pick up a six-pack of Pepsi, and his hand clasps my shoulder.

Fletcher Greel, he says. Well, hey there. I used to fish with you as a kid.

I look over my shoulder at his tan face. His eyes are as familiar as Shelby's brown ones. Riley White. I smile. How you doin?

He's grown taller than I am. Just seeing his face makes a laugh come up in me. We shake hands and grin at each other.

I been real good, he says. He lets loose my hand and stands back, looking me up and down. What in hell are you up to, Greel?

I shrug. Whole pack of nothing right now, I tell him.

You staying awhile? he asks.

At least the summer.

Oh yeah? Riley's eyes go wide. You and I, he says, we gotta do some fishin.

Sure thing, I tell him.

Riley White, Elsa calls from the front. You fixin to buy that beer or just stare at it making my freezer warm? Cause no one lasts in my store without a shirt for more than half a minute.

All right, Miss Elsa, I'm just deciding here. He closes the freezer door. Well kiss my ass, Fletcher Greel, you look like a goddamn Bean catalogue. You ever been back here since you left?

I come back sometimes, I tell him, but never for this long.

Riley looks down at my Pepsi. You enjoy yourself while us fuckers sweated our asses off down here? he asks.

I laugh. Nah, I tell him. It's cold up there, snows two-thirds of the year.

And you survived it, he says. He opens the freezer again and picks out a six-pack of Bud. Houser Banks ain't much, he says, but it sure beats snow. Now go on, get yourself a beer. He points his thumb in Elsa's direction. She don't give an ass crack how old you are. When he holds the door open, I lean in, grab myself a twelve-pack of Bud and put the Pepsi back. He watches me. You graduate this year? he asks.

I did, I tell him. I stand back from the freezer. You?

He hauls his six-pack up so it's sitting on one shoulder and says, Sure as hell did, almost didn't make it for all the whiskey I'd drunk the night prior. Went up there with my cap and gown and nothing else on, it was hot as a boiled furnace that day. He starts to walk down the aisle, motions me to follow. Got suspended more than I went, he calls back, but I'll not be taking a finishing course from my mamma's couch. Boy's got to have a little education under his belt. He yanks up his fall-down denims. How the hell you been, Greel? You must be a goddamn Yankee by now.

I'm no Yankee, I tell him, but my T-shirt feels too stiff and my denims too long and my shoes too new.

He bangs his beer on Elsa's counter. She tilts her head to one side, looking at him like a mother looks when her son has gone and spilled the milk again.

What, Miss Elsa? Riley asks. He looks at her like his feelings are hurt. Least I'm buyin it, he says, huh? Keeping you in business. He turns to me and says, I keep this woman in business.

Elsa rolls her eyes. You boys so good at lyin, she tells us, why can't you be as good at lovin as you are at lyin?

I'm twice as good, says Riley. He digs around in his pocket and pulls out a bunch of crumpled bills. Me and the Yankee here, he says, you can put ours together.

I take out my billfold and he throws his hand to it. You can buy the bait next time we go fishin, he tells me.

Elsa shakes her head, puts his bills in her drawer and closes it with a ring. She hands Riley change. You boys be good, she tells us. She picks her nail file from behind her ear and says, You stay out of trouble, you hear? I know how old you are, don't think I don't.

We both say, Yes ma'am, in unison, like we were born together.

The screen door bangs shut behind us. The sun is still abusing the sidewalk, and it makes me squint. Riley looks at the men on milk crates and the orange-haired woman. Hey there, Lizbeth, Catch, Freddy, how you?

They tell him hello and that they're hot and then they watch us cross the sidewalk. Riley throws his beer in the backseat of a red Roadrunner convertible stayed at the handicapped spot right outside Elsa's door.

I stand looking at it. This isn't your car, I say to Riley.

He takes my beer from me and puts it in the passenger's seat. Sure as hell is, Yankee. Got it out of the junkyard two summers ago, put in an engine and a muffler, ain't got glass for any of it except the front. Riley takes a cigarette from behind his ear and commences lighting it with a match from his shorts pocket that he rips on the side of the car. My brother Jimmy, you remember him? He had a transmission and all the parts I needed to make the engine go right. He walks around the car, smiling. The sun glints off it in a blinding way. I painted it, he says, and patched up the vinyl. Runs good. Sounds like a Harley but runs like a charm. He leans against the passenger door and looks at me.

I run my finger over the chrome on the side of it. Nice ride, I tell him.

He smokes, looks over at the courthouse and asks, How's your daddy? Doing well, I tell him.

He nods. Good, he says. Striped bass are spawning strong this time a year, he tells me, and they all take to Elsa's jigs. They say it'll be a dry summer, keeps away those mosquitoes. Last summer I quit fishing it got so hot. He looks up at me and smiles. We got that weather here, Yankee, punches the shit out of you. Two tornadoes, a hurricane and a goddamn forest fire in the north Mississippi hill country last year.

I know it, I tell him.

He wraps his hand around his bicep. Makes you tough, he says. Gesturing with his cigarette to the east where the river is, he says, We got to go down to Ole Cranky's piece of river. Remember him chasing us with that shotgun? I bet you a fat man he couldn't have got us if we stood two feet before him and didn't move a muscle. Riley shakes his head. Yeah, we used to sit on that big old log, held our white butts for hours, bass biting for bream, bream biting our bait and the chiggers biting us.

That log's wore out and rotted by now, I'll bet, I tell him.

It probably is, he says.

By now my back is sweating, and I could go for one of those cold beers. Riley doesn't sweat at all. He smokes and looks around.

Fishin is pretty tolerant, he says. Even if you do it wrong it's a hell of a lot of fun. You workin? he asks me.

I nod toward the courthouse. I'm helping my old man out.

That right? Riley flicks his ash. He leans up from the side of the door. Well then, Little Judge, you and I need to find some purpose in life if you're going to be holed up in Houser Banks's dusty old courthouse for days on end. There's piss poor to do around here, this town ain't worth bat shit, but I think we might could dig up a little fun. He jumps into the driver's side of that Roadrunner, turns the key in the ignition. The radio blares out a baseball score. He turns it off. Hop in, Yankee, he says.

I look at him.

C'mon, Greel, he says. I'm gonna whip you if you stand there and shoot you if you run, six holes through your Yankee ass, now get in.

Backing out, Riley asks me, Ready for a joyride?

Bombs away, I tell him.

We roar down Houser Banks Road at thirty miles over the speed limit and head for the country while I pop the tops of two Buds and hand him one.

At first Riley's quiet with ride, but it isn't long before he starts to storytell. He could make conversation with a wall if he had to and knows how to keep it going better than any talk show host. I half listen and half think what a great thing it is that Riley and I are all graduated and riding around together in his convertible Roadrunner through the back roads of Fresh County with cold beers in our hands.

The first time I got drunk was with Riley in the seventh grade, off a pint of old tequila he'd found somewhere. I puked my eyeballs out off the side of the tree house while Riley sat beside me patting my back. In his drunken slur he told me, It's all part of it, you won't always puke, Greel, just beginner's luck. This took my shame away. While I screech down the roads with Riley White, I get that same feeling I always used to have when I was with him, that anything at all can happen and it's bound to be a good time.

He turns north up Highway 12 past Mud Creek Farm onto a side road called Hillbury. Kudzu covers both sides over old oak and gum and catalpa trees big around as three men hand to hand. Riley stands with his head up over the windshield, his smoking hand on the wheel and his beer spilling down his arm. Wahooooooo! he yells.

I let my head be pinned to the passenger's seat and my shirt go flat against me. There are bare-naked roads sided with corn and cotton, full of stubborn heat. We pass car junkyards circled by green plastic fencing roped with honeysuckle and jasmine. Shotgun shacks with Christmas decorations on them sit in the middle of stands of pine. It makes for dark, haunted-looking landscape.

Riley puts in a tape and B. B. King sings out *The Thrill Is Gone*. And Riley tells me the story of how he got arrested in Memphis last March for drinking underage. He had to hitch all the way back to Houser Banks at dawn without any shoes on since steel-toed boots are considered a weapon in Tennessee and they took them away from him in the county jail. He hauls a beer down his throat. Ninety-five dollars those boots, he tells me. Let's you and me go try to get them back, huh? Tennessee cops are wussies, I'm telling you, we could bribe them with *Playboy* and they'd be happy.

Buzzards sit on every fence post, waiting for the smell of a dead thing rotting. Just after the Fresh County line, on the side of the road, a white-painted sign on raw plywood says *Hey! You Wasn't Hungry?* Fifty feet later the next sign reads *You Just Missed Arlena's Soul Food. Our Fish Fry Goes On All Night and Into the Day. Also Selling Plastic Covers and Furniture.* The curved road is sided with longhorns and horses grazing in a hollowed-out bottom next to a lake the color of mud.

He guns the Roadrunner and throws another beer can out. I hate to litter, he calls over to me, but if Sheriff Hill caught us, he'd know immediate as a good piss how many beers we've had.

The smell of cow shit is bitter in the air and the night goes breezy with nothing like cool, but still some relief away from beating sunshine. My beer buzz is doing a great thing, too. It's working to kill the despair of spending a summer in Houser Banks. I sit back with the wind in my face and let myself feel good.

Sometime later Riley slows the car and I'm deafened from the sudden quiet. He looks around him, gestures to the wood on either side and says, I wouldn't mind having a deer camp somewheres out here. Not to hunt, just to play cards, drink, pee outside and lie. Tell enormous lies.

We turn and the land clears and flattens to farmland again. Riley rolls to a stop at an intersection of three cornfields, shakes his head like a dog after he swims and looks over at me. What do you say, Yankee, did you like that ride?

I did, I tell him. Where are we?

He reaches under his seat for another beer. We're about fifty-some miles east of Houser Banks, I believe. He sucks the foam off his Bud, puts the gearshift in neutral and lights a cigarette. A mutt of a hound dog hobbles along the fence in front of us. We watch it without saying anything.

In an altogether different voice than I have heard from him during the past two hours, Riley says, I been meaning to call you, Greel.

When I look over, he's studying his side mirror. The engine sings idle. I'm real sorry about your mamma, he tells me.

I watch the mutt sniffing the fence rail. I appreciate it, I tell him.

Riley nods. She was a great woman.

I know it, I say. I start to raise my beer to drink it, then rest it on my thigh.

He smokes. I went to the funeral, he tells me.

I'm surprised as hell at this and try to remember Riley at the church, but the service blurs in my mind and I can't picture anything except standing at the grave site with Pops kneeling beside me, crying. When he got up, he had grass stains on his knees.

I stood in back, he says. I never knew your daddy so well, and I didn't think there'd be a hell of a lot of time to say hello . . . whole lot of people there. She knew the town.

We're quiet for a good while. My beer's gone warm in my hand, but I don't yet reach down for another. The only sounds are tree frogs and Riley inhaling his cigarette. Finally a car's headlights appear in back of us.

Riley looks in his side mirror and says, Life has a way, don't it, Judge?

That it does, I tell him.

Riley throws his cigarette out the window, shucks the gearshift down and moves the car to the left. A junkit with missing hubcaps and a colorless paint job rolls up to our side and takes a right.

That's why God created whiskey and the blues, says Riley while he turns left. You get drunk as a pig and play hard as you can, and then it goes away.

What goes away? I ask him.

Riley looks over at me and says, Why, the pain, my friend, the god-damn, hard-earned pain.

He pulls a cassette tape out of the glove box in front of me and puts it in the deck. This one I don't recognize. It's the deep-down voice of a woman singing about love.

You like the blues, Yankee? he asks.

What I know of it, I tell him. Pops used to listen to B.B. when I was young. That's about it.

What did you all listen to up north? Riley wants to know.

I shrug my shoulders and tell him, The Stones, the Dead, some Bob Marley.

Riley sips his beer and says, All these Houser Banks boys listen to is country. He raises his beer can to me. Country and blues, Yankee, not much different in terms of subject matter, both sad, only blues got soul. Whitey music lacks soul. Not enough bad shit has happened to us. Ever heard this one: What do you get when you play a country song backwards?

I shrug and look over at him.

He smiles. You get your dog back, your house back and your wife back, he tells me.

I laugh.

You haven't heard that one, says Riley, then you have been missing awhile. You need to get some Mississippi in you. You need to hear you some sliding bottlenecks and backbeat drummin, you need to witness some crossed-harp harmonica. It still goes on all over this here country on weekend nights. It's just us crackers ain't usually privy to it. You got a thing to do tonight?

I got Pops waiting on me at home, I tell him, but he's forgetting what his name is around eleven.

Riley looks up at the moon following us on our right and says, That gives him about two hours of headaching where his boy might be.

Aw, I say, he'll be all right.

Good, says Riley, then we're going to check out some of the best music east of the delta. We'll go hear us some fine stories about crap-shootin men and cheatin women. He looks in his rearview, where two men are riding the Roadrunner's tail, and sides the car for them. They come roaring past, a pickup with its top sawed off, two black guys in it. They're hauling trailers hitched together that say *Dixie Land Barbecue* across them. The truck leaves us with black exhaust and kicked-up tar.

Riley eases back onto the road. When I was sixteen, he tells me, I'd listened to country all my life, never cared much or thought about the blues. Then I went to work for this company in Sardis, made sinks, tubs, toilet seats and the like for hotels and motels. Made em out of epoxy resin. You got to scrape that shit out of your eyelids in the mornings, get the crud off. I had a Superglue smell coming out my armpits. Riley speeds up around a corner. I worked in setup, he says, on the black boys' side, cause I was too damn weird and open-minded to park it with the white folks, and that was a hell of a lot of fun. But after two weeks I went in the front office and said, I'm quitting. You all are poisoning me. I read the chemical kill sheet and everything in it says this place causes cancer. I won't leave now, waste everyone on the line, but come Monday you won't see my sorry ass here. Riley throws his cigarette out and checks his rearview. I went back into where the boys were workin, that particular day I was measuring shower walls, when this big ole fat white guy, pink as pink get-out, mean boss, we called him Uncle Tom, came up and said to me, You ain't quittin because we're poisoning you. He pointed his chubby heart attack finger at me and narrowed his eyes, all punched into his face, and said, You're taking your trade secrets over to Tupelo to Bubba, boisterous, ugly, big-bellied asshole, is what you're doing. Riley looks at me and laughs, Uncle Tom got his hand around my neck, and he would have liked to squeeze the shit out of me, but this black guy in pouring pulled him from me. Emmett Fry was his name, muscled as a bull and fast as a racehorse. He got fired that day and we went home and drank his mamma's muscadine wine and talked about the shitheads who think they're going to retire from there, but they ain't gonna retire, they're gonna be dead. Riley shakes his head. Fry introduced me to the blues, used to play it in a chicken-scratched voice that would blow your heart out. I felt like I'd finally come home when I heard that music. There's nothing else in the world like it.

At the end of the road we stop at a soy field and turn right. Swarms of blackbirds alight from a caved-in barn roof and come like one mechanical black machine over our heads.

And now I'm addicted, he tells me. He goes five miles per hour past a rust-spotted tin roof building leaning on its side and held up by the unused wheels of a semi. Black men are hanging their limbs off the railing of the porch, smoking cigarettes and cigarillos, holding pints, wearing hats and long sideburns. They watch as we go down the road.

I start to sweat. What are we doing, Riley? I say.

Ah, he tells me, just hold on. It's harmless. He parks the car after a long line of vehicles, silences the engine and looks over at me. You, Greel, are as fresh as a cut lawn in summer. Hang by me and you'll be fine. All's it is is drunks and good music and fine ladies in there, nothing to be worried about. He sits his beer on the dash and gets out.

I help him move the Roadrunner top over the car, and we walk up together.

A few men on the porch recognize Riley, clap him on the back and say, How you doin, white boy? You backin up the music?

He says he sure is.

They look at me but they don't say anything, and I try not to look tough or weak, just plain neutral. Invisible as they come. There's a fry pan hanging on the side of the door, someone's scrawled on it in chalk, *Mamma Hatchey's Juke.* On the wall underneath it says *If you got your mind on fight or betting, go somewheres else. No drug selling or smoking. If caught will be locked up. That's the law.*

It costs four dollars to get in and the man taking the money has on a top hat tall as a forearm. He has one silver tooth and rings on every finger. He smiles wide and says, You boys have a fine time, now.

The place is a swarm of hot, sweating black bodies. I've never been in a place with that many black people in it. There's a stage along the right wall with a band playing and a pool table in the middle of the room. The felt's worn through and one corner pocket is missing, so someone has to catch the balls or they bounce on the floor. Lightbulbs dangle by long cords from the ceiling.

The singer onstage calls out, It's my turn now, but if you want to come up here, do it. He has a walking cane across his lap.

Riley leans into me and says, He fills his cane with moonshine and drinks straight from it till they have to carry him out of here.

The man with the moonshine cane picks up his guitar and says into the microphone, One, two, three, then he yells, C'mon, black Nanny, and he starts playing, *You said you loved me once, but now you gone and changed your mind. Give yourself a little more time.*

Riley and I walk to the back corner, where two strong-looking ladies are fixing fish sandwiches on Wonder bread. There's a sign up to the left: *Burgers and cheeseburgers, grilled chicken and catfish $1.00. Canned beer $2.00. You want moonshine ask Slim Henry.* The bar is an old door to a house held up by two wooden sawhorses.

Riley leans into me. Best food you never did eat, he says.

The woman behind the bar has a chiseled-looking face and eyes that look straight into you. She's wearing a man's tie around her head to catch the sweat. She looks over my head and asks a man behind me his order.

The man says, Jazzy already got it.

She looks at me. What you want, baby?

Riley puts his hands on the counter. Two grilled chickens and two Budweisers, he tells her.

She points to me and says, What, he can't talk for hisself? Some girly ate your tongue? She laughs. She calls over to the other lady, We got a mute white boy wants two Buds and a couple of grilled chickens. What you want, Troy? she asks a man next to us. He's wearing a green bowling shoe on one foot and a red one on the other. He states his order.

Hot as a furnace in here, says Riley. He points to an old claw-foot bathtub that's got hunks of ice in it. Hanging from the ceiling by rope are three metal fans blowing as hard as they can over the ice. Air-conditioning, he says.

The woman comes back with our sandwiches and beers. I give her seven dollars. She drops one on the counter and sticks out her tongue. I stick out my tongue back at her and she laughs at the ceiling, a strong, deep laugh that goes through you.

You just met you Mamma Hatchey, says Riley. Later she'll be on that stage burning up the wood she stands on.

It's so hot in there if you rub against someone their sweat comes onto you and makes you wet. It smells of that sweat and of spilt beer and hard liquor and fish sandwiches. The women dancing in front of the band are something I haven't ever seen before, and they make any discomfort worth it. They have muscled thighs and heels as high as porch steps. They dance with their arms above their heads and their eyes closed, their hips swiveling and their flesh leaking out of their shirtfronts. They don't pay me and Riley a lick of attention, they shimmy with their lady friends and their boyfriends and they laugh with their mouths open and their white teeth showing.

Riley and I stand to the side of the stage next to a doorjamb with a bunch of tinsel hanging off it. The guy onstage sings, *Well, I'm going out to Texas, black woman, to hear that wild ox moan. If it don't moan to suit me, black woman, going to drive my bell cow home.*

The bassist can play with his teeth and the drummer puts his drumsticks in his mouth and plays with his hands. Riley stands behind me and says goddamn over and over while he watches them.

A man in a purple suit stands right next to me. He nods. How you doin? he asks.

I'm all right, I tell him.

Good, he says. Hey, he yells over the crowd. Hey, Charley, where's Redman?

Charley comes toward him hauling a loose suspender over his shoulder and flicking a steel nail between his teeth. You didn't hear it? Charley says. Reddy got hisself run over by a ambulance while he was drivin last Saturday. Got his knee broke, his face broke and his arm broke.

The man in purple says, He just dumb as hell, ain't he? He can't help it. He nudges me. Dumb as a tree trunk, he says.

I smile at him.

Onstage the music dies down, the man lifts his cane and another man, wearing a tank top and a straw hat that looks shot through by a shotgun, takes the microphone. Give it up for them, he says. The applause gets louder. Give up the sweat, he tells us. Give up the towel.

A girl with hair piled up on her head goes up with her bottom shaking and hands the man a towel. Come on up and play, he says to the crowd. Eddie here can't play all night. Ifn you want to play, though, you got to do it good. We don't want to hear us no rackety shit.

Singers come up out of the crowd and do sets. Sometimes Riley goes and gets beer and sometimes I do, catching the razz from Mamma Hatchey and loving it every time.

Once when I come back a woman in a little red dress with breasts hanging out it is talking to the man in purple, who's been standing next to me continuously. He's trying to sneak his arm around her bottom. She turns around and slaps his hand. Don't you do that, Frank, she tells him. I'll tattle on you to Regina. She catches sight of me, lifts her chin and turns up the corner of her mouth. Well, she says, and looks me up and down. Her lips are big and painted. She licks them. There ain't nothing like the smell of innocence. You either real young or you the law.

I'm not the law, I tell her.

Good, she says. She smiles, puts a long fingernail in her mouth and looks at me sidelong. Essie, she calls. She grabs a woman's shirt without looking at her. Girl, come here.

Essie comes over and stands next to her. What you want? she asks.

The woman in red points at me. Will you get a load of this white boy?

Essie says, Get a load of him? She throws back her head and laughs. It'd be a mighty big load, cousin. I bet you he ain't never had a woman, he still a newborn. Ain't you, baby? She tousles my hair with her hand.

The man in purple says, You leave this boy alone, he ain't botherin nobody.

The first woman raises her eyebrows high and says, Why don't you cool it, Frank? Ain't nobody talkin to you. She bounces away with Essie. I watch their dresses stretch across their backsides.

The crowd starts to cry out for Mamma Hatchey, who is making her way forward. They stamp their feet and bangs their hands together and call her name.

Once onstage, she takes the microphone from the man and says, You better get back from me, feel my strength, boy.

Raise the roof, yells the man in the straw hat. Give it up for her. He walks away with a jig in his knees and his left hand flicking at his side.

Mamma Hatchey keeps a cigarillo between her fingers while she sings. Her voice takes up any leftover space in that crowded room. The skeleton of raw wood that holds the place together shakes. Her sweat comes off her in sheets, and surprisingly, she is able to move that strong, tall body in a fluid way. Her voice is the deepest and most soulful I've ever heard. Riley is about down on his knees in worship.

Around us people clap and holler. Drinks spill and dancing bodies get thrown up against one another. Mamma Hatchey sings two more songs. At the end of the second song, a girl in a blue dress comes and stands about ten feet away. She lights a cigarette and sips out of a straw in a Coke can. Riley watches her and I see her glance at him. Mamma Hatchey announces that she's finished. She's wet and her breasts are heaving.

I see that young un down there, Mamma Hatchey says. You want to sing a song, honey? She looks directly at the girl in blue, who smiles, kills the cigarette on the floor with her shoe and starts forward. The crowd breaks into claps and pats the girl's back and helps her onstage. Mamma Hatchey says, C'mon, baby, come up here, the mens and womens are wanting it.

The crowd starts to shout her name: Crystal.

The girl has long black braids down her back. Her blue dress is tight to her ankles. She is shy with the microphone cord. The bass player and Mamma Hatchey help her straighten it. The girl's dress leaves enough room at the sleeveless armhole so you can catch a glimpse of what's inside. She stands before the crowd and looks right out at us with her mouth closed. The room quiets.

When she opens her mouth to sing, she's got a smooth voice, deep as a well, and the notes she holds go on forever. I thought Mamma Hatchey moved her body well, but this girl's body makes music when she moves it. Riley stands rigid, grips his beer and watches her with unblinking eyes. Her voice goes smoky and low and then it hits high notes without strain. When she sings she looks like she's making love slow enough to drive you crazy.

A woman with curlers in her hair and a net over them comes to stand next to the guy in purple. He says, She damn good.

She's Jazzy's sister's kid, says the woman in the curlers. Not more'n sixteen.

Riley looks at them.

That one of Nash's? says the man. Well, shit on a stick, I didn't knowed he had a girl. The man has a pint of something and rips on it every few seconds, holding it limply as if his wrist were broken.

Rest are boys, says the curlered lady. She's born late. The lady catches me looking at them and gives me a hard stare. I turn my eyes to the floor, then back at the girl onstage.

Talent like that, says the man in purple, could damn near ruin a chile.

It don't ruin her none, the woman in the curlers tells him.

During her slow song, people are quiet. While she sings, they all sway together in their drunken way. I want to ask Riley who she is, but he doesn't look like he wants to talk, so I keep my mouth shut, suck on my warm beer and fantasize that the girl onstage is warming my twin bed on Elm Street.

When the girl stops her song, she smiles and looks back at the drummer, who salutes her. Then she looks at the guitarist with the harmonica pinned to his shirt. He nods and grins and tells her to come on with another one. The crowd chants her name again and she begins another one, a fast, clippy tune that makes you feel like you have to dance.

The curlered woman and the purple man get on the floor and twirl around each other.

I lean over to Riley and say into his ear, Who is she?

He doesn't answer.

After she has gone through four songs, she smiles, waves shortly and hands the microphone to the straw-hatted man. When she steps off the plank, she holds her dress up to a fine pair of legs. The crowd is already lonely for her, and they try to make her stay up there for one more song. She smiles, and ducks her head and steps through the room. You got it, girl, they tell her. You could move mountains with that voice, baby. You goin on making yourself famous. She walks up next to us and looks right at Riley. Then she heads to the back of the room. I see her skirt around the bar and disappear through the door to the left of the refrigerator.

Riley kills his beer, hands the empty can to me and says, I'll be right back. I watch him weave his way to the front of the room, say something to the doorman and move through the door.

I am alone. The only white person in there. In all my years away at school, I never was anywhere like this and if Riley White didn't exist, I believe I'd have died not knowing about it.

A toothless man in a Panama hat gets up onstage, sits in the chair, smiles, waves and commences playing a guitar. The drummer sings and the music starts again. The beat of the instruments seems to come up through the soles of my shoes from those cracked and splintered floorboards. I want to dance, but I couldn't dance half as good as anyone around me, so I try to root myself in one place. No one looks my way or notices me. I glance around for the girl who sang, but she doesn't come again. The lady in red who thought I was the law is dancing close with a man who has four gold chain necklaces on. He is two heads taller than her, and so drunk his neck isn't working well enough to hold on to his head.

Just when I'm starting to get worried about Riley, he comes back in. It's been three-quarters of an hour. His face is red and his shirt's untucked. His temples are wet with sweat. He takes the empties I am still dumbly holding and places them on the railing in back of me. Let's go, Yankee.

So we go, out that sweating room through the crowd of bodies. When we come out the front door to the porch, a cool, quiet night slaps me in the face. Bye now, Riley says to no one in particular.

Y'all come back now, you hear? the top-hatted man tells us.

We'll do that, says Riley. We go through the front lawn under an almost starless night with a sheer cloud cover.

When we climb into the Roadrunner, the interior smells like sex.

Riley begins to crank the engine, then gets out and tries to haul the top back. I jump out to help him from the other side. We strap it to the rear of the car and climb back in.

Circling the car around, Riley heads us back in the direction we came, puts a hand through his hair and doesn't speak until we get to the end of the straightaway. He turns right. His voice is quiet. Get me out a beer, will you, Judge?

I grab one, pull the tab and hand it over.

Keeping his fingers on the top of the wheel, he kills that beer, then throws the can to the road. He fishes in his front pocket for a cigarette and ends up squooshing the empty box between his fingers. Goddamn, he says, you always got to run out of smokes when you're near starved for one. He throws the empty pack on the floor and checks his ashtray, pulls out a half-smoked Camel and puts it between his lips. In the same voice he used when he spoke of my mother, he says, You want to know who I wouldn't kill to be with that girl all the time? You want to know what I wouldn't do?

I watch him, careful, so I could know that. I think of the girl onstage and I realize he doesn't have to say a thing, I could near guess what it must be like.

He turns his head toward me and looks for as long as the car will let him until we start to crawl onto gravel. Then he turns back to the road. You wouldn't want to know that, Greel. He turns the radio on, then off again, runs a hand through his hair and finally says, You ever been knocked down, dragged out for a woman?

Like you are? I ask him. I'm quiet for a second, looking up at the cloud cover moving fast toward the north. A half slice of moon appears. No, I tell him. I don't think I've ever been like you probably are over her.

He murmurs, Lucky goddamn piece of Yankee shit. Then he smiles at me, and I smile with him.

The Roadrunner hurls us through the night. Out of the side of my vision I see Riley in a whole different way. A man is always greater for whose body he is touching, and Riley has become larger than life.

5

HALEY

From the bread aisle in Elsa's store, I watch Bo Dickens's eyes moving from face to face. He has a hunk of tobacco on the inside of his bottom lip and a Coke can in one hand for a spittoon.

The store is to the left of the courthouse. Wives and girlfriends can usually find their men there if they've lost them. At breakfast, Elsa will skiddle them hash browns and grits and bacon and sausage, eggs any way they want and Texas toast and pancakes big around as dinner plates. They come back at lunch for po'boys and steak sandwiches and corn dogs and hamburgers. On Saturday nights she opens up her basement to country singers and poker games and whiskey drinking.

It's the first official day of my summer vacation. Daddy and Bo, Joe Frielly, Calley Pearl and T. Fingerling are all standing around in the heat of Elsa's store with sweat licking them up, listening to Bo Dickens tell a story. Elsa's behind the register blowing wide, pink bubbles that pop against her lips like satin. Her youngest brother, Calley Pearl, jobless and usually jailbound, rubs a finger in his teared eyes and tries to break a laugh. Dickens, he says, how the hell did you shit your pants and beat the hell out of the guy at the same time?

The men stay their eating and watch Bo and wait on an answer. Elsa leans over the counter and keeps her gum chewing steady.

Bo picks the tobacco out of his lip and sticks it in the soda can. He points an unlit cigarette at Calley. Pearl, he says, you ever been in Jackson's Twin Winnie bar after stealin money from a black delta boy who has a sawed-off double-barrel at your back?

Nope, says Calley, shifting his feet.

The men smirk, take guzzles of their sodas and bites from their lunches and drags off their smokes.

Well, let me tell you, Bo says, narrowing his eyes. You got a shotgun at your back, and I don't care what kind, but especially one held by a two-hundred-and-fifty-pound nigger sonofabitch—scuse me, Elsa—and madder than a stick of dynamite, then you'd know. You gotta get around fast as a greyhound, grab that gun, wing a fist across the mister's jaw and while he's on the floor, pray to Jesus and the devil that his gun's tight in your hand. If you got it, point it at the motherfucker's face and kick him in the forehead before he can holler for help. Soon as you kick him, you best be using the same foot to run out that door quick as a shot with five hundred bucks of his gambled money in your back pocket. At that minute, your shit's going to be warm in your pants, but you got to get your truck moving and haul ass eighty-five miles per hour out of that joint's driveway, piss stone drunk and praising Mary's high heaven that you're still alive. You do that, Calley Pearl, and then you tell me if you wouldn't mess your pants, too. Problem is, Cal, you done mess your pants when the gun's hot on your spine, the motherfucker's gonna shoot you, not for no five hundred bucks, but cause you smell so bad.

The whole store leans back laughing. Bo lights his smoke and smiles. The men start eating again. They say, Christ, Dickens, that's better'n the last one.

Elsa pops a bubble and tells him, You're plumb crazy, Bo.

Then what happened? Calley Pearl wants to know. He follow you? But no one pays any attention to him.

Daddy looks at his watch. Joey, he says, we fixin to do some work today, or you just want to sit around making Elsa's store hot listening to Bo's bullshit?

Let's go, says Joey.

The men begin to move, throwing food wrappers in the garbage, draining drinks and giving money to Elsa. I pretend to study the racks of bread. Bo caught my dress sleeve on my way in here. Don't go, wait on me after this, he said fast. Not one man saw. Daddy's at the counter, tallying what he bought. Hey Haley, he calls, you about ready?

I look over at him. Gwyn gave me a list long as a schoolbook, I tell him. I should stay and get it all for her.

He takes a swig of his soda, throws it in the trash and wipes the back of his hand across his mouth. Long as a schoolbook, huh? He squints at me. Well how you plannin to get home, seein as I got the truck?

I finger a can of tuna. I'll go to Gypsy's shop, I tell him. She'll drop me.

Daddy bangs a new pack of smokes on his thigh. All right, he says, spitting something from between his teeth. See you at home later. He nods his chin to Bo. See you, Dickens. Bye now, Calley. When he and Joe slam the screen, they leave dust and quiet behind them.

The phone rings and Elsa says into it, It's about time you done called me.

Bo gives me a slow, tight-lipped smile and gestures his head toward the door, squashes his cigarette in the sand ashtray and says, Well, I got some things to take care of, Cal. When Elsa gets off the ringer, tell her I said good-bye. He places his cowboy hat on his head and is gone.

Calley takes a newspaper from the steel rack beside the register, leans his bum to the wall and makes like he's reading it. I can feel him watching me while I search the aisles for the things Gwyn wants. Gwyneth's script is elegant, like the Declaration of Independence we used to see in school-books. Even the word *bread* looks beautiful.

I go fast because I know Bo is waiting. Milk and OJ and tuna and toothpaste.

Calley folds the newspaper and puts a hand in his pocket. Hey Haley, he calls.

I look up at him.

He glances at Elsa, who's still on the phone, and nods his head at me. How old you gotten to be? he asks.

I'm sixteen, I tell him.

Calley Pearl's got that look about him that he might mistake you for an ice cream, lick you up in one sitting and then wipe his mouth clean without an extra thought about it. He's a man whose arms flap around him like useless things and he's most of the time in bar fights or getting in trouble for stealing car radios. I study the floorboards. They're patched over by a two-by-four and someone has written $A + H$ on it in black marker.

Calley walks forward and stands next to me. He fingers a can of dog food and looks at my list. You've gotten so pretty, he says. I saw you a couple of nights ago at the Hothouse Barbecue with your daddy, grown men wantin to dance with you. You were just a little girl, last I knew.

His denims are dirt stained and they're held up by a fraying leather belt around a pudgy belly that not too long ago must have been skinny. He's got nice blond hair, streaked to white, and blue eyes that look like the ocean must. Daddy says he used to be a lady-killer. Dumb ladies, he says, but still ladies.

I pick up a box of crackers, throw them in the cart and walk toward the meat case. Calley walks behind me.

I bet you breakin all the boys' hearts at school. He does a kind of jig and plants himself in front of me. When I try to go around him, he dodges me one way and then the other. He says, Ha ha, and messes the hair out of his eyes. You a jewel, he says. You know it, you're a bona fide piece of pretty.

When I come forward to the deli case, he looks down into it as if he were choosing something and says, low so Elsa won't hear, Gus is starting me at the station when Rickie leaves, bout another ten days, if you want to stop by and see me sometime.

I'm working at the stables all the time, I tell him.

Well after work, he says.

Elsa glances at us and says into the phone, Billy, I got to go. Ellyson's girl is here and she needs some meat.

Calley backpedals to the door. In the grinder mirror I see him pick up a newspaper and pretend to read.

Bye now, Elsa says into the receiver. She rolls her eyes at me and smiles. Men, she tells me when she hangs up. Sometimes I wish I was a homosexual.

Calley calls from the doorway, I heard that. You don't wish no such thing. Some people are born like that. You should be countin your blessings.

When I turn back to look at him, he smiles.

Elsa rubs her hands on the thighs of her jeans and ties the strings of her apron behind her. You want your half a pound of turkey, honey? she asks me.

I nod yes and she rips off a piece of Saran wrap and starts to cut the meat into thin slabs. She licks her fingers and peels off a sticker to seal it. Don't you got somewhere to be, Calley Pearl? she yells over to him.

Right here where I am, he says. I got to watch all the pretty ladies who come into your store.

Look out for them men, she says. She nods her head to her brother and goes to the register. They must be like flies to butter on you, honey.

I watch her painted fingernails ringing everything up while I bag quick as I can.

It's fifteen dollars and fifteen cents, she says. She chews her gum while I count out change. Auburn pieces of hair stick to her neck in the heat. How's Gwyneth feeling these days? she asks me.

She's fine, thank you, ma'am. I grab the bag and start toward the door.

You got that okay, sweetheart?

I'm all right, I tell her.

You going to Gypsy's?

Yes, I tell her.

You wanting Calley to take you over there?

Calley stands straight up and throws the newspaper on the floor.

Seems he hasn't a thing to do, she says.

Calley opens the door for me and looks down the length of my body when he does it.

No ma'am, I call back. Thank you, though. I don't look at Calley.

Look out for that heat, Elsa calls after the screen slams, and those boys. I turn once and Calley Pearl winks at me.

Outside of Elsa's store nothing's going on, there's just one boy sitting on a bicycle holding the tree beside him for balance. Lo, he says to me.

Hi ya, I say and start across the center of Main to Water Street. It's deserted. On one side is an old building site where a half-finished house sits with holes for windows and a dirt lawn. Other than that, it's just blacktop. There isn't a single piece of shade.

Bo's pickup rumbles by in less than a minute. He slows and puts his hand out the driver's-side window. Let me take your package, he says.

I can carry it, I tell him.

Come on, little lady, let me take that bag so you don't waste yourself from heat.

There's no reason why Bo should believe every time he wants to see me, he can. I'm going to Gypsy's, I tell him.

He inches the truck up. Well, let me carry you, he says. Hop in.

There's a tight crick in my elbow from holding the bag. Sweat drips down the back of my legs. I want to get in, but I keep on walking. He leans into the rearview to watch for cars. Let me see what all you got in that bag, he says.

Without looking at him, I walk over to the truck and put the bag on the sill of his window. Instead of seeing what's inside, he drags the bag over his lap to the passenger's seat, smiles and points a finger at me. Gotcha, he says. A car comes around the corner of Water Street and Bo's face loses its smile. Meet me at the old hunting camp up on Oak Street, he tells me, and then he is gone. His tires kick up dirt and grit behind him.

At the corner of Oak, there's a closed-up gas station with holes in the ground where the pumps used to be. The building's boarded up by graffitied plywood. *I love Eric. Karen will you marry me? AC's pussy's sweet to eat.*

The Browns live halfway up Oak in a mustard-colored house. One of the Brown girls is standing at the jamb in a red dress that's safety-pinned at the shoulder. She has a tall-boy Coors in her hand and is smoking a cigarette. A hound with bare spots on its back is tied up to the wash line. It bites its leash and growls at me.

Dog, the girl says, hush up. She doesn't say it with any force.

At the top of the hill, fire ant homes are piled around and long wheat-colored grass is growing through splits in the cement. Bo's pickup makes a clicking sound like motors do when they've just been cut off. He isn't anywhere around.

A four-wheeler road cuts into the woods. The path smells of sour urine and new mud. I walk down it until I get to the clearing. Insects skate on top of the swamp and dragonflies skirt in midair, having sex. Or at least Daddy told me that's what they do. To the left is the deer camp, where men sit around in winter bragging on their hounds and drinking whiskey. I call Bo's name. The woods stay still.

The deer camp's roof is green with moss and the boards are splintered and half rotten. I try to see through the peepholes and knots in the wood. Finally I go in the door, which is hanging from rusted hinges like a leaning drunk. Inside it smells like mold and dead animal. I'm half blinded from sunlight and can only just make out Bo's form sitting on a bench against the far wall, smoking a cigarette.

This scares me, I tell him.

Come here, then, he says. A sliver of light cuts across his face in a thin streak from his eye to his chin. I stay where I am. You mad at me, little lady? he asks.

Through the door, wind blows and trails up my sundress. I reach my hand back, open the door more and lean into it. I didn't like coming here, I say.

He cocks his head. Why's that?

That road is hot, I tell him. And those Browns are creepy. You shouldn't have taken Gwyn's groceries, they'll rot in this heat.

He ducks his head and laughs. Come here and tell me that, beautiful girl.

I do it, stand before him with my arms across my chest. It's hard to look him in the eye, so I look over at the old steel sink to the right. The dry faucet is curved like a person bending with his mouth open.

He reaches up with one hand and takes my wrist. How you been, Haley?

I been good, I tell him.

He throws his cigarette down and mashes it with his boot. You running from me, or what?

No, I say. Someone has engraved the word *fuck* on the bench beside him.

He holds tight to my arm. There's a splash in the swamp outside, and he jerks at the sound, then relaxes. Sweat drops down the small of my back. He pulls me so I am between his legs, the inside of his thighs touch the outside of mine. With one finger he makes a trail down my stomach. You and me, he says, this isn't bad, I won't hurt you. He puts his mouth against my stomach. I wouldn't do a thing to hurt you. I just want you a little, Haley. I watch you, he says. I can't not see you. I wish I didn't want it. But I do.

He tells me I am too beautiful for this world.

I swallow, study his black, curly hair and his gray eyes when he looks up at me. His mouth is the color of a raspberry stain.

He whispers, Why can't you come to me more? I want that.

You're the one, I say and then stop. He tips his head back and watches me. Who is scared, I say. You won't hardly talk to me or look at me, then all of a sudden today you want to see me. Why today? Why not Tuesday or last Saturday, when I was alone in the tack room and you knew it?

He half smiles, his hands go up and down on my hips, then he leans over and puts his lips to my stomach again. I ain't taking chances that could take me from you, he says into me. Don't think I don't want to see you. All the time. His fingers bunch my dress sides. He lifts it from my thighs. Haley Ellyson, he says.

One of my hands comes up and trails the vein running his left temple, my other hand clutches his hair. Slung in a U across my belly are my violet silk underpants. He picks up their elastic. I take a sharp breath inward.

On the split wall above him, a spiderweb waves like a limp hair net. I focus on it while my body goes liquid with want. I wish this were not Bo. Why couldn't he be someone else I was allowed to love in the wide open with people watching so I wouldn't have to whisper in the hellhole of a winter deer camp?

He has me take a step back, pulls his T-shirt off and puts it at our feet. Then he wraps his hands around my arms and pulls me down so I am kneeling between his legs on his shirt.

You're shaking, he says.

I nod. He pulls me to him. His chest smells of smoke tobacco and horse lather. He moves two fingers around the neck of my dress and then drops his hand down as if he were trying to steal something. He squeezes my left breast with his callused fingertips. His breath comes heavy and fast. My eyes close, I part my lips

You okay, Haley? he asks. And then his lips are on mine, tasting of salt and smoke. While my dress is raised from me, I keep my eyes shut, feeling him licking the sweat from my shoulders and collarbone. The Brown girl in her red dress enters my mind, clear as if she were there spying, sucking on her cigarette, calling her dog.

I open my eyes and Bo and I watch each other while he touches every part of me, neck and face, thighs and belly, as if he were searching an injured animal for what's broken. Hard wood bites through the cotton of his T-shirt and stings my knees. Somehow the pain is good. I am groaning and my groin opens to ache. I don't want to ask him to touch me there, but without his touch, it hurts like something swelled to busting. My back arches and my eyes close again. I am saying something, I don't know what, and then I hear myself a third time. I hate you, I am telling him.

His hands stop moving on my body.

He slacks his arms from me and leans his head against the wall. He looks once at my breasts and then back into my eyes.

I got a bay stud, he tells me, worth forty-five hundred dollars that I could've gotten on a dime if I had gone up to Tunica today. They're selling good cattle-using horses cheap. The old man who owned them fell down with a stroke last week with a shitload of debt and they got to get rid of them quick. They gave me a chance to go out there for a pick before the sale and I came here for you instead because I hadn't got the chance to see you in awhile. I wanted to be with you more than we have. At the sale all that'll be left is crow's bait, but I was worried on you and wanting you. And now, he says, you gone and told me you hate me. He runs his tongue quick around the outside of his mouth, leans back and looks at the ceiling.

Even in the heat, a wet chill comes over me. I'm sorry, I tell him. We stay like that for some time. Bo is bare chested and I am naked save my panties. He does not even glance my way. Finally I pick my dress off the floor and put it over my head. Tears come without warning and I bite my lip to try to keep them away. They slick my face and my nose runs. He looks down at me and then starts to get up, but I reach for his arm. No, I tell him. When he sits back down, he sighs.

Haley, he says, soft. He takes me in his arms and starts to rock back and forth. Hush, girl, he says. You're all right, there ain't no need to cry.

He hugs me too close so I have trouble breathing. When he strokes my head, I can feel the hair pulling my scalp. Even so, I hold his arms and touch the coarse hairs, wrap my fingers around his tensed muscles. The tears come quick like storm and then they stop fast as they came and leave me shaking. I am weak and limp feeling, leaning against his bare chest.

He moves his arms from around me, puts his hands on my cheeks and looks into my eyes. My face gets puffy and red when I cry, so I try to look away, but he keeps a firm hold and says, What are you crying for, girl? You're likely to make a man crazy acting like you did today.

I look away from him. I know, I say, quiet.

Let's go, he says. He looses from me and goes to pick up his T-shirt. Let's get out of this stinkin woodpile before it falls down on us.

Bo drives us back in late afternoon. The sun looks like a fat yellow stain in the sky. He makes me lie on my back on his hot vinyl seat so no one will see me. His denimed leg is beneath me. I can feel it flex to let up or push down on the gas. Out the top of the window, woods go by in a green blur. His rearview is hung with the twisted bendings of old coat hangers vibrating while we drive. There's a green air freshener hanging off it in the shape of a curvy lady. She smells of pine.

Why didn't that man have an arm? I ask him.

Bo's ashtray is out and it's full up with old smokes that smell like a chimney fire. It takes him three tries to bang it closed. Then he says, That man wasn't from Houser Banks or anywhere near here. I don't know his story, little lady, and we ain't bound to know it now. I watch his jaw flex. He glances down at me. What? he says when he catches me looking. I bat the curvy air freshener lady with my hand and watch her swing.

I knew a man once who used to run the Twirly-Whirl at the fair, I say to Bo while he smokes out the window. He lost his leg in the Vietnam War. Liv and I used to visit him the summer we were twelve. He'd hold his hand like this—I make a fist to show him. He'd put quarters in there and bang them around like a rattle.

Bo is quiet. It is a long while before he tells me, I don't love you because you helped me that night. His voice is gruff. I loved you long before that.

He doesn't touch me. The whole way home I wish he would. The crying and the wishing leave me lonesome and trapped-feeling. Between us the air feels heavy and silent.

By the woods at the end of our street, he sides the truck in an inlet and looks in his rearview. Okay, he tells me.

I lean up, hoist Gwyneth's bag in my lap and slide off the seat, slamming the door behind me without looking at him or saying good-bye.

6

FLETCHER

The heat comes in around six in the morning and sticks to my bedsheets. I don't sleep half well after that and at seven twenty, just when I'm too tired to stay awake anymore, Pops pokes his head in my room and says, I'm going in, son. See you at eight thirty.

The Fresh County Courthouse sits smack in the center of Houser Banks. It's old, with high ceilings and wooden benches. The balcony where black people used to sit hangs over the back. Pieces of railing are missing and it needs a paint job. Saloon-type doors separate the general public from the plaintiff's and defendant's tables. I walk through them to the doors leading to the judge's quarters.

Pops is behind his desk with a folder and a cup of coffee in front of him. He motions for me to sit down in the chair to his left, picks a piece of lint off his robe and watches me put my hands on my knees.

You ready? he asks me.

I nod.

Firstly, he says and picks up some papers and waves them at me, we have a custody case, Becky Hartle versus the State of Mississippi. He looks at the door and takes off his glasses. Oh, come in, Julian, let me introduce you to my son, Fletcher Greel.

A guy over six feet tall with a unibrow and black frizzy hair comes in. He's got a wide heavy-boned face, and he's wearing an industrial green work shirt. I was just about to start in on a day's work, Mr. Fletcher, he says to me, gesturing with his large hands to a mop and water bucket in the doorway. When I look up at him, I see he has eyes the color of nothing. He winks.

Pops sits back down, straightens the papers in front of him and says, Fletcher will be working here this summer.

Julian smiles. Sure thing, he says. You working on being a judge someday like your daddy?

Before I can answer, he says, Good for you, Mr. Fletcher. Seein how long I been here, I might could be a judge myself, ain't that right, Your Honor?

Pops clears his throat and laughs once, a kind of bark. I think you'd make a fine judge, Julian, he says. How was your vacation?

Julian walks to the back of the room, touching the papers and books on Pops's shelves as he goes.

It was fine, thank you, sir, he says. I did a whole lot of nothing, which is what I like to do on vacation. He stands at the end of the room slopping his mop up and down in the water bucket. Then he pushes the handle down and squeezes the water from it. He looks back, salutes me and says, See you later, Mr. Fletcher, it was a pleasure. He pushes his mop like a rudder and disappears around the corner.

When he's gone, Pops says, An okay fellow. Was in trouble with the law a couple of times. He's making an effort to straighten up, though. We hope he'll learn to fly straight.

Pops picks up a yellow Magic Marker. I have been meaning to tell you, son, he says while he fingers the marker, we have a little salary for you, not much, but you will be paid every two weeks about four hundred and fifty dollars.

Thank you, sir.

You might prefer to be interning at an attorney's office, but I think it's all right to have you here, learning from this end of things, plenty of time for the other later. He undoes the top of the marker, swivels his chair around and puts a yellow X on today's date on his calendar. There are two Xs on the two days prior to today.

He turns around again, leans back in the chair with his hands around his head and stares at the door. Third man this week executed in Louisiana, he says. This one was a twenty-year-old boy. Killed an elderly couple in rural Louisiana. They don't know why he did it, no prior convictions, but the jury and the judge saw fit to have him executed at twelve fourteen A.M. this morning, when you and I were sleeping. Four fifteen-second jolts of electricity. They don't even let them see, cover the face with a canvas mask and lead him to the death house in leg shackles. My father rocks harder in his chair and his lip twitches. I shift in my seat. Twenty years old, he says again. He puts both feet on the floor and rests his elbows on the desktop.

He starts to say something else when a girl in a wheelchair rolls herself in a good distance from his desk. Before she can state her business Pops says, Robin, how are you today? This is my son, Fletcher Greel. He's working with us this summer.

Robin has straight black hair the color of a wet eel and thick brown lips. Her legs are thin and limp before her. She raises her chin and looks at me. I stand and come to her with my arm outstretched. She watches her lap while we shake.

Pleased to meet you, she says. She tosses her hair and looks up at my father. Your Honor, they wanted me to come in and tell you, Attorney Fredricks would like a word with you.

Pops sits back down and says, He can come see me in ten minutes. Thank you, Robin.

She wheels herself out backward then turns around at the door and looks once more at me before she starts on her way down the hall.

My father opens his desk drawer and rummages around. She's a Chickasaw, he says, adopted at seven from a family your mother knew from the church. Hardworking girl. If she needs a thing, you try to do it for her.

I find I am still standing up and sit down suddenly, struck dumb and damn depressed about my summer, which so far consists of dusty courtrooms, cocky janitors, beautiful women with nonworking legs and Pops's yellow *X*s marking executions across the days on his calendar.

When we walk out of the courthouse that afternoon, heat is warping the air, sweat drains out of me. Pops and I come around to the parking lot. Robin is wheeling off in front of us, crossing the street to Rose's Boutique.

We haven't seen the whole of it, Pops says to me. Sad thing is, Becca Hartle doesn't know herself anymore.

Yes sir, I say, for something to say. A woman opens the door for Robin and she rolls in. The curtain hanging behind the display hides the front window, so I can't see what's in there.

Pops sighs. Something seems to go from him. He slumps in his walk. His face looks slack and tired.

Long day, huh? I ask him.

He smiles a little. It was that, wasn't it, son?

We stop at our cars. What's that shop over there? I point to where Robin has just gone in.

That? Oh, a Creole woman owns it. I don't know what all is in there, jewelry and maybe some fixes or something. I believe she's from New Orleans.

Fixes? I say.

Well, he says, you know, like voodoo or what have you.

Oh.

He puts his briefcase on top of the Lincoln and starts to wriggle out of his jacket. She doesn't know that she did it, he says. She believes a lie. He slings his coat over one arm.

I put my hand on the car door. Who? I ask him.

Becca Hartle. You can't work justice with anyone who believes a lie. She can't remember what she does when she drinks. Even though she can see the burn spots, she doesn't believe she did it to him. She's blaming everyone else.

The handle of my car is hot as a working griddle. Who all is she blaming? I ask him.

Pops leans across the roof of the Lincoln. She's blaming the law for taking it up, he says.

I look down at my hands and bite the sides of the flesh around the thumbnail.

It's irritating, says my father, to watch a person blaming the law. We're trying to protect the children, for God's sake. If she'd just give them a chance to stay elsewhere.

I shake my head slowly. Maybe she is blaming someone else, I tell him. I look down at my keys.

Who'd that be? he asks.

I shrug. When I look up at him, I find he's handling me with a focused stare. I don't know, I tell him, but I'd say she's probably blaming her husband, somehow, for dying on her.

Pops nods slowly and watches me. Then he says, Why don't you hop in here with me? He points to the Lincoln.

He doesn't say a word while we drive down Church Street past the Episcopal church. When we hit the dirt path into the graveyard, I catch sight of a new burial, the dark brown mud laid over in a rectangle with fresh flowers around it. A man in an undershirt is standing over the grave with his head bowed. I watch him while we wind past three old oaks and turn left. Thinking of that man's empty words to a new grave site makes my mouth dry.

The way Pops steers lets me know he drives this route all the time. I watch all those headstones go by and think how for every one of them there's a whole pile of people left living who have to hurt and miss somebody and sometimes they forget to be sad about it for a while, and so then they have to feel guilty.

My mom's grave is atop a hillside all the way at the other end of the cemetery.

The day we went to the shop to pick out her gravestone was a bad day for her, her face was paler than usual, and she had to stop twice to catch her breath when I walked her from the house to the car.

My grandfather and I sat in the back of the Lincoln, and he kept rubbing his palms together as if he were cold. Every so often, my mom would look back at him and say, You doing okay, Daddy? They squeezed each other's hands over the seat back.

Grandpa stayed in the car when we went in the store.

I want something feminine, my mother said while we walked with a toupeed salesman through the rows of stone pieces. Pops kissed the top of her head and looked down at her. He didn't say anything. The salesman kept pushing his index finger over his two front teeth as if he were cleaning them. He pointed to pink granite stones in each row. It's a soft pink, he said about twelve times.

When we got to the statues of angels, my mom looked up at Pops, and her eyes got wide and panicked. We won't find anything, Jonathan. She backed away from him. There's nothing here, she said. Her voice sounded hysterical. I hadn't ever heard it like that before.

When Pops went to her, she put her hands against his chest and said, Don't touch me. Then she tugged the kerchief off her head. I ran to pick it up and tried to give it to her, but she wouldn't take it. She just looked at me and one of her eyes seemed to fly off in another direction. I'm going home, she said, and she turned around and walked down the aisle. The overhead lights made a white spot on her bald head. Somehow one of her heels had come out of her tennis shoe, so she limped.

Ellie, Pops called while he ran off after her.

I stood there holding the red kerchief. The salesman stood beside me.

Yes, he said, well. He coughed once. His voice was oily, and he smelled of wet cigar. Here, he said, pushing catalogues of gravestones at me. Have her pick one out from home, and your father can call us.

I took them without thinking.

When I came to the car, Pops had the engine started. I dropped the catalogues on the gravel drive and got in. My mother was in the back, curled into Grandpa's chest. He kept his palm on the back of her bald head, and I thought he looked brave.

On the way out of the parking lot, I watched the catalogues turn over in the wind and paste themselves to the side of the building.

I think about your mother every breathing minute, says my father. His voice surprises me. He has parked the car under a tall pine in front of her grave and turned off the ignition. The car goes stale with heat.

I nod. I know, I say.

He looks out toward her grave. When she couldn't have more children, she cried quite a bit, he says. Then one evening three or so years later, after you had been put to bed, we were sitting having a brandy after dinner and she said how she'd thought she wanted more children but then when she had you, she realized you were all she needed.

He opens the door. A drone of insects comes at us. Pops walks up there first with his hands in his pockets. He bends down, picks a twig off the ground and throws it to the side, then squats on his haunches and wipes the stone with the palm of his hand.

A plane hurls itself through the sky. I wonder what it would have been like if she had gone that way, split second, her body evaporating in engine fire. It would have spared her the knowing that the end was close.

I open the door and put one leg out, sit there and watch Pops out the bug-spattered front window of the Lincoln.

It was only one year ago that I was in Houser Banks and didn't even know she was sick. She would come into my room every morning, wake me by flipping up the shades. Come on, sleepy bones, she'd say. There's a day going on out there without you.

When she leaned over to kiss my forehead, she always left her mouth there for a couple of seconds. Hmm? she'd ask all soft. You gonna come down and bless this day with yourself?

I would pull my sheet over my head, turn to face the wall and tell her, A few more minutes.

Sometimes I'd go back to sleep while she stood there. Or I'd hear her footsteps across my floor and the door clicking when she went out.

When I think about that, it makes me crazy. I wake up in the middle of the night wishing I had gotten up those mornings and watched her make breakfast and read the paper and water her flowers. I tell God or whatever it is that looms around up there, if she were here this summer, I would memorize her hair and her eyes and her hands and every word she spoke. I swear I would ask her about every year that had passed in her life.

Pops rocks forward on his haunches and lifts to standing. The sun is swollen and white in the sky behind him. Fletcher, come on over here, he calls.

I get out of the car. When I climb to the top of the hill, I stand directly in back of him. There are wet sweat circles around his armpits.

You been here much? he asks without looking at me.

I kick at the lawn. No sir, I tell him, I haven't.

In the silence a crow yells and flaps its wings for lack of wind.

Well . . . you need to do that.

Yes sir.

Don't do it for me, he says, and don't do it for her. She's either here or she's not. We aren't going to know a thing about your mother anymore. I've had a mother die. I don't know all of it, but I know what it is to boil up inside and then have it boil over. All you need to do is just pay some attention to it now. He turns and stares at me until I look up. He says quietly, Understand?

I nod.

He begins to walk away. I am going to turn the car around, he tells me. I'll sit in it, you stay here and come when you're ready.

Yes sir, I tell him.

I wait until I hear his car door shut. The engine starts, and I walk forward. A black bug crawls across her stone. Sitting on my haunches like Pops did, I close my eyes and think I'm a selfish, piss-poor son. I know I am. Because what I most wish for is all that time I had before I knew she was sick, when riding around with her and eating lunch with her didn't mean a thing except what it had always meant. I feel guilt a mile long about it. I am glad for the time I had when I didn't know, and maybe I kept myself from the knowing because of all that pain it brought on.

Two days before I left for Spain last summer, when we were on our way to Tupelo to buy a backpack for my trip, I couldn't ignore it anymore. She swerved the Lincoln to the side of Highway 12 and stopped so quick, I grabbed the air ducts. Then she opened the door, leaned out and threw up. I heard it split the gravel. A beat-up Chevy passed us and gave a long honk.

Excuse me, I heard her say. She choked and spit and then she threw up again. After that, she just stayed there with her head hanging. Her voice was weak. There are Kleenexes in the glove compartment, Fletcher. Will you get them for me?

I leaned up and opened the glove. There was a plastic travel pack of tissues in there, and I put them on her lap. She took one without looking at it, wiped her mouth, threw it on the ground and got another. She did this six times. I watched her soak her tongue with one and blow her nose with another. She put the back of her hand across her forehead and then she sat up, closed the car door and looked in the rearview. We got back on the road. Her hands shook on the steering wheel. She cried quietly and wiped her tears away when they came.

I remember she wore a red dress that day and one spot of throw-up had landed on the collar. I kept worrying about it, wondering whether or not I should mention it to her.

7

HALEY

The sidewalk on Cricket Street in front of Crystal's house smells like steaming wet cement. Wiry black kids run through fire hydrants outside of square homes squooshed up next to one another. Torn-up living room couches sit on porches and black women stand around them in faded cotton dresses calling to one another across the street and jostling diapered babies on their hips. Men lean against doorjambs behind them, smoking cigarettes and watching the road out of heavy-lidded eyes. They look at me with some interest when I ride slowly down their street.

I park in a vacant lot where a house got burned down. Piles of broken glass and pieces of a kitchen stove and bed frames and blocks of black wood are lying around. From there I cut down a small pathway and walk the backyard alleyways to Crystal's. She's waiting for me on her back porch. I watch her dress skirt swing while I follow her to her room. She's barefooted and her tiny braids sway down her back.

I am still awestruck by Crystal Nash. I have a thought that her mystery is something she was born with and she will all her life get to live with it. She is hypnotizing to be around. I believe that hard as he tries, Riley won't ever lose his love for her because of that.

Her room smells of smoke and dust and Crystal's musky perfume. I flop down on her bed and she stands in the center of her bedroom. Before you came, I was practicing, she says to me. You want to hear it?

I nod at her and watch her carefully while she puts the needle on her record player and then waits in the center of the room for the music to begin. When the song starts, her body sways with the music. She puts her head back and closes her eyes and starts to sing. It looks like her body is feeling the deepest pleasure. Her hips move, her hands dance and her mouth bellows out sound and then gets soft in a matter of seconds. Listening to her makes me want to love someone so bad it hurts my insides.

When the song ends, Crystal's body goes slack. I clap hard for her. The record player needle ticks, and she smiles, raises the needle off and pushes the cassette's play button. A woman's deep voice comes on and sings *Ice man, ice man, come on up . . .*

That's how I practice, she says while she lies down on her bed next to me. Her dress skirt is cloud gray. She picks something off it.

Crystal, you're so good, I tell her. You could be famous.

Yeah, well you should come hear me sing some night at Mamma Hatchey's with Riley, if you got the nerve. She runs the tip of her pointer finger over my thigh and whistles. Girl, she says, you're going to turn black with the tan you got going on. You got some muscles too, don't you? She points her finger into her own leg and makes an imprint in the velvet brown of her skin. Maybe I'll go on ride me some horses, get strong like you. At least I got to do some aerobics or something. I'm getting all chubby.

I laugh. Aw, Crystal, I say, you'll be fat when Stitchy turns mayor. Which is absolutely never.

She rolls her head to look at me. Her black braids fall between us on the lime-colored spread. Reach me a Virginia off the bedside, would you? she asks.

I pass her two so I can smoke one.

She leans forward for a lighter off the windowsill, takes the cigarettes from me and lights them. The room fills with smoke. She bats the air to make it clearer. We lie on our backs and smoke. On the ceiling there's a tan water stain in a lopsided circle the shape of a half-moon. The memory of her voice rises in my ears. If I could sing like that, I'd find a place out in the woods where no one ever was and listen to myself all day long.

Smoke comes out her mouth in one long stream. Through the window a cloud passes, a column of dusty sun comes in hot on our skin. She gets rid of the ash on her Virginia into a Coke can beside the bed and says, You still with . . . what's his name? Riley's cousin, that older boy?

Hannaford? I say, Nah, he turned out to be mean down to his bones. And he's all full up with himself. I stand up to get away from the window heat and go over to the bookshelves, where she's got tattered and ripped songbooks with faded music marks in them. I turn their soft, weathered pages.

I could have told you he was mean, Crystal says. And those good-lookin ones are always full up with themselves. How old is he?

Nineteen, I tell her. I run my finger over the rough seam of a book.

And you're sixteen years old? she asks, craning her neck to look over at me.

I nod.

Damn, girl, you like em better old, don't you?

I think of Bo and don't say anything. Crystal smokes.

I guess there's no one I care on going out with at Banks High, I tell her. Hannaford was good-looking and he seemed like he'd be a pile of fun, but he wasn't anything more than the others. Now that I'm through with him, he's gotten crazy, callin my house all the time, comin to the stables any hour even though everyone knows he couldn't mount a saddle if there were Crazy Glue on it. He's been botherin me while I'm doing the feedings and once he even stood next to me a whole lesson, pleadin like a sorry beggar that I should go back with him. I told him to go away and forget it and don't come around no more. I can't tell him anything, though. He isn't listenin to me.

Shit, says Crystal, he's kicking up so much fuss you'd think y'all had been married. You should just tell him you'll go back with him and then shoot him so he dies happy.

I laugh. There's something kinda scary about him, too, I tell her. I never thought it before now.

Crystal ashes her cigarette and nods. He's got a evil look about his eyes, she says. You don't want to mess with a man who has evil eyes. Riley thinks he may be one of the ones ran us off the road after he picked me up at the Jitney that night.

I know it, I tell her. I finally told Di and Stony, the stable managers, about how he was coming in all the time. I didn't tell Daddy cause Daddy'd probably shoot him right off without thinking. Daddy never did like me going out with him. Stony'd be more levelheaded about it.

Did he do anything? asks Crystal.

Stony?

She nods.

Yeah, he went out to the driveway last Tuesday when Hannaford drove in. He didn't even let Hannaford out of his car. Stony went right up to his window and told him my daddy didn't like unwelcome boys hanging around me and that he'd take a pistol to him if he ever bothered me again. Said Daddy was fixin to kill him without a care in the world of the consequences.

Crystal raises her hands over her head to stretch. What did the poor lovesick bastard do? she asks.

I put a songbook back on the shelf, take a pull off my cigarette and tell her, He tail dragged it out of there so fast, he about ran a fence post. Damn coward, what he is, when it all comes down to it. And Daddy didn't even know a thing about it. Lately he's been too occupied with Gwyn being pregnant to take notice of a thing like Hannaford.

Those cocky ones are always cowards on the inside, says Crystal.

Out of nowhere the deep red of Bo's mouth comes to me, the feel of it on my neck, sweat dripping down his face. Through my body, the veins pulse. I will the memory away by shutting my eyes as tight as I can and breathing low into my belly.

I remember the first time I met Hannaford, says Crystal. I open my eyes and look at her. She puts her cigarette butt in the Coke can beside her bed. Riley and I were taking a drive in the Roadrunner last April on Highway 12. Hannaford saw our car and did a U in the road. He followed us until Riley pulled over and then he came up to the car like he was the sheriff. He didn't even look at Riley, he just stared at me. Finally Riley introduced us and that boy looked straight through me like I was made of air. Riley never said much about him when I asked except to tell me to stay away. Bad blood is what he said.

I raise my eyebrows at her. They share blood, I say.

Not the same kind, says Crystal. He's got a different, meaner kind than Riley.

I nod. Well I always thought since he was kin to Riley, he couldn't be bad as Riley told me he was, but now I know Riley was right.

What about Ford? she asks. She moves her foot up her calf to scratch it.

Ford is nice, I tell her, but I can't go out with him. He's too whiny for me.

He's too in love with you, all's it is, says Crystal. She leans up to open the window. A thick hot breeze comes in. I move toward it.

Crystal nods at it. I don't know whether it's warmer with the window closed or open, she tells me. Mamma says you keep it closed, the cool from the night stays in.

What cool? I say.

A woman leans out the top window of the house next door, rests her elbows on the sill and looks around. She's got a clothespin pinching her bangs together. We stare at each other for some seconds, but we don't smile.

You're gonna marry rich, Haley Ellyson, I can feel it, says Crystal.

I bend over and fizz my Virginia in the Coke can. Why do you say that? I ask her.

I don't know. She pulls her shoulders up and narrows her eyes. I got a feeling you are. Some highfalutin rich boy, she says.

I pick my hair off my neck and turn my back to the window to see if the air will find my sweating skin. Falutin, I say. What does that mean?

Damned if I know. Proud, I think. Fancy, says Crystal.

No one from Houser Banks, I tell her. I am so sick of Houser Banks.

You're sick of breakin hearts is all. She's quiet for a second, then asks in a soft way, News on Riley? She chews her bottom lip and I give her the note, crinkled from my jean shorts pocket.

She opens it carefully. When she reads it, her eyes get wide and her mouth turns up. She shakes her head slow and laughs at some places, all the while holding the paper like you would a fragile piece of antique lace. Riley's handwriting is blue scribble. I don't know how she reads it. When she's done, she folds it as it came, puts it under her pillow and says, I've got to see that boy.

He's still coming to hear you sing? I ask. I expect he could get in a pile of trouble if they knew he was after you. I stand above the bed and look down at her.

Aw, it's just a skin-ballin, crap-shootin little juke house over at the edge of Fresh County, she says. No one knows me there except my great-uncle Spam and his wife, Jazzy, and they're too busy with their own selves to watch my goings-ons. Aunt Jazzy makes catfish sandwiches at the back and Uncle Spam runs the liquor. Mamma told me they used to sing for chicken and chitlins at Saturday night rent parties down in Jackson when they were younger, but now they're older than magic, and he's deaf as a two-by-four and blind in one eye. She's losing her memory fast.

Crystal scratches her calf and frowns at a welted bug bite. They're the ones hooked me up to sing, she says, and they bring me home at the end of the night. I don't talk to Riley in there. We sneak out the door about ten minutes apart from each other and meet in the Roadrunner. Crystal breathes in so her chest swells. Then she exhales in one gust. Hell of a way to meet, she says.

Jesus, don't they think it's crazy, Riley coming in there? I ask her.

She shrugs. They don't give his white ass the time of day.

Would they do anything to Riley if they knew he was after you?

She crinkles her forehead and looks up at me like I just told her I never heard of my own name. She says, If they knew that white boy was sneakin off to make me high off his love on the side of Mamma Hatchey's juke? Shit, girl, they wouldn't shake his hand and ask him to supper, that's for sure.

Don't you get a scare in you about it?

You want to know the living truth, Crystal says, I'm more scared of being without him. Her mouth goes down at the corners, and she looks at her toes rested against the wall. Her toenails are painted fluorescent red. Only reason I liked school last year was for Riley, she says, gazing out the window.

The woman's voice through the speaker sings still. Between the notes the woman laughs like she knows something that is the secret to the whole of life, and she won't ever tell. I pick the cassette case off Crystal's bed. Memphis Minnie, it says and shows a black woman with a hairdo from a long time ago.

Most of the time, Crystal says, I hated it there. I wanted to be like any of y'all who'd grown up together and then I wanted to be back at my own school. Even though Mamma and Pappa said I couldn't learn patoot at Fresh and I should be happy to be able to go to Banks because they paid special money to put me there on account of my grades, I felt familiar at Fresh. At Banks I was lonely. Except Riley. Riley was the only one. He could make me laugh. Oh, that boy made me laugh so my insides shook. And he would watch me and wait for it to die down so he could say another thing to keep me smiling. He'd leave me notes in my locker and wait on me after sixth period in the science courtyard. I was the one who had to be hush-hush about it. We used to go to the Roadrunner and make love during study hall. Did you know that? She turns her head to look at me.

I put the cassette cover back on the bed and say, No.

Well, she says, I'd be half crying the parking guy would find us and I'd get run out of there straight back to Fresh County High. My mamma and pappa would be so mad. They don't want me messing around some white boy, they want me to get an education and get out and raise myself up with a black man. Daddy's always saying how he and his older brothers went through hell during the sixties to try to make it as safe as it is right now. They say the attitude is ingrained in the South even if the laws are changed and to be real careful of anything that happens to make you think it's different. She looks at the ends of her braids and says softly, But it did happen. And those were the happiest of my days, you know it?

I guess they would have been, I say. I sit down next to her.

I never let a single boy do anything but kiss me before I met Riley White, Crystal tells me. I thought I would wait till the day I was married, just like Mamma said. And I sure didn't think it would be no white boy. She sighs. I don't want to go back senior year with Riley graduated. But if I go back to Fresh everyone there will act like I'm too good for them or too bad for them, one. Mamma and Pappa say going to Banks will make college a whole lot easier, but they look down on any friends I have there. I feel like I don't have a home. Whole thing makes me lonely. She takes a hand and runs it over her braids. Her eyes have the shaky look of cry to them.

You don't even have to go to school, I tell her. You could just sing and make millions and then you and Riley can be off doing whatever you want.

Crystal shakes her head. I'm only eighteen years old and Riley's only nineteen, she says. He's going to fall in love with some woman years older than now, some white woman who can love him with people watching it. Someone he doesn't have to sneak around with all the time. Now, though, I think he likes it. It gives him some kind of excitement. She looks up at me with a smile only on the left side of her mouth, the other side trembles.

I straighten the bedspread with my fingers. He loves you, I tell her.

A dog barks somewhere, then stops and starts again. I look up for the woman with the clothespin, but she has gone. A yellow T-shirt hangs off the sill with the words *Tallahatchie River Fest* written on it.

When Riley isn't around, sometimes I don't care one way or the other, Crystal says. But when I am with him, then it's all I care about on this whole earth. It's like I'm onstage when I'm with Riley. She sighs. Mamma always told me, Men will mess up your life if you let them. Don't give yourself to them. She said it so easy, like you could help it. You can't help it. You know, there isn't any helping it.

The phone rings in the inners of her house and Crystal starts up, then waves her hand at it. I'll just let it ring, she says. Only person I'd want to talk to is him, and he's at the river dam. She spins around on her buttocks and unfolds herself to standing. The phone rings three more times, then stops. She turns to look at me with her hands on her hips. What would your daddy do if you came home with a black boy? she asks me.

I couldn't ever do that, I say quick. Then I feel hot color come up in my face, but I can't think of a thing to say that will ease or erase it.

Crystal nods slow and stares at an iron's burn spot on the rug. The music stops. We stand in silence. She twists back and forth in place, watching the bottom of her dress swing. Riley and I aren't going to get a blessing from anybody, she says to her skirt. If I'd have made only B's or A minuses, then I would have gone to Fresh County High like everyone else and I'd be in love with some crazy-assed black boy. I probably would've fallen for Semmes Jackson or someone. She stops turning and looks over at the clock on her bedside. Oh Haley, she says. You better get your white bottom out of here. They're gonna be home in a half an hour or less and they're not trusting even you anymore. They're suspecting all the worse after the Jitney that night. They think they can keep me safe with their watchin—she studies her fingernails—but it's a whole lot bigger than that.

I nod and breathe in her musk smell. All right, I say.

Crystal follows me to her back porch and sits on the first step with her hands underneath her. I head down the stairs and walk the dirt path next to the wrought iron fence, turning once to wave at her. The sound of playing kids comes from the front street. I hear a woman say, BJ, if you don't stop draggin on my dress, your butt's gonna be in a sling.

Three girls are playing jump rope on the other side of the fence, singing a tune of clippy hopscotch variety.

> *I yo flipped his toe,*
> *give her a kick and away she'll go.*
> *I love coffee, I love tea,*
> *I love the pretty boy and he loves me.*

A small girl stands by the side of the fence, watching with her head tucked. She's carrying a goldfish and water in a plastic sandwich bag.

Hi, I tell her, you got a new goldfish?

She smiles, purses her lips and nods, staring down at it.

All the way to the pickup I can hear those girls singing. Their voices get thinner in the air while I walk away.

> *Went to the river, couldn't get across,*
> *paid five dollars for an old gray horse.*

He wouldn't pull, got it for a bull.
Bull wouldn't holler, sold it for a dollar.
Dollar wouldn't pay, put it in the grass.

Six houses from Crystal's, I turn left at a long alley leading to where the pickup is parked in the old dirt lot.

One favorite thing of coming to Crystal's is walking that piece of alley through this neighborhood where no one knows my name. Sometimes the boys of my age who live on Crystal's street will follow behind me a few steps and say things just under their breath. Hey white girl, they say, you want to give me some, you lookin for it?

8

FLETCHER

Arlene Hool looks torn up. She's got two bruised eyes and bald patches from where her ex-boyfriend pulled her hair out. She can lift her sleeve and show the cigarette burns and not cry. She says what happened to her in a worn-out tone, and after she is done with the telling, she asks Pops if she can smoke in the court-room. He says she cannot. I glance at Robin, she's watching the lady care-fully. She doesn't smile and neither do I.

Pops gives Arlene a three-year relief-from-abuse order against her ex-boyfriend, who hasn't even bothered to appear in court.

Just to get the hell away from how depressing domestic abuse cases are, I go to the bathroom. You have to look at yourself while you piss in the courthouse because there's a mirror above the urinal. The haircut ole Spier gave me last Saturday makes me look like a second-grader on his first day of school. While I'm zipping up, I see something move in the reflection to the left of the toilet stalls. When I walk over there, I find Julian Mars sitting on his upside-down cleaning bucket, crammed into that little space between the wall and the toilet stalls. He's got a magazine on his lap.

I loop up my belt. What are you reading? I ask him.

He puts both of his giant tan hands over the magazine. You a nice kid? he asks me. He narrows his shit-colored eyes.

I don't know, I tell him. I guess I am.

He looks at me sidelong. You wanna be a man, not a kid, is that it? he asks.

I watch him. His expression doesn't change. When I look down I see the face of a girl on his magazine. It occurs to me he is reading porn. I step back and run my hands under the sink next to the urinal. Then I turn off the water and get a paper towel.

He's still watching me. Best place to janitor is a courthouse, he says, fingering his bushy black hair. You might want to consider it when you grow up, Fletcher. You can get your chores done and then hide out in the john all day long doin your schoolwork. Judges and lawyers, they'll hold their shit and their piss forever if they have to. That's why so many of them are fat. They get bloated from holding it so long.

I chuck my paper towel in the garbage and start walking toward the door. I'll see you later, Julian, I say.

Course, your old man, Julian calls after me, he's not fat. He's the exception. He might be some kind of God. I don't think he has to piss or shit at all.

I have an urge to hit his ugly face, but I keep walking.

Hey, college boy, he calls.

I stand there holding the door handle and don't turn around. What? I say, quiet.

You gonna tattle to the girlies in the office on me?

Nope, I tell him, and open the door.

Hold up, he calls me. I turn around to find him standing with his legs apart. The magazine is hanging off his left hand. It shows a girl dressed up in a cowboy hat and boots with spurs on and nothing else. I glance away quick as I can.

What about your old man? he says. He flicks something at the left side of his waist. At first I think it is a lighter. When I glance down, I see it is the shiny flat steel of a knife blade. I look up at him and he smiles, one tooth on the top left side is missing to a gaping hole.

You aren't gonna need that, Julian, I tell him. This kid isn't interested in talking. And then I move through the door. It sways and closes behind me.

At lunch I piss in Square Diner's rest room and stay in the courtroom with Pops for the rest of the day to avoid Julian Mars.

Robin's sitting in the elevator when I come out at five fifteen. As many times as I've been in that courthouse to pick Pops up from work, I've never seen the inside of that elevator. It's got cracked linoleum floors and gray walls. We look at each other. She has her finger on the button.

You want a ride? she asks me in her soft voice.

I step inside. She lets her finger off the button and the steel doors come clanging shut. They're the kind with crisscrossed bars in front of them.

Takes awhile, she says, it's an old one. Her long dark fingers are curled around the ends of the chair. I lean against the far wall and will her to look in my direction. She does not.

That was a sad day in court, I say. The elevator lurches downward.

She takes one hand from the armrest and inspects her nails. How so? she asks.

I am aware that I don't know exactly what was sad about it, but it seemed something that would instantly be agreed upon. The elevator slows. I don't know, I tell her, all those women, it just seems too bad, is all.

We thud to a stop and the doors clank open. Robin starts to wheel herself out. I put my hands on the back of her chair and push her over the elevator entrance. She does not stop me. I wheel her to the front of the courthouse and turn her around to open the door with my back. The sun assaults us when we come out. My top lip mustaches with sweat. Her skin is smooth and brown in the sun. I can see partway down her blouse to the side of her white lace bra. Even standing behind her I get a feeling she can tell what I'm doing, so I look away. While I take her down the outside ramp, she pulls her hair from her neck. It's a long neck with four scarred indents across it. When we get to the parking lot, she says, I'm fine here. I got a friend works on the other side of the street. I'm going in there.

I can wheel you, I tell her.

She shakes her head. No thanks, she says. She looks up at me and I catch her gaze. She watches my eyes carefully and then she says, You think those restraining orders hold anyone away?

I can't tell if it is a rhetorical question. I shrug. I suppose sometimes they do, I tell her.

She looks away from me, stares hard at the sidewalk and says, It's only the wimps it keeps away. The real dangerous ones don't care nothin about a piece of paper.

I can't think of what to say.

Your daddy's a good judge, she says, if judging worked. But it don't always.

I guess not, I say.

Most women, she says, you won't even see their faces in that courtroom. The real ones, they're too scared to come in here.

I fidget with my hands in my pockets and look toward the window of the courthouse where Pops's office is.

Those women, she says, flicking her chin to the upstairs courtroom. They don't even know what it is to be beat.

She raises her head slightly and looks me up and down. I'm glad you don't know that, she says, it makes you nice. She puts her hands on her wheels in a hurried motion and turns herself around. Bye now, she says, and she rolls away from me down the sidewalk, stopping at the side of the courthouse. When she crosses the street, a car brakes a good distance from her so she can pass. I watch and wonder on her until she is gone through the door to that store.

Riley White's parked a note under my windshield. *Hey Judge, I'm at my brother's shop if you want to track me down. Riley.*

Smacky's Transmission smells of gasoline and grease and rubber and gears. On the office desk is an oil-grubbed Houser Banks telephone book and an appointment log. Checks are pinned to a cork above it, and pencils hang off the wall by dirty strings. There are gone-by calendars up there with half-naked girls on them.

I go out of the office and into the garage, calling Riley's name.

He appears out of the back holding a six-pack of Bud and charger cables. Greel, he says, now I know you can read.

There's a Cadillac hanging from the ceiling like a Christmas ornament and Riley stands beneath it, fiddling with the cables. How you doin? he says to his hands.

I'm not complaining, I tell him. I lean against the office door.

Then I'm listenin, he says. I got to steal these cables for the Runner, the lights and radio are dimming sometimes. Hold this, would you? He throws me the six-pack of beer. I catch it just barely. He looks at me and grins. You look the spitting image of your daddy in them khakis, he says.

You work here? I ask him.

No, I sure as hell don't. I despise this shit, man. I hate the inside of a machine, it depresses me. Riley slings the cables over his left arm and takes a pack of smokes from his shirt pocket. He comes over to me, claps a hand on my shoulder for balance and swipes a match on the bottom of his shoe sole. You going to college next year, Greel? he asks me while he lights his smoke.

I guess so, I say, quiet.

You guess, he says around his cigarette. He shuts off the lights at the side of the garage. The place goes dark, and we move toward the back. Did you do an application? Riley calls back to me.

Yeah, I tell him. I go through the door when he opens it for me.

He locks it behind us with a key on a string around his neck. Well, where you going? he asks.

Place called Tufts, I tell him, in Boston.

The Roadrunner's sitting at a diagonal next to the back door of the shop. Boston? he says. Shit, Judge, that is Yankeetown. Riley throws the cables in the trunk, hops in and tells me to help myself to the passenger's seat. He cranks the engine. Above its roar he says, There's a bag of boiled peanuts at your feet. Mamma made them last night. Take some, they're damn good. I snuck tequila in one batch, thought they'd be a good drunk, but I ruined the whole lot of them and she was sore at me for the entire night. I had to steal that bag.

I pick a couple out and try passing one to Riley, who says he's too damn full of them to eat another.

I need something real, says Riley, a meal at some point or another during the course of this evening. He heads the car out to the front. While we are sitting waiting on traffic, a little red pickup comes down the road going 120 miles per hour. It screeches to a halt in front of Smacky's.

Well Christ bite my ass, says Riley, if it ain't Haley Ellyson.

The truck reverses and turns in next to us. She sticks her head out the window. Riley White, she says, looking at me. She's the same girl I saw at Spier's the day I got my hair cut and I been lookin for her ever since.

Ellyson, Riley says, you're gonna kill your goddamn truck.

It's already half dead, she says. She smiles at me with a set of white straight teeth. Where y'all going? she asks.

We're going to catch ourselves a smile, Riley tells her.

Haley raises her eyebrows. Well, you want to drag me along with you? Hannaford's on my tail, I might could've lost him, though. She looks in her rearview.

No, you sure as hell didn't, Riley says, leaning over and looking down the road. Is he in Durfel's rig?

Oh no, says Haley.

She pulls her pickup forward and parks it next to Smacky's front door.

Hell of a driver, Riley says to me. Mind if she joins us?

Not at all, I tell him.

He throws his cigarette out the window and says, Don't go falling in love with this one, Yankee, she's a live wire without a fuse box.

Haley Ellyson walks toward us in bare feet, holding her shoes in one hand, wearing a tiny little sundress with a mess of honey-colored hair around her, a sight to see, I can't stop looking in my passenger's-side mirror. She climbs over the driver's-side door and into the back just as a brown four-runner pulls up with two guys in front and a guy in back. The guy in the bed jumps out before they stop. He's got overalls on and no shirt.

Oh hell in a wastebasket, Riley says under his breath.

Riley White, where you been? says the guy in overalls. He walks slowly toward the car, watching Haley.

The driver of the truck says, He hasn't been hanging tough with us.

They've got country blaring out their speakers. Riley cups his hand around his ear. What? he says. I can't hear you over that rackety shit you got playing on your radio.

The driver turns it up and jounces up and down in his seat. The guy in the overalls comes to my side of the car. He stands looking at Haley, but he speaks to me.

What's your name? he says.

Riley sticks an unlit cigarette in his mouth and says, Fletcher Greel, meet my cousin Hannaford. Riley's cousin is about six feet tall and broad across, with blue eyes set far apart and eyebrows that look white bleached from sun. He's tan, without a chest hair on him, and has an easiness about him he must have taken a lifetime to acquire.

Hey, I tell him.

He keeps looking at Haley. A pleasure to meet you, he says to me. He puts a hand on the back window. Riley adjusts his rearview and watches him.

The boys in the truck glance at me as if I were something they'd been told not to look at, then the passenger door opens and a guy in leg braces gets out and starts making his way over to the car.

You still workin the dam? Hannaford says to Riley. They still payin you ten fifty an hour to dig in the goddamn dirt?

That's what I'm doing, says Riley. He watches the boy in braces.

Whose pussy did you lick to get that job? Hannaford asks, but before Riley can answer he says, You got a smoke on you, cousin?

Nope, Riley says, lighting his own.

What in hell's in your front pocket then? asks Hannaford.

Those are mine, says Riley.

The guy in leg braces is about five-five, with rust-colored hair almost covering his eyes. Riley White, he says, pulling out his hand, I haven't seen you in a while.

Riley puts his palm out. Hey Letchy, he says.

Letchy smiles and says, Hey Haley.

She leans up on the seat back and says, How you doin?

He says he's fine and glances my way.

This here's Fletcher Greel, Riley says, home from Yankee country to get the hell some Rebel in him.

The judge's son, says Haley, soft.

I raise my eyebrows and look back at her.

Aren't you? she asks me.

I nod. Hannaford's standing next to my side of the car, watching me.

How you doin? Letchy asks me. Your daddy got mine out of a misdemeanor. He smiles a little and keeps his eyes on mine as if we are in a private club.

A line of brown chew spit pisses in between the two vehicles. Riley looks down at it. The driver smiles, he turns the radio down. Riley, what are you doin tonight? he asks. Come on over to Letchy's. His parents are in Biloxi for two weeks.

Hey—Hannaford punches my arm—you got a cigarette? I plumb ran out.

I don't smoke, I tell him.

He looks me over as if I have just told him something that is either an outright lie or the worst truth he's ever heard and he can't decide which.

I turn away from him.

We just got back from Jackson, Letchy says to Riley. He points to the truck. Stretch bought a Colt compact .45 enhanced officer's edition.

So, judge's son, Hannaford says to me, you know Haley?

I just this minute met her, I tell him.

Well, he says, it sure as hell seems like she knows you. He nods to her, the way she's leaning so close like that. Haley doesn't turn around. He squats next to the car with his hands on my window and watches her while he speaks loud enough so she can hear. I went out with her last year, he tells me, but she gone and done me in. He nods his head to her. Nice lookin, huh? And fun as the night is long, boy. But she's a heap a trouble. Know that. He points a finger at my chest. She'll be after you next. Sixteen and going at two hundred miles per hour toward trouble.

His face is all of a sudden red and one eye twitches until he puts his pointer finger up and stills the lid.

I don't say anything. Haley keeps her eyes on Letchy, who is saying, You can come by later if you feel up to it. We're trying to get a bunch of people over there.

So, you don't smoke, Hannaford says and looks at me, what do you do then, Fletcher Greel?

Haley turns to face us and says, Hannaford, leave him alone.

Hannaford stands up off his haunches, backs away two steps and puts both hands up in mock respect. Oh Haley, he says, sorry, honey pot. I was just trying to get to make conversation with your new boyfriend, are you jealous?

She narrows her eyes and turns away.

He leans in the car and tugs at her dress. Hey, come here, he says. I just wanna talk to you a minute.

She looks at his hand as if she were about to get snakebit and says, I don't got a thing to say to you.

He places his hand around her waist. I got some stuff to say to you, he tells her.

Haley moves over some in her seat and says, You need to let me alone.

When I turn to face front I see Riley's watching them in the rearview mirror. Letch, he says, we gotta go, maybe we'll see y'all later. Hannaford, he calls, you want to back off, I'm gunning out of here. Hannaford trips forward when Riley hits his accelerator and we lurch toward the road. See you, boys, he says.

Hannaford follows a few steps. Hey! he calls. He punches the car tail once. Hey! But Riley is turning right onto Highway 12 and we're flying fast as that motor will take us.

Haley leans back. All three of us are silent until we hit Banks Boulevard, then Riley slows. He's a bona fide asshole, Riley says. He glances in his rearview at Haley, who has her arms crossed in front of her.

He's worse than that, Haley tells him.

Riley leans into me and calls out, Haley here is the best horse handler in Fresh County. You should have seen her in the high school rodeo last week, placed first in pole bending, second in girls' cuttin, first in saddle bronc and third place in bareback.

Aw Riley, says Haley, I placed first in bareback.

I look at her. I would have liked to have seen that, I tell her.

She smiles at me.

I am sorry, little lady, Riley says, how could I have been mistaken? First in bareback, first in bareback. He repeats it to himself like a cadence.

Where we going? she calls out.

We're going to Big Bertha's Barbecue, Riley tells her.

Out in East Neigh? Is Crystal coming?

No, she ain't and don't ask no more questions, I got to concentrate on how it is you get there.

We ride past vacant concrete block gas stations and abandoned houses with their shutters hanging off a nail and their windows shot out. The sun falls in a kind of crimson color to our left. We don't say anything at all while horn-scratched voices blow through Riley's speakers. I am more than conscious of how fine looking Haley Ellyson is, gracing the backseat of the Roadrunner.

Big Bertha's restaurant is really only a fifty-gallon barrel cut in two with a torch and held together by a rusty hinge. Big Bertha looks like the human equivalent of a water tank. She's wearing an American flag wrapped around her head and comes right up when we side the Roadrunner in front of her house.

How you boys doin? she asks us. She stands by Riley's door, and when he jumps out, she wraps her arms around him. Her cheeks are beaded with sweat. How you, honey child? She lets Riley go and looks at us. I know you. She points to Haley. You come out here once before, but I don't know this a one. She points to me.

This here's Fletcher, says Riley. He's a . . . a Methodist. If you can't love a Methodist, who can you love?

I'm an Episcopalian, but I figure it's better if I keep my mouth shut.

Big Bertha is carrying a spatula that she waves in the air while leading us through her yard, littered with sinks and one bathtub and a toilet with its top ripped off. Riley hangs back with me. They sell used bathroom fixtures, he says. If you go to build a house, you can come here, get whatever it is you need.

A sign leaning against the house reads *Big Bertha's Barbecu, At 4:30 am, We Open R Doors, We Have No Certain Time to Close, The Cook Will Be Glad to Serve U.* There's a goat tied to a privy not far from the house and a pregnant black girl is sitting on the porch watching us with an ear of corn in her hands. She's got a baby tucked into her arms by a sling made out of an old towel. In front of us, Big Bertha waddles, swatting flies away with the spatula. Smoke floods from the barbecue.

Haley's dress skirts around her when she walks and I can't stop looking.

What you got? Riley asks Big Bertha.

We got chicken, Bertha tells him. All's we got today is chicken. You want three of em?

Well, says Riley, I eat so much chicken, I can't hardly turn my head on a rooster. We'll have four, he tells her.

She slaps four thighs on the grill from a Styrofoam cooler next to her.

A man in a tan gardening hat sits on a sided soda machine a few feet from the grill. He nods to us, sucks in on his teeth. Hidee, he says.

Hello there Lean, says Riley, how you?

Lean's got one long tooth in the front of his mouth, and far as I can tell, that's it.

I'm doin good, he says and starts talking faster than a trained auctioneer. Auntie May's on the phone this mornin, she lives out yonder near to the Petersons, her son Walter he run around with that little Peterson boy. The Petersons can't hold theyselves together.

The pregnant girl sits shucking her corn and watching us. She moves the towel around so the baby can nurse.

The man licks his tooth and says, Big James Earl Peterson, that boy's daddy, he gone shot himself through the mouth last month. Just last Sat'day that little un done the same thing, .22 on his tongue and pulled the trigger right there on back of Walter's daddy's home. Walter gone and have to watched it. He ten years old.

Sonofabitch, says Riley.

The man rubs his hand over his head and looks to the west, where the ball of red sun's descending. That boy's fat as a hog, too, Lean says. Dead fat kid on a back porch in this heat's a goddamn buttache.

Yup, says Riley.

Lean sucks his tooth and looks at the ground. And now her Wallie, he hollerin like to won't stop. His eyes gone blind. He just rubbin em and rubbin em.

Big Bertha pulls off a piece of gritty black meat from the barbecue and passes it to Lean. Here you go, old Uncle, she says.

Lean takes it and nods to Bertha, who rubs her arm across her forehead and says, Hot enough to kill a mule.

Haley watches the girl on the porch.

With his mouth full and spitting food, Lean starts to talk again. Possum come up our bathroom floor, he says, set a trap Friday evenin. Sat'day mornin, dead as a nail. Skinned, gutted, washed it right up. Auntie roasted it. Tasted good. And that there meal was free as air.

Bertha flips the chicken. Lean keeps on talking, but he's hard to understand and I stop listening.

When the chicken is done, Big Bertha puts the thighs between pieces of bread and wraps them in tinfoil, throws them in an old plastic Wonder bread bag and hands the bag to Riley.

Eight dollars, says Bertha.

I pay and tell Haley and Riley not to worry about it.

They thank me and then Riley says, Lean?

Lean throws his chicken bones on the ground and looks at Riley, then at me, then back at Riley. Okay, I got you, he says. I ain't entirely persnickety, but I got ways about me. Trust some of em, not all of em, black, white, colored, not colored all come on here, wanting this, that. Two, three, forty of em. They tell this one and that a one, somehow word gets out, good for greenbacks not for my back, got to make my own way in the world, can't be takin chances from here on in, as is I ain't assured of heaven. God almighty might see fit to work the wonders of the law on me. Lean stops talking but continues to mumble.

Riley looks at us. Can y'all wait in the car? he says. I'll be along in a minute.

We head back across the yard. Haley holds her hand up to the girl shucking the corn. The girl waves back.

At the Roadrunner I say, You are welcome to sit up front.

She gets in the back. You're sweet to offer, she says, but I like the back, I like all the wind.

I nod.

We sit in silence for some seconds. And then I look at her. I'm sorry I didn't help you out more before with Riley's cousin.

She leans up next to me. You didn't need to do a thing, she says. It would have just made a mess. He's a messy boy. She looks into the thick treed darkness across the road and sighs. Daddy always says if you ignore somebody like that, he'll go away. Only for him seems to add kindlin to the fire, doesn't it? She's got a husky voice that crackles when she speaks.

I don't know, I tell her. How long has he been after you like that?

She shrugs. A month maybe. I went out with him last year.

I nod, look back at the road and try to think of something to say.

I've seen you before, she tells me. She pulls all her hair atop her head and holds it there with one hand, watching me.

I look back at her. At Spier's? I ask her.

Yeah, at Spier's, but also before that, vacations and all.

I'm jiggered by this, feel red hot crawl up my neck and hope it's too dark for her to see it. I've seen you, too, I start to tell her, but Riley arrives, hands me the plastic Wonder bread bag with our sandwiches in it and a paper bag full of bottles and hops in the front seat.

When we peel away, Haley calls out, You got us some moonshine, didn't you, Riley?

Riley puts his finger to his lips and says, Shh. Goddamn psychic women of the South, he tells me.

She leans back in her seat.

Why's it a secret? I ask.

Five to ten years in Parchman State Penitentiary is why, says Riley.

Halfway back to Houser Banks Riley says he has to go pick someone up. I was going to go get her alone, he tells us. But now that y'all are here, I guess we'll make a party of it.

Haley claps her hands together and shakes her hair from her eyes and says, Hooray, Crystal, in a singsong voice.

We go to the Jitney Supermarket between Houser Banks and East Neigh. Riley parks under a tree next to broken shopping carts, away from the spotlights at the back of the building.

Haley says, Riley you are plain crazy coming here.

He looks in his rearview mirror at her, pats his shirt for his cigarettes and says, There aren't very many other ways, Hale. He starts to put the cigarette in his mouth, then takes the smoke out and rests it behind his ear. Hit the back, will you Greel?

I hop the seat, and Haley moves over for me.

Somebody's running toward us from the back of the building and when she gets closer, I see it's the girl who sang at the juke joint the other night. She's carrying a deli smock, and she's breathless from running. Hi! she tells Haley and me. She looks twice at me, a flicker of recognition comes across her face.

Riley pats the seat next to him. Lie down, baby, he says, and she does, putting her head on his lap and riding like that all the way back to Houser Banks. I hear Riley say, Where does your mamma think you'll be?

Marva McClure's, she says, then she picks up her head and looks at me. You saw me sing, she says.

It was unbelievable, I tell her.

She smiles, tosses her head and then disappears down on Riley's lap. He looks down at her, almost loses the road and swerves back on it at the last minute.

Riley goes so fast on Banks Boulevard that when we hit corners Haley and I bump into each other in the backseat. She laughs and says, Faster, Riley. Then she turns to me. Put your head back like this, she says, and look for the brightest star you can find, it will run along beside us and you can make a wish on it.

So we ride with our heads back, and I try to think of a wish to plant on the star I find to the right of the moon. The only one I can think of is to somehow make it so Haley Ellyson wants to hang out with me more than just this one time.

Riley heads the car up Highway 12 to Leete Circle and parks it where the new dam's being built. Sup's on, he says. He rummages around in the glove, picks out a tape and kisses it. Ah, he says, dinner music. When he plays it, I recognize Crystal's voice.

Crystal! says Haley. She leans forward to listen. Crystal shakes her head at Riley, leans over and kisses his mouth many soft times. His eyes close and his hands reach for her waist, and then she backs away.

Bertha's chicken is tender and juicy. The moist of it drips down my chin. During dinner moonshine is passed around in a glass corked bottle. It makes you fly with your feet rooted.

At supper's end, Haley and I sit together on two flattened twelve-pack boxes from Riley's trunk. We dangle our legs off the edge of the bank and look down at the white-capped shadows running the river and the half-built dam. Riley sits on a rock and Crystal leans between his legs. He announces the full moon. We all look up at it.

Hale, you remember that Dulles boy drowned out here three summers ago? They found him on a full moon.

Haley nods. Yeah, she says, I remember.

I look up to see Riley kiss Crystal's neck, she tilts her head for him to do it and smiles at me when she sees me look.

John Dulles, Riley says, taking his lips from Crystal. He was catfishin. They think a moccasin got wrapped around the pole, bit him in the face. He was whipping around in this here gully when they found him, between the bank and that cypress, his left leg ripped off at the hip. Some-one must have fished that leg up. Riley spits on the ground, wipes his forearm across his mouth and says, They found him cause Harry Kyle ran off the road here, ricocheted off that streetlamp and smashed into the phone pole. His head and eyeballs, full up with splinters. He ain't right in the mind now. Can't move from the neck down.

I know who it is Riley's speaking of, he's bald and keeps a brown paper sack next to his leg in his wheelchair. A light-skinned black girl runs the chair for him. He is who I thought of when I first saw Robin, and I wonder if they speak to each other.

He was slated to be married that spring, says Haley.

Riley takes a drink of moonshine. Really? he says. To who, that girl who wheels him around?

Oh no. Haley picks up a stone and throws it down the bank. It hits the river and splashes lightly. She says, This other blond girl who used to be a cheerleader, went to school with Daddy.

That so? says Riley, lighting a smoke. Then there was that girl hung herself by that rope we used to swing off over there and down a piece, he says.

Jenny Setchel, says Haley. Through the leaves above us, a piece of moonlight has found her calf and I can see her legs are tan and muscled.

Riley passes the moonshine to Crystal, who swirls it around in front of her and takes a sip. Death ain't pretty, Riley says, watching the river. A face blows up and gets purple like nothin human you'd ever want to see.

I think of my mother and wish Riley would think of her too and stop talking on death. He says, Baby Judd and me were here right after it happened, everyone all crowded around her. It was sick to me, like watchin someone touchin themselves in public.

Haley closes her eyes and then opens them and looks at Riley. What was she wearin? she asks.

Naked as a jaybird.

Shit, I say.

Riley looks at me. I know it, Judge.

I ask them if they think anyone could have saved her.

Riley smokes for a while, then says, I doubt it. Those people I think are born like that. None of them can be helped. Sometimes somethin in you just wants to die. You can't fight it.

Crystal bends down and hands us the moonshine. Lightning bugs tear up the air. Haley leans her head on her hand and looks up at Riley. Even drownin? she says. You think anyone ever wants to drown?

I was talking about people who killed themselves, Riley tells her, but I think there may have been a choice, yeah, when you're drownin and you decide not to fight anymore, just let yourself swallow water. Riley leans over Crystal and shucks his smoke down into the river. What do you think, Yankee?

Haley looks at me. I pick up a stick and make lines in the dirt with it. Maybe so, I tell him. I couldn't say for sure. I imagine some people just fight like hell, they don't ever give up till they die.

I think it's sad talking about dyin like this, says Crystal. When I die I want to be burnt up to fine ash and thrown in a river like this one.

We keep passing the moonshine, and I think talk of death is over. Soon enough, someone starts in again, speaking about what happens after you die. Crystal talks about heaven and who goes. Riley says he thinks some wander invisible on the earth. Haley asks who might go to hell, what sorts of people. Crystal says she thinks rapists and murderers go.

Not murderers who have to fight in war because they are told to, though, says Crystal.

What about self-defense? asks Haley.

Crystal leans back and puts her hands on Riley's knees. She says, Not self-defense either. Even serial killers, lots of them are just sick. They don't mean to do what they do, they just can't help it.

Bullshit, says Riley, you can always help it.

Well, says Crystal, maybe there ain't no hell at all, maybe bad people are made good in heaven.

Haley and I stay quiet.

Riley says, I don't think that thing they call God would have any kind of rules about heaven and hell, it isn't like he points his golden finger and says, Down the basement for you sorry fella, up those holy stairs for you. Riley puts a hand on Crystal's shoulder. Her head is cocked, listening to him. I grew up in the church, I know religion, he tells us. Christians think they know what God is, but I'll wager a bet they got it wrong. You think those guys who bow down to the east and drop everything to pray five times a day are going to hell and some crooked-ass Baptist preacher from Mississippi is going to heaven? He laughs and sips the moonshine, wipes his mouth with the back of his hand and says, Our job is to quit talking heaven and hell and look for our own spirituality, and it don't have to be Christian. Two-thirds of the people in this world who are religious ain't Christian.

We all go silent. He bends forward with the moonshine and passes it to me, then leans back, wrapping his hands around Crystal's waist.

While I sip the moonshine, I think of Riley's words, wonder on the stars overhead and watch them blur and the trees sway in one slight hot breeze. The liquor's hitting me so my eyes don't focus quite right and the river sounds far away. The moon looks to me like a fat, smiling Humpty-Dumpty.

After a while, I ask on Letchy's legs and Haley says he was born with it and the doctors tell him he won't live past forty-five.

He can't ever have sex, says Riley.

This hits me like a bag of quarters in the chest. Wow, I say.

Ain't that the fucking worst? asks Riley.

I can't think of anything worse, I admit.

Haley smiles and raises her eyebrows.

I wonder if Robin Fuller is the same, I say.

I don't think so, says Riley. I've heard some stories.

Haley wants to know who Robin is and I tell her she's a wheelchaired girl who works at the courthouse, and Riley tells the girls they ought to behave or begin performing sexual favors for me because I am bound to be the next judge of Houser Banks.

Haley says, You are? I'll give you a kiss if you promise to never commit me to jail.

I tell her I promise heart and soul and make the sign of a cross over my chest. She comes at me with her mouth open and ends up kissing the side of my cheek, right next to my lips. My face warms and my spine goes hot.

She pulls away and smiles.

Riley breaks my shyness by talking about boxing. We agree on Sugar Ray Leonard as the next middleweight champion.

Then Riley starts in about the bream bedding down under the full moon and how we should be fishing.

Crystal interrupts him. I want to dance, she says.

I realize her tape is stopped and the only noise we have is river sound.

You should see this girl dance, Riley says. She moves like she's got a rattlesnake in her bosom.

He jumps off the rock and runs to the Roadrunner. In a few seconds the air is crowded with the sound of heartaching, soul-moving blues and we are killing the dirt with our feet.

When they dance, Riley and Crystal touch each other's waists and necks and sides of bodies, they hold each other and kiss long and spin around while they do it. Haley takes my hand and twirls under my arm and around me. She presses her back against my belly and I hold her shoulders. During slow songs we hang on to each other's necks, and I try not to think about her body so I don't offend her with a hard-on. Above us the moon cuts out an indigo sky and makes shadows out of the trees and the boulders and us. All my inhibition disappears, and I know for the next few weeks I will be forced to wonder what the hell I looked like and if Haley was watching me close enough to laugh at the way I moved.

Around midnight Crystal says she wishes the streetlight weren't so bright because it takes away from the beauty of the moon, so Riley gets a .25 caliber pistol out of the tackle box in his trunk and commences to work at shooting it out. After a couple of tries, he makes it. Glass shatters everywhere. Crystal ducks her head and runs. Haley yells, Wahoo, Riley.

And then we hear sirens.

Riley slams the gun in the glove and says, Hellfire, jump in, kids, we'll eat waffles at the Huddle House in Oxford, they won't ever catch us there.

He rams the Roadrunner down dirt and gravel roads through the outskirts of Houser Banks. Just before Highway 6, in front of a roadhouse with a blinking red Budweiser sign in the window, the Roadrunner flies off the gravel. We wind up parked on the side of a cotton patch.

Let's rest awhile, he says.

He sinks against the driver's-side door and Crystal snuggles up next to him with her hands around his waist. Haley and I lie back across the seat, her head on my shoulder and my arm in back of her.

When I wake up to the coming eyesore of the sun's daylight, I can still see the moon, one small pinhead in the sky. My drunk isn't gone, and because it makes me brave, I turn and kiss Haley on the lips. She shifts against me.

I'm sorry if you didn't want me to do that, I whisper.

I see her eyes open, the lids heavy. She says, No, no, please don't apologize, Fletcher Greel. I been waitin on that all night.

9

HALEY

Trailerloads of new horses came from Mexico three days ago, fifty-three quarter horses, thoroughbreds, mustangs and geldings: wild, raw and green. Bays, browns and sorrels, grays and gold palominos.

One is a red roan with a lot of white sugar frosting on her that Daddy has taken a liking to, started calling her his Gorgeous Hussy. Near five minutes after they'd emptied the trailers of stomping, blowing horses, the boys found Gorgeous Hussy because she was a lactating mare, which meant her foal back home would have to die with no milk, and she'd be that much harder to bring around. Gwyneth sitting at home about to fill up with coming milk is the sure reason Daddy has fallen in love with this mare. He's taken to all but ignoring Hemingway, the gelding from Salinas he usually rides, so I try to go around twice a day and hang out with him, whispering sweet nothings into his ear and feeding him apple pieces.

The horses came with five men from Mexico, who are here for just a week through some of the first breakings. The Mexicans stay in small wood shacks not far from the stables. They speak Spanish softly and smoke Marlboros from the packs tucked in the sides of their baseball caps. They know horses like I know my own name. Yesterday morning, I watched them cooking beans and rice, frying tortilla shells and boiling coffee over an open fire for breakfast. Before eating, they bent their heads to pray and crossed themselves.

A feeling like Christmas come in June enters the stables when new horses arrive, but a part of me feels sad deep down about it. I try to imagine what it's like for them to have this two-legged animal coming at them with a rope, trying to make them do things they don't know a lick about.

Those horses aren't ever going to be wild again. They most likely miss some land they loved and friends they had there and the feeling of being barebacked and crazy free. I've woken up from sleep thinking of it. Those times I pray to God that they don't have memory. But I believe they do.

In early morning, before the horses are brought out, Bo and Daddy and the other men stand in a circle smoking and drinking coffee out of old mayonnaise jars. Di and Stony fry redeye gravy and cheese grits and bacon and sausage in the apartment upstairs from the barn. The smell of their breakfast is everywhere and it mixes with the scent of horses and new manure.

The height of the talk is about Billy Towle's house getting burglarized last weekend when he was gone to Memphis. That sonofabitch, they say, stole everything he owned. The robber took Billy's shotguns, pistols and rifle, the tires and rims off his truck, his stereo, TV, air conditioner, two push mowers and a bathroom commode, plus his whole supply of whiskey and bourbon and one smoked ham in the freezer. A goddamn ham, the men say. They blame and curse the people of East Neigh. They swear they'll sleep with their 12-gauges by their pillows, put their dogs out and shoot any motherfucker makes the dog bark. The rivalry between Houser Banks and East Neigh has been around for as long as I can remember, so the talk doesn't surprise me any.

Their second favorite subject is how the Mississippi legislature has made dogfighting a felony when it used to only be a misdemeanor. They argue into the coming daylight about whether or not Sheriff Hill would write them up or let them go if they found out about the dogfights they have out at Kelby's basement on the second Saturday of every month.

I put water in the troughs and feed in the boxes and rake the dirt out of the front corral while listening to Daddy and the other breakers stall their day by kicking stones around and talking. I can feel Bo watching me, and when I chance to look up at him, he stares for one long while, then drags his eyes to the group, and I get that hot thing through me of secrets untold.

At around eight, the men stamp out their cigarettes and drain their coffee and pull up their suspenders and the day begins with the smell of leather lead lines and fresh hay and the horse lather and feed and men's sweat.

The breakers are working with what they call herd-bound and barn-sour horses and their patience is tried. It's a contest of tired, and right now the horses are winning. They stomp around the corral, snorting and galloping, with their eyes rolling in their heads and big fits of air bursting out their snouts. Their ears lay flat against their heads and they shuck the spurs and whips and bits, kicking up dust and ducking saddles and bridles.

Bo went to Salinas four summers ago to train with old Indian riders and cowpunchers and circus trainers. He learned to break horses the quickest way possible and with the least resistance and manpower. Then he came back and taught the breakers to turn pussycat while they train, to whisper to these huge philistine alpha-male breeding stallions that it is all right and not to be afraid. Softer you go, he says, sooner you train. He knows how to convince these horses, with sweet-talking words and light fingertips, to be roped on lines thirty feet long and to adjust to snaffle bit, saddle and pad, stirrups, halters and bridle.

Bo is the best breaker. His time is five hours even.

Goddamn, that Bo Dickens, the men say, shaking their heads. I don't know how he does it, crazy sonofabitch.

I watch him in the corral roping and riding, overpowering those horses with his smooth voice. Those are the times he forgets to look at me. He is looking at the horses' flanks and how their ears separate, concentrating on standing upwind of them and watching which way their eyes roll.

It makes me want to be with Bo. Through these days I try to imagine when I'm going to be alone with him next and I go over the times I've been with him already.

By the end of the week, I feel tired from thinking about it, and wish it was just what it used to be, Bo Dickens the same to me as my own daddy and Archie and Stony, T. Fingerling and Billy Towle. The woods nothing more than trees and brush and mud and rocks.

On Friday, I rope a lead line around Daisy's neck and head her toward the stable doors. Riding makes me forget and we've been so busy, I haven't had a chance to ride Daisy at all. When I step outside, Daddy has his elbows on the far fence, his hands hanging loosely in front of him. He's smoking a cigarette and watching Billy Towle loop ropes around the fence posts.

While I am walking Daisy toward the woods, Daddy calls my name and comes at me in a slow jog. He shades his eyes from the sun. Where you going? he asks.

Ridin, I say.

Daddy's chaps are dirtied and a seam on them is ripped to a hole big as a finger. He brushes them with his hands when he sees me looking, then smiles up at me, his blue eyes crinkling. I need new ones, he says. He palms Daisy's neck. Water her, he tells me, don't let her get too hot. You going to be back for supper?

I shrug. I don't know, Daddy.

Shifting my feet in the stirrups, I look ahead at the woods, then back at Daddy. I'm just going to see Riley over at the new dam, I tell him.

Are you?

Yeah. I pat Daisy. He's working there. He'll be off in a little while.

A space of time passes. Finally he says, He still with that black girl?

I look at my reins, twist them around in my hands. I don't know, I tell him.

You know what happened at the Jitney over in East Neigh a couple of weeks ago?

I nod my head yes and comb through Daisy's mane with my fingers.

That boy's gonna get himself killed, Daddy says. They were lucky they only got pushed off the road.

I know that, Daddy, but it wasn't Riley's fault.

Daddy watches me skadily. Then whose fault was it?

I shrug my shoulders and look at the woods. I don't know, I say, maybe the boys who chased him?

Daddy says, But if he hadn't've been with her—

I know, Daddy, okay. He's not driving around with her, don't worry. Riley isn't stupid.

A horsefly lands on Daisy's neck, and I bat it away for her.

Daddy says, I don't think Riley is as stupid as his daddy, but he ain't smart enough not to take up with a black girl either. Don't go getting yourself tangled up with anyone like that, wind up in the graveyard with a bullet through your throat. I can't watch you every minute. With Gwyn pregnant and needin me, I been havin to trust you a little more. He looks down and moves the dirt around with his shoe toe. I can see his neck redden up his face when he says, Miss Gwyneth says it's the only way you and I are going to make it through your growin-up years. I'm tryin to trust trouble won't find you and you won't go looking for it.

I'm not looking for any trouble, I say. I'll be okay.

He nods and then Billy calls his name. Daddy turns, lifts a palm at him and says, I got to move some stuff for Billy, you gonna be gone long?

I'm just going to ride over and say hi, see what all he's doing tonight.

Daddy nods and slaps Daisy. All right, he says slowly, as if deciding whether to leave this word with me or not. Now go on, he says, be careful.

The opening to the woods swallows me up, and I go loose with ride and rhythm. Daisy's hooves kick up the ground's earthy smell. I lean over her, put my head against the side of her neck and I whisper, Faster, like Gwyneth does in the MG.

Daisy goes quick, jumping over fallen pine logs from this spring's storm and running dirt roads of clumped mud tracks from four-wheel drives. I ride low down on her neck so I can smell her and think how Daddy worries about those boys in town who chase people around, holler loud and shoot their pistols in the air. The men of the town do bad things, too, but they don't get looked down on for it. Their bad things give them a pace of pride to walk to. I wonder when it is that boys start turning into men and it is okay to be bad. Sometimes I feel like Daddy is crazy, letting his friends help raise me, but then the boys of town who will grow up to be just like them aren't even allowed in our living room.

At Clover Road I slow Daisy so she can walk over the tire-busted mud from logging trucks. She lathers and I sweat and catch my breath and speak to her about how good she is.

Once we hit Leete Circle, I can hear the river rushing just over the hill. Daisy dips her head for the water she smells. Three Ford pickups, an old Toyota Forerunner and Riley's Roadrunner are parked in the circular drive just above the hill heading downriver. The bank is a steep pile of small-growth pines, shrubs and overgrowth. It looks different now than it did the night of the full moon when everything was shadowy and blue and I was beside Fletcher Greel, drunk on moonshine, waiting for him to kiss me.

The workers stand by the dam yelling to one another over the sound of rushing water. They're wearing yellow, red and green hard hats and bright orange safety vests. The river's logged at either side, ready to meet at the middle. One guy takes off his hard hat and I see it's Riley, walking up the hill first, the others following, carrying tools and loosening their vests.

I dismount Daisy and lead her toward the Roadrunner, parked at an angle like Riley got there hurried and had no time to put it straight. I lean against the fender and wait. When I reach out to pat Daisy's stomach, it's steaming.

All the men are sweaty with work, wearing stained T-shirts and black rubber boots wet with river and faces soiled and deep tan. When they see me, they say, Riley, you got you a visitor, and pat his back and nod toward me. Beautiful day, one bearded guy calls over to me. Nice horse you got there.

Riley walks to me, smiling wide with his hard hat in his hand. Hey Hale! He pats Daisy's flank. Daisy girl, you still going strong, aren't you?

Daisy whinnies, studies him out the side of her head and stamps her back left foot.

We watch the men hitch into their pickups and throw their hats on the seats next to them. They set smokes between their lips, crank engines and yell, See y'all tomorrow.

Riley raises his palm up. They leave us with the smell of exhaust and dust. Then there's silence minus the sound of the rushing river.

Riley sits on the Roadrunner's hood, puts his chin on his chest and squeezes the back of his neck. You're a sweet sight after a pisser of a day, he tells me.

Hard one, huh? I put one foot up on the fender next to him.

He raises his eyebrows. You ever tried to build a river dam? he asks.

I smile and shake my head.

Your daddy mad after the other night when we didn't come home? he asks.

He never knew it, I tell him. Gwyn's been staying with us cause our house is cooler than Gypsy's and they've been goin to sleep early. I snuck in the back sliders and up to bed before he got up.

Good, he says.

What about Crystal? I ask.

She was home free, they thought she was sleeping at Marva's. I don't know about the judge. He winks at me.

I look down, toe the dust with my foot. Crystal's family still pissed about the Jitney? I ask him.

Yeah, they are. He unrolls his shirtsleeve for his pack of smokes.

Daddy just mentioned it when I said I was coming out to see you, I say.

That so? he asks. Whole town is always in on every little thing. Houser Banks is just achin to be better than somebody else, ain't it? And East Neigh's the perfect bait. He stands with a cigarette between his fingers, shakes his head, looks out at the river and says, I got to see her sometimes, Haley, you know it? Like the other night, we have to do that sometimes, keep ourselves sane.

Riley scrapes his match on a stone, throws it toward the river and says, Sheriff Hill found the guy who owns the pickup that rode me and Crystal into the ditch that night. He lights his smoke.

You got the license plate?

No I didn't, I was attending to Crystal. She scraped her leg, bad. But it was the same truck, green Dodge with a dent in it. Pulled him over cause he got a smashed taillight. It was one of the Piersons. Jerry. You know him?

I know who he is.

Riley smokes. Well he's a friend of Hannaford's and Letchy's older brother and all them Broder boys live down at the end of the river. Hill outright accused him and Pierson didn't deny it. But Hill didn't do a damn thing to him.

I look hard at Riley, who stares at the river without glancing up, and then I say, Why would he let him go like that?

Riley shrugs. Racist do-gooder is why. He takes the cigarette out of his mouth with his pointer finger and thumb. Plus there wasn't just one guy in the truck the night they chased us, there was three or four.

Daisy stamps her front leg from a fly. Riley pats her without looking at her. He sighs out.

Still, they should have done something to him, I tell him.

Riley shrugs. Didn't have to be Pierson who was driving that night. It could have been anyone, they share their vehicles like they share their women. You know what Sheriff Hill said to me?

I shake my head.

He told me, What do you expect, a boy like you taking out a girl from East Neigh?

What did you tell him? I ask.

I didn't say a goddamn thing. One smart-ass sound from me's what they're lookin for, says Riley. It was all I could do not to come at him. I bit this here flashy tongue and said, Yes sir.

We watch an orange-breasted robin land not three feet from Daisy and poke its head in the dust. The air is heavy with afternoon light coming between the tree limbs in thin white streaks of heat. Nothing stirs.

Hell, Riley says, kicking a stone toward the bank. It ain't all bad, least I got her. He grins at me and puts the smoke between his teeth, reaches back to get the elastic out of his hair and shakes his head around. His hair's golden with blond streaks in it from working under the sun. He scratches his scalp, then puts the elastic back in.

I'm surprised you don't get beat up with hair as long as that, I tell him. I prop myself up to sitting on the hood of his car.

Riley smooths his hand over his ponytail and says, That's not what's going to get me beat, Ellyson.

You ever think of not seeing her? I ask.

He looks at me, then he looks at the end of his cigarette. Sometimes I wish I never met her, he says. Sometimes I wish there were no such thing. But there is such a thing and it ain't that easy to just stop. The clear answer is no, I never think of not seeing her. You might as well stick a pistol in your mouth if you're gonna let someone else tell you who you can and can't see. He's quiet and his eyes are red and tired looking. Then Riley's grin comes and he tousles my hair and says, Shit, girl, all you been doin is riding, I been workin harder than the day is long, what you say we go and have a nice cool one?

I nod my head, slow, but I don't get up. Tell me about Fletcher Greel, I say.

Aha, Riley says, this is why you come to call. He puts his hand out palm up and says, You gonna give me something for that information?

C'mon Riley, please.

He grins. My dear Haley Ellyson, he is head over heels in love with you, first time he ever did lay eyes on you.

How do you know that?

I could tell it right from the get-go.

He called me last night, but I was over at Gypsy's with Gwyn. Does he ride horses?

Riley looks at me under his eyebrows. He probably rides them, but not like you ride them, Hale. He wasn't born on a horse. Go easy on him. Riley puts an arm around my shoulders and dips his chin to look into my eyes. He's an old buddy of mine. He drops the arm from me, jumps off the hood and stretches up with his hands, reaching as tall as he can make them. I'm looking out for him, Riley says to the sky. Don't do anything crazy with that boy's heart.

Riley bulges with new muscles. When he pulls his head down, he sees me looking at them and makes a right angle out of his arm, wrapping his hand around one bicep. Like that, huh? he asks. I'm getting somewhere in life.

I laugh. Then I say, I'm not doing anything to Fletcher Greel, Riley. He's different.

He comes to sit beside me, makes a drumbeat on the car hood. Don't tell me about differences, I know we're all the same. You know Greel lost his mamma this year?

Did he?

Cancer. Ate her right up in a matter of months. Riley reaches over and pats Daisy's neck. Mamma Greel was always nice to me. I'm comin from a house on the riverbank full of grease monkey mechanics, and she's always inviting me in and saying to stay for dinner.

Where do they live?

Elm.

Oh.

We are both quiet.

Finally I say, I didn't know y'all were friends.

Since a long time back. Until he up and went north for school and guys aren't writing each other love notes like y'all girls do. We'd just say hey when we ran into each other once in a while. Fact, I don't think I've seen him in years. He was off to Europe for summers or the Bahamas for Christmas. His mamma was from Virginia, had a whole heap of cash in her family. Anyway, I just went to forgetting about Fletcher Greel until the other night I saw him at Elsa's and dragged him down to see Crystal sing.

I pull my hair from my neck so the flesh can get some cool. Did he like it there?

Yeah, I think that Yankee loved it, says Riley, running his finger over the red chrome of the Roadrunner. Jesus, Hale, I been wanting you for years and now you run on with some judge's son just got the hell into town.

Aw Riley, I say, you and me are like brother and sister.

Riley clucks his tongue. I bet you say that to all the boys, he tells me. He picks his keys out of his pocket, throws them up, catches them behind his back and says, What you say we head on over to that little piece of swimming river? You're so interested in the judge there, I might swing by his windshield and stick an invitation on it to come find us. So get on that little red stringy, Haley girl. Daisy—he lifts up her snout—I'll race your owner to that flat piece of river near Ellyson's wood.

Before Riley can get off the hood, I jump on Daisy and say, Did you say race?

He grins and kicks his heels over his door. Riley White said race, he tells me.

★   ★   ★

It's not three minutes how the crow flies back to our house, and I put Daisy in our stable out back, get on my bathing suit and make it to the swimming hole before Riley does.

There's a rock shaped like a seat in the middle of the river, I think it's the only one in Mississippi. I lie there letting the sun bake me, watching for people. When I'm sure I'm alone, I touch my nipples to get that rush of feeling, do it underneath the cool water while a breeze kicks up gentle. Then I go down to touch the velvety piece of skin buried in hair. I shut my eyes. One bird sings five times and then one long beckoning time. Bo's face comes into my mind. *You're so fucking beautiful.*

I open my eyes and watch the green puzzle of leaves above me, sharp light glitters in and out and blinds me some. As I'm rocking on my hand, Riley's Roadrunner screams up and parks on the other side of the trees. He hops out and runs down the bank and into the water without pause. I can't stop, and I climax while Riley swims like someone on fire, not calm or slick but with splashes and yelps and hollers. The water goes into riot with his movements. I am languid and sleepy and my eyelids are hot.

Riley hasn't caught me touching myself. He is all hyped up about swimming. Damnation this feels good, he yells while he swims. Shit, and hell's on fuckin fire. He makes his hands paddles and doggie-styles to me, swallowing water and then spitting it out in one long stream. He splashes me and pushes himself up on the dry part of the rock. Water falls down his chest. His green boxer shorts are transparent and even though he picks the cloth off himself in a quick, careless way, I can still see the patch of hair there.

He lies down on his belly over the rock. Ouch, he says, hot as a fry pan. Cupping water in his hand, he wets the rock and slurps out of the river beside him.

You'll get sick, drinking this water, I tell him.

He grins at me. Woulda died by now if that's true, I drink it all god-damn day. He lifts himself up and pats his belly. Got a stomach like iron, Ellyson. He lies back down, rests his cheek on the rock and closes his eyes.

Tiny waves slap beside us and the breeze is warm. The sun slides its hazy self down the sky. I duck my whole head under to see if I can get the horse smell out of my hair and the creases in my neck. When I lift up, I swing my hair back with a jerk of my neck to spray Riley.

Without opening his eyes he says, Ah, that feels good.

That morning Daddy had asked me to ride a new horse to see how it felt. The reins were tight in my hands, so now the place between my thumb and pointer sting in the water. That stallion had been big beneath me, and I check the insides of my thighs to see the red stinging welt of him. I'm always trying to ride the ones Daddy picks so someday I can ride as good as the men at the stables. I've gotten thrown from quite a few of them. This one rode well, though, and he never bucked once. Riley's bottom lip drops, his eyelids twitch.

I hope Fletcher comes and think of what Riley said about his mamma dying. I wonder if he's broken up inside about it, and who he talks to when he's sad. The sun slices across my legs hot as the edge of an iron and I dip myself back under.

About fifteen minutes later, Fletcher comes down the slope toward us with his khakis and a work shirt on. Hi, I call to him.

He jerks his head so his hair goes out of his eyes and says, quiet, How are you? He pulls off his shirt and throws it on the ground. It's a button-up white one and he doesn't seem to care about getting it dirty. Fletcher's chest is a golden color. He nods to Riley and asks, Is he sleepin?

I tell him I think he might be.

He pulls his socks off, one at a time. I clasp my hands together, splash water down my front and watch him. All he has on is his khakis. He is fiddling with the belt buckle. Is the water cool? he asks.

It's real nice, I tell him.

Riley stirs, lifts his chin up and rubs his eyes. Judge Greel! What in hell you doin here?

You wrote me a note on my goddamn windshield, Riley White. What do you mean, what am I doin here? I'd know your handwriting anywhere. Hasn't changed any since the fifth grade.

Shit, brotha, says Riley, get's the job done.

Fletcher looks out in the distance at the trees not moving and says, That it does.

You gettin yourself wet or what, Little Judge?

Aimin to.

You don't wanna go bare assed with the lady here? Haley, turn your head. Riley gets up on the rock in back of me and puts his palms over my eyes. He tells Fletcher to take his pants off, then he makes a show of splashing and slipping on the rocks and tells Fletcher that I am battling him to get a look-see. I laugh and I hear Fletcher laugh. When Riley looses me, I see Fletcher swimming in the river, his white bottom shimmering under the river and all the rest of his body coppery and smooth.

★   ★   ★

Riley and Fletcher and I take to swimming together those first few weeks of summer vacation. Fletcher's a good swimmer, he uses hard, long arm strokes that look especially fine next to Riley, who makes the water come alive, splashing all over like a hurricane.

Sometimes Riley goes deep and gets me by the thighs and picks me up and throws me through the air. Mostly I lie on that rock and watch them and wait for Fletcher to come over to talk to me with his lips wet and his eyelashes damp and color on his cheeks. Hey, he says, how are the horses?

I say back, They're good. Then I ask him, You been judging all day?

He grins and says, Hard at it.

Later we cruise in the Roadrunner and get to feel the speed of the air on our wet bodies. I smell like river and water drips off my hair down my breast and onto my belly. It keeps me cool. Fletcher and I sit in the back-seat with our swimsuits on. He holds my hand loosely. I ring my hair out so it lies in a puddle on my leg, then pull a finger through it and make my skin wet.

While we are riding in the Roadrunner, Riley always wishes aloud for Crystal, talking of her like a person just new to religion talks about Jesus. When the situation'll hold, he says, she's comin swimming with us. Fletcher, man, you gotta hang out with her more. You'd love her. He says it to the sun, cutting out on the day, leaving us with shadows of oaks and pines and hanging cypresses and that kudzu that used to scare me as a little girl, when I thought it would swallow my house up. Daddy said it killed everything.

Swimming with Riley and Fletcher every afternoon after the stables brings some kind of relief to me. It makes me new inside, like a baptism is supposed to. During the day while I am working, I can't wait to go to the river, feel it slick up my legs and belly and lick away the hot and sweat of the stables. I think about Fletcher's face and hands and his quiet way of talking. It takes my mind from Bo, so that I start to believe I've discovered a secret to life. What you need is just to find somebody else who can fill that deep aching hole inside that you are always trying to kick dirt over and pretend isn't there.

One Sunday night, Crystal comes with us. We pick her up at the Jitney and drive her through the sunset to the river. The heat hangs thick and heavy. It feels like we're breathing water. Under her clothes she has on a yellow bathing suit the color of canary feathers, but she can't swim, so I sit with her at the edge of the river, our bottoms in the sand, feeling the cool water up our legs. The river gets drunk up in her flesh like wet in silk.

How you been? she asks me.

I splash water on my face. I been good, I say. Riley's been missin you so bad, he's like to drive himself crazy.

Crystal throws her braids over her shoulder and looks out at him. We had a long time talkin about it last night, she says, and we decided all this bein careful ain't worth it. I'm gonna see him when I want to. That night at the Jitney's braggin for how much it did to keep us apart.

Careful, I almost say to her, then I don't because I wish for her almost as much as Riley when she isn't around. She brings us a kind of magic when she comes.

Fletcher swims by and splashes us. We both squeal and put our hands up.

When he floats away on his back, she pokes her elbow in my ribs, flicks her head toward him and says, So, girl, you like that boy?

I have a crush long as this river.

She whistles low. How's he for a kisser?

I only know from one time. I haven't ever been alone with him.

Well, hurry up, Crystal tells me. Christ, you got it bad if you haven't even kissed him and you like him this much.

Riley can't stand not having Crystal in the water, so he swims up to us and takes her out by the hand. When it's up to her chest, her eyes get wide with a kind of panic, and she says she wants to go back.

No, baby, please, he says. He picks her up in his arms and carries her through the water and promises he won't ever let go.

Later we go out to the barn Daddy built, tucked into the woods behind our house. It's overgrown with vines and smells of horse and hay and old cracked manure. There are rotting lead lines on the walls and worn-out saddles and a freezer frozen to a temperature just enough to ice beer and not cold enough to bust it. It's Daddy's reserve. He comes here if they run out on a Sunday or late at night during a poker game.

We each get one, then climb the loft ladder and sit down on hay-covered slatted pine boards with our hair leaking water. Swallows and bats swoop and fly and it's pitch dark because there's no moon. All we have is Riley's lighter.

Crystal sits between Riley's legs and I sit next to Fletcher and feel his hand right close to mine. He looks down at it and touches my fingers. When he glances up, I smile at him.

Riley tries to light up a smoke.

No smokin in here, I tell him as I ease back against the barn wall.

Aw Haley, I'm not gonna burn the place down.

But Crystal hushes him, and he puts the cigarette behind his ear. We all tuck beers under warm body parts and wait for them to heat up some. I can feel Fletcher breathing beside me.

Riley says he feels these woods are full of ghosts.

We sit and listen. There's only the singing of tree frogs.

Then Riley says, Black men.

My body goes rigid. Fletcher must feel it because he puts his hand over mine, and he whispers, You all right?

I nod.

What are you talkin about, Riley? Fletcher asks. His voice vibrates beside me.

I'm not funnin, Riley says, I can feel it, all the spirits of those guys died out here in these woods. I watch Riley and Crystal's silhouette. He has his lips to the back of her neck. He lifts his head and says, What's it like up north terms of race, Judge?

Fletcher weaves his fingers through mine. I can't say for sure, he says. There were about six black kids at our school, I didn't know any of them too well. Unless we have classes on it, none of us ever talked about it. I don't think anyone'd be chasing you down in the north for it. But I don't know. I couldn't say. I guess you'd have to be from there to know what they believe. Fletcher shifts against me and coughs once. I'd get roused on for being from the South, though. They'd say shit about the Klan and the Civil War and being back in the slavery ages and all that. His voice trails off.

Riley nods silently. His nod lasts a long time. I watch how still Crystal has gotten, staring out the barn window at the stars in a moonless sky, thinking thoughts she doesn't share and I would be afraid to ask about.

Finally Riley pops his beer. Hell, he says, I can't wait, I'd chew the ice off it.

10

FLETCHER

Before going to pick up Haley, I change my button-down four times and finally decide on the blue one before I see Shelby across the hallway pretending to clean the baseboard.

I stand with my hands in my denim pockets and my shirt unbuttoned and look at her. She comes into my bedroom and straightens the shoulders of the shirt. Mr. Fletcher, she says, shaking her head. I can see tears start in her eyes. Shel cries at sappy TV commercials and even when she's saying bye to you if you're going fishing for the day. It's one of the things I love about her.

I do believe my boy has a girl he's crazy bout, she says.

I just got a date, I tell her. Hot crawls up my neck.

She palms my cheek. Ain't no girl in her right mind wouldn't fall in love with this one, she says.

I stamp my foot against the floor to get my heel on correctly. Aw Shel, I say, come on.

I'm telling the truth, she says. You handsome and smart as a fresh dollar.

Haley's house is on Clarendon Road, the last on a dead-end road. Stands of pine and magnolia crowd around it and the front porch is cement and about as big as a pool table. When we'd spoken on the phone, she'd told me to come around back.

There are sliding doors back there leading to a combination den-kitchen area. In the den, rifles line one side of the wall and there's a sling-shot over the door entrance. Vince Gill is singing out of a stereo. On the table is a glass half filled with what looks like bourbon. A woman's sandals are in front of it. I rap my knuckles on the side of the house and look around. There's a full ashtray on the deck railing.

I wait for what seems like eternity and hope her father doesn't come in because he's rumored to be hard on her boyfriends. More than that, I hope she didn't forget. I get hung up on the thought that she might have forgotten and think of all the things I could do that would make me half sane if she did. None of them involve sitting with Pops in the TV room at home watching sitcoms and witnessing his serial scotch drinking.

Finally she appears down the stairwell at the far end of the room wear-ing a dress the color of milk and silver hoop earrings big around as a baby's wrist. Her hair's down around her, curled wild. The ends are wet. When she walks toward me, she seems to float on her bare feet. I am half afraid a strong wind will blow through the screen and take her from me. She watches me while she fiddles with the door latch. Hi, she says. I can't breathe for how she looks and try to concentrate on just her collarbone while she works the handle. She runs her eyes down my shirt and ironed khakis and says quietly, This always sticks. And then the screen is open and she is standing before me. Her skin looks a warm tan and waxed from shower. When she shakes her head, all that hair falls behind her. You look so handsome, she tells me. I'm just used to you in your swimsuit.

I nod and swallow.

You goin to give me that? She points to the gardenia in my hand and smiles. Or keep it for your lonesome?

When I pass it to her, she smells it with her eyes closed. Then she comes forward, stands on her tippy toes and brushes my cheek with her lips. Thank you, she says. The words on my skin make me half hard.

I wish this was a beautiful fast car to take you out in, I tell her when I open the passenger door of the Honda. Before I'd left, Pops offered the Lincoln, but I didn't want to appear to be trying that hard.

She bends down into the seat. I watch her adjust her dress beneath her. I like this car, she says. You should see the pile of metal some boys have taken me out in.

I close the door and come around the driver's side thinking I don't want to know anything about other boys taking Haley Ellyson anywhere at all.

On the way there, I turn the radio on and then off again. Highway 12 is dark green with coming night.

You ever been to the Yocona Inn? I ask her.

She looks out her window. No, she says, but I've heard of it. She clasps her hands in front of her. I love to go out to dinner, she says. She looks like a little girl and just half a second ago she looked like a grown woman and the combination about does me in.

In the backseat is a pile of gardenias and a bottle of red wine I stole from the cellar. I was shy to bring all the flowers to her. But what I'd like to do is cover her body all over with the petals of the other ones and have her tell me what it feels like on her skin. I haven't ever had a thought like this one and the idea comes out of me before I have a chance to stop it. She listens and tilts her head, keeping her eyes on the road. My voice trails at the end and my body goes hot having said such a thing. When I am done, I watch her raise her hands, touch her stomach and her arms and then come up and pull her palms over her breasts. Finally she holds her throat and smiles with her eyes closed. I about lose the road watching her, with that fierce wish that I could be those hands and that milk-white dress, and then she says, quiet, I wish you hadn't told me that, cause now I'll be wanting it the rest of my days.

I try to think of how to promise her this when she takes a hand from her throat and wraps two of her fingers in mine. Her hand feels small and delicate. The skin is soft.

I don't want to slow or stop because then I'd have to let loose of her hand, and the car almost stalls once as I am trying best I can not to shift. When I absolutely have to, I pick her hand up and shift that way.

On the way there, she speaks of the new Mexican horses at the stables and tells me about a baby her daddy's girlfriend is preparing to have. I ask her all manner of questions about the horses and how long she's been riding and if she likes that girlfriend. The questions aren't to be polite, I ask them because I love the sound of Haley's voice, like crackling leaves in fall, and I want to know anything about her she is offering to tell.

Finally we are quiet. I put up the window to keep it from blowing her hair too much, then find a radio station that plays songs like *You've Lost That Lovin' Feeling* and *Joy to the World*. She says, It's nice, you and I are by ourselves because . . . She shrugs her shoulders and looks out the window and sighs and doesn't say one word more.

I am selfish glad that she's out of words because so am I. Sitting in the car with just her and no words might be all the happy I can handle.

The Yocona Inn is full of golden light. It has books lining the walls and upholstered chairs. The men are in suits and the ladies have on dresses. They glance at us when we walk in. Out of the corner of my eye, I watch Haley straighten her back and smooth her dress. She checks both earrings and then puts her arms at her sides and lifts her chin. I take Haley's hand and tell the waitress, Two, please. The menus are in leather folders and there are candles and flowers on the tables and red tablecloths. When we sit down, Haley pulls the tablecloth toward us and smells the flowers like she did her gardenia and then opens the menu. Running her finger down each item, she studies them before she says to me, I don't know what to order.

We lean over one menu, hers, and I tell her the duck is gamy, like chicken but thicker, and the steak is good if she wants a big meal. The fettuccine will make her mouth water and the only bad thing about it is you want to keep eating it no matter how full you are. I tell her if she wants two things, she can have two, and she looks at me like I've just told her I bought the place for her.

She says, I think I want the fettuccine.

The waitress has tight little breasts and hair the color of iron and her eyebrows are painted on. She calls me and Haley sweetie and I about think she's going to offer us the children's menu. Haley orders her entrée and her salad with Italian dressing. She asks for a large Coke. She glances at the waitress while she speaks and fiddles with a corner of the menu. I order my steak and all the other things that don't make any difference at all since Haley is beside me. And then the waitress goes away.

Haley watches me as I pick up my napkin and unfold it on my lap. She does the same. Her earrings make curved shadows across her jaw. There's faint dinner conversation all around and glasses clicking and the sound of easy laughs. I bend down and take the wine out of its paper sack and put it on the table before us and then I do the same with the two wineglasses, which smell now like gardenias. I offer one glass to Haley to smell and she smiles and flirts her eyes at me and says, It even sticks to glass, that scent.

I take the bunch of gardenias out of the bag and spread them before us like a fan and she says she hasn't ever seen anything so beautiful against that deep red tablecloth.

I have forgotten the corkscrew for the wine. The thought makes my teeth cold, and I get some mad at myself and try to think what I can do so I don't look like a fool. We look at the wine for a while. I watch a leathery-skinned, silver-haired guy at the next table open his wine with a corkscrew from his jackknife. I didn't bring my jackknife here tonight.

Haley picks the bottle up and tips it toward her and says the color matches the tablecloth. She rubs her hand over the bend in the bottle and says, Should we drink some?

So I have to tell her. She isn't bothered and sees the man with his wine at the next table. Without a thought, she leans back and asks the man for his corkscrew. She blinks her eyes when she does it, and her voice drawls sweet as breakfast syrup. He appears to mind not at all.

The wine is warm. For all that hot inside, it makes me hotter. I raise my glass and say, To Haley Ellyson.

We drink and she puts the glass down and rubs the stem up and down with two fingers. She tells me it's delicious and then she looks around and says this is the fanciest dinner place she's ever been to. I tell her I wanted to see her treated to a nice place and that I am not at all disappointed. I tell her I wanted to feed her the best food I knew how to get and watch her eat it in a room like this one.

Her eyes go wide, and in them I see my own reflection, my glass raised, my hair over one eye. And then she is raising her own glass. When she sips the wine, it stains her lips red.

Haley eats delicately and slowly, she chews well and licks her lips a whole lot. After she takes a bite, she puts her knife and fork down until she is done and takes a small sip of wine. I am fairly sure Haley didn't learn this from somebody teaching her manners, that she has natural elegance running in her like a beautiful vein.

And then she is a girl again, leaning close and telling me about the flavors in each thing. She tells me she can't eat the whole meal and she wishes she could because she will want for it later. She says food is something the whole of earth should celebrate more and that some of the best things she ever ate include a yellow watermelon one thirsty July Fourth, fresh shake-and-bake bream and a mango her daddy's girlfriend brought her fresh from the tree. She says she'll eat Tabasco on just about anything and won't ever smoke full-time because it ruins your taste buds.

We order three desserts from our waitress. By this time Haley is flushed with wine. When dessert comes, she takes the filling out of the pie crusts and licks the frosting off her cake and holds the ice cream in her mouth until I suppose it is melted.

I think there isn't a person in the world you'd rather take out to dinner than Haley Ellyson.

Over dessert, Haley tells me she read somewhere there were places where people lounge around on couches and cushions while they eat and musicians come and play instruments and there are fifteen courses and the meal takes all night. I tell her that is most likely an Arab country and she says, Best of all someone feeds you so you don't have to do a single piece of work.

I glance around and when I think no one's looking I take a piece of peach pie on my fork and say to her to put her hands behind her back. Then I feed her and when she eats it, one drop of juice comes down onto her chin. She waits for me to wipe it off.

We drive back with the windows open because Haley says she ate too much and drank too much and a little wind would be good. She tells me to drive as fast as I am able and then she lolls her head back in the seat. I almost side the Honda twice from riding the corners so quick, and once I have to swerve to miss a deer. We make it back to Houser Banks in forty-five minutes. Without opening her eyes Haley directs me to a party down near the piece of a river where Riley White lives.

The place is lit up like a matchbox on fire and the moon looks like a hangnail above it. People are smoking on the porch and music is coming out the windows. The underside of my car slams on rocks in the driveway. We stop and I go to turn off the lights, but Haley says, No. She touches my other arm. I wait and look at her.

I don't want to be here after all, she says. Let's don't ruin a good night.

On the top porch step I see Hannaford. He's smoking a cigar and wearing a pair of cut-off jeans without a T-shirt and his baseball cap's on backward. He's squinting at our car to see who's in it.

We back out and hit the dirt road and watch the dust billow up in front of us. I hear Haley breathe out.

Where do you want to go now? I ask her.

She shrugs. I don't know, she says, but I'm bored of that crowd. You know I got two more years with them.

I don't say anything. The road splits and I take the left fork to town.

She doesn't look at me when she says, I wonder if you'd be a whole lot different than you are now if you'd stayed in Houser Banks. All the boys are the same. Except Riley. I guess you and Riley would have been a crowd of your own, do you think?

I am about to say I'm not sure what I would be like if I went to school here when Haley says, Don't tell me, I want to imagine that you'd be just like you are today if you stayed in Houser Banks.

So I swallow my words and when Haley tells me to take a right, I do it, and when she says for me to turn left onto Highway 12, I do that, too.

Not long after that, we're at her street and she tells me to park in a wooded inlet on the left side. We walk down the dark street holding hands and she skips a little and asks me if I can hear the mourning doves. I tell her I can and she says they make her sad sometimes.

The house is as we left it, without any cars in the drive. I stand on her concrete porch uncertain of whether she wants me there. She wrangles with her key in the lock. Then the door swings open and she is inside, opening the door wide and saying, You can come on in.

The den light and the kitchen stove light are on and that's it. She calls hello, but immediately afterward she says her daddy is playing poker out at T.'s and Gwyneth is staying at Gypsy's, so nobody but a burglar would be home. She shivers visibly after she says it, then shakes the shiver off like you would water.

Her dress is sleeveless and when she picks her hair up on top of her head, I see the curve of her breast. She smiles her white, perfect teeth at me and says, If you come up with me now, you might have to sneak out later.

I can't tell if it's an invitation or a good-bye, and I don't want to seem careless with her, so I say, I'd love to come up, but I can go now if you want me to.

She takes her knit purse off her shoulder, sits on the bottom step and takes off one shoe at a time, rubbing the arch. I can see partway up the dress and even though I know I shouldn't, I study the curve of her inside thigh. She looks up and I glance away, down the hall at the den and the closed sliders and the wall with its clock ticking.

When she stands up, she reaches for my hand and then we are walking up those stairs, past a closed door into a darkened hallway. She flips a switch and one hall light burns down on us in a cone. We pass a bathroom on one side with a hairbrush on the basin and one of Haley's dresses slung over it. Across the hall is a bedroom, we turn into it.

She has a dresser with anything on it you'd care to think of, barrettes and Polaroid pictures of a sandy brown horse, a Coke can, a coffee cup, a pack of Virginias and a straw hat with a fake flower on its band. Haley drops my hand and walks over her floor, strewn with riding pants and T-shirts and shoes and loose change. The rug is one of those circular braided ones. It's frayed at the edges. Her bed's unmade. She goes right to the closet at the far end of the room, kneels before it and starts to throw out clothes and blankets, uncovering an old wooden box with metal hinges.

I look at a photograph on her desk of a woman who looks a lot like Haley, the same hair, but the woman's lips are thinner. This your sister?

No, she says, I'm an only child. She looks up briefly. That's my mamma when she was a little girl.

Oh, I say, quiet. You want to tell me about her?

Haley keeps rummaging in her box and says, I want to tell you about a lot of things. Come here, she says.

I walk to her. She's naked under her dress. She must be because I am sure I can see the dark circle of nipples. Maybe she has underwear on. Maybe.

When I kneel beside her, I find the box she sits in front of is filled with bones from small birds that she unwraps from dark-colored fabric. There are fish skeletons and the whole skull of a deer. One thing looks like a dog's jawbone. When I ask her about it, she says, That's Shep, the old German shepherd who used to chase cars on Highway 12. He died in our woods.

I don't know which dog she is speaking of, but I nod anyway.

She pulls out blue jay and cardinal feathers, seashells and butterfly wings.

Then she takes out a leather-bound photo book and tells me it was in Spier's barbershop when Gypsy went to clean it. It's Mr. Little's old album, she says.

You can tell which one he is, the tall, shy-looking one with light hair and crinkly eyes. He didn't look much different as an old man. His hair went silver, that's about it. When she turns the pages, the glue comes undone in places, and the black-and-whites slip crooked on the paper.

She rights them and says, No one came to the funeral when he died, isn't that sad? Gypsy said it was just the preacher and his casket and the guys from the funeral home that the town hired. Her voice is young and soft and something in it makes me sorry for her. She says, No one wanted any of this. On the last page is a picture of Little as a teenager, holding the handlebars of an old Triumph, smiling like his mouth will quit on him if he grins any harder.

She takes it from me and studies it long. Then she puts it back and commences showing me beehives and hornets' nests and pieces of birch bark the color of her dress.

I know it is important to her, this treasure chest, so I look long and finger everything. There is an old leather-bound French book with gold on the edges of the pages.

When I pick it up, she says, Will you read it to me?

My French isn't so good, I tell her.

I don't care, she says, make believe it is.

I open to the middle of the book. *Ó mon Dieu,* I say, *en union avec les mérites de Jésus et de Marie, je vous offre pour les âmes du purgatoire toutes*—

She puts her hand over the page. Her nails are choked low from riding, but the fingers are still beautiful.

Say I love you in that language, she tells me.

Except with Pops and my mom, I haven't ever said the words I love you out loud and it is a hard thing to say even in French. But I put my palm across my heart and smile on the left side of my mouth and say, Je t'aime.

Oh, she says, and then she tells me she wants to record it into her box and play it when she feels sad. Say it again, she tells me, and I do. I think to go to her, to kiss her on the mouth a long, long time without ever stopping. Maybe to lay her down on that messy bed and kiss her other places and feel her body and tell her how undone I am for her, but she is saying, Hold on, and getting out another cardboard box. She places it in her hands behind her back and tells me to pick which hand.

When I do this, she hands it to me and watches me carefully while I open it. Inside is a crinkled piece of paper and when I unfold it, I recognize my own handwriting.

I finger the note. It's a poem I wrote when I used to write anything down I thought about. Got to believing I'd be famous someday. I had written,

> At midnight there is loneliness, a feeling like hawk wings
>   outstretched.
> At dark there are times when warmth comes, explodes, when all
>   you care about is a little misery.

The writing isn't careful, it's black ink and scrawly and the words don't make any sense to me anymore. In the bottom corner is a list of Christmas stuff. *Mom: scarf,* Town and Country *subscription, wildflower mix. Dad: desk blotter, Faulkner biography.*

Do you remember that? Haley asks me. Her voice is small, as if I am going to be mad at her.

No, I tell her, I don't remember it at all. It must have been a while back because my handwriting is some different now.

You were fourteen, says Haley, leaning over and looking at it. Her shoulder blade is smooth and curved and it brushes against my arm. Her hair falls slowly and she puts it back with one hand, so I can see that side of her neck. I was twelve, she says. It was right after New Year's. I was waiting outside Elsa's for Daddy and you were on the curb in a blue jacket. You were all hunched over cause it was raining, and you took this out of your pocket, looked at it, and then threw it in that big garbage barrel near the mailbox. It missed, but then a car came for you and you got in it. So I picked it up.

Jesus Christ, I tell her, I'm embarrassed as hell.

She shifts so she's sitting on her knees. Why? she says.

I shrug. I just am, I tell her, cause I don't know what all this means, but 'I must have thought I did back then.

She nods. Well, she says, I do stuff like that all the time, and wish somebody would pick it up by accident so I don't have to show it to someone first.

She takes the note from me and folds it carefully and then puts that trunk together as it came. I watch her pile up pillows and one brown blanket on top. She closes the closet door and then we both come up to standing and I almost knock into her. She looks down at the ground, and I look there, too.

Thank you for going out with me tonight, I tell her.

She looks up at me. Thank you for inviting me, she says. She takes my hand and comes to me. The kiss is mostly breath and waiting. My heart about stops for it. Haley says, softly, Oh.

There's an animal comes up in me wants her so badly I have to open my eyes and look at her forehead, her closed lids and her mouth, which is right up close to mine, and her closed eyelids. I keep that animal at bay and kiss her as tenderly as I know how.

She offers her neck to me and I kiss that and the earlobe and her chin. I run my hand over her shoulders and try to think of words to say to her that she is everything, but no words come and so I kiss her throat and she says, So soft.

And I am about to say, I'm crazy for you, when she looks up quick.

Did you hear that? she asks.

I say, I didn't hear a thing. Which is true since I am deafed for her. Wouldn't have heard an elephant walk into the room.

She puts her finger to her mouth.

I try to still my breathing while she stands rigid and waits. Finally her body relaxes and the hand that was holding mine goes limp and she smiles at me. Sorry, she says. I thought I heard somebody, this house creaks something awful.

I guess your daddy'll be home soon, I tell her.

She nods. He might be, she says, and I don't want you off on a bad start with him if we are going to be together sometimes.

I hold her chin and kiss her again and tell her I hope it's more than sometimes and that I think about her every minute and would give up a thousand minutes just to have her for one. These are words I haven't said to anyone before and didn't know I had them in me. When I say them, she grips me tight and kisses the space of skin beneath my ear and says my name like I didn't know it could be spoken.

We kiss more and she bites my lips and runs her fingers between my mouth and hers and I am hard and aching for her and she is not righted on her feet, so I have to steady her.

Finally, after I am dizzy and we have to stop to steady our breath, she ducks her head and places her hair in back of her and takes a step from me, staring at our hands. I feel it's a sure good-bye in light of her daddy being on his way. In order to be respectful I say, I guess I should go.

She breathes in. I don't want you to, she says, but I guess it's better than havin Daddy come home and kill you. Or me.

Even though I want to tear my hair out for the unfairness of it, we are walking back down the hallway and down those stairs and she is standing at the open door. She says, Thank you so much, it was delicious. Am I going to see you at the river tomorrow after work? I hope you weren't out too late to get up early.

I tell her thank you for coming with me and that I will wait for her at the river tomorrow and that I don't care how tired I am. All the while I take only quick glances at her so I don't die from how beautiful she looks and how boyish I feel and then I am down those concrete steps, walking over magnolia leaves, turning to say, Bye now and sleep well. And she is shutting the door so that rectangle of light disappears. I have to walk her road in the pitch dark.

11

HALEY

It's hot. There's the oily heat of the sun during the day, and the still, musty heat at night. The heat comes rolling in one flat expanse over growing cotton and cornfields and dares all the dryness of hay bales and crab weeds and wheat grass that grow close to people's houses.

The horses buck the heat by slowing, they lather well and want for water constantly. Daddy and the men hose them down and press them with cold packs and wet blankets and walk them more than they run them.

On a day like this, Riley tells Fletcher and me to meet him at the river, that he is taking us to a blues fest in Arkansas and we should make up things to tell our daddies so we won't get in trouble if we stay all night.

Fletcher and I swim and afterward wait for Riley up near Battle Creek, our bodies still wet from river and mud clinging to the bottoms of our feet.

The wind against our skin feels good when Riley starts to drive. Fletcher and I sit in back and watch the road peeling out before us in a long black strip and the river running beside us with its glittery sun-kissed body.

How you doin, Riley? Fletcher asks.

Riley smokes and looks at us in his rearview and says he hasn't been with Crystal in eleven days because someone reported to her parents that they saw her leaving work early with him and they're mad at her cause they don't want any trouble.

She's been misty eyed about it, Riley tells us.

I've got a feeling of softness for Riley that grows inside me like a thing rooted. I lean up and put my hands around the driver's-side back. Crystal's gonna be all right, I tell him.

He looks at the road and nods. I watch him bite the side of his lip. She's gonna be just fine, he says, long as she loves me as the honky man I am. Long as that ain't stoppin.

I know Crystal isn't stopping her love of Riley for anyone. It is in the all of her when she says anything, in the way she walks to him or leans up to kiss him.

You couldn't stop her if you wanted to, I tell him. I see that he has held his breath to hear me say this. He exhales and loosens his grip on the wheel. Then he reaches a hand up, messes my hair and says, Shit, girl, you aimin to lean back with that boyfriend of yours? I'm sure he's been anxious on you all day.

Fletcher looks at me while I lean back. I put my head on his shoulder and he kisses the top of my head. It makes me feel sleepy and drugged. He says, Has anyone ever called you anything but Haley?

My daddy calls me Turnip, I tell him, cause I hated greens so much as a little girl.

Fletcher nods and I watch his slow smile, then he turns and looks out. Houser Banks Baptist goes by in a blur.

On the way there, we watch the highway turn into lush swamps and flatland without any hill as far as you can make your eye go. I think of Bo and the smoke coming from his cranberry-colored lips. Of the hot, empty places he has taken me to, the sweaty guilt and shamed wanting. He's away now and I haven't seen him in five days running. With his absence, there's a relief I can't describe and it makes the sun sweet on my face.

I reach over and take Fletcher's hand and he slings the other arm in back of me. Fletcher smells of lemon and clean, something like goodness. He is like no boy I've ever met. He's not rough, but he seems to me braver than any of those other Houser Banks boys who wear knives on their waists and carry guns in their boots and drive their pickups drunk down Highway 12 at 2 A.M.

You can tell he's different from the things he does. Just yesterday, he fixed me a picnic dinner by the water. We sat on a blanket he brought and he pulled the food out of a big brown basket. There was a long loaf of uncut and crispy bread and fancy cheese that tasted like butter and mangoes he sliced and fed to me. He brought along fried chicken he said was Shelby's best. There were two cloth napkins and one bottle of wine the color of gold. When I was tired he said, Lie down and tell me when you're thirsty and I will pour some in your mouth.

Later he bushwhacked through the woods to pick me a wildflower so I could wear it in my hair.

It's only been three and a half weeks since I've known him, but as far as I can tell, he doesn't seem to care about thanks or gratitude or wanting a thing back for his sweetness. Afterward we walked through the woods not a hundred yards from the body and I thought to show him it, but there wasn't any time and it was getting dark out.

I had to meet Daddy at eight to go to a horse auction, so I kissed Fletcher good-bye in the inlet on Clarendon. The kisses were so fine I went wet from them, and my stomach curled whenever I thought of them the whole night through. When we kiss, we do it tender as if we were both breakable or drowning people.

Bo has hardness to his kisses, a desperateness. As if he were in prison and I am the walls and he half likes it and half wants to be free and it is all my fault.

When we get there, the field is spot-colored with tents. Men stagger around drunk. Women laugh with their heads back and sway their hips to the music while their boyfriends stand behind them holding their waists. Trailers encircle the place, selling fried pork and barbecue and beer and bumper stickers and fair jewelry. Christmas lights are strung at random around the side stage, where Crystal is going to sing.

Blues blare out of loudspeakers, and the front stage is big as a house, with costumed ladies dancing backup and men in dark shades and top hats and rings on every finger doing the singing. At the side stage, we sit on hay bales and stacked tires and drink beer out of plastic cups that Riley buys us for a dollar. Written in black paint on nailed two-by-fours are the names of the singers. Crystal Nash is number six.

On the side stage, shirtless drummers drink sixteen-ounce Buds as sweat drools off black bodies. The women are in sequins and the men are in seersucker suits.

The hay bales rock with clapping and the musicians tell stories. Almost all the people in the tent are black except for me and Fletcher and Riley and a few others with cameras around their necks and big fat sunglasses atop their heads and knee-length shorts and short-sleeved shirts with collars. They are the tourists.

Above us, the stars come out by the millions and the quarter moon rises and we lose Riley to a school bus painted purple that is supposed to be backstage. Fletcher and I dance to the music and hold each other tight. His arms are familiar and his breath is sweet. I tell him I don't want this night to ever end.

Riley comes back. A breeze blows in and billows up tent folds and ladies' dresses and my hair. My neck cools. The grass gets sodden and beaten below our feet. Men turn their baseball caps around so the bill is in back, women get even looser in their bodies and people holler up to the stage for encores.

At a quarter till midnight Crystal sings in a molasses-colored dress one shade darker than her skin. It shines in the stage lights. Her mouth is a blood color and her nails are painted red and her braids drip onto her arms. She fills the tent with her voice, so I think for a minute that even the main stage has quieted to hear her. The crowd rides her rhythm in dance and clap.

Crystal acts a little shy when she is with just Fletcher and Riley and me, but when she is singing like that, she looks brazen and unafraid, with a gleaming smile and her body moving and her mouth open wide. She looks like she is already a famous person. The three of us stand at the side of the stage, mesmerized. I feel a proud light inside me because she is ours.

The plywood beneath her shakes with the drummer's feet stomping. The guitarist watches her as if she is making his hands play and he's just the tool. She and Riley catch eyes through one whole verse. Then she looks back at the crowd and shakes her hip and twists her body to look at the guitarist in his solo and I realize for one horrible second that Crystal Nash isn't ours at all, that we have no time left with her. She is a glittering island and her life will move on and away from us to somewhere bigger, where even her sound couldn't fill it.

When I look back at Fletcher and Riley, they are still smiling and moving their feet. Riley winks at me and Fletcher sips his beer. It appears that moment came to me only, so I keep dancing like I was and push it out of my mind best I can.

After Crystal sings, she has to go home in the back of a station wagon with some relatives who have been watching the main stage. She looks out the window at us without waving, and I see her watch Riley long and turn her head to do it. He stands there staring after the car like it is all he can do to not run after it.

Riley and Fletcher and I sleep in a pup tent in the middle of the field. Through the night we hear people in other tents making love and drunks tripping around the unlit trailers.

It's so hot it feels like we are sleeping in invisible Jell-O. Riley lies sprawled out in the middle of the tent in his boxer shorts. Fletcher is on his right side wearing yellow boxers and a white T-shirt and looking like he is faking sleep for how he keeps his mouth closed and breathes so quiet next to Riley, who rips up the air with his snoring. I am on Riley's left, wishing I could have slept next to Fletcher. Riley had come to the tent to fall dead asleep right away. Fletcher and I walked around some, watching the trailers fold in on themselves. We watched the lights burning in the family tents. We shoved napkins away with our shoes. He bought me a corn dog and a Coke from the one man who was still selling. Y'all married? the man asked us and Fletcher turned to me and put his arm around my neck and told him we were just fresh married that very day.

When we came back, Riley was already asleep and there wasn't any room to lie down but on either side of him.

It's so hot I can't sleep. Somewhere a radio plays blues the night through, sad and drowsy, and it mixes with the sound of whippoorwills and insects. Humid air moves in through the screen of the tiny back window. I look out to see the blackened windows of the trailers and the littered lawn and the tents and lean-tos and people scattered in sleeping bags under stars.

While I look, I wish that Bo Dickens would disappear forever. I would be left with only the memory of him, and I could live whole and pure with Fletcher and Riley and Crystal for the rest of my days.

When I lie back down, I chance to look over at Fletcher. He is watching me. I turn onto my side and we watch each other over Riley's sleeping chest, going up and down in rhythm. Fletcher lays his hand on the ground above Riley's head and I bring my hand there, too. We stay like that for what seems like hours, holding hands and waiting for sleep.

In the morning we drive back tired and dirty and sleep deprived under a clear blue sky. We forgo breakfast except for drive-through coffee, and by midday blanching, seething sun is hitting the Roadrunner. When we reach Houser Banks, we need cool drinks and food and new clothes and a shower. But most of all, I want to be next to Fletcher. I am afraid of the way my skin will be lonely when I have to leave him. While we ride down Highway 12, a panic comes up in me for my empty house I will enter and for the end of our trip and for the sad feeling I will have when the Roadrunner drives away.

Riley stops at the inlet on Clarendon, leaves the motor running and turns around in his seat to look at me. I gaze down at the long street and the tiny square of my house at the end of it. The MG and the truck aren't in the drive.

You gonna be all right, Ellyson? Riley asks.

I don't say anything. Fletcher takes my hand and Riley looks down at it.

I don't want to leave y'all, I tell them.

Riley says, I gotta go get my brother Judd. You can come along if you want to.

I shake my head no.

Riley faces front and shuts off the radio and Fletcher bends toward me. You want to swim a little bit? he asks me. I can get the Honda and we can meet at the river in a half an hour.

My stomach lifts its nagging and I kiss his cheek fast and watch him grin. I say, Okay, meet you there.

Riley roots around for his pack of smokes and says, Goddamnit if you two ain't the spittin image of true love.

Fletcher is already sitting on the edge of the river when I come. He has brought a yellow rubber raft big enough for two bodies and is blowing it up with his cheeks puffed and his face red. I come running up beside him, pulling off my sundress when I do it so I am just in my red string bikini.

He holds his thumb over the opening and watches me come toward him. Hey, he says.

The sun beats down in white, dusty rays over the water, which looks solid as a mirror without any wind. I squat beside him. He says, I'm glad I got here before you.

I tilt my head. Why's that?

He caps the plastic top and says, Because I hate for you to ever have to wait for me.

With one hand he splashes the boat and makes the rubber slippery and wet and cool with river water and then we hop onto the raft and float. Fletcher lies with his face to the sun and his hands cupping the back of his head. He has a pile of gold hair traveling from his belly button to the waist of his pants.

Doesn't this feel good? I ask him.

He says nothing ever felt better.

We pass a white-haired man with glasses fishing off the bank. A little boy is sitting next to him pulling a willow branch through the water. Hi ya, he says when we pass and, Nice day for it.

Fletcher and I float without saying anything and then his hand is on my back and my hand is around the waist of his shorts and we are holding on to each other in broad daylight. He is breathing hard, but he stays like that, facing me, with his arms around me. The water moves us in slow waves and I realize I haven't ever touched a boy like this, where he wasn't trying to swallow my face or grab me hard in a place that was supposed to be soft. I raise my head to his chest and say, I haven't ever felt like this with anyone before in my life.

Fletcher says, I haven't either and I have a feeling I won't ever again.

The man who is fishing is a speck in the distance and I wonder about getting back, but Fletcher says his arm muscles are strong and I can laze around while he paddles when the time comes. When I look at the shore, I realize we are passing Battle Creek and the body is above the bank from us and though I hadn't planned it I say to him, I want to show you something.

He watches me and nods.

I sit up, the raft sways and almost tips. His hand grips me so I won't fall.

Fletcher, it's a secret, I tell him, and I don't want you to say anything to anyone at all.

Fletcher shrugs and says, Okay. I won't.

You have to promise.

He half smiles and looks at me. He says, I promise. I'm good at secrets.

I have a moment of doubt, not that Fletcher will be able to hold the secret but that it is somehow mean to let him in on it. I want to do it now because I am afraid I will lose my courage.

We side the raft and hide it underneath a pile of brush and Virginia creeper vines. We are just in our bathing suits and our feet get partway cut up when we walk. He says, You sure you want to do this now?

I nod. When I take his hand, it is cool from river. I turn him to me and take a piece of river sludge off his chin. Fletcher, I say, no questions either, okay? I know somethin about these woods, but you can't ask me about it or we won't be friends again.

It takes Fletcher a long time to nod and when he finally does, it is a slow nod like he is deciding more than just this one thing. And then we are walking through the brush and sapling and roots to the body.

We stand ten feet from it and I point at it. He bends down on his haunches and studies the mound in front of us and then he stands and puts his hand through his hair and says, I don't get it.

I am shaking and my armpits are damp with sweat.

A body is buried there, I tell him.

Almost as soon as I say it, he takes a step back and has to right himself from stumbling. He sniffs the air, then walks toward the grave and stands real close. Memory comes to me of Bo doing the burying, his red, angry face, how he dripped sweat and didn't talk and grunted at the effort of it. I am weak with the thought of that arm out, that it will make Fletcher startle and run, but he does not. He toes the mound once and then he turns and looks back at me. How do you know it's a body?

Silence comes like a clanging door inside me. I lift my chin and say thinly, I said no questions.

He squints at me, turns back and looks the length of the grave.

I hear myself saying, I can't, Fletcher, you promised.

He nods and then comes walking toward me with his head bent, studying the ground. He does not stop walking when he gets to me, just takes my hand so that I turn to follow him.

When we get to the bank, he pushes the leaves and vines over and places the raft back in the water. He holds it steady with two hands so I can climb on. Then he gets on, too, lies flat on his back and shades his eyes from the sun. His other arm he puts around my back. We drift for some time farther out from where we came. There aren't any words between us.

He flips over on his belly and begins to paddle us back. Our legs and sides are touching, but I don't hold his hand or drape my arm over his back. I stay on my side of the raft best I can, afraid that now that I have shown Fletcher such a thing he won't want to be with me anymore. Maybe he will go and tell his daddy that it's there. The thought makes me mostly scared, but somewhere deep in me, there is also that lure hook of what will happen next.

His arm muscles flex while he paddles and once he splashes me and tells me he is sorry.

That's okay, I tell him. I inch up next to him and lay my head down, drag my hand in the water and say, What makes you so quiet?

He keeps paddling until we get to the still part of the river, then he stops. His voice is soft. He says, I can't talk right now because I want to

know how you know it's there. I have a thought we should tell it to someone. Only I promised you I wouldn't ask any questions or tell anyone at
all, and I'm not a person to break promises to you, ever. So I don't have a
whole lot to say right now. My words'll come back directly if you'll wait
on them.

I tell him I will. But I hope you still like me, I say.

He rolls over next to me and puts my head on his chest and whispers
into my hair, Are you kidding me? It'd take a whole lot more than that.

After a little while he says, Are you all right? You feel okay?

I nod and a calm comes in me because I am lying next to Fletcher
Greel, and he is free and innocent of all the bad in my world. I can show
him just little snippets here or there so he knows to comfort me. All he
really knows is a mound in the woods and not what's attached to it. I feel
suddenly safe and the sun feels good, the river sounds peaceful and the raft
is like a mother carrying her two grown babies into heaven.

12

FLETCHER

The Roadrunner hauls us out toward Atlanta on Highway 78. Riley's driving with his arm resting on the car door, his dirty blond hair blowing out of his ponytail. He whistles and holds a cigarette in his left hand. The ashes get ripped off while we go.

There's two hundred miles until we hit South Carolina. Riley and I are high as the stars on Biloxi marijuana. I pull the visor down against strong headlights. On the visor mirror's left-hand bottom corner is a smudge of lipstick I recognize as Crystal's. She must have touched her lips and then touched the mirror to adjust it. I feel it now, but it is all dried up. Riley looks over at me. Admiring yourself? he asks.

I push the visor up. Nope, I tell him.

Bullshit, he says.

On the rearview, he's hung a bunch of keys off a string. When we get where we are going, Riley will put them around his neck. Now they bang and jangle in front of us.

We are both wearing our best worn-down denims and white T-shirts. I look straight ahead, focus on the road, which wastes away to black around the corners, and say, We look like goddamn twins.

That we do, Riley says. Grow your hair and we could call each other Bobbsey.

My hair is growing itself without me, I tell him.

Riley smiles. Good, he says. You'll catch hell. But who wants to twin up with all them baseball-hatted look-alikes?

I just hope where we're goin they don't call us faggots for dressing in the same outfit, I tell him.

Riley lifts one hand above his head so that it is a wall for wind and says, With this hair, it wouldn't be the first time. But nobody's allowed to call us faggot, Yankee. You can bet all your courthouse paycheck on that.

We stop at a place east of Atlanta called Bull's Beer House. Smoke comes out the front hall like a chimney. Waitresses are dressed in black bow ties with white collars, their hair frames their faces like lions' manes. They're wearing skirts that wrap around their thighs and ankle-high boots with heels and bodysuits that squoosh their breasts together so you want to put your hand in the soft of them and make it hot.

Hey, an auburn one says to us. She's holding a corked drink tray and she twists her hips to lay a napkin on a table. Y'all can sit wherever you want.

The floor is made of wide unpolished wood boards. On the walls there are deer heads and blinking stoplights and old road signs that say *Stop* and *Yield* and *Slow Children*. A mirror hangs from one side and makes the room seem double in size. The bar takes up the whole left wall and four bartenders walk around with unsmiling faces and unkind eyes, so you'd have to be brave to ask for a drink. Menu cards are stuck to the tables by silver holders shaped like ladies' legs. The women in there carry themselves like they are proud of their bodies and might like to share them with anyone who is willing to try, and the men have deep voices that sound like they weren't ever boys in all their lives.

These men shoot pool with the cue in back of their waist and don't shut one eye or move the cue back and forth. They shoot the balls straight as a gun. Then they watch the balls hit the pockets as if the balls are their subjects and they themselves are royalty and this is their kingdom.

Riley points to a booth underneath a plank that hits one wall and travels across to the other wall. Girls'll dance up there if you come on a lucky night, he says while we sit down. They look like her, he points to a blond waitress. But the outfit's different.

The table is raw pine and people have carved initials and hearts and pictures of penises too long to be true and words like *Linda sucks good dick* and *Nigger lovers eat me raw*. I trace my pointer finger over the grooves of the words and think about writing my name and Haley's name here. I wonder how long it would stay there, and how many people would sit and look at it and run their fingers over it.

The waitress slips napkins in front of us and Riley tells her to get us two shots of whiskey and two Budweisers. She puts a black plastic ashtray in front of us. Riley bangs a new pack of Camels against his palm and looks around. He says, My brother Sammy and I used to come here when it was called Fat Matty's. It was a gambling biker bar back then and these guys'd to hang out wearin chains and sportin tattoos.

The waitress comes back with our drinks. Riley tells her to start a tab. She walks away.

I guess she doesn't care how old we are, I tell Riley.

He knocks back his whiskey and grins. I guess not, he says. They never cared. He looks around and tells me, We'd come in here when I wasn't fourteen years old, geeky and tall as a cornstalk. Sammy was about eighteen. I guess he'd bring me along so he wouldn't talk the upholstery off the car seat. I was a young un without a hell of a lot to say and not old enough to tattle cause I knew if I did, I'd get my ass kicked. I used to stand right there, Riley says, pointing to a staircase, and flirt with a girl named Desde, looked only a spit older than I was, brunette with tits like water balloons and a nose of cocaine that made her horny as hell. The gamblers played downstairs with dollar bills instead of poker chips. Cards slung on the table of Fat Matty's were the love of Sammy's life. Riley shakes his head and smiles.

The stop-and-go light flickers red to yellow to green over and over again. I watch a big-muscled man with cut-off shirtsleeves throw a woman across his shoulder and spank her bottom. What happened to Sammy? I ask Riley.

Riley peels the label off his beer bottle. Sammy's in the pen, Judge. Got caught for armed robbery last year. Always had veins full of cocaine and a shitload of gambling debts behind him. It wasn't his first offense and we didn't have the money for a fancy lawyer. He's got some time to do.

Riley takes a smoke out of his pack and lights it. There's whiny country coming out the speakers and a drunk lady at the bar uses a spoon as a microphone and sings along.

Jesus, I tell him, I didn't have any idea. I'm sorry, Rile.

I think of my father and wonder why he hadn't ever told me.

Yeah, says Riley. Well. In Sammy's honor, I'm still into the quick money. I want to do it legal. A hole in the floor for pissin and a cell big as a six-by-six doesn't appeal to me. I'm into the dog idea. This guy in South Carolina we're goin to see made a bunch of money in dogs, now he's losing it all on account of bad-check charges. Ten days to rid himself of a breed of coon dogs, walker, redbone, bluetick, black and tan. All I'll need to do is build em little houses in the shade. They'll dig themselves some trenches and rest their chins in the dirt all day until nightfall when I'll run em. I can run em for a season with a good tracker and if one of em's a good trailer I can sell him and trade high. They sell for about five hundred each, I think.

I nod. I want to talk more about Sammy, to ask him what it feels like to have a brother behind bars and whether he ever goes to visit him. Only I can tell Riley's done talking about it.

He leans back with his smoke in his mouth and his elbows over the sides of the booth. He smokes without taking the cigarette from his lips. If I sell the lot of em, he says around his smoke, I can go to Jamaica or somewhere sunny once Crystal graduates.

You leaving the country? I ask Riley.

Riley shrugs. I don't want to, I've always been happy as a boy could be right here in Mississippi. Houser Banks is where I belong and I couldn't think near serious of leavin it. But Crystal says she won't stay here. She wouldn't be caught dead livin out the rest of her days in a bright red convertible with a white boy in the U.S. of A. more than she'd be caught in Houser Banks square with just her panties on. Riley takes his smoke out and ashes it. That is a thing I'd like to see, says Riley. But if she wants to go somewheres besides this country, I'll fly to Timbuktu if need be.

That's in Africa, I tell Riley.

He raises his eyebrows. Yeah? he says. Well so be it. All I need is Crystal Nash on my side and I could handle a barrel of rattlesnakes. He picks up my hand and looks at my watch. It's a quarter till midnight, he says. Two hundred and eighty miles till we hit this little South Carolina bumfuck town in the middle of nowhere. We can yack at the convicted man for an hour or two, make him a proposition he can't refuse more than he can refuse heaven on this green earth and be back by two tomorrow afternoon with some coon dogs to train and sell. He nods his chin to my drink. But for now happy up, boy, we got time.

Riley and I wind up doing three more whiskey shots and drinking three more beers. We play pool with two girls from Macon until three in the morning. He partners with Sally Jane and I partner with Lisa. They are twenty-one years old and Lisa has bubble-gum-colored lips. When she wants to say anything at all to me, she whispers and runs her tongue around her lips. She's got a bulge of belly busting out of her jeans and plump upper arms and I imagine she's the type who gets guys to come home with her and then they leave in the morning without a phone call or a nice word. The thought makes me sad as hell, and I try to be as nice as I can without leading her on.

Sally Jane's husband's out of town and she keeps telling us that. She laughs with her mouth open whenever she misses a shot, and I see the fillings in her back molars. She tells Riley he's a real good shot at pool and maybe he could teach her to be better. He does this by standing at the other end of the pool table and pointing to a place on the ball she should be shooting for. She's a terrible player and Lisa and I take two out of the three games.

When the bartenders turn on the lights and start hollering for us to clear the place, Sally Jane sidles up to us and brings the collar of her shirt back a little. Y'all want to come back to our house? she asks. We could smoke a joint. I got a good record collection. She leans against the cue stick. Oldies but goodies, she says.

Riley and I excuse ourselves to piss off the back deck, which is littered with empty kegs of beer and cigarette butts. While we are pissing we decide it's a bad idea to do anything more with Lisa and Sally Jane. Then we sneak around the side of the building, jump in the Roadrunner and leave that place with a twenty-seven-dollar tab we won't ever pay.

South Carolina's got billboards up that say *Pregnant? Don't abort your baby.* Riley and I decide a blanket statement like this one makes us mad as hornets, but more than mad, we are sleep deprived and cranky, so we park the car in a Krispy Kreme parking lot and sleep until eight the next morning.

By 9 A.M. the sun's hot to blistering. We can't figure out if it's hotter with the top down or up. In debating it we get lost on rural routes and byways and old Highway 7s. Riley stops and calls the dog guy from a staticky phone booth north of Columbus and comes back to the Roadrunner to tell me about a joint in the glove box that he needs to smoke if his nerves are going to survive the day.

The highways are full up with nothing, and so hot the air looks liquid on top of the pavement. We light the joint going seventy-six in a fifty-five, Riley with his dark glasses on and Louis Armstrong on the cassette player. He lolls his head against the seat and says, This ain't half bad.

It takes me three drags before I realize something important we hadn't ever thought of. How many dogs are there? I ask Riley.

There are about ten of them, says Riley. He takes the joint and looks at it. Maybe twenty, he says, I don't know.

I nod, look at the backseat and then back at Riley, who's sucking in good and heavy. Where you going to put them? I ask.

One long puff comes out Riley's mouth. His eyes go wide. He says, Shit, Greel, damned if I know. I hadn't even bothered to think about it.

And then the sirens start.

The blues whirl around in the rearview and against the white seats. Riley says, Shit, fuckin hell Jesus Christ, while he tries to kill the joint on his pants leg best he can. Finally he puts the still-smoking and half-done joint in his mouth. He coughs and sputters and swallows five times.

The Roadrunner hits gravel when we slow. Then we sit and wait. Riley's face is a the color of glue paste and he stays rigid while the officer gets out of his car with big dark glasses that make him look like a coon. He's wearing a tall hat and he doesn't have any lips as far as I can see.

Howdy, he says. He stands there looking at Riley and me.

Riley turns his head slowly and says, Howdy Officer.

The guy looks down the road in front of us, puts his palm up and looks back at Riley. License and registration, he says. And take your glasses off.

Riley fumbles with his shades and manages to get them off. He blinks his eyes four times fast. I got bad allergies, he tells him.

One car hauls past us in a cheery way, probably thanking God they're free and not the poor bastards with the sick luck in the bright red car.

The officer stares down at Riley for some time, then he says, It's the license and registration I'm waitin on son. I don't got all day to stand here starin at you.

Riley reaches in his back pocket for his wallet and gives his license to the officer. By this time, Riley's face is splotched red and I see his cheeks blow out twice. He swallows continuously and breaks out in a sweat. He passes his registration over.

While the guy is looking at Riley's papers, Riley grips the steering wheel. He shuts his eyes tight. Suddenly he says, Ah, excuse me. He opens the door so fast it whacks the policeman in the shins and then he leans over and throws up. I watch puke spots splatter onto the guy's boots and listen as Riley's insides power-hit the dirt. His barf smells like the worst heated nightmare and I almost have to get sick myself.

Step out of the car, the policeman says to Riley when he's done. He looks over at me. And you too, he says.

We stand there in steaming heat. Our hands are behind us in hand-cuffs. The air is hot and smells of tar and Riley's already-eaten Krispy Kremes. The first guy calls a second guy, who comes with his sirens blaring and his lights cutting up the air. They commence ripping everything out of the car looking for drugs. The floor mats lie on the side of the road and pretty soon everything in the glove box is placed on top of them. They get Riley to open the trunk. They take his fishing gear and rip through his tackle box. Luckily, Riley'd taken his gun out of the box. I don't know if that would've been legal or not, but it wouldn't have helped our situation any. Riley gets sick one more time while we stand by the brush and scrub and litter in the blaring sonofabitch sunlight.

They give us a Breathalyzer test each, which shows a trace of what we'd had the night before but not enough to do any damage. Then they throw us in the back of the first guy's car, leaving the Roadrunner to split paint in the sun. We sit with our wrists in the bracelets, looking out the front window through the bars of a cage like the hounds Riley intends to make himself rich with.

Riley says he's looking forward to the bright orange citation sticker.

They don't have a goddamn thing on us, says Riley while one cop stands bending his head toward the other cop out the front window. That joint's the only thing I got and I ate it and I threw it up. If they want to start rummaging in my puke for evidence, they can start now.

At least this car is air-conditioned, I tell him.

The South Carolina holding cell is twenty-five-by-thirty-feet big with sixty men in it. It's ninety-five degrees and no one is wearing shoelaces.

How come they took our laces? I ask Riley after the guard walks us in and leaves us there.

They want us alive, he tells me. Be a lot easier if they let most of these guys rot on a shoestring noose, though, says Riley.

The place smells like piss. There are bare-backed men wide as a county in there and twenty-pound crack addicts and businessmen sweating fear out their Brooks Brothers armpits. I try to breathe through my mouth. Riley sidles us up to a piece of cement near the door and the red-faced men watch us and spit on the ground and look angry as pit bulls.

A light-colored black guy with a stub of a leg and a splintered crutch comes and stands in front of us. He has a cocaine smell coming from him and his pupils are so big you can't tell what color his eyes are. He opens his fly and takes out a droopy, shriveled-looking prune cock. Riley leans his head against the wall and shakes it back and forth slowly. Go away, he says in the deepest voice I've ever heard from him. A shirtless guy with a shaved head and a swastika carved into his stomach watches us.

The man with his dick out turns to me. In a raspy voice he says, Couldn't you suck me for a dollar? I edge away from him. My hand hits a mucous pile dripping down the wall, and I wipe it on my pants. The bald man with the swastika chews his fingernails. When I look around, I see a bunch of them watching us, stopping what they are doing to see what all we are going to say next. Riley leans up from the wall. He stands with his feet splayed and his arms crossed in front of him.

Two things could happen here, Riley says to prune dick. A guard could walk in while we are fighting and we'd get worse than we are now or a guard could walk in and wonder why you are sleeping and won't wake up.

Prune dick's brows curl, his mouth goes jittery and he asks in a whiny voice, Why you cracker ass think you could make me sleep that way? He is still holding his penis.

Riley shrugs. I been fightin all my life, he says. I've run from as many fights as I have hair on my body, but I been in twice as many. Ain't no South Carolina nobody gonna make me suck his dick.

Another black man in a fancy pin-striped suit comes over and stands beside Riley. Looking at prune dick, he says, I'll help you make him sleep, that shithead gives me and mine a bad name.

Prune dick stuffs his penis back in his pants and hobbles away, mumbling all the while. The big black guy in the suit sits on the floor across from us and raps his knuckles on the ground next to him as if to toughen them. One of his eyelids looks burned shut.

I'm hoping he has a cigarette hid somewhere, Riley says to me before he goes and sits down next to him.

I ain't your friend, white boy, the man says when Riley sits, so don't s'pose it.

Riley raises his eyebrows, stands up again and comes to lean on the wall next to me.

There ain't a decent guy in the place, says Riley.

We look over to our left at a guy jumping around like a flea and calling out the name of his mamma or his girl, Wanda Blake, Wanda Blake. At first I feel sorry for her for ever having to be associated with the likes of him and then I come to hate her for ever being on this earth in the first place.

Men rattle the door's barred window and the handle and try to kick it with their feet. Every fifteen minutes a guard comes by with a joystick and a gun on his waist and a neck so fat it's got rolls in it. He tells us all to hush up in a violent way that makes you think he might pipe-bomb the place before the day's over. My skin itches and my mouth is dry as paper and I want to know am I getting out of here and when. I think Pops could get us out in a heartbeat, but I hate to have to call and tell him where we are. I haven't been in trouble with him since I was ten years old and I can't imagine what he'd be like in that situation. I imagine he would be quiet and cold.

I turn around and face the wall. Riley looks over at me. Bending my head so no one can read my lips, I say, Rile I'm scared as shit. My old man isn't gonna like fishing me out of here.

Riley nods. I don't think your old man ever has to know you were in here. They don't have nothin on us cept a speeding ticket.

I shove my sneaker toe against the wall. They could pin whatever they want on us, I tell him.

Look around you, Judge, says Riley. They don't care a rat's ass about us. Believe me on this one, Yankee.

I breathe in deep and smell the foul urine smell and say, All right. You haven't ever lied to me yet.

Riley spits on the ground and rubs it with his shoe sole. While he's looking down at it he says quietly, And I don't ever plan to.

We stand for a long time not talking to anyone. No one much bothers us and we wind up sitting down on the floor with our backs to the wall. I fall into a sort of heat-induced stupor until I hear a man say, I'm Big Boy so-and-so from so-and-so street in so-and-so, I'm gonna make the first person who tries to sleep eat his own eyeballs. I open my eyes quick and look up at him. It's the guy with the swastika on his stomach. He's got a lopsided head and he looks muscled as an ox and meaning business. I'm trying my hardest not to blink at all when a little brown-skinned guy slumped in the corner stands up. He's got flat black hair down his back, and he looks like an Indian. I believe he is blind. His two murky-colored eyeballs stare at nothing at all. He turns his eyes in the direction of Big Boy and says, I'm Jay Count Little Blind and I'm from Florida and I'm going to sleep wherever and whenever I goddamn want to. Then he sits back down and closes his squirrely eyes.

Big Boy breathes in, his chest puffs out. The din of the place quiets some and men turn to look. Big Boy takes three steps toward Jay Count. When he kicks him, he leaves tread marks across his arm. He turns around and heads toward the door and without breaking his stride, he kicks it so hard he aches his foot and goes to howling like a birthing lady. Guys resume what they were doing before, pissing against the wall and watching the door while they do it so the guard doesn't catch them. My own piss has been pushing on my groin since we got stopped.

Riley walks toward Jay Count and I follow because I don't want to be left alone. Jay Count's cradling the arm that was kicked. Riley leans down next to him and says, Jay Count Little Blind, how you doin?

The little man smiles, his teeth are rotted yellow. That's not the worst of it, Jay Count says. People have died in here.

Riley stands up and nods his head. I lean against the sweating cement wall. That'd be bad, says Riley. It stinks enough in here already.

Jay Count Little Blind invites us to sit with him. He turns out to be a talker. He's from Tampa Bay and he tells us about his mamma and his three sisters and how their house got tore away in a tornado. He can't remember when, but he thinks it was '67. He went blind in an electric fire during it and then wandered around without food, unable to find his family. He took to begging on the streets. While he talks I see the side of his neck is scarred from fire and one earlobe is lobbed off. He has a dirty rope around his neck with seashells strung on it. His pants don't have a zipper and are hung up by a torn-apart white plastic belt.

I remember colors, he says, but they're fading now sure as the tune you think you won't ever forget or the touch of a girl you once loved. You boys from where?

We're from Mississippi, says Riley.

Well tell me about the colors, Jay says.

Riley sits on the floor next to him and I squat on my haunches. There's a guy next to us hunched over sleeping with a string of drool out his mouth. Big Boy is kicking the door in a steady rhythm. Riley looks hard at the ground, thinking.

A guard comes in and lets a man out and tells Big Boy to cut it out.

Riley starts to talk. He speaks of goldenrod and honeysuckle, blooming cotton fields and full-up corn and rows of soybeans, the bream going silver in moonlight and in hunting season the skies so blue it hurts the eyes. He tells him the rivers run black when they're high and in spring the magnolias look like girls ready for a party.

Boy, you are in love, Jay Count tells him.

Riley and I look at each other. Riley lifts his eyebrows and asks Jay, How so?

Jay says, Tell me about her.

Riley looks at the floor. She's five-eight, he says.

Jay Count nods his head.

Beautiful enough to knock you over, says Riley. Skin smooth as cherry-wood, and she can open up her mouth and sing the blues like there ain't no tomorrow and all she has time for is to love you right today.

Jay Count laughs and then gestures his hand in a way that means he wants more.

She moves like slow honey, says Riley, and if I could love her the rest of my days, I'd get down on my hands and knees and lick this dirty floor with my tongue.

Jay Count Little Blind is quiet. His head doesn't quit the nodding and he stays like that for some time. He starts to speak so low Riley and I have to bend to hear him.

What did you say? asks Riley.

I said, What's the problem?

Sir? says Riley.

The blind man leans forward and gropes with his hands. When he feels Riley's thigh, he makes a fist and pounds it on his leg, hard to bruising. There's anguish in your voice, boy, he says. There's hell to pay for her from the sounds of it.

Riley nods. Well, he says. He looks around at the cell and then back at the man. I'm a white boy. She's a black girl. And there's hell to pay for that where I come from.

The blind man shakes his head back and forth four times and says, I knew it. He spits a piece of white saliva on the floor. Some lands on his bare foot. While he's brushing it away, he tells us, There's always anguish if you love someone like that. Be glad of your problem, boy, cause without it, the love goes dull.

The three of us sit there for a long while, looking at the men and watching for the guards to come. I don't hear what else the blind man says because I'm thinking so hard about what he told Riley.

Finally the guard comes and calls our names. Riley steps to the door first and I'm almost through it when I get kicked in the ass so hard my nuts ache.

They let us go.

Night has come and turned a kind of crimson color on the horizon. We hitch back during a beautiful sundown. The woman who carries us to

the car has groceries in her front seat. She looks like a candidate for a Tup-
perware party and I can tell she thinks we smell bad.

I always feel so fortunate, she says while she glances in the rearview. I
want to help those who are disadvantaged. Are you boys homeless?

Yes ma'am, says Riley, and I try not to laugh while he sticks his whole
head out the window and yells, Wahooooo, thank you Pappa God, free at
last, to the South Carolina air.

Once in the Roadrunner, we tell the scene of the holding tank over
and over again to each other, from when we smoked the joint to when
we got back to the car as if neither one of us were sitting right there when
it all happened. Wind blows the hair from our heads while we drive and
the night air leaves us heatless.

We get on Highway 78 toward home. Fuck the hound dogs, Riley
says. We're goin back to Houser Banks and Crystal Nash and a world that
doesn't smell like piss gone sour.

In my elation at being free, I am also sick with envy. I keep thinking of
what that blind guy said and I'm jealous as hell of Riley and his problem
and how it will make his love last.

13

H A L E Y

Bo is leaning against the corral fence, drinking water out of a quart jar and watching T. long-line a new stallion inside the perimeter. I wait until T. is on the far side of the ring and walk up beside him. Heat's coming off his body. He's got his T-shirt sleeves rolled up on top of his shoulders.

When I say his name, his arm freezes and the water jug stays suspended in air.

He is tight lipped and rigid. Then he slugs the water down. I watch his Adam's apple while he swallows.

The stallion turns clockwise midcanter and T. faces it. Bo lifts his head slightly. Go to the outside barn, he says to me. Now. Then he yells to T., Not so much to the right, try and stay upwind.

I stand in the outside barn for what seems like a long time. It's dark and hot in there and smells of wet wood. Leaning against an empty stall door, I listen to the horses shift in their stalls and the birds beat their wings against the rafters and wish I hadn't gone to him. Riley and Fletcher are still in South Carolina, and I was looking at an afternoon stretched out lonely and wide, too hot to ride. And no one's home either. Gypsy took Gwyn to Memphis to look at baby clothes. Daddy and some of the other men are off for the afternoon, stacking two-by-fours by Battle Creek now that the mud's dry.

When the heavy door creaks open, a strip of light comes through and then blinks shut. Bo's shadowy form walks down the corridor, his boots hit the hay and the loose floorboards. He stands in front of me. We look at each other in dim, slat-board light. He lifts my chin with two fingers, then squats down on his haunches and holds my legs with both hands. Haley, he says, looking up at me, you can't do that, walk up to me like that.

A crow squawks near the top vent.

I didn't do anything, I tell him. Nobody's gonna think anything if I come up to you once in a while.

He ducks his head and looks at the floor.

You been ignorin me, I say quietly. I peel a wood sliver off the wall to my left.

I haven't been ignorin you, Haley. You're the one who leaves fast as lightnin every afternoon, and I got these Mexican horses to train, and goddamnit, girl, I don't wanna do what I'm doin. Whenever I spend time with your daddy I want to shoot myself for thinking about you like I do. You don't understand what it's like for me. I can't have you around me like that in broad daylight with people lookin. I'm in for you. I can't say why, but I can't stop it.

I make myself step forward. He lets go of my legs. The stall door creaks when I lean up from it. I liked it with you gone, I tell him, cause I didn't have to wonder when you'd come to me.

I start walking away from him. I am fairly sure Bo Dickens will follow me, and I can feel him watching while I go slowly through the barn, trailing my hand over the wood of the wall.

Haley, he calls after me.

I keep walking.

He jogs up beside me and grabs my waist and then his mouth is on my mouth, hungry and wet, and he is groaning. His callused hands are around my neck, and he whispers in my ear, Girl, I want you and I shouldn't. Can't you understand that? His breath is moist and quick, he puts his tongue around the outside of my ear. He tells me, I have to bring in some new saddles I ordered from South Haven, they're at my place. I'll tell Di I need your help and that you're comin with me.

Bo and I ride out to his house together in his truck with Dolly Parton on the cassette player. Wind rushes out the air vents. It's the hottest day of the year so far and my body goes wet all over, the sweat comes out in silent moans. At the stop sign off Highway 12, Bo turns to look at me. My heart beats crazy fast while our eyes stare at each other.

Finally he takes his foot off the brake, and we keep driving.

Down deep in me, I know this isn't right, that swimming with Riley and Fletcher feels like comfort in the face of this. Even though I know it isn't fair, I am half mad at them for going on a road trip and leaving me to do something like I am doing now. The road curves before us. Bo drives it fast, with the limbs of the trees bending over from last night's storm. Their green's so dark it looks like a stain on the sky.

We don't say one word to each other.

At his house, we climb out of the pickup. He comes around my side before I can start toward his front porch and takes my hand in his. His hand is large and it has hair running the length of it. I walk a little in back of him. He is tall as Daddy and muscled, without a piece of fat on him.

Once inside he calls his dog and puts her out. The front den is cluttered with newspapers and half-done drink glasses, a full ashtray and scattered beer bottles. A gun's lying on the table next to the couch. He picks a shirt off the floor and throws it on the easy chair. I live alone, he tells me. And I ain't got money for a maid.

It's the first time I've been inside Bo Dickens's house since I was a little girl and I used to ride along with Daddy when he came here. It looks smaller and the walls are yellow. I remember them as white. I follow Bo down the hall to his bedroom. To my surprise, it's neat and cleaner than the whole rest of his house. The bed is made with a plain blue spread. There's nothing on the bedside table. His room is undecorated except for a couple of spurs hung on the wall and a saddle mounted over a fifty-gallon oil drum in the corner. There isn't a stitch of clothing in there. Above the bed is a black-and-white picture of a man who looks a little like Bo, long-lining a horse in a corral. I walk up to the photo. The man's got a belt buckle big around as a grapefruit. That your daddy? I ask.

Bo takes a step toward me. Yup. He's dead now, he says. That same horse kicked him in the head and left him in a coma. Nine months. Mamma finally had to pull the plug. I keep that picture up to remember the power of a horse.

When was that? I ask him.

Before you were born.

I take a step back. Bo watches me while he slowly unbuttons his shirt. When he takes it off, the muscles quiver. His chest has black curly hair on it. I look up at his eyes, they are glittering and his mouth is wet. He is breathing quick. He comes and stands before me. There are two red scars across his belly and I touch them. Holding the back of my head, he kisses me, runnng the inside of his tongue around my teeth.

I keep fingering the scars. What are these? I ask him.

Lie down, little lady, he says to me.

I lie down, riding boots and all, across his bed with my head on his pillow. It smells like Bo, stable dirt and smoke.

He lies on his side next to me with one leg over mine. I was a stupid boy once, says Bo. Those scars are from then.

What happened?

Bo grabs my chin. Shh, he says, no more questions. He licks my lips, tells me to close my eyes and then he kisses my eyelids. His hands go up my shirt, and he kneads my nipples.

I want Bo in a grasping, hair-pulling, biting way. It occurs to me I want to hurt him and to be hurt by him. It's that feeling you get when you put your hand over a candle flame for as long as you can without taking it away. I put his neck skin between my teeth and bite.

He rears back and swats at me.

Ow! Fuck, girl. He rubs his neck with one hand and holds my jaw with the other. Something like laughter comes into his eyes. Why'd you do that?

I don't know, I tell him. His pupils get bigger while I watch him.

He says, You're a lot like your mamma, you know it?

Daddy says that sometimes.

He lifts my T-shirt, pulls it over my head and throws it on the floor. You gonna hurt me again, let me know so I'm a little prepared, he says.

I shrug. Maybe I will, I tell him.

He smiles. Feisty, he says. That's from the Gorham side, not the Ellyson side. While he's unfastening my bra he says, We used to have some fun, me and your daddy and your mamma. She was wild. He puts his nose to my breasts.

We'd go down to Jackson, he says, with his mouth muffled against me, to this honkey-tonk had these fake bulls she'd ride like a cowgirl. He lifts my arms and runs his lips over my armpits. Your mamma'd get herself prizes all the time. Hundred bucks, two hundred bucks. He covers my body with his so the breath goes out of me. We look at each other and he kisses me long and hard. I think of Fletcher, how soft it is with him. Bo's lips are soft too, it's just he uses them in a hard way.

I want to be inside you, he tells me while he's fingering my bra strap. I'm dyin to. I wouldn't do that to you but I don't want you doin it with someone else, either. I don't ever want to hear about it or I'd do somethin you might hate me for.

My breath freezes and my belly clenches. He drops his hands from the bra, lifts up and looks at me. I felt that, he says. I didn't say you had to do what I tell you. I'm just lettin you know.

What about those girlfriends you were always havin? I ask him.

He raises one eyebrow. I've had girlfriends, he says. I never felt a thing for them like I do now.

But have you been in love with them?

He runs his teeth over my breast and murmurs, Shh.

The ceiling is paintbrushed in swirled circles. Light streams into the window to my right while Bo makes his way down my breasts, licking me all over, so my skin goes wet with his tongue. Even in this heat it makes me shiver. He licks my arms and my belly. He keeps my arms pinned to the bed by his hands. I think of what he said about me not being with other guys. And then I think of Fletcher. When we are together, Fletcher is always so careful with me, lets me lead and asks me to say what it is I want. Fletcher wouldn't ever hurt me, doesn't ever want me to have to wait for him. It makes me want to cry out, and a sick feeling rises in me about myself. *Bo* makes me wait all the time, makes me be in hot, lonely places. For one strangled minute I wish I could leave my body on this bedspread for his pleasure and go walking outside or swimming in the river or be back home to wait for Gwyneth. Now that I am here, I don't know how to go from him, and leaving is what I most want. While he rolls me over and runs his tongue up and down my back, I think something dirty has come inside me, something unwanted and strange feeling, like a food you eat that isn't setting right with you, but you don't want to get sick either. You just wish you never ate it in the first place. It's how I feel whenever I'm with Bo and also right after I go to that dead body.

I breathe in the cotton smell of his pillow. Bo, I say.

Mmmm. His mouth is on my spine.

Are you ever going to tell Daddy?

He stops, rolls me over and rests his fingers around the rim of my jean waist. About that night? he asks.

Yes.

Bo sighs. It's not a thing that needs talkin about, Haley. He was just some fool nigger shouldn't have been in your house in the first place. Nobody's gonna miss him except the law and his junkie brothers. Drug-addicted felon is what he was. Bo undoes my jean button and I hear my zipper go down. He lifts my bottom and pulls the pants over my thighs.

What happened? I ask.

But Bo won't answer me. He has scooted down and put his warm mouth on me. He begins sucking and then he is on top of me, the bulging zipper of his denims against my crotch. He calls my name. He wants me so bad I am almost afraid of him, only I can't help the rush I feel, watching the blood fill his neck and face, his closed eyes and the vein on his forehead. I see again how I can make desire so strong in him. Oh Jesus, he says. His breath comes quieter and quieter, his thrusting slows to a rocking. I can feel the wet of his denims from where he came. His cheek is next to mine and his hot breath is in my ear.

Oh Haley, he says. He rakes his hand through my matted hair, kisses the sweat off my forehead. You are so fuckin beautiful, he says. So, so beautiful.

A hot flush comes up in me and this time I kiss him back, his waiting, warm, searching mouth. He kisses me and says my name and pulls his fingers through my hair and then he puts his head beside mine.

It stings where he rubbed against me.

Sweet girl, he says to my neck.

We lie together for some time. Finally he gets up and pulls me up with him. I sit on the edge of the bed and he kneels in front of me, holding my arms. You drive me wild, girl. How can you drive me so wild?

I watch Bo Dickens while he says it, his rough, handsome face. He is a man who can tame feral Mexican horses, the same man who taught me to ride and was at all my birthday parties when I was a little girl. He could have any woman he wants but can't decide which one, Gwyn said of him two years ago. Now I look at him and think I must be something if he wants me this bad, red faced and breathing hard and thanking Jesus.

Though I wish I hadn't come here, I can't imagine not coming here. I believe all my life will be strung up with incidents of Bo Dickens and me, and the hot secret of what we have become to each other.

Outside the sun glares at us. Fifteen saddles sit dusty in his barn, and my body feels made of water, shaky and unsolid.

14

FLETCHER

Haley is waiting for me at midnight near Feldman's stables. One horse is saddled. She's sitting bareback on the other one. When I'm mounted and holding the reins, she whispers, Are you ready?

We pass through the stable yards and enter a hollow divide in the woods, thickset with foliage on either side of us. The air is windless. I watch Haley lean over her horse and squeeze her boots against its flanks. Okay, Daisy, she says.

She has given me an easy horse, it aims to please, and there's a good rhythm to its gallop. In front of me Haley arches her body over her horse's neck. I follow her on a path big enough for a four-wheeler. Grass is growing up on the tire tracks. Trees lie across it. Sometimes Haley warns me by yelling back, There's a jump up ahead!

Once, by an almost dry creek bed, I watch her lift her hands up, pull her hair on top of her head and hold it there. She bounces along no-handed, the Y of her legs separated for the wide flank of sandy brown horse.

At the end of the wood trail, we ride through a small pond with moonlight across it in a thick, swaggering column. There are fireflies everywhere. The horses wade across with water up to their bellies, and I watch her wipe sweat from the back of her neck with her forearm. Our jeans shed water when we climb the far bank, and my legs hang from my body like wet weights.

I follow her out by the river dam on thick dirt, split by tires. Riding up beside me, she says, This is where we came with Riley and Crystal that first night. She holds her hand out to me.

I reach over and grab her fingers. I'd bend to kiss the lady's hand, I say, but I'd fall off. I loved that night we came here with them, I tell her.

She watches me. You can kiss it later, she says. I loved that night, too.

On her thumb is a turquoise ring a Gypsy gave me in exchange for my windbreaker last year in Spain. It's too big for her, so she wears it on her thumb. Turquoise is my favorite thing, she told me when I gave it to her.

She takes her hand from mine and puts it on the horse's neck, then leans backward with her head to the sky and says, Listen to this echo. Fletcher Greel, she calls out. I hear it coming back at me, bouncing off river bottom and rock sides. I yell her name, too, and she smiles when she listens to it. She says she loves that song where the man goes away and wants the girl to come with him, so he promises her he'll make his *I love yous* echo over canyons. She says, I'd go with him just for that.

We both know the song, but we can't think of the name of it.

Our horses snap twigs when they walk, and when we gallop through the last part of the road, their hooves sound like drumbeats and kick up dust that comes and hangs on my wet denims. I feel like a cowboy.

Up past Leete Circle, the old Leete land sits fallow with grown-over fields of corn and cotton turned meadow. Haley lies belly down on her horse and looks over at me. I'll race you, she says.

I say, I'll race you back, which I do badly, the horse under me working what it can, but I haven't ridden since summer camp three years ago and my hands get all cut up from the reins cause I'm holding them so tight. Also, I have a hard time concentrating. Haley has no saddle and there isn't anything sexier than Haley riding bareback. I keep imagining her naked on that horse. Against all my will, my cock swells in my denims and I swear at myself and try to think instead of how to make the horse go faster and what way I should be sitting in the saddle and whether my heels are down. I am clumsy as hell, but that horse rides me for another hour before Haley says she is tired and the moon's too high to see right. Let's turn here, she says. We can take the little path that cuts to the back of the stables.

When we get there, she puts both horses away for us and does up the stable door and comes to stand by me next to the Honda. My body is still sweaty from riding and the temperature has dropped some so the wet cools on my skin. I stand before her. We look up at the moon, a lopsided, bleached slab, high up there and working its way back down. Haley touches my shoulder and when I look at her, she runs a finger over her lips and says, Here.

She's hungry for it when I kiss her and her body presses against mine. There's a rush in my head so I can't think clearly. When I come to, I find my hands on her breasts. She's kissing my neck with her mouth open. Her hands are wrapped around my waist. She looks up and ducks her head slightly, then she smiles. She kisses my chin. What time do you think it is? she asks.

I think it is about two in the mornin, I tell her. I pull the side of her T-shirt down, put my lips on her collarbone and say her name.

Say it again, she says.

And I do.

Again.

Haley.

Again.

Haley. I kiss her mouth. Haley.

She breathes deep, puts her face in my neck. I love how soft your mouth is, she says. I want to sleep beside you, in your house.

I'd sleep with you anywhere, I tell her, a bed of nails if I had to.

She drags a tongue down my neck and I close my eyes and grip her tighter.

Will you get in trouble, she asks, if I come there?

No, I tell her, pulling my head over so she can kiss my neck more. Will you?

She has my earlobe between her lips and she looses it to say, My father is sleeping with his girlfriend and he hasn't waited up for me in two months. If I get up early enough, I'll be fine.

I promise I'll wake you up whenever you need me to and take you back.

While we drive the Honda to Elm, she leans her head on my shoulder and kisses my ear more until I forget I am driving. I shut my eyes and stop breathing. I feel her grab the wheel, laugh and say, Fletcher! When I open my eyes, tree limbs are brushing the Honda's front window. I swerve back onto the road.

We sit in the driveway at Elm looking up at my house. I tell her, My father sleeps at that end of the house. I point to the west. He's on the first floor. We'll just go around back to the patio. We can take the kitchen stairs up. They're carpeted. You ready?

Haley tells me she was born ready.

When we get to the top of the stairs, I show her where the door is to the bathroom in case she wants to go. She doesn't.

She moves through my door and goes to sit on my bed. Pops keeps the outside porch light on all night, and I can watch her in the shadows without flicking my bedroom switch. Come, she says. She pats the bed beside her.

I sit there.

Lift up your arms, she tells me.

Haley takes off my T-shirt, squats in front of me and pulls my wet boots off one by one. She tells me she wants to be the one to do the undressing, that I shouldn't help her at all. Then she peels me free of my socks and leans forward to unbutton my jeans. I take a breath in and watch her hair falling across her face, and her lips purse in effort. My zipper sounds loud as she undoes it and she has to do it slowly for how swelled up I am. I don't wear underwear and when she takes my denims off, I sit there with quick, jagged breath, completely naked.

Lie down, she whispers. She sits on the side of the bed with her back to me, lifts up her arms and pulls off her shirt so I can see her long tan back. She reaches back and unfastens her bra, slips it down her shoulders. I put a hand on her spine and am about to go forward to kiss it when she leans over to pull off her boots and Levi's. In one swift motion, she swings her legs onto the bed and is lying next to me. She's wearing her panties. And that's it.

My heart jams blood into my veins. I can't not touch her, and start to run my hand over her stomach, her breasts. I reach down and touch her panties softly. The material is slick as oil. Then she's pulling me toward her and kissing my mouth, soft, long, languid kisses that get deeper and make my head swim with nothing like sanity. And then she is over me, her mouth on mine. She is kissing my throat and then my stomach, wrapping her legs around me and saying my name. Her body is tight against me. I can feel myself against those panties, not inside her, but still I am almost coming. I want her so bad I feel like crying. Then I hear her putting on the brakes. She says, Wait. Stop, Fletcher. I say to myself, Gentle, easy. I hold any movement of my hands and my mouth so she knows I've heard. I swallow and say slowly, Okay.

When I pull back to look at her, she's got fear in her eyes. When I smile, she smiles back, and I am relieved.

I'm sorry, I whisper.

She lays her head on my shoulder. She's breathing hard and her fingers are wrapped around my arms. She takes one deep breath in and looks out the window, then back at me. I thought I wanted it slow, she tells me, but I couldn't stop it once it started. It's like . . . She doesn't finish, and her mouth stays open as if looking for words.

I nod, pull a piece of hair from her mouth. I know, I tell her. I'm sorry. Her weight feels delicious on me. Her legs smooth, intertwined with mine.

It's okay, she says, it wasn't just you. It's us. I've never been like this, she gestures to herself on top of me. Crazy for someone. She is silent and I push her hair back from her face gently as I can. She looks into my eyes and says softly, Is it cause we waited so long to be together like this?

I don't think it has to do with waiting, I tell her. I think you and I might just be like this. No matter what.

Her eyes go wide.

You want me to just lie next to you awhile? I ask her.

She nods and rolls off me and puts her hand in mine.

I been with boys, she says and leans up on her side to look at my face. But I've never felt like that.

My stomach goes into my throat at the thought of Haley with someone else. I don't say anything.

Not a lot of boys, she says. Hardly any, but those times I felt like I was kind of watching the whole thing happen. She puts her hand on my cheek. Her fingers are hot. Even if I like it, I don't ever forget who I am. But you and I are . . . fire.

Parched grass, I tell her, picking up her hand and kissing it, with a match.

She watches me kiss her hand, then she lies on her back with her face to the ceiling. Partly it is that I'm safe with you and so I let myself. I can hear surprise in her voice. It's like dissolving, she says quietly. She waits and we breathe in the blue shadowy air without speaking. In the half-light, I see her smile.

Out my window, Elm Street is empty, one line of curved black. I want to ask her how many boys, but then I don't want to know. There isn't anyone else for me but Haley. Nobody existed until now. I haven't ever felt that fire either, but now I know it was there all the time. Haley pulled it out of me. The thought strikes me dumb, and I don't know how to tell it, so I don't say anything. My cock stays hard up my stomach and I want to wrap my hand around it to relieve it, but I make myself be still for her.

Haley rolls toward me so her warm breath is on my chest, her voice is muffled. You know how I gave you that note you wrote a long time ago? she asks me. Well, I been watchin you. All vacations you come home, I look for you.

When I can get my breathing collected, I say, I've seen you, too. My voice has holes in it for the breath it needs. I want to scream out with her body this close.

She leans over and puts her head on my chest. Her hair's all over it, and her voice is lazy. For some reason, she says, I always wanted to have you like this. There's somethin about you, she tells me, that is a kind of perfect.

My bones feel weak. I stroke her back, try to steady the vague shake in my body. It's you who's perfect, I tell her.

And I mean it. I want to tell her she can have my mouth on any part of her she wants, right now and the rest of the night through, only I don't want her to be afraid. Lying there with her naked body draped over me is torture, but in all the world I can't wreck what we've started. And I love her here, I don't care that much how it is, as long as she's here. She circles my nipple with her finger for a good while until her hand stills and goes limp. Desperation rises in me thinking she's asleep, then she lifts her head slightly and says, Daddy hasn't taken kindly to any of my boyfriends before.

I know it.

She puts her head back down. You already heard that? she asks me. Are you afraid of him?

I never met him, I tell her, so I don't know if I need to be afraid of him.

She's quiet for a minute. Do you know who he is, though? she asks me.

I know who he is, I tell her. He doesn't look that mean to me. I wait a couple of seconds, then I ask, Is he ever mean to you?

She doesn't say anything for a long while, and I start to think she has decided not to answer and wonder if it was fair of me to ask it. Then her hand starts trailing my stomach hairs. I grip the side of her waist, I don't intend to, and I let it loose when I realize I've done it so she won't feel any pressure at all.

He's not really ever mean to me, she says. We fight, but he'd never hit me or do anything terrible, he's just mean when he thinks man's done him wrong or tricked him or somethin. He's protective of me, too. Sometimes I think I do things to get back at him for keeping such a close watch. Not wide-open things, things on my lonesome so I know he doesn't have a hold of every single part of me. She doesn't wait for me to respond before she asks, Will you have bad dreams?

I kiss her head and say into it, Why would I have bad dreams?

Because of going to Battle Creek again today.

The body? I ask her.

She nods.

Naw, I say. I'm not that creeped out when we go to the body. You?

She is quiet, then I feel her nod. I might have nightmares, she says. Her voice is small. Sometimes I have them. She nuzzles closer. But with you I bet I won't.

I stroke her long back, touch where it widens to hips and trail my hand up again. I'm here, I tell her, if you want to wake me up.

Okay, she says, and then she says quietly, Fletcher?

Yeah?

I want to be with you all the time. When I'm not with you sometimes I feel afraid.

I hike her thigh up closer to me.

My mamma, Haley says, and I listen close cause she hasn't mentioned her mother before, she writes me every so often from places, tells me about where she is, and one thing she always says is that I'll fall in love someday, and I shouldn't go drowning in anybody . . . Her voice trails away.

I'd save you, I tell her.

She doesn't answer.

Haley, I say.

Hmm? she murmurs.

How do you know that body was there? I ask her. Then I remember again how I promised her I wouldn't ask any questions about it.

But she doesn't answer. Her breathing goes rhythmic, and I don't think she's heard my question. A small wet spot begins on my chest from her drool. I watch out my window as a green Porsche speeds down Elm. Dr. Anderson's kid. A quick breeze passes through the screen.

My head is only halfway on the pillow and my arm beneath her is a pile of numb weight, it aches along the elbow. But it doesn't matter because she is here. As soft as I can, I run my thumb along her spine and up through her hair to her neck. I stay awake for a long time, staring at that empty road, waiting for morning, wishing it might never come. She has made a restless ball of want out of me. I don't know how Haley can sleep with this want all through the night. But she does, and then I start to wonder if this is some kind of test. Maybe she wants to know how much would I go through to be with her. I'd like to wake her up and tell her I would swim across any ocean she named, and hike through rivers of leeches and kill a den of rabid animals for her. Only I am afraid it isn't really a test at all, and I would scare her away.

After that night I don't have to worry about tests, because I am seeing her whenever we can. Anywhere and anytime we can get next to each other, we do. When I am with her, the whole world is a drug. She is like a spit of wanted magic in my life. Houser Banks isn't a living tomb anymore with Haley Ellyson pulling me back to the living like an anchor.

She is the kind of girl who likes more to be without clothes than with, loves drinking tequila and eating the worm and can sing all the words to Neil Young's song about his dead hound named King. She has a way of dragging her tongue over your body so you go drunk with it and touching you so soft you think your flesh might be on fire.

I work on memorizing her, the mole on her right rib and the feel of her tiny hairs growing around her nipples, the smell of her lady, which is like moss grown up on stones.

Always when I am with her, even though I'm high off it, I have a thought that I'm afraid of: Somewhere deep in me I'm scared that if I lose her it will be like losing a limb off my body and I'll be left crippled for life.

15

HALEY

Out Highway 12, east of Houser Banks, there's a gray split-wood shack, twice as big as a privy, with a tin roof and no yard. It's built so close to the road a drunk man driving in a moonless night might easily run it over.

A black man with a white beard, an eye patch and four teeth owns it. His name's Happy Harrison and Daddy says he's been around a million years. He stands at the jamb of his door in clear weather wearing cut-offs and knee socks and fake leather shoes and smoking a corncob pipe. A homemade sign hangs above him by two bicycle chains. It reads: *Fireworks for Sale.*

When I was little, I couldn't wait for that hot summer day when Daddy came home from Happy's with firecrackers packed in the back of the Ford on wooden crates. He'd lift me on his shoulders and hold my knees and I felt like I was floating while we walked down the wood trail that goes to Battle Creek. Daddy's steel-tipped boots, made of the finest worn leather, would snap the tree twigs in two while we walked.

When we got there, Archie, T. and Bo, Stony and Billy Towle would already be there with their wives and girlfriends and food and cartons of beer and soda. From the riverbank we would watch the sky explode with greens and yellows and pinks and blues bursting, cracking, popping and winding down to a dribble in the sky.

The men ran sideways after they lit the fireworks, watching over their shoulders and yelling, with their hats pinned to their heads by a palm. They said things like *Jesus H. Christ* and *Kiss my ass, you see that one? You think I'm not deaf now?* Their eyes always lit up like men's will in desire.

After I grew up, I spent Fourth of July on the bank of the river where Riley White's family lives. In those backyards, shallow water jets out into streams and turns to swamp. The houses are swarmed by mosquitoes and flies, which come to bother lights and ankles. Some of the houses are fall-apart, with porches coming down on the side like a cripple. Around mid-summer if there hasn't been much rain, there's a stink to that part of the river and it looks a tan, listless color. It's grimed at the top, the foam at the sides collecting things like dead branches and beer cans and parts of cigarette cartons.

People bunch together in the yards of these houses on Independence Day, standing in clusters, blowing the breeze, stirring dirt with their boot tips, eating barbecue and drinking beer in the dim light of dusk. By nightfall they are lighting homemade crackers, which last only half a second, then disappear into shrinking crystals. Cheap, dangerous fireworks that take off people's fingertips and blow their eardrums. Riley's second cousin Cue Boil got defaced by one, it singed all the hair off his head. Riley told me the story while we sat in his dinghy last July Fourth, past midnight, sipping Pabst Blue Ribbon. He ended up bald and shit ugly, said Riley, with nothing to live for, so he went out, washed himself with gasoline and struck a match. Finished the job. He told me Cue had taken a liking to Hannaford like no one else in the family had. Taught him how to shoot a pistol and took him dove hunting. Cue's funeral was the last time Riley'd seen Hannaford cry. Hannaford was ten years old when it happened and he slept on the dirt of Cue's grave the night of his funeral. Hearing this from Riley may have been what made me finally go out with Hannaford. The knowledge that he had a tender spot in him made me think maybe he was a combination of a bad boy and sweetheart. That mix can be worse than irresistible.

This Fourth of July, I am standing on Riley's porch at two in the afternoon with a can of Schlitz in my hand, my thumb over its opening and my eyes and mouth squeezed shut, waiting for Riley's younger brother Judd to finish spraying bug kill all over me. Judd is one year younger than I am, skinny and bare-chested with denims hanging off his hips. His boxers show up over the waist. He's wearing a baseball cap with the bill ripped off. The sky is clouded over to dark gray and fat drops have already started to fall. Riley bounces on the bumper of a white Chrysler held to the yard by cinder blocks. Judd's tryin to look up your skirt, he calls.

I open my eyes and turn to glance at Judd in back of me. He stands up and reddens. Shut the hell up, Riley, I'm not lookin up the lady's skirt.

Goddamn right, says Riley, bending over and placing his hands palm down on the car's hood. Judge Greel's son'll kick your butt.

Judd sprays the backs of my legs and my ankles.

You startin trouble again Riley? I ask him.

I am, says Riley.

Judd shakes the bug kill, squeezes the top one more time, then throws the can in the yard. It's finished, he says.

Inside the house, a phone rings. Riley jumps off the car and starts to walk toward us.

Mrs. White opens the screen door and says, You boys know where your daddy's got to? He has a telephone call from Mr. Roach.

No ma'am, says Riley.

Judd shrugs.

The screen door's hinge is broken. It bangs against the house when she comes out it, drying her hands on a dish towel. Baby Judd, she says, you might know what all Mr. Roach could want. You were with him on Tuesday, why don't you take it?

I don't know what he could want, says Judd. Why don't you take a message?

Annabelle White stands there in a green apron, staring out at her yard. She's itty-bitty and not tall enough to be five foot three. You wouldn't have thought she could have birthed five boys and lost one. She goes inside, pulling the screen behind her.

Riley plops himself on the porch swing. You should've got it for her, Riley tells Judd. He lights a smoke.

You get it for her, if you want to help so badly, Judd says. He sits next to me on the porch step, studying the sky. A moist wind blows.

Riley rocks the porch swing. It's gonna rain, he says.

Judd nods. It'll storm before the day's out.

The phone rings again.

It ain't gonna storm, Riley tells him, it's just gonna piss on us and then stop. We won't get a bit of excitement out of it so ease your woody, brotha.

Judd picks the balled-up T-shirt beside him and throws it at Riley, who reaches up and catches it.

Mrs. White comes to the door again. She says, Riley that phone's for you and the girl sounds long distance.

Riley's up as if his pants were on fire. The swing bangs against the porch railing and the front door slams hard. I know it is Crystal.

Judd looks at me. What are y'all doin today? he asks me.

I shrug and sip my Schlitz, watching the layers of clouds. It might rain, I tell him, so I don't know. You ever been to a parade? I ask him.

I don't really think so, he says.

Riley's older brother Jeffrey comes out a side door, gets in an old Ford truck in the dirt next to the driveway and starts to try to crank it.

Every Fourth of July I wish Houser Banks had a parade, I tell Judd. I love parades. They got these fife-and-drum bands, so loud they play you from the inside out. I beat my chest to show him, and he smiles. I say, They got these eighteen-wheeler cabs haulin floats down a main street with little girls and boys on them dressed like Betsy Ross and Benjamin Franklin and baton twirlers with sparkly boots and big hats. When I was little we used to visit my mamma's mamma in Oxford and they always had a parade.

Judd nods and smiles, his dimple creases. I touch it and tell him he was kissed by an angel at birth, that's what a dimple means. He colors and ducks his head down, then lifts it and looks at me with eager eyes. You want to go to a parade somewhere? he says. I bet there's a parade I could take you to. He shoves his hair from his eyes and sits grinning at me. He has the same straight white teeth as Riley's, without the smirk. What do you think? he asks.

I laugh and tousle his hair. I can't do that, I tell him, sipping my warm Schlitz.

His face falls. You got a boyfriend, don't you? He picks up a twig on the step beside him and cracks it in two. He says, Riley told me you do.

Jeffrey stops trying to crank the truck and calls over, Baby Judd, get the hell over here and help me look at this alternator.

Judd throws the stick down, picks up a two-by-four lying by the porch and brings it to his brother. They cram it lengthwise between the hood and the motor, then bury their faces in the mechanics of the thing.

Riley comes out the door, and he isn't smiling. He sits one step from me. When he lights a cigarette, his hand is shaking.

I can't think of what to say, so I say his name.

He blows out smoke and studies the end of his cigarette. Fuckin Hannaford, he says.

I raise an eyebrow. Hannaford? I thought that was Crystal on the phone.

It was Crystal. She said Hannaford came along into the Jitney last night while she was workin and went to hasslin her. Asked her what she was doin and how late she was workin. He told her that he was my cousin and maybe he could see her later. Riley's fingers grip the cigarette until they whiten. He picks up my beer and swallows, then makes a face. Piss warm, he says.

I lean back on my elbows and watch him.

You know he must've been with those guys at the Jitney, ran us off the road that night, Riley says.

You think that, don't you? I ask him.

I do. How would he know she worked at the Jitney? What sonofabitch from Banks ever goes to the East Neigh Jitney? He's had a bug up his ass ever since he found out about me and Crystal and then you quit him and that made him double mad.

That's sick, I tell Riley. Jeffrey goes around and cranks the truck.

Hannaford's sick and his daddy's sick, Riley says. Whole damn family is sick and sick people don't only mind their own business, that's what in hell is wrong with them.

Judd bangs down the hood and starts walking toward us. Riley stubs his cigarette on the bottom of the porch's railing. He takes another cigarette from his pack and lights it.

Mrs. White comes to the screen. Riley, she says, come on in here a second.

I ain't, says Riley plainly.

She opens the door and looks at him. Riley Coleman White, am I speaking to you?

You are, says Riley. Cousin or no cousin, Mamma, Riley turns around to face her, I'm gonna whip his ass—

She says, Riley!

He's gonna get a goddamn beatin, Mamma, says Riley, I swear it. He runs a hand through his hair.

You talkin bout Hannaford? Judd asks when he comes over.

No one answers him.

Well then, mister, Annabelle White says, shaking a spoon at Riley, you better get off the property cause the whole lot of them are coming for barbecue in just a little while and I'll not have any fights on the Fourth. You hear me?

Yes ma'am, grumbles Riley.

Mrs. White turns back to the house.

Riley unfolds his body, stretches and says, C'mon Haley girl let's get the hell going. I'm gonna pop my head open from thinking evil thoughts if we hang around here too long.

Judd watches us walk past him and through the yard. He calls, Hey can I come with you?

Nope, Riley says. He doesn't even look back.

I turn and wave to Judd and shrug my shoulders like it's not my fault he isn't coming.

We drive through hot, heavy air. Above us a thick layer of clouds is wanting to cry over everything. Riley says, The magic of a convertible is you can drive right through the rain without getting wet. He eyes the sky. Unless it's a storm that don't have space between the drops, he says.

We drive for a while around the outskirts of Houser Banks, drawing on the rolling Buds underneath Riley's seats and throwing the beer cans out. The green looks deep in this light and the leaves flash their silvered underneaths and rustle in wind. Riley smokes and says nothing. I think of Crystal at the Jitney deli, her face hardening at Hannaford's advances, his square-shouldered cockiness. I can't believe I went out with Hannaford, I say to Riley.

Riley leans toward me and tells me, I warned you, Miss Ellyson.

I know, I say.

Aah, says Riley. He looks in his rearview and then pats my leg. We all make mistakes. You got a good one now, girl.

I nod and think of Fletcher. My whole body starts to relax. We pass the Battle Creek inlet, where just about a third of a mile up, there is that subtle deer track that leads to the body. Where we going? I ask him.

He shrugs. I don't know, he says, I was just driving.

The wind blows a noise tunnel around us and his hair whips and my hair whips and the car makes a kind of hooing sound. Drops start to splatter the windshield and the beer begins to make me sleepy.

You want to go see about the judge? Riley asks me.

He has some picnic to be at with his daddy, I tell him. He won't be back until eight o'clock. He said he'd call us then. I think I need a nap, though, Riley.

Riley shrugs and nods his head. You go take one, he says. I need to think awhile. I'm not good company. He does a U-turn on the road, tires squealing. Then he heads back toward Highway 12.

Before we reach my house, the rain's coming down in streams, pounding the pavement and wrecking driving vision. Riley and I park along the side of the road under a magnolia and pull up the top. When we get back in, our clothes are soaked through and we are shivering in our seats.

I listen to the Roadrunner pull out and stand dripping in the front hall. The house is empty. Daddy has most likely gone to Elsa's for the day to mourn the passing of independence with the boys. Gwyneth is at Gypsy's. I go up to my room, tear off my clothes and slip between my cool sheets, listening to the rain on the roof and feeling the damp wind blowing through my screen. When I fall asleep, I dream the man at the Twirly-Whirl and the black man we buried are intertwined. One becomes the other. The black man is standing before me, one arm outstretched, the stump flying disembodied in the sky. His eyes are white as marbles and rolled up in his head. I am lying on the ground beneath him, my heart kicking in my chest, unable to move.

When I wake the sheet is wound around my body in tight twists, and the phone is ringing. I can't get to it in time and it stops. The house is empty and still. I walk downstairs through the den to the kitchen and turn on Daddy's transistor. It's playing *Baby, baby, I'm fallin in love, fallin in love with you* . . . In the kitchen the windows are open, and the screen door's wide to the drone of insects and the uneven patter of occasional rain. The breeze is cool like it hasn't been in days and the house smells of wet grass. The phone rings again. It is a weighted rotary phone, sitting on the counter.

Hello? I say and hope it's Fletcher.

It's Gypsy. Her voice catches itself on her own name. She is crying.

Hey Miss Gypsy, I say. What's the matter?

I hear her inhale on a cigarette. It's Gwyneth, honey, she's lost the baby, you go get your daddy.

I stare at the streams of gathered water on the kitchen windowpane.

Haley, she says, you there?

Yes.

I can't hear you, such a racket here, darlin, it's bad, she's losing blood. Can you go get your daddy? I couldn't get through at Elsa's. We're at Memorial, birthing ward. She'll be okay if your daddy can come. Hurry now. There is a click, the line goes dead.

The phone starts to beep loudly, and I hang it up. Our kitchen clock reads seven fifteen. When I tell the empty house that Gwyneth lost the baby, all goes on as it did before. The rocking chair stays still and the sliders are partway open. On the radio a man sings *Get ready, get set, get wet, your very own patio pool, July Fourth sale* . . . I reach over and turn the knob to off.

In Elsa's basement, men gamble their lives away and drink whiskey by the bottle. The only women who come there are ones who are loose in their bodies from being entered so many times. The basement door is around the back of the store. A St. Pauli Girl poster is on the door. Across her crotch someone has scribbled *Come on down, boys!* I walk down the stairs, which are lit with a single hanging lightbulb covered with dead flies. The steps curve in toward a doorway and Jackie's leaning against the bottom wall. His bald black head shines in the light. He's stacking dollar bills in his right hand. In the corner a drunk in a wool winter cap lifts his heavy-lidded eyes, and says, Hotternajackrabbit, then goes back to his stupor. A bourbon bottle tucked like a baby in his arms. *Enter for a buck,* the sign above him reads. *Minors stay out.* From here the sound of men's voices and country tunes comes clear.

Hey Haley! Jackie's eyes go wide when he sees me. You growed up on me. You a real woman. He leans back on his heels, tilts his head and frowns. You don't look so good, child.

I need to find my daddy, I tell him.

He steps toward the door and points inside. Right that way, he says.

The room smells like whiskey and tobacco. The low roll of men's voices come from drunk throats and bellies full of liquor. Billy Towle, Freddy Lie, T. Fingerling, and their crew are sitting at the middle card table. The yellow light above them makes haunted shadows under their eyes and lips. I think to go to them, but they are studying their cards with a tight look akin to anger.

Men stand around the room with bottles in their hands. Joy's old husband is in the middle, storytelling. A woman with coarse blond hair holds his arm and looks up at him with her hard middle-aged face. Twanged country pours out the juke, and I try to remember what Daddy was wearing when I left that morning.

Elsa's pouring whiskey into a shot glass, her dishrag tucked into her skirt waist. I stand at the far end of the bar and wait for her.

Hey, Haley Elllyson, how you? she says when she comes over. Her eyes skirt around the room, a gray part halves her cinnamon-colored hair. She looks back at me. Don't stay too long, okay, honey? Much as I want you here, you're too young for the sheriff. She pats my hand and smiles at me. You want a Coke or somethin?

No thanks, Elsa, you know where Daddy's at?

She leans over the bar and puts two fingers on my chin, dipping it down and looking into my eyes. Her eye makeup is violet. The mascara is caked in places. She is familiar and the sight of her makes me want to cry. You all right, honey? she asks.

I nod. She stands on the tippy toes of her high-heeled sandals and looks around the room with two quick jerks of her head. Your daddy done disappeared, honey. I haven't seen him in half an hour, and with a handsome man like that I'm always lookin. She waves her arm to the room and tells me to mill around a bit. It's sometimes hard to see someone unless you mingle. Okay, honey?

I nod.

And Haley— she starts to say, but a man with eyebrows thick as a rug calls Elsa's name and hits a shot glass against the bar top. You want your regular, honey? she asks, pushing her dishrag in his face. Then you wait a cotton-pickin minute. I'm gettin it.

When I wander, men turn to look at me. One has a flannel shirt cut at the shoulders and a shaved head. Hey pretty thing, he says. Someone says to him, Leave her be, that's Ellyson's little girl.

Well shit, the man says, how was I supposed to know?

Another man tries to dance with me. He's wearing jeans with the belt loops tore off and a white T-shirt that says *Heaven's Palace* on it, a masseuse parlor men talk about east of Houser Banks. He's so drunk he doesn't stand up right and I push him away easy. I go up to the men I know and pull at shirttails and sleeves, asking where Daddy is. They strain their necks to see above the crowd and say they don't know, they saw him earlier, but . . .

I lick my lips until they are dry and chapped. Finally I have to walk to the middle table, where the gambling men are rubbing their temples, staring down at their cards and dodging their eyes around the group to see if anyone is watching them worry. They have bills and coins piled in the middle and brown drink bottles set next to each elbow and glass ashtrays between them with butts and ash spilling out.

You in or out? Make up your mind, someone says.

Someone else says, I'll fold.

I squat down next to Billy Towle's metal chair. A man I've never seen before with greasy blond hair and blue tattooed words across his knuckles raises his chin and squints an eye at me. Billy's body turns before his eyes do. Oh, sweet Lord, Billy says when he sees me. You near scared the crap out of me, Haley. What are you doing down at Elsa's?

The stranger says, Towle, you want to play or talk to the lady?

Billy throws his cards on the table. Fold, he says.

I see he has a terrible hand. He turns back and looks down at me. The jukebox quiets and there is just the dull noise of drink bottoms on the bar's wood, ice cubes against glass and the constant hum of voices.

I squat lower. Listen, I'm sorry to bother you, Mister Billy, but I got to find my daddy.

You hurt, Haley?

No, I'm not hurt. You know where he's at?

Billy turns to watch a blond woman with a cowboy hat step up to the microphone and say into it, Testing, testing.

Someone at the table says, Erickson, your turn.

Billy moves his chair back and stands. I stand with him. He hitches his denims up, tucks in his T-shirt and looks around. All right, you give me the message, Haley. I'll go on, tell your daddy.

I bite my bottom lip until I can taste blood, cross my arms in front of me and think how I never knew a man to leave his cards long enough to deliver a message to a lost somebody. From the looks of it, Billy Towle's down on his luck and not going to give up anytime this side of midnight.

You can't tell me where he's at? I ask him.

Towle, says the man with the tattoo, he's looking at me, not at Billy, you setting up here? The man puts a toothpick in his mouth, twirls it around in his teeth with his eyebrows raised. The word LOVE is spread over his four knuckles. He looks the opposite of that.

Billy says to him, Hang on a minute. Okay, he says to me. He points to a door by the band's stage. He went down there near hour and a half ago, but if I was you, I'd just wait a spell. Why don't you set down at the bar a bit, let Elsa make you—

Billy, for shit's sake, you in this game or not? says T.

I walk away quickly. Behind me Billy's saying, Haley! Haley Ellyson! But he gives up, and I keep going straight to that door, close it behind me and walk down three concrete steps to a wood-paneled sliding door at the bottom, which I open. Once I am in, there is silence, just a soft beating sound above me. The room smells of cheap perfume. To my left is a lamp made out of a Jim Bean bottle. There's a rust-colored easy chair, three couch cushions on the floor and a pile of pale green sheets in a cardboard box.

The door to my right opens, and I start back. It takes me two breaths before I realize it is Bo Dickens standing in the frame. He closes the door behind him so it clicks softly into place. He stares at me while he buckles his belt.

Hey, little lady, he says. His white T-shirt is soaked through at the belly and underarms. It is the first time I have seen Bo Dickens's bare feet. He finishes with his belt and starts toward me. His hair is either wet or drenched with sweat. I thought I heard someone come in, he says. Never in the world expected to see you here. He watches my face.

There's a line of light under the door he came from, and I glance there. I manage to say, I came to find Daddy.

He nods. We stare at each other.

He here? I ask him.

Bo shakes his head. He ain't here. Left about a quarter of an hour ago.

Where'd he go? My chest feels like something is pressing against it.

He went out with some other folks. I don't know where he went to. He takes a step toward me.

It occurs to me Bo may think I've come looking for him, followed him here. I need to find him, Bo, I say. Bad.

He narrows his eyes, puts his fingertips together in a bunch and runs his tongue over them. I see flicks of sweat on his top lip. Three loud bumps sound at the other side of the door. He glances there quick, then takes two strides forward until his face is right next to mine. I watch his black-stubbled chin and his turned-right front tooth. I can smell something moist and familiar on him. The inside of a woman. He puts his hands on my waist and grips hard. I duck my chin into my chest and tell him, I need to find Daddy, now. Let me know where he is.

He steps back, leans against the wall and puts a hand in his denim pocket. What is it you want your daddy for so badly? he asks.

I need to tell him something.

Oh yeah? What about?

Gwyneth, I tell him.

He stands from the wall and frowns. Gwyneth? he says. What is it?

She's lost the baby.

He watches me to see if I will take it back. Then he starts to nod, slowly. Okay, Haley, I'll get your daddy. You go on home case the phone rings. Where's she at, Memorial?

Yes. I feel my muscles go soft and shaky with relief.

He puts a hand around my back to lead me out. At the other end of the room, he brings me up some cement stairs. Pushing open the heavy metal doors, he holds them wide for me so I can climb out into the damp night air.

He says, I'm goin to use the phone a second and then get my truck and go to the hospital. Don't move from the house till we call you up.

All right, I say. Above me is a sliver of moon in clouds. The rain's stopped.

Behind me I hear Bo call, Don't you worry now, sweet girl, everything's gonna be just fine.

16

FLETCHER

I watch Haley's father at the Square Diner register. He's wearing muddied boots. His blue eyes look out from under his cowboy hat at the waitress. Frannie, he says to her, if it won't set you back any I could use five ones for a five.

I crane my neck to look for Haley out the window, but she isn't there. I haven't seen her in three days because of Gwyneth being sick.

Pops takes a bite of his sandwich and glances at Haley's father, who pockets the bills in his denims. He leaves a faint trace of mud on the carpet when he goes out.

Pops pokes his salad with a fork. You know who I was on the phone with this morning? he asks me.

I shake my head no.

Sheriff from Calhoun County. Their circuit court judge from Annison has been charged with raping the thirteen-year-old grandson of one of the judges during a child abuse conference in Providence this past weekend.

I look at Pops. Is that right? I say.

Pops nods. Must have stirred up something or other, he claimed he couldn't help himself.

Probably wasn't the first one, then, I tell him.

No, he says. Not even close. He swallows and picks up his sandwich.

What are they going to do to him? I ask.

Pops looks at his food. Well, he says, he needs treatment, but they'll send him to prison. Now Parchman's going to be the third-largest prison in the nation if this projected expansion goes through, and you think those men are getting any better? Pops chews and swallows before he says, They're sending a bunch of those Jackson gang members they caught last summer to a thousand-acre farm just north of Austin. No girls, no cigarettes, no alcohol, no weapons. That might work, I'd like to see what happens with that. Pops clears his throat. It's reform that's important, making sure the crimes aren't committed again, not punishment.

Frannie walks by. How y'all doin? she asks us.

We're just fine, thank you, Frannie, says Pops. We'd love some coffee to help us through this afternoon.

After lunch we have to sit four hours through a divorce case with only one recess. At the end of the day, Pops is too tired to speak and leaves in a hurry in the Lincoln. I stand next to the Honda and watch Robin wheel across the street to the corner shop. The older woman comes and opens the door. I smile. She smiles back and waves her hand to me in a come-here gesture. Then they both disappear.

I've heard the woman sells turquoise and I would like to get some for Haley. It takes me near five minutes to get my courage up. Five minutes in Mississippi July blinding heat that can make you sick. I walk over there sweating down my back and neck, my temple throbbing dully, cursing my shyness.

A bell rings on the door. Inside it's cool and dark. I can't see a thing save the shape of two heads and the counter.

Well, well, a husky voice says, our little friend finally made it into the shop.

It smells like herb and smoke and finally my eyes adjust. The short-haired, dark-skinned older woman is standing behind the counter with her hands on her waist. Robin is seated to her left, smoking a cigarette. The smell is sweet and lingers over the tiny room. The woman spreads her hands over the display case. Welcome, she tells me.

I stare at the green lava lamp on the counter and start to get a weird, hypnotized feeling.

Maybe you're too young to remember these, the woman says, following my gaze to the lamp. They were popular in the early '70s. She pushes it aside and leans her elbows on the counter. How are you, sweet? she asks me.

I'm fine thank you, ma'am, I tell her.

Her display is mostly turquoise and some orange stones and crystals lying next to wrapped cloth bags of different colors. In the far left case are various kinds of cigarettes and glass pipes and rolling papers. She has a tiny fountain going behind her and silver bracelets like armor up and down her arms that clang when she moves.

You want a clove cigarette? Robin asks me.

No, thanks, I tell her, I don't smoke.

You don't have to smoke to like one of these, she says.

The other woman laughs. She commences tying a bright blue scarf around her head like a turban. She says, You wantin to buy some jewelry, hon?

Robin looks down at her lap and doesn't say anything.

I walk over to them and look into the glass. I'm Fletcher, I tell the woman, for something to say. I hold out my hand to her. She takes it loosely. Her fingers are long and cool.

I know, she says. That's a nice strong name. She withdraws her hand. My name's Rose. It's not my God-given name, but I'm not a Christian. It used to be Mary Elizabeth. How's that for biblical? Are you a Christian, honey?

I shrug and put my hands in my pockets. I guess I am, I say. I like the idea of heaven. The impulse to say this was strong, I couldn't have helped it, but once it's out I redden fiercely. Neither one of them seem to take notice. Rose slides the case doors apart and pulls out chokers and long necklaces and earrings and bracelets. Robin reaches out and fingers one necklace. I glance at the door to see if anyone is coming in. I don't want Pops to find out I came in here after work, but I guess anything is hard to hide in Houser Banks.

Rose says, I know who you are. You have a good daddy and your mamma was sweet, she'll grace heaven. That makes a grand concoction in a man. She smiles and watches me. Robin flicks her ash in the ashtray and doesn't look at me. In this light her skin looks a kind of golden.

Why don't you come sit with us, baby, tell us all your stories? Rose motions to a chair beside Robin. You guiltless-lookin ones always have more stories than you let on. Don't you think he's got treasures, Robin? Rose squints her eyes, looks at her red fingernails and says, Don't you think sweet needs his fortune read?

Robin smiles wryly. I could read it, she says.

Rose watches her. I stay where I am.

Robin takes out her hand and starts to count on her fingers. Five easy steps, she says. She flips her shiny hair back on her shoulders. First he'll go to college, she tells us. Second he'll marry a lady in Houser Banks with a weddin reception in his own backyard. Third he'll be an attorney-turned-judge. Fourth he'll have three lovely children, who'll go to those fancy schools he did. Fifth he'll die.

Heat swelters up my neck and my breath waits in my chest. I watch her take a drag of that cigarette. She looks at me with her chin lifted and her eyes half lidded. Rose raises her eyebrows.

No one says anything.

Finally Rose says, You okay, baby? She leans over the counter and touches my cheek with a cool hand. Cause no one's allowed to get too sad in my shop. We got a cure for anything that lacks joy. Don't we, Robin?

Actually, I tell them, I better go. I start to turn toward the door.

Rose says, Well, it's true, that *was* one of the nastiest things that's been said in my shop. And let me tell you, nasty things have been said. Madder than rabid raccoons, some of these women.

I reach the door and manage to say, I'll see y'all another time. I can't quit the feeling that I'm going to start crying and I don't have a good handle on why.

Rose comes out from behind the counter and says, Wait just a second, sweet. She walks toward me quickly and grabs ahold of my arm. Now come back here. The phone rings and Rose drags me back in the store. Still holding my arm, she picks up the receiver and says, Hello, as if the person were interrupting.

Robin looks at the ground.

Yes, says Rose, she's here. She cups a hand over the receiver and nods her head to the back. Take it out there, sweetie, she tells Robin.

Robin wheels around. She turns once and looks at me, and I see she is sorry. Then she's gone through a black curtain.

Rose looses my arm and goes back behind the counter. I stand there awkwardly while she watches me. The lava lamp goes on in its obscene, slow-motion way, like unearthly planets rotating. Rose says, You got a girl, sweet?

I look her in the eye and don't speak.

She sighs, tilts her head and smiles. I know you do, Fletcher Greel, she says. You're too handsome not to. Pick out what you want for her. I'll give you a discount.

I look down at the things in the case. Rose waves her hand toward

Robin. Don't pay her a dime's worth of attention, hon. She isn't hard on the inside, she's so soft it about kills her. I've known her since she was this big, Rose says, putting her hand two feet above the ground, I was friends with her mamma. Her pappa was meaner than mojo, nothin worked. The man was the devil, I'm telling you. That girl wasn't treated right a day in her life. I won't tell you about her legs, those are hers to tell, but I'll tell you he was awful. All her mamma could do was love a whiskey bottle and hope for a strike of lightnin to kill him dead. Rose leans far over the counter. I see the fold of her breasts and smell her strong, earthy smell. She whispers, Don't tell her I told you, she wants to appear tough as nails. But just don't get your feelings hurt by someone like that. They barely know they do it.

I run one hand through my hair and think of Robin coming from a bad place. It hadn't occurred to me to think about her family or how her legs had become like they are. I'd thought she was born with them. It makes me sorry inside. I stare at a turquoise star on a silver chain that Robin had been looking at earlier.

Rose watches me. I point to the necklace and say, I'd like that.

Rose nods and wraps it. She says, It's fifty dollars, honey. To a regular customer it'd be sixty.

I take out two twenties and a ten. I'll have those turquoise earrings, too, I tell her.

Rose smiles. That's ten more.

I hand her another ten, pocket the earrings and hold on to the wrapped necklace with the other hand. When Robin wheels herself back in, her cheeks are flushed. She doesn't say who it was on the phone. She just sits and glances up at me. Rose starts in on a story about the two sisters living in New Orleans she buys her charms from. She says, One'll steal your boyfriend out from under you and the other is old and mean, but they're not hurtin on pennies. Those people down there are more generous with their money than the Houser Banks folks.

I put the box on Robin's wheelchair seat next to her left knee. I know Rose sees it.

I need to get going, I tell them. I look at Rose. Thank you, ma'am.

Robin fingers her package.

Rose walks me to the door and opens it for me. Thank you, she says. She strokes her neck while she says it. You come back now, you hear? I mean it.

All right, I say, I will.

Robin says softly, Bye-bye.

I wave a hand and leave. The door closes on me. I'm sixty dollars poorer, and my shirt smells of herb and smoke. I think about the lonesome, haunting look in Robin's eyes and I feel scared and sad for her.

When I look over at the parking lot, Riley is sitting in the Roadrunner, grinning, with two poles out the back. The passenger door is open. Come on, Yankee, he calls. Quit deliberating. Let's you and me get us some supper.

I jog across the street to him. His hound is sacked out in the backseat with his tongue dripping onto the Roadrunner's floor and a breeze ripping through his fur so it stands up like a fan.

Once I'm in the car, Riley asks me, You associating with that crazy lady in the corner shop?

Yeah, I bought earrings for Haley. I haven't seen her much, she's been taking care of Gwyneth.

Does that Indian girl work with her, the one in a wheelchair? He starts to pull out of the drive and waits for a line of cars to pass.

Nah, she just hangs out with her.

Riley pulls out into traffic. Shame about her legs, he says.

How'd she do it? I ask him.

Riley shrugs. Biggest secret in Houser Banks. You could sell that one if you ever learn it, it'd make you rich, boy.

We slide into silence and don't say a word all the way to the old dam at Battle Creek.

When we get to the inlet, Riley jumps the car door, then opens it. He has a smoke between his teeth. Mutt, he says, come along. The dog jumps out. Riley bends down and undoes his collar, sticks the car keys on there and then buckles it up again. He takes the crickets and tackle box and two poles out of the backseat and piles them into my arms and gestures to the river. Start toward that fall-apart jonboat, he tells me. I'll be along in a minute. I just got to get my motor and battery and we'll be good to go.

Fifty feet from where we park, we can look downriver to the slats that made the old dam. Out of its chipped, splintered wood come gushing waterfalls that look swollen as the fat bottom lip of some watery God. Water gushes twenty feet down and parts the river. It finds its way over rocks and gullies and comes out smooth and placid, still as glass with a jonboat and a dock out its bank. The jonboat is bone colored with red paint scrawled over it. There's a wind and it bangs a little against the mud. The air smells of the moist heat smell akin to dead fish.

Riley comes down with the mutt trailing along behind. He says, I'm always expectin this little boatty-boat to have come unknotted or stolen.

He pulls the back of the boat up, screws on the boat clamps for the motor, lifts out a battery and a gas can, rigs up the gas line, mixes oil in the tank, attaches the battery cables and gets in it. He tries it near seven times before that little shit-for-nothing starts. What the hell you waitin on, Judge? He grins at me. Climb the fuck in, he says.

After I get in, Riley goes up to the car once more, comes back down with a cooler, puts it in the boat between the back and middle seat and tells me, You got your drink of choice, Judge. Bourbon, Bud or whiskey. This here cooler might sink us, but at least we'll die drunk. Hey mutt, he whistles to his dog, who's aiming on getting in the water. Get the hell over here. The dog does as told and promptly falls asleep under the rear seat.

We lollygag out to the middle of the river. The heat is ugly. Riley kills the motor when we get far enough out. He picks up the cage of crickets. Elsa's best, he tells me and commences baiting our hooks.

In the next forty-five minutes we haven't caught anything worth talking about. Riley declares the crickets lemons, too sour for the fish to want. He throws his line toward a shady part of shore. The sun's inching down the sky, bleeding its white heat. The water is black in the center and green around the sides, shimmering with wind. Riley picks a cigarette from behind his ear and lights it with a lighter from his front pocket. Where in hell are the goddamn fish? he says around his smoke. Too hot for em? He slaps his arm and flicks away a horsefly big enough to leash up. With much effort, Riley makes his mutt get out from under the seat and tells him to sit on top of it, then he leans back so his head is resting on the dog's belly. He stares overhead at two mallards circling.

Wish I had my .22, he says. I remember the first time I killed a bird with my BB gun. Nine years old, trudging through the backyard woods like a soldier, or so I thought, and saw a bird up in the tree, little brown sparrow making a peep noise, a kind of one-two rhythm. I told myself if that bird didn't quit the noise, I'd kill it on the spot. Course it went and chirped again. I aimed, hit that little fucker in the tail end and dropped it like a sack of rice. It was still breathing when I got there. I hunched down and cried like a schoolgirl. Then made a proper burial for it. Said a few Our Fathers, Hail Marys, whatever.

Riley gets a tug on his line. He stands up quick. His cigarette falls and floats in the water. When it's reeled in, the line is empty. Damnit, says Riley, some teeny-weeny stole my bait. Without rebaiting, he gets back in his position with his dog as pillow. Anyway, shootin got easier and easier. I was an addict, Judge. I damn near had to kill somethin before I went to school in the morning. It was scary. Then I discovered girls and the birds threw a party. Who wants to kill a bird when you can grab some tittie? He laughs.

I try to pull in but my line won't tug. I take to standing and pull that way.

Riley says, Greel, I think you're hung up, unless you've hooked a Loch Ness. He grabs my line from me and with three jerks looses it. Cast out near that mess of shrubs, he says. We got to fish like the rednecks taught us, fish are dirty animals.

I cast out there.

He drags his line all the way in and goes to taking off the hook.

Mike Tyson and Tony Tucker, says Riley. Who you got your bets on, Judge?

Tyson, I tell him. All my bets are on that mean motherfucker.

Mine too, Yankee, mine too. So, you workin with the Indian girl? he asks me.

Yup.

What's she like?

She's all right. I'm damn sorry for her.

Riley casts and reaches in his overall pockets for his cigarettes. He looks at me. You're sorry for her in what way?

I shrug. I don't know, I tell him. A lonely kind of way.

Riley smokes and stares at the water. You got a tug, Judge.

I pull but there isn't anything there. When I reel up, my cricket's half gone.

Your cricket lost his ass, says Riley. He baits me and throws the line and says, You want to know my take, it would make me goddamn in the loony bin not havin my legs. Maybe she's a whole lot stronger than that, but you don't want to take any chances, Judge. You already got a crazy girl in your life.

I throw out farther, into a space of water next to a gray rock that shadows into the river. Haley Ellyson? I ask.

Damn right, Haley Ellyson.

Crazy how so?

Riley smokes and reaches in the cooler for the pint of whiskey. I don't know, Judge. You seen her ride a horse? She must have something crazy in her to ride like that. Riley takes a sip of whiskey. But I can't tell you nothin about her, she already has you.

Yes she does, I tell him.

He looks long at me. Now you know what it feels like, says Riley. He doesn't smile when he says it. Finally he says, We're not catchin even a appetizer. He stands up and looks around at the water. The dog raises its head, too. Don't even think about swimmin, mutt, says Riley. To me he says, I think we should motor on over there to that piece of shore. Them little sonofabitches bitin here are too small to get hooked, they're robbin us blind of bait. Over yonder hasn't gotten sun since about one this afternoon.

The wind doesn't help any, I tell him, and I think I might need a smaller hook.

We sit on the other side of the river. Riley says, Hannaford got himself beat at Letchy's party last Saturday. Split his rib in two. He had to have it wrapped.

Who split it in two?

Some asshole.

Hannaford's an asshole, I tell him. Cousin or no cousin, he don't know how to keep his mouth shut.

Shit, Judge, don't I know it.

He's broken over Haley, I say.

Who hasn't been broken over Haley?

There is silence between us, then Riley says, You got a girl up north, Greel?

No.

You ain't got some Yankee pussy waitin for you up there?

Nope.

None to be had?

No, there's some to be had, sure as hell. I went out with a girl named Francie this past year, but it was just for the hell of it. They are all wanting you to boyfriend them for life.

Francie? That's a hell of a name, says Riley. He smiles at me.

She looked better than her name, I tell him.

South's like that too, Riley says. All the girls wantin to marry you. Crystal ain't. But if she wanted to marry me tomorrow I'd do it. So now you got Haley Ellyson, prettiest thing ever did walk the earth, and I haven't seen her as sweet as I see her with you.

Something lifts inside me, but I keep a look on the line.

She's different with you, Greel, says Riley. She's stickin to our little judge here. I don't know how you do it.

I breathe in and look up at the wind blowing in currented streams across the river. I don't know either, I tell him.

Hannaford's been bothering Crystal some more, he says.

No shit.

Riley smokes. Uh-huh, and he ain't got no kind of good in him. Got his mean from his daddy, my mamma's last brother, Uncle Frank. He reels in and casts out, drags the line toward him in the water. Frank killed a man once, Riley says. Three of them did it, with a hammer, to see if they could. They ended up strangling him with a vacuum cleaner cord. Riley's line jerks and he reels in quick, but nothing's on his hook. He rebaits, casts out again and says, Afterward they wrapped the body in curtains and put it in the bottom of a sofa, nailed a piece of plywood across the bottom, hid it in a weedy area off of 12. The sheriff found out about it three weeks later when a driver came into the brush to take a piss and smelled stench in the air. He leans his pole against the side of the boat, puts both hands in the air and stretches long. Hannaford's daddy was seventeen then, says Riley. Got almost no time to speak of. He's runnin free. I can't even look in his eyes for fear somethin will break in me and I will kill the man. Aimin not really to kill him, but to end the meaness that runs in him.

I look over the side of the boat for fish bubbles. There aren't any. Hannaford ever done anything akin to that? I ask Riley.

Not as bad, Riley says, but close. He doesn't speak for one long while and then he says, I'll tell you somethin I haven't ever told anybody. I seen Hannaford in the pants of a thirteen-year-old girl, an orphan Mamma let stay with us awhile. He looks at me and narrows his eyes. She was a mute, skinny, pretty little thing that slunk around the house so quiet you forgot she was there. Hannaford was eighteen and I was fifteen. I came up on them during a Memorial Day picnic, shacked in the back of that Ford used to be parked on cinders out a ways from our house. Riley looks over the side of the boat and sneers his top lip like he can see the memory in the dark of the water. She had the look of a ghost, he says. Her eyes were as scared as a once-shot-at deer. So I went to hauling Hannaford out. We fought for near quarter of an hour while that girl ran away. Riley picks up a cup and commences baling some of the water out of the boat bottom. After the fight I went directly to the house and sat down on my bed for near two hours thinking how sickness runs through men so much even your own cousin has it and you have to bear witness when you don't want to. I kept thinkin of that little girl wearing a hand-off yellow dress, tore at the shoulder, and wonderin what to do about an eighteen-year-old with his dick in her. He stops baling and looks at me. And Hannaford wasn't better for the cracked jaw and broke finger I gave him. It just made him meaner.

I breathe in and think that all Pops's prison reform talk and lash against the death penalty couldn't make me not want Hannaford locked up or shot dead.

Finally Riley throws the bucket back on the boat bottom and asks, How's Gwyneth?

I only know from what Haley tells me, I say. I think she's going to be all right, though. Just down and out and sad as hell.

You ever seen her? Riley asks.

I shake my head no.

She's a beauty, Judge. Steal a goddamn look whenever you can.

That won't be for a while.

Nope, it probably won't. I don't know what boyfriend's ever crossed the thresh of Ire Ellyson's house. But you're a whole lot cleaner and better behavin than the rest of them. Riley frowns. He has a tug on his line and he stands again. His cigarette drops on the boat bottom and when his line is tugged up it's a big yellow-throated bream. The mutt raises up and perks its ears, but doesn't come off the bow. Riley yells, Wahoo, dinner!

For a while we cast out by a fall-down log near the swamped edge of the river where Riley caught his. We catch a good ten in a row. Our crickets get low and Riley pulls out some chartreuse bait. We sink those instead, and our boat gets full of thrashing yellow glinting bream, which we throw in the cooler for later. We whoop and holler. The dog gets overwrought and jumps out and splashes us. He swims toward shore. Riley yells at him that he's scaring all the fish away. Now you're out for good, Riley tells him. So the mutt stands there sopping wet on the side of the bank looking sorry and skinny as hell. When he tries to swim in, Riley yells at him to quit. The bream stop as suddenly as they started. We pat each other on the back and take a breather.

I get a Bud from the cooler and Riley stays with the whiskey. Sullen, stinking heat scorches us.

We sit for a while and drink. Riley smokes.

How'd you meet Crystal? I ask him.

Riley half smiles and shakes his head. You remember I told you about Emmett Fry takin me to Hatchey's that first time? Well, in walked Crystal Nash the middle of that night and never was this boy the same, Judge. You can set back all your money on that. He trails a hand through the water and says, And then I'll be damned if she wasn't in the halls of Houser Banks High that next year. They paid to send her there cause her grades were so good. Her family's got their pride and hope on her. I threw out all the charm I could muster to get her to me and by some work of the devil or God I got her. He raises his eyebrows. No one can leave it alone either. Why is it you get a good thing and the whole world wants to bother it? He stares for some time at nothing in particular.

I try not to watch him, but I can't help it. It is the stillest I've ever seen Riley White.

After a while, he shifts his feet on the tackle box and says, Some of those boys in school, they couldn't handle having a hard-on for a black girl. They'd follow her around and say rude shit. They just about stopped it when we started in. I mean we didn't call any attention to ourselves, we were quiet about it. Still you can't hide it all the time. But it isn't done, he says. Hannaford's a prick. He and I have been into it since we were up to here. He points to his knees. This is his perfect chance to get me, seein as I'm in love and it's a black girl. He can have a fuckin field day.

We sit and watch the sky. The heat eases while that fat, big-bellied mister of a sun hits the lower horizon.

With a full-up cooler of fish and the mutt asleep beside it we drive home along the curves of Highway 12, where there isn't anything but a mess of kudzu, and the Roadrunner sputters and dies. Motherfucker, says Riley. He bangs his hands on the steering wheel. How strong's your thumb, Yankee?

The road is hot and dusty.

Shit, that car ain't nothin but trouble, but I love it so, Riley says in a singsong voice. The mutt trails behind us with his head low. A trucker comes at us, raging down the hillside with all steam and power and no goal to stop. My mouth is dry from heat and my armpits sop wet from it. When the truck blares by, Riley shrugs his shoulders and shakes his head and lights a smoke. I think of all the fish rotting on melting ice in the trunk.

That car's like Crystal is for me, gets me into trouble, but I can't stay away, Riley says. He looks at me, his long hair's stuck to his forehead. He clasps his hand on my shoulder. Sorry about this, Yankee. I gotta get that car fixed up good. He turns and looks back at it, disappearing into a red dot in the distance. I gotta get a better mechanic than just my screwy brother. Good thing Crystal's not with us now, he says.

I don't say anything, but I can still hear the jeers of those men behind us the other night when we drove the Roadrunner out Highway 12 at the brink of dusk. They followed us four miles in a beat-up Chevy calling, Nigger lovers! Hey girl you givin it away? Pass her over here.

Riley went white with mad.

Beside him Crystal stared straight ahead saying, I'm the one who knows here, Riley, I'm the one who's had experience. You drive! You don't do a thing but drive, Riley White.

I heard Haley say under her breath, I wish I had a gun. I'd shoot those bastards.

Riley drove not fast like you'd think but slow, as if he weren't one bit scared as I believed he must have been.

When a gray flatbed slows on the roadside before us, Riley says, I think we might have a taker.

A man in a beard and dirtied white T-shirt with a pack of smokes rolled in his sleeve leans his head out from the passenger's side. Hi ya, boys, he says.

Hi ya, says Riley, we're goin on to Houser Banks near as you can get us. Thank ye kindly mister.

He makes like to go toward the back of the truck.

Hey, the driver calls.

Riley stops and looks at them.

Y'all wanna ride in this here truck? The driver has an unlit cigar twirling between his front teeth. His mouth is a smile of sorts, but in it is a sneer. He looks mean as a snake.

Riley hesitates. Yes sir, we sure would. My car ran off the road awhile back there and we just need a ride up the road a piece as far as you're goin.

The guy in the passenger's seat looks at the driver, then out at the horizon, and says, It's pretty damn hot out to be walkin.

Riley nods. Yes sir.

Well, says the passenger. He adjusts his mirror. What do you say, Henry?

The driver shrugs, clenches his cigar between his teeth and revs the truck. Dirt spits up from under the tires and they swerve out to the black-top so we have to jump back. The mutt scuddles into the side brush. The man in the passenger's seat leans out his window and looks back at us. While they drive off he yells, Then get a fuckin haircut! And they are gone, treating us to dust in our eyes and mouths.

17

HALEY

We run the baby's ashes over the river at noon on Monday not a hundred feet from where the body is buried in the woods. I think how odd it is that I know about that body and no one else here does. I close my eyes and say a prayer for the baby's spirit to stay away from the buried man in case he is dangerous.

Daddy's wearing his blue suit and I watch while he holds on to Gwyneth. Her legs buckle beneath her. He whispers in her hair, Shh, baby, shh. She doesn't cry at all.

Gypsy and Spier and I stand by the oak looking out at Battle Creek while the minister says words to make the baby's soul go straight to heaven. A sinless child, he says, born of no guilt.

Born dead, I think, and hate myself for it.

I feel sure having a baby die right at the moment you think it is getting born is one of the worst things that could happen to a mamma. No one but Gwyn could say for certain, though. And Gwyn isn't talking.

Later Daddy orders a stone and has it put next to the Ellyson plot. He buys flowering plants that will last through the seasons. Near dusk he and I muddy our knees with the planting. We drop sweat on the newly turned dirt and don't speak at all.

That night I lie awake staring at a hazy half-moon and the boughs of oak out my window tapping against my screen and think of the black hole growing on my inside that feels like it is taking the all of me down into it. I wonder on life. Why do we do those simple things like brush our teeth and get dressed?

That baby had already become a sister to me and I realize I had been talking to it in my mind for some time now, that I was promising it things for when it came to live with us. I guess what I had wanted most of all was for us to be a family. I hadn't so much wanted it as believed it to be already true. Even when I think of good things like the sweet pile of bliss that goes with riding a horse, I can't get a fix anymore on why I love it. I think of Fletcher going to college. Now there'll be no baby in the house for me to busy myself with when he's gone. In that dark, sleepless night I start to believe that life is just a duty you do until something unknown takes it away from you in the middle of a Fourth of July day when you are least expecting it. It makes me know you can't count on anything at all.

I don't want to but I imagine my own funeral and who would come and what they would say about me. I think of Daddy dying and how he would go, what person would do the telling, and what I would do. Then I think of the death of everyone I know, Fletcher and Riley, Gwyneth and Bo. The imaginings are so real I sob into my bedcovers. Finally I sit upright in bed and turn on my light because I am afraid in the dark I will disappear, melt into some watery substance and become like that girl Riley says he saw out at the river, hanging by her neck. Naked, he told us, as a jaybird.

I leave the light on. Sleep comes with rising mist and the call of doves and a faint grassy wind that breezes in my screen and ruffles my hair and my sheets. At seven I get out of bed feeling drugged, as if my veins are made up of some sluggish syrup.

When I pass Daddy's room, I stand for some seconds listening at their door.

You gonna get up today, sweet lady? Daddy asks Gwyn.

She murmurs something back that I can't hear.

I'll holler at you at ten, he says. If you want to get up when I call and you can't do it on your own, I can drive back home and make you some breakfast or send Haley to do it.

There is a whisper of sound while Gwyn speaks and then I hear his boots come toward the door.

In the kitchen we stand drinking black coffee and Daddy smokes a Winston. Gypsy calls him to ask about Gwyn and I go out to the driveway and climb in Daddy's truck instead of the Ford I usually drive. At a quarter to eight Daddy pulls himself in on the driver's side, pumps down the gearshift and says, You riding with me today, Turnip?

Yeah, I'd sure like to. I adjust the passenger's mirror.

Well, he says, turning around to back up, I'd sure like to have you.

We ride together in silence. At the stop sign after Highway 12, he places one of his big palms on my knee and squeezes, then chokes on a word and shakes his head.

I swallow, look through the front window at Houser Banks square, spread out before us with its dew-soaked cars parked at an angle. Becca Hartle is walking up the courthouse doors and Miss French is leaning against Elsa's car talking to Cal. The courthouse clock has been forty-five minutes fast for as long as I can remember. It rings for eight thirty. I lean my cheek against the window, close my eyes and focus on my breath because it seems too shallow, like I can't get enough oxygen in me. Daddy says, You doin okay, Hale?

All I can do is nod.

I feel him push off from the stop sign. I know how you're feelin, Turnip, he tells me. I damn well know it.

The men in Elsa's store get quiet when we come in. The only sound is the rickety fan in the corner behind the cash register. From the freezer I get an orange juice and then wait at the counter while Daddy picks out his jelly roll and pours his coffee. The men look at their boots and smoke and don't speak at all. It's not a mean quiet, it comes out of deference and love for Daddy. They are using silence as a rescue from words they don't know how to say.

Hi ya, Elsa, Daddy says when he goes to pay.

Hey Ire, she tells him. She watches him when she takes his change, but he doesn't look up and we go out without saying anything else.

When we get to the stables, Daddy turns the truck slowly in the drive and cuts off the motor. Stony is haying in the left field. Daddy lights a cigarette. In back of us the men stand in a circle, drinking coffee, shoeing the dirt and taking sidelong glances at the back of the truck. I open my door. Daddy doesn't look at me. See ya there, kiddo, he says. Have a good one.

Throughout the day, between riding classes and feedings, I stand at the door of the stables eating the apples and carrots meant for the horses, and watch Daddy working with two cattle horses. He is gentle with them, but he doesn't smile or call to them or run much. His legs are like two lead weights meant to drag him down. He seems not to notice the dust and heat. When he sees me, he picks up a hand or touches his hat, and a tightness comes to my throat for the sad and worry in his squinty eyes.

He works through lunch and quits late.

Later I lie by the river on the denim blanket we keep under the rock next to the gum tree, and wait for Fletcher. He comes up running, unbuttoning his shirt. When he sees me, he slows to a jog, then stands looking down at me. His shirt's sweat soaked and when he takes it off his skin is slicked. He sits next to me, picks up my hand and kisses the fingertips. You doin okay? he asks. He looks at me. I wasn't sure you'd be here.

Gypsy's with Gwyn today, I tell him.

Fletcher nods. Out of his pockets he brings four wildflowers, a blue jay feather and a pair of turquoise earrings. He puts one of the wildflowers behind my ear. I hold the earrings in my hand and look at them. These are beautiful, I tell him. Where did you get them?

He tells me he got them from the Creole woman's shop behind the courthouse.

My skin looks tan next to the turquoise. The stones are cool feeling, and the turquoise is what Gwyneth would call crude, with brown lines running the length of it, and all different shades of blue. You could look at the stones for a long while without feeling tired of them.

Fletcher watches me look. When he lies down on his back, I trail the turquoise over his belly and chest and neck. He says it feels good. He opens his eyes and looks at me and I smile. Maybe it's the first time I've smiled since the Fourth of July.

In about an hour Crystal and Riley come. Crystal wades in and talks to Fletcher by the shore while Riley and I swim out to the rock. We lie on our bellies with our legs in the water and stare out at the far bank.

How's Miss Gwyneth hangin on? asks Riley.

I shrug, and before I can say a word, warm tears come leaking down my face.

Riley lifts his arm from the water and throws it around my shoulders, squeezing me. Nothing wrong with some teardrops salting up our river, he says. It needs a little spice.

I put my cheek to the rock and let those tears melt into its hot. Riley keeps his arm around me and pulls me closer. That's a way, Haley. Good for you, girl. You got some cry in you after all.

★   ★   ★

That second sleepless night, I steal out the back sliders and drive the red truck to Fletcher's, where I whistle up to his window. He lets me in, silently. His house is big and holds all the air you'd ever want to breathe in a lifetime. He leads me up those back carpeted stairs to his room. His sheets are cool and crisp and they smell of him, mint and soap.

You okay? he whispers. He stretches his body long against mine.

I nod.

He kisses my lips and cheeks and holds my hand in his. He's wearing cotton boxer shorts and no shirt. I lean against his chest. Fletcher?

Mmm?

Tell me about your mamma.

He breathes in and lays his head on his pillow so he is facing the ceiling. Running his hand through his hair, he starts to talk about the things he misses.

Simple things, he tells me. She used to keep a pair of earrings on the ledge of the coatrack in the front hall so if she was in a hurry and forgot some, she could put them on.

What kind were they? I ask him.

Pearls, he says.

I want to know her favorite color and he says it was red. He tells me her favorite singer was Smokey Robinson and that she and his daddy would sit at the kitchen table listening to his record albums some summer nights in their T-shirts and denims, eating hot peppers and chasing them down with beer. They'd talk and laugh and the tears would fall down their cheeks from the hot. He says at the time it made him feel left out, but now that she's gone, he loves to remember it.

She got real mad sometimes, he says, and she'd holler out, Fletcher Thomas Greel go outside and run around so I can have time to cool off a spell.

So did you? I ask him.

Sure as hell I did, and if I ever got pissed off about something, she said, You go in your room and lie down on your bed and kick your wall hard as you can. He points to the wall next to his window. She used to have that wall painted every year up until I was twelve cause there'd be black shoe marks on it. Helped to get the mad out so we wouldn't have to fight.

What did she smell like? I ask him.

He leans up and looks at me. You want to know that? he says. Hold on a second. He lifts the sheets off the bed and climbs over me, then goes to kneel at his dresser. The outside light shines on his backbone when he bends over the bottom drawer. He takes something out and walks back to the bed.

Close your eyes, he says to me, and then there is a faint sweet smell in front of me. When I open my eyes, a pink satin something is next to my face. He puts his face into it and then folds it neatly and places it back in the drawer. When he climbs into bed again, he tells me, She smelled like that. She used to sleep in it, he says.

He talks into the night about her and we give her mention space and some silence. I ask how she met his daddy and what her voice sounded like and if she laughed a lot or was more serious, what food she liked and what colors she wore. Fletcher's fingers run over my palm while he speaks and we both watch the red lights on his digital pass from minute to minute. After he has been silent for some time, I tell him, I want to be buried in New Orleans.

Why's that?

I want to be buried above ground. I like that idea.

He is quiet.

I think it'd be terrible, I tell him, getting dirt thrown on you.

For a long while Fletcher doesn't say a word. And then he is touching me. It is the slowest we have ever been together, soft and asking, and he says over and over again, Is this all right? You tell me if you want me to stop.

Later Fletcher falls asleep with his arms around my waist and his head on my chest. I don't sleep at all that night. Fear comes to me again and this time it is about Fletcher. I saw a letter on his dresser the other day that said he was slated to be at college on the twenty-fifth of August. I know people like him don't stay put in places like Houser Banks. I am most of all afraid of this vision I have of myself, sitting in a house when I am a middle-aged lady, sleeping beside a man who handles me rough and doesn't hold me when he dreams. I imagine I will feel dead from loneliness and my only happiness will be when I close my eyes at night and think about the summer Fletcher Greel loved me.

Two days later I stand at the stable door watching Daddy with his back to Gorgeous Hussy's nose. He is letting her scratch her neck and face by rubbing them against his shoulder blades. He stumbles forward sometimes with her strength and then rights himself. You gettin all that scratch out, girl? he says to her. Go for it.

I haul the saddle I am carrying to its hanging place on the wall. He watches me. Hey there, Haley, he says.

Hey Daddy. I sit on a hay bale and pick out a piece of straw to hold between my two front teeth. The barn smells of horse manure and dry wood and hay.

He pushes Hussy's head away, pats her neck and reaches into the bucket at his feet to take out a brush. Then he starts to go at her flanks with it. Dust comes off in clouds.

That's a good horse, I tell him, swinging my legs from the hay bale seat.

She was a hard one to crack, he says, but now I reckon she's the best on the farm. He runs the brush around Hussy's belly in circles. Mad as hellfire when she came out here minus her young one. He leans into Hussy's ear. But now you're right at home with a rider, ain't you Hussy girl? He runs his knuckles across her back.

I take the straw out of my mouth and examine it. Daddy? I say.

Yup.

You think Gwyn will be okay?

I don't know, he says. He goes around the back of the horse and starts to brush out her hip. But I do know this, Turnip, God made women strong. A man might have some big old muscle and know how to handle a weapon, but on the inside he's made of mush. He can stand breaking a thousand mustangs better than a heartache. Women know how to grieve it out and build up again. He throws the brush in the bucket and gets out the polishing brush. Gwyn's had heartache before, he says. She lost a daddy when she wasn't even twenty. Not six months later she got married to one of the richest men in Texas. They had a baby. Three days after her son's second birthday, Gwyneth was walking with him to the mailbox and he got away from her while she was bending for the mail. He ran right into the street. A garbage truck driver, drunk on whiskey, was coming around the corner at full speed. Gwyn didn't get to her boy in time. Daddy spits on the ground, rubs his toes over it and wipes his mouth with his sleeve. Her boy was killed, he says.

My God, I say.

Daddy and I are silent. Afternoon light shifts through the cracks of the barn walls. He brushes the horse's flank and says, I'd say she knows pretty well how to survive pain, is why I told you that.

What happened to her husband?

Daddy looks up at me over the horse's back. Gwyn went a little crazy about it, Hale, and her husband put her in Blue Gate, where people shit themselves and their teeth rot out their heads. That sonofabitch oil pimp just left her there to play checkers in the rec room. She says she slept every day for six weeks and dreamt out all her grief.

While I sit and think on this, Gwyneth turns into a whole new person. I want to run home and look at her again. It is a miracle to me that she had a life before Houser Banks and I never thought to ask about it. But it's also a new thing to think that you can go crazy once and you don't have to stay that way. The thought shocks me into silence for a good while. Daddy glances up at me a few times, but he doesn't say anything. I wonder if Daddy's hiding hurt. Maybe one day he'll break down and not be able to eat or drink or go to work anymore. I watch him carefully, for where the hurt might show itself, but he looks like Daddy still. A little tired around the eyes. That's it.

He eases around the horse's flank, and I ask him softly, How about you, Daddy? Are you all right?

He begins to polish Hussy's side. I'm going to be just fine, Turnip. I learned to get over a loss once, and I know I can do it again. I thought I'd never stop grieving your mamma. I'll tell you something, I used to read those letters over and over again to myself after I read them aloud to you when you were little. I'd wait for them like a hungry man waits his dinner. And then it ebbed, slow as rain. One day I woke up without the pain. I was grateful as hell for what I had, this little girl I'd die for, he says, winking at me, and a woman who came into my life like no one has before. Gwyneth Fox.

Did you want real bad to be a daddy to that baby? I ask.

He stops brushing and says, I wanted it for Miss Gwyneth. She wanted that baby. I'm more sad for her than I am for myself.

I watch a crow beat its wings in the rafters and then settle. But did you want it? I ask.

Daddy comes around and holds Hussy's jaw, brushes her neck. Daddying's a hard job to do, he says. Reach me that comb, will you, Haley? When I pass it to him, he tells me, I wasn't afraid of the raising. He combs through Hussy's mane. It's Gwyn who worried me.

I go back and sit on the haystack and watch a daddy longlegs making its way to my thigh. I try not to move because I like how its legs feel on my skin.

Gwyneth, says Daddy, is like one of those wild horses you never quite break. He goes around the back of the horse and starts to untangle the tail. No matter how long you've been with them or how many times you put on the saddle and ride them, a part of them stays wild and you always get the feeling it might run from you. You have one hope with a wild horse, though. Daddy fluffs Hussy's tail. It's a herding animal, he says. So is Gwyn. She doesn't like to be alone. When she got pregnant, I think she was most in the world happy that she would always have somebody to herself. Daddy throws the comb in the bucket. I wasn't sure once she had a somebody, a baby girl, to be with her all the time, she wouldn't just up and run off on me.

I pick out a piece of fat hay, draw a line across my thigh with it and say, She isn't just with you because she wants to be with somebody, Daddy. She loves you.

Daddy walks around Hussy, brushing her with quick strokes of his hands. Love ain't everything, Turnip. You think it might be when you're sixteen, but it's a whole lot more complicated than that and sometimes you just do want to run from it.

The daddy longlegs starts on down the hay bale. *You* don't ever run from it, I tell him.

He looks over the horse's back at me. I have, when I was younger. Before I met your mamma I ran like the devil into the bottle and into the bed of other women. After I met your mamma, I started to know a simple fact about life, there's runners and there's stay putters, and I decided to be a stay putter, stick around, do what I'm doing, let someone else bust their gut running. He goes to the bucket and gets out a shoe pick.

I suppose, I tell him, if you think somebody's going to run, they might just do it.

Daddy picks up Hussy's front leg, leans against her chest and starts to chunk the mud out of her shoe. They aren't gonna run because of what you believe, Haley, they're gonna run because that's the kind of people they are.

We are quiet.

When he is finished with the last shoe, he stands up, brushes his hands on his denims and looks at me. What are you thinking there, Turnip?

I was just wondering if I was going to be a runner or a stay putter.

And? He goes to the barn wall and gets down a lead line.

I'd rather be a runner, I say. Being left seems terrible to me.

Daddy loops the line around Hussy's neck. Well just make sure you can run fast enough. If you think you're not quick enough to get away from someone, you might as well not even go near them. Now go on, he says, take the truck home so you can sit with Gwyn, she's waitin on you. I'll get a ride from Stony later.

The phone's ringing when I come home.

I pick it up.

You alone? Bo asks.

My breath stops, he hasn't ever called me at home before. I look over the counter at Gwyneth, sitting in the rocker staring into a glass of Wild Turkey. No, I tell him.

Gwyneth there?

Yes.

Anyone else?

No, I say.

I want you to meet me outside in an hour and a half.

Okay, I tell him, and then he hangs up.

Gwyn takes a sip of her drink. I'm sorry I didn't answer that when it was ringin, I'm just too damn tired. Who was that, darlin? You have some admirer? You wantin up some boy's attention? She swings one bare foot with chipped pink paint on the toenails and gets a cigarette out of the pack beside her. She asks, You want to tell me about him?

I will, I tell her, but I want to fix you some lunch first.

You got a letter waitin on you upstairs, honey.

I tell her I'll fix her lunch before I read it, but she says she's isn't hungry right yet and a letter shouldn't sit around getting stale.

The shade's drawn in my room. Dim yellow light comes out the sides. I turn on the lamp above my bureau. The letter's lying flat on its back. I can tell by all the loopy script and foreign stamps it's from Mamma. I look up at myself in the mirror.

Bo wants to see me so badly he called my home.

There's an old pack of Virginias on the dresser in front of me and I take a stale one out and smoke it, watching myself through the haze, my messy hair and blue eyes. There are dirt creases in my neck from being at the stables. But I don't care. I won't wash myself for Bo like I do for Fletcher. I won't put perfume on my press points and look pretty for him, won't brush my teeth of the tobacco smell. I tell myself I am not going to do anything different just because I am going to see Bo. In a secret part of me, I want my body to be raw for him, earthy. I want him to think of me as almost wild, untamed and lacking fear.

I lie on my bed with the rotating fan going on my dresser and slit the letter open with an old dinner knife on my bedside.

Tuesday, July 12

Haley Sweetheart,

I'm sorry I haven't written since March. It just seems time goes by so quick and every time I sit down to write you, I start to cry so bad, I can't. Today I think I can finally get through a whole letter.

I've been thinking of you lately and wanting to come see you. It's only I am in Amsterdam without a dime to my name for a plane fare home. Plus, I am so damned scared to come back, every time I arrange to do it, I botch it up.

It is airy here in summer and there are old buildings with fancy engravings on them. The streets are full of people who speak Dutch and are real polite, but not so generous and sweet like they are in Mississippi. I miss the South. Make sure you are eating enough, the food is better in your hometown than anywhere else in the world.

I am seeing a nice man named Rikel. He's got a tattoo of Africa across his shoulder blades. He's lived in Liberia, worked for some revolution there. I don't know what it's all about. I could never bring him home for too long, he doesn't like the politics there and they wouldn't understand him, so I guess I'd come by myself if I were going to stay awhile.

We went to see a band the other night called the Nevils and danced till five. I ripped my stockings and lost my shoes, had to go home barefoot, but we saw a sunrise and it looked like the sky was on fire. I am sick now from it because I was tired to begin with and just wore myself out. I've been drinking tea and eating toast and trying to get well. I don't much like the food here and everyone drinks black beer, thick as syrup. I don't like that either. I am a wine girl.

How are you? If you have a boyfriend treat him well, but like I always say, don't go drowning yourself in it, you are your own girl. I hope you have lots of friends and are keeping yourself real busy.

Uncle Hetchel sent the photo of you in the riding competition this past May. You've gotten so pretty. It made me cry for three days straight without stopping. They almost had to put me in a hospital. Hetchel tells me Daddy is seeing a younger blond lady. I hope she is nice to you. Don't let anyone but Daddy tell you what to do and don't listen to him all the time, either, just trust your own self.

I love him very much, Haley, you know I never stopped. But I needed to smell the world. Your daddy and I loved each other in a way that wanted to tear us both apart. We started a fire every time we were in a room together and that can make a life tiring. We took too much out of each other. I know I have told you this all before, but the words always fall wrong. I do miss you. I used to sit you on my lap and sing you Patsy Cline's *Crazy* and you'd play with those hairs along my neck. Do you remember? I want to come this fall to see you. I love how Houser Banks smells in the fall. I know I keep saying I'm coming, it is just I am afraid if I see you, I will never leave, and I don't have a place there anymore. Oh, now I am all teary eyed from writing to you and picturing you.

I love you, don't go breaking my heart by hating me. I will write more when I get a chance. Do you still have the sapphire I gave you before I left? I still have mine and I wear it around my neck on a chain and think of you every day. I don't ever take it off.

Love you. Be good to yourself. Always stay my little girl somewhere inside.

Yours,
Ann Marie (Mamma)

P.S. You can write me care of Hetchel whenever you want to.

Folding the letter up neatly, I go to my closet and place it with all of Mamma's other letters at the bottom of the trunk.

Then I peel off my riding clothes because they are hot. Whenever Mamma writes she always says she wants to come visit, but she doesn't ever. I used to hold the letters in my hands before opening them to weigh them and see if there might be a plane ticket inside for me to come to her. There never was. One time there was a picture of her and a man named Michael outside in a café, but I couldn't make her out, the sun was right in her face and the hat she wore made a shadow. I looked at it so hard, it got worn and tired and finally Daddy put it in my photo album downstairs so it wouldn't get ruined.

I put on a summer dress from my floor, wrinkled and damp from when I stepped on it that morning after I showered, and think how most of all I want Mamma to know I am dating Fletcher Greel, whose daddy is the town judge and who treats me fine. I want to tell her I go swimming with him in the river. And that Bo Dickens is crazy for me. I want her to see me ride a horse. A part of me is like an empty hole for Mamma. But I know that for her hurt lives in Houser Banks, and she is too fragile to come home and look it in the face.

I go downstairs and sit on the arm of the couch across from Gwyn. She is about to put a fresh cigarette between her lips. She takes it out and looks at it. Oh shit, honey, I got to stop this. Here you are in love and all I'm doin is smoking my life away. She tilts her head at me. You think I'm a sad lady? she asks. I watch Gwyneth and think of what Daddy just told me about her. I guess you're a little sad right now, I tell her, but I bet it will pass.

She rolls the cigarette between two fingers and says, I think it will, too. Her hands shake when she lights the cigarette. She blows smoke out and takes a last sip of her drink. With one hand she picks her hair off her neck. Hot, hot, hot, she says and passes me the empty bourbon glass so I can refill it, which I do from the liquor cabinet in back of her.

And then that's my last, she says. Cause a lady shouldn't be drunk before three.

In the kitchen, I pile tuna and celery and mayonnaise in a bowl and watch her over the counter while I'm doing it. She leans her head on the chair back and stares out the screen. Her voice is lazy. I think there's a God out there, she says, who hates and loves me. He keeps giving me things and taking them away.

Some God, I say, spreading the tuna on bread.

I wish he'd dote on me for once, she tells me.

He dotes on you, I tell her, and then I think of her baby boy. I say, Maybe any mishap's the work of the devil.

I bring her the sandwich, knowing she will only have a taste, maybe two tastes of it, then smoke her cigarette and drink her drink.

She sits the plate on her lap and looks down at it. Thank you, honey.

I lie across the couch opposite her. That letter was from Mamma, I tell her.

She looks up at me. How is she doin?

I pick at my cuticles. She's in Amsterdam, I tell her.

Gwyn holds up the sandwich and looks at it. That make you sad, sweetie?

I shrug my shoulders. I don't know, I tell her. I guess a little.

Gwyn puts the sandwich down and takes a sip of her drink. Isn't it funny? Her voice is see-through and smoky. She says, *Men* take off like that all the time. But when a woman goes, it just feels so different. She sighs and says, I guess she had to go.

Gwyn has never spoken of Mamma before. I stop picking my cuticles and listen. She swirls her drink back and forth in the glass. It's not my place to say any which way about your mamma, but you were so little and maybe your mamma felt like she couldn't make you secure and safe, like little girls are supposed to be. She must have just known your daddy loved you and wouldn't ever let go. Gwyn smiles at me. Your mamma was a baby herself when she had you. Some young people get a fear in them that they aren't filled up enough and they go out and try to make themselves full up so they don't have to die empty inside.

A plane goes by overhead and she waits on the noise to pass before she tells me, You always think somethin's going to be *the thing* to fill you up. You know, when I was young I took jazz dance at this studio in the Quarter on Saint Catherine. My teacher was a little queer man named Albert Fresky. He called me Heavenly as if that were my name. Gwyn imitates him with her arms out and her voice high. Oh Heavenly, marvelous, what movement, what grace. She laughs. He told Mamma I was going to make it big, so I was always daydreaming about the flowers I would get and my audiences and all the costumes I would wear. And then it was such hard work to get there. So I quit when I got to high school. Plus, by then there were all those boys, and God, they were important. That was when I began to think boys were *the thing*. Gwyn picks up her plate and puts it on the table beside her without taking even one bite from the sandwich. She sighs. You always think you found something that makes you feel like a crowd clapping and flowers at your feet, and then, poof, it's gone. She gestures vaguely at the screen with an unlit cigarette and says, That's why they make you wish on things that blow out, like candles.

While she is lighting her cigarette, I suddenly remember Bo. I stand up casual as I can and say, Miss Gwyneth, I have to run an errand, will you be all right here?

She shakes out her match and blows smoke through the air. Oh honey, she says, I'm going to be just fine.

When I close the front screen, I hear her say, Have a good time. Don't be long now. Her words are drawn out and quiet.

I say back, Okay, Miss Gwyneth, even though I know she doesn't keep time for anything since she lost the baby.

Bo is sitting in his truck waiting for me on the corner of Highway 12. He isn't looking toward the way he knows I will be coming. His browned left arm's across the open window, and he's watching in his side mirror for cars.

When I open the passenger door, he still doesn't look my way. The seat is eating up the heat and stings the back of my legs. Before I have the door closed he tells me to lie down. It's as if he's talking to someone he picked up that he has to bring along like a package. I lie down lengthwise across the seat with the top of my head flush to his thigh and my eyes level with the AM radio.

He starts to pull onto the road without saying anything else to me. I feel the hot sticky seat and look at the Styrofoam cups and the empty cigarette packs on his truck floor. He glances over his shoulder and takes a left. I can feel his blue-jeaned leg tensing to the gas. The sun beats in the passenger's-side window and my body starts to pour out sweat. We have been driving three minutes by the truck's dashboard clock before he asks, You ever been huntin?

I try to look up at his face but can only see his stubbled jaw, tensing and releasing and then tensing again. Sure, I tell him.

Yeah, he says. He glances in his rearview. You know how to track?

I can tell he's mad at me for something. I don't want him to think I am afraid of him. I reach up and bat at that cardboard lady air freshener hanging from the mirror. She waves crazily. No, I tell him, I never really learned how to track.

Oh yeah? he says.

Yeah.

How come?

I shrug, look up at him to see if he will glance down at me. He does not. I don't hunt much, I tell him.

You don't hunt much, he mutters. I can feel the truck turn. We accelerate and hit dirt, my body jounces. The truck gets darker inside with the tree shade on either side of us.

Well, I hunt all the time, he tells me. His voice is steady. The jaw keeps flexing. I know how to track real good, he says. And you know what I think, Haley?

What?

The truck goes faster. I hold the seat and make my body stiff so as not to be tossed forward. Above the noise of the truck's speed he says, I think someone's been goin to the body.

The coppery taste of fear comes into my mouth.

He grips the wheel harder. In fact, he says, I think two people have been goin to the body.

I lie totally still.

And I just want to know, he says. The truck sighs into a skid, road dust clouds up around us, and the world goes silent. He bends his face near mine, his breath so close I can taste it.

Is it you? he asks me.

He studies me hard without blinking, and I feel as if his stare will break me into little pieces. But I don't want to be broken. I know almost as much as he does. He's lost without me. I pick up my right hand and move it toward him. He doesn't let his look follow it. The tip of my finger reaches that jaw, puts itself on the hard, bristled stubble of his chin and then I say, Yes, it was me.

18

FLETCHER

The door to Pops's chambers is closed when I come in, so I stand in front of it, drinking a coffee from Elsa's that tastes like cream and sugar and nothing else. Extra sweet for my sweet, Elsa said when I paid for it. I hate coffee, but I was hoping to run into Haley there. If I'm early and she and Mr. Ellyson are late, I can catch a glimpse of her before she goes into the stables, and that makes me set for the day in the way a strong cocktail makes you set for a boring as hell dinner party.

Julian comes out of the bathroom pushing his mop bucket in front of him. When he sees me he stops, looks at my father's closed door and leans against his mop. Hey there, he says.

I lift my chin in greeting.

He looks both ways down the hall. His black frizzed hair's matted on one side. Where's Miss America? he asks.

I sip my coffee. Robin? I say.

Julian raises his eyebrows. Ah, yeah, that'd be the name her mamma gave her.

She isn't here yet, I tell him.

No? He wheels his bucket out and the door closes behind him. I thought you might know, he says. He pushes the mop up and down. Soapy water slops onto the floor. I guess y'all are gettin real cozy. I saw you goin into the witch's shop last week. He looks up and stares at me. His eyes are bloodshot and tired looking. He says, I called up from that pay phone right there. He points out the window, makin sure you weren't causin no trouble. I would have come visitin but the witch don't like me. He grins wide enough to show me a black gaping hole where his tooth's missing.

I don't say anything. He pulls his mop and bucket behind him, crosses the hall and stands not two feet from me, then leans in so close I can smell his breath. It's like a banana gone by. Let me ask you a question, little Greel, he says. He licks his flesh-colored lips.

I look down at the swirls in my coffee and try to keep my voice steady. What's that, Julian? I ask.

He pushes his head toward me. I lean away from him, but he comes in closer and whispers, You ever dream of gettin a legless lay?

The door behind me breezes open and Julian trips back, the mop falls out of the bucket and puddles water on the floor.

Pops looks down at it. Good morning Julian, he says. Fletcher, would you come in here a minute? We have quite a day ahead of us.

All day we watch the mayor of Tunica dig himself a hole big enough to bury his head and his ass under. Fifteen years back he slept with a black woman named Sadie Hart who got pregnant with his kid. Now he's neck deep in it.

The black woman's got a deep husky voice that doesn't fit her slight frame, and she's hell-bent on getting some help in raising her kid. I don't blame her.

The mayor's wife is dumb as a stick. Pops has to ask one of the secretaries to give her a sweater from the front office because she is wearing a halter with no bra, and her nipples are sticking out like marbles. You could fit two hands in her cleavage and not a slice of paper between her thigh and skirt. She wraps the sweater around her like a cape.

At five thirty, the squeaky-clean lawyer for the black woman stands at the podium for his closing argument. When he looks around, his oiled hair doesn't move. He adjusts his tie and says, I understand the racial and political sensitivity of this case, which is why we're in Fresh County's courtroom instead of Tunica's. Every man has a maggot in his past that will devour his future if he lets it, but this child is not a maggot. He is flesh and blood. Squeaky-clean fists the podium and says, His father is the mayor of the town he lives in. I can't tell you how proud I would be if my father was the mayor. But because this boy is a different color from his father, he's not allowed to be proud. He cannot even tell people who his daddy is, he can't go to lunch with him or enjoy a baseball game. Squeaky-clean looks around expectantly at the eight of us.

I watch Robin nodding quietly to herself. She doesn't stop when she sees me looking.

My father leans back in his chair, takes off his glasses and says, Proceed.

Afterward, the attorney for the mayor gets up and tries to say there is no evidence showing material change in the nature of the child since this case was already decided eleven years ago, and so no more money should be granted. As it stands right now, the woman gets $250 a month.

Pops says, Excuse me, counselor?

Weeble-wobble looks frightened.

My father bends forward and points his glasses at him. Counselor, please tell us something in your closing argument that we can use to help us make a decision here. No material change? This child was four when the case was ruled, he's now fifteen. How is that no material change?

The mayor feels the pulse on his neck while his wife bends down with her folded cleavage and whispers in his ear.

When I look up at Robin, she is smiling at my father.

At a quarter to six, I sit in the judge's chambers watching Pops write. His air conditioner hums behind us and his pen scribbles. Other than that, there isn't any sound. Finally he glances over at me, takes off his glasses and says, You want to go now, son? He smiles.

Anything more I can do? I ask.

He looks back down at his papers and says, Nope.

Pops, I say.

Hmmm?

You ever get scared?

He stops and glances over his glasses at me. Scared? he asks. Of what?

I pick up a pen off his desk and turn it over in my hand. I don't know, I tell him. Scared of making all these decisions. That last guy, he looked like if he had a good .45 in his glove box, he mighta come at you.

The mayor?

No, I was thinking about that guy yesterday in here for domestic.

Aaah, says Pops. He commences writing. Life is one big scare son. You can't stop yourself from saying truth and saving someone's justice because some buster might have a .45 in his glove box. Anyway, I don't know if justice is such a bad thing to die on. He looks up and stares across the room at his door. I guess that's what you have to figure out, what you want to die on and live life accordingly. He pauses, looks down at his desk, turns a page. Truth is a mighty thing, he says, then he waves a hand at me. Go on now, I'll see you eight forty-five tomorrow morning. Or maybe I'll see you tonight.

Gwyneth and Gypsy have driven up to Memphis for the day and Haley's father has gone to Freely's farm north of Holly Springs, where they bring horses in wild and tame them. It takes seven minutes to drive from the courthouse to her house. Once I'm there, she takes me upstairs to her dark shaded room and is wild for me, urgent like someone just loosed from fire. She pulls off my shirt so the buttons pop from their holes and pushes my jeans to my ankles. She lifts her dress with her panties still on and pushes me inside her where she is hot and waiting. When I enter her, everything spins crazily around me. I can feel her underwear like a silk divider and then she is saying my name and my breath is out of me like a kick in the gut. I am pulling myself from her, coming onto her brown smooth belly. Below me her face is red and her lips are swollen. She keeps her eyes closed. Her hair is stuck to her forehead by sweat. She looks beautiful.

I slump down beside her, put my arm around her waist and my face in her wet neck and try to steady my breath, place my palm on my heart to calm the beating. My God, I say. I can feel her beside me, working to calm her own breath.

Before we are all the way slowed down she says, Have you ever only fucked rich girls?

I hold my breath, then let it out in one long stream. What does that mean? I ask her.

She lifts up on her elbow so my hand slides onto the pillow. She looks right into me without blinking. It's just a question, she tells me. Her eyes blink quickly and her chin is turned up.

My temple throbs from thirst. I don't know what she wants from me and wish it were seconds ago, when I was inside her. I pull her head toward to me gently, kiss her and say, Haley, you're the richest girl I ever knew.

She watches me and then she lies down and turns her head away. She starts to peel some paint off her wall. How come it's money that makes you get big, fancy things? How come it can't be something else? she asks.

The sun's coming through the blinds in dusty streaks across her bed and makes my back sweat. I reach a hand there to wipe it off. Like what things? I ask her.

Like I go by your house sometimes, she says while she peels one long strip of paint to a caulked underneath, when you aren't home I go by and look at it and I can tell it's old.

I lie faceup and stare at the ceiling. It is, I tell her. But everyone has old things.

Yeah, she says, but your old things are the ones that matter, they're taken care of. Paint flutters onto the bedspread.

Don't say *your,* okay, Hale?

She turns from the wall and looks at me. Her voice is just a murmur. Why's that? she asks.

Because that makes us separate.

She rolls over, puts her face in my collarbone and drapes her arm over my chest. We lie there in silence and I stare around her room. It has clothes thrown all over the place and riding boots hung on the wall by some string and a nail. She has a dinner plate with crumbs on it on her floor. Her bed isn't made. It smells like Haley in there, this faint smell I can't ever put my finger on.

Finally she says, Daddy and his friends built this house when I was six years old. We lived in a camper in the yard. Mamma would sit in a lawn chair and sing me songs and we'd watch them work and feed them beer and sandwiches when they were hungry. They'd leave after my bedtime when they were too drunk to be useful and Daddy would stay up with a big generator light and work till dawn.

I stroke her arm. That's better than something old, I tell her, something hand built.

She lifts her head and looks at me. I'm sorry I asked you that, Fletcher, about the rich girls. She runs her hand over my stomach. I don't know why I get like that, she tells me. I just want to know, now what? Now that you're all graduated, what are we going to do? We don't ever talk about it.

Be with you, I tell her.

She is quiet, runs her thumb up and down my thigh. No, she says, I mean after the summer.

I don't want to talk about going away, I tell her.

I'm afraid Haley will pull away from me if we talk about it too much, and I can't stand the thought of it. I about stop breathing so as not to talk. Crickets start up out her window.

She talks anyway. You'll go up to college, she says, and you might never come back from there. You might be the next judge of Boston.

She licks my shoulder and then blows on it. I guess I could visit you, she tells me. You could take me to dinner and make love to me in stretch limousines.

She says it as if in all the world that's what she should do, leave me lonely in a strange city, waiting for her to come to me.

I look at my jeans around my ankles, at Haley's wrinkled dress. Underneath it I know the come is hardening on her belly. I want to tell Haley about the sick feeling I have inside me whenever I think of being away from her. I don't know how to talk about it, though, so I don't say anything. Finally for lack of any other words I tell her, Just because my father wants me to judge doesn't mean I'm going to. Plus, I'm not wantin to live in Boston my whole life.

She sits up in bed and looks down at me. You'll have fun, she says. There'll be all different kinds of things to do and you'll meet tons of new people. I'd love to go there, Boston, or anyplace I've never been before.

She climbs over me to get off the bed. I try to pull her back, but she bites my arm playfully and wriggles away.

She stands in her wrinkly dress, flips her hair over and makes a knot with it on top of her head.

I bring my pants up to my waist. I hate meeting new people, I tell her, I'm shy as hell.

She puts her hands on her hips and watches me fumble with my belt buckle. You could send for me, she says quietly. Maybe I could make you hate it less.

She sits down next to me and stares into space. I'm grumpy, she says. Her voice has a childlike whine to it that I haven't ever heard. Looking down at her hands, she says, Before you came along, everything felt kind of useless. Why else do you think I'd have—Haley stops short; she hesitates—done things and been with people I'm not much proud of? She breathes in deep. Now you'll leave, she says, and it will just go back to being that lonely way again. I want you to stay with me forever so I don't have to have that feeling anymore.

When I talk my voice is hoarse. We can do anything we want. You don't have to stay at Banks High, there's other places in the world to go to school. And I sure as shit don't have to go north to college, yet. There's plenty of time for that.

She puts her head on my shoulder and whispers, You think?

Yeah, I say, I do.

I put my arm around her waist and lay her down on her back. She closes her eyes. Putting my chin on her chest, I watch her face. The red is going down in it so it is that golden tan color again. Her eyelashes make a shadow on her cheeks. I try to think what else I could do but go to college and where else she could go besides Banks High, which is hard because I know her father doesn't have all that much money. My mind knots itself around these questions while we lie like that in silence. Finally I lay my head back on the pillow next to hers and let my thoughts go numb. It's some cooler now and a perfect temperature for doing nothing.

Just as I am trailing off to sleep, Haley says, You promised we'd go to the body today. She leans over and runs a finger around my lips.

And I never broke a promise, I tell her. I keep my eyes closed. A wind goes through the tree outside, the sound comforting or lonely depending on which way you are when you lie by it. An audience of frogs begins their bull sound. Why do you always want to go there, Haley?

She waits for a long while. The house creaks with floorboards and ceiling beams settling. Haley says, I got to prove to myself that I'm not afraid.

I open my eyes and look at her. Before I can ask her another question she says, If someone did somethin bad to me, would you kill him?

Like what? I ask her.

She sits up beside me. I don't know, like what if someone raped me?

Her perfect legs are crossed Indian style on the bed. She fiddles with her dress hem.

I imagine Haley getting shoved in the back of someone's beat-up Chevy. Haley would be almost impossible to pin down, but if he did, if he had a gun . . . I picture a man unzipping his fly with a greedy, squirrely look in his eye, sporting India ink up and down his arms. I realize I'm thinking of the guy who was in for domestic last Thursday. The thought makes me feel like I'm going to retch on the carpet.

I'd kill him, I say, without thinking.

Really? she asks. A light comes into her eyes.

It makes me hesitate. If I could, I tell her, I would, I say.

When she kisses me, it is with her tongue in my mouth and her hand on my cock, and I am hard for her immediately before she pulls back, smiles, gets on her feet and tugs at the sheet beneath me. Come on, lazybones, she says, get up.

I stand and shake the hair out of my eyes while Haley opens her door. She goes in the bathroom across the hall and splashes water on her face. I walk to the doorjamb and say, Was that a test?

She turns off the water, takes a towel from the rack and watches me while she dries her hands. What I just asked you? she says.

I nod.

She dries her face and shoves the towel back without looking at me. If you are afraid it was a test, then maybe you aren't telling the truth.

I go over and put my hands on her shoulders. Haley Ellyson, I say. I look in her eyes. I'd do anything for you. That isn't a lie.

She holds my waist and puts her mouth on my heart. I know it, I hear her say against me. That's why I love you.

We walk that narrow snaky trail alongside a row of young pines and Haley says, Isn't that messed up? You can get jail time for stealing food when you're hungry or for killin someone who was a killer. You know what I think? she says. I think jail's stupid anyway, it doesn't stop anybody from doin anything. Feral, she says, as if she is testing the word. I think prison makes men feral. If a person or even an animal is locked up too long, and then they get with too much freedom, they'll go crazy, kill more and rob more. Prison and all, it's the wrong way to do it.

I push back a tree branch to let her pass. You're talking about prison reform, I tell her. You should hang out with my old man.

Haley's silver bracelets I bought for her at Rose's cling against each other while we go. I watch the leather of my loafers, wanting to take them off and throw them in the river along with my dress socks.

We are almost there when Haley runs in front of me on the path, picks up her dress, bends over and moons me. Her ass is round and shining. Before I can get to her, she pulls her panties up and her dress down, giggles and says, That's for later.

From the large catalpa, I can see the pile of pine and creeper, grown up to a shadow of a mound about three feet high. This is the fifth time this summer we've walked this trail, and the woods keep growing around it like a jungle gone crazy.

Haley squats down and looks over at me. Come here, Fletcher.

I kneel down next to her. This is when I always want to tell her we need to tell somebody, that it's an obvious murder. Only I promised her something before I ever knew what she wanted to show me. I said I would keep quiet and not ask her any questions. I promised, and I can't break that promise.

She whispers something I can't hear.

What did you say? I ask her.

It's gone, she says.

What's gone?

The arm, she says.

I stand up and wipe my hands on my pants. The arm? I say. What arm is that?

She stands up, too, comes next to me and looks into my eyes. Her eyes are unblinking and her face has gone white. Didn't you ever notice? she asks. His arm was sticking out of the grave. Just a little nub of one. Now someone's gone and buried that, too.

I hold Haley and kiss the top of her head. I feel suddenly scared. There wasn't any arm, ever. Haley has either dreamt it up or told herself something that isn't true. I don't know what to say and so I hug her in front of that dead body and listen to her breath coming quick and jagged.

At home Pops is sitting on the front porch in the rocking chair holding a drink.

Hello, he says.

I walk up the steps. Hi Pops.

You have a good night? There is a slur to his words a stranger might not detect.

Fine, I say. I jam my hands in my pockets.

It's beautiful out, he tells me.

I don't say anything. The air is stock still, no breeze, just a heavy humidity. He rocks in the chair. I try to think of a thing to say. I cannot. Finally I start toward the door and take a breath in to tell him I am going up to bed when he says, You been with the Ellyson girl most nights?

I stand still. Yes sir, I manage.

He rocks in his chair, takes a sip of his drink. Her mother grew up around here with me, he says. Ann Marie Gorham. He looks back at me. I'll tell you, Banks High was up in flames for her. She was quite a bit younger than I was, but I remember her well. A girl men fought for, that kind of face and disposition. He looks down at his drink and stirs the ice with an index finger. Then Ire Ellyson, five years her senior, married her right after her graduation. About a year later that little girl was born. And what did Ann Marie do but run off on them when that child wasn't more than six years old. I kept thinking she would swing back here and want custody of her, but she never did. Pops shakes his head. Whole town felt sorry for Ire. I don't know that crowd, Elsa's crowd, but I know when a little girl is left alone with her daddy.

A screech owl sounds and Pops looks toward the side yard. He seemed to do a good job, though, Pops says. He's a rough sort, but he's hardworking. That little girl of his was always cuter than a card, but while you were away at school, she got downright beautiful. I used to tell your mother, She's going to be quite a handful, and your mother would always say, She probably already is a handful. He laughs quick and then quiets. Pops gestures toward me. He says, Figures the first time you come home for a while to stay she's the one you find.

I can't find admiration or insult in what he has said. He turns all the way around to face me. I wonder what Ire thinks of you, he says. The judge's son.

I look down at my knuckles and bite the side of my thumbnail. I can taste Haley still in my mouth. I don't think he knows, I tell him.

Pops nods. Well, men like that don't like to be blind, son, it makes them mad as hell. He takes a sip of his drink. Be careful.

Yes sir, I say.

He faces front and starts to rock.

I guess I'm going to go up and get a good night's rest, I tell him.

His right hand lifts in dismissal.

When I climb into bed, I look at the red letters of the digital for a long time, turning from one number to the next. I hear Pops come in and lock the doors. The house goes silent, and I keep an ear out for Haley's whistling. I think about her mother being a beautiful girl, can't imagine how Pops could be in the same town with her and not have wanted her. Maybe he did.

19

HALEY

When I was a little girl, my friend Olivia and I went to the fair every day, sunup to sundown, when it came to town in August. We ate funnel cakes, got sick after the roundup and kissed sixteen-year-old carnival boys behind the food trailers, wishing they would hurry up and kidnap us so we could run away with them.

Houser Banks's fairground is out on old Highway 12 by the fall-apart cement bridge and train trestle. When the fair people come to town, they set up tents and trailers on the grass and then drive into Houser Banks, taking over Elsa's and Square Diner and lounging all over the sidewalk's benches. They stare at us without shyness and snap their gum and smoke cigarettes like it's an insult. The women have seven earring holes to an ear and they go braless in tank tops with shiny words ironed on them. They buy one-load laundry detergent and boxes of tampons and sticks of ice cream they eat in the store before paying. The men have long sideburns and wear fat rings on their fingers and faded tattoos of ship masts on their arms. They buy cases of Pabst Blue Ribbon and cartons of cigarettes and T-shirts off the wall that say *Houser Banks, Mississippi, the friendliest town that never did bite you.* Elsa made them up three years ago just for the fair people, and they cost $10 each.

Even though they all look like they haven't loved or been loved much, and have traveled too long and stayed awake too many nights through, I still want to be one of them. They never have to stay anywhere for long.

Every two days they get to have a new home, living in highway HoJos and rest areas and hauling nine pieces of trailer down the interstate driving toward their next chance to set up bumper cars and dunking pools, pig races, corn dog stands and country dances.

By the second week in August, signs for the fair have been pasted on telephone poles, bulletin boards, Elsa's front door and the Square Diner's window. Fletcher, Crystal, Riley and I pass them by when we ride out to the old bridge on Sunday night. The fairgrounds are on the way there. Fletcher's got his arm around me in the backseat and I am cuddled up to him. I look over at the one lone Porta Potti and the weedy grass surrounded on all sides by a sagging split rail fence that will have to be covered by plastic and raised to eight feet high so no one sneaks in without paying.

The fairgrounds disappear and the road peters out to a gravel drive. Riley lets the car idle, goes and moves the orange sawhorses with the word *Danger* stenciled on them in black. When he hops back in, he takes us through to the end of the road and we park in front of the old bridge under a half-dead oak that's been split by lightning.

Crystal has brought candles, and she wraps their bottoms in tinfoil and sticks them in the grass while I spread out the denim blanket. Fletcher tries to open the wine with the corkscrew on his pocketknife. Riley runs down the grassed slope, tucks his T-shirt in the back waist of his denims and jumps onto the foot-wide cement railing that walls the bridge. A good way below him, the water runs quick and clear over rocks and eddies into caverns along the banks. I stop at one corner of the blanket and watch. He balances on the cement piece and looks down at the river. Putting his hands out on either side of him, he begins to walk.

Fletcher stops turning the cork.

When Crystal looks up from grounding a candle, she gasps. Without a laugh in her she says, Get off there, baby.

But he's too far away from her to hear. He inches his feet forward like someone on a trapeze, his arms wavering in balance. The water rushes below and I watch one buzzard circling the east bank.

Riley White, Crystal says. She takes two steps toward the bridge.

Fletcher goes to stand a little behind her. He's not such a fool that he'll fall, he tells her. He'll be all right.

He doesn't say it firm, though, and his eyes won't move from Riley's feet. Riley makes it to the middle of the bridge where it is broken in two, so he would have to jump to get to the other part of the wall. Beneath him water rushes. He puts both feet together, pulls his arms in and sways. It looks like he is about to jump.

Crystal holds her throat with her hand.

Just when I think Riley is going to try, he leans his body to the right and lets himself fall off the railing to the bridge below, righting himself on a slab of cement and jumping up in the air. When he turns around, he is laughing, and he hops the cement's crumbling holes and the rusty steel bars that hold it and comes running up the grass.

Hey, he says, y'all got that wine open?

Fletcher doesn't move. He is still holding the bottle by its neck, the knife tucked into his pants pocket. Riley walks up and puts his hand to Crystal's waist, she crumples down on her knees and lets her head drop.

Riley looks from me to Fletcher with his forehead wrinkled and then squats beside her. You okay, baby?

In a husky voice Crystal says, You big show-off.

The bridge? He leans into her and tries to get a look at her face. You didn't think I'd fall there, did you sweetheart?

Crystal doesn't look at him. She shrugs.

Riley hugs her head against his chest and pats her hair and says, I wouldn't do that to you.

Picking the knife out of his pocket, Fletcher turns from them and starts walking back toward me, twisting the screw into the cork while he comes.

The night drops out stars and a half-moon. Fletcher pours wine into Dixie cups and passes them around. Lying with his face to the sky, Riley smokes a cigarette straight up so the ash doesn't fall and Crystal leans over him. Riley White, she says, like she's lullabying a child. She traces a finger over his hairline.

He closes his eyes. That river is damn low, he says.

I sip my wine and listen to the water's tinkly sound. We haven't had any real rain since early July and Daddy says farmers will begin to shit bricks soon and then sell them so they can make a buck. Gwyneth is always sitting in her rocking chair with sweet tea that melts its ice for how long she holds it. If the earth would only rain and relieve itself, she says. Her words sound wilted and she puts a hand across her forehead so the bangs stick to one side.

Where'd you get this wine, Yankee? Riley asks.

Fletcher mashes the cork down on the bottle and underhands it over to him. Crystal catches it and looks at the label. It's a blue bottle with curly words all over it.

Riley leans up and looks over Crystal's shoulder. The ash on his cigarette falls. Damn, Judge, all's I know is it's French. We givin ourselves a little taste of the high life?

Fletcher says, It's from our wine cellar. My old man's allergic to grapes. All the wine was my mother's.

Riley looks up at him and nods while Crystal plants the bottle firmly in the grass at her feet. The light of the candles flicker.

When Riley lies back down, Crystal takes his cigarette from him. Smoke exhales in a cloud around her.

Crystal, baby, feed me some of that wine, Riley tells her. When she lifts the cup to his lips, it spills around his mouth and she leans over and licks it off, laughing and kissing him.

Crystal and Riley have gotten careless with their want for each other. She is with us more than not and tells her parents outright lies about when she's working and whose house she's going to. She pours more wine in their Dixie cups and passes the bottle back to us. I drink straight from it. When I dip my head back down, Riley's got his face turned toward me. That's the idea, Ellyson, he tells me. The bottle's more classy than these here Dixie cups, I feel like I'm at the dentist.

I swirl my wine around in my mouth, swallow and say, The opening night of the fair's this coming weekend.

Riley raises his eyebrows. Shit. I hate the fair.

Why's that? Fletcher asks him.

Because, Riley says, lying back down and rubbing a hand along Crystal's spine, it means the summer's almost over.

Crickets clock their sound, and I see one red blinking light over the treeline giving warning to planes.

I want us all to go, I tell them.

Yeah? Riley says with his eyes closed.

Yeah, I say, I love the fair. I wouldn't ever miss it in this whole world.

So be it, says Riley. County fair, Saturday night. These two squires, he gestures to Fletcher with his hand without opening his eyes, will be on the arms of you two ladies.

Crystal watches the candle flame in front of her and for one brief minute something comes into her eyes that makes her seem like a little girl. She looks up. When she sees me watching her, she raises her eyebrows and smiles. Then she turns and kisses Riley on the cheek. He grins wide and says, Thank you, Miss Nash. Thank you kindly.

★   ★   ★

I am not sure if I am dreaming that night when something comes and covers my mouth.

My throat closes. I look up to see Bo leaning over the bed. He has his hand over my mouth. Shh, he says. He sets himself on the side of my mattress. The digital on my bedside reads 1:12. He smells of smoke and whiskey.

Pulling the sheet up to my chin, I lean back against my wall. How'd you get in? I ask. Daddy locks it up tight and sleeps with a shotgun next to him, I tell him.

I know that, says Bo. I helped build this house, and there are more ways than one to get in it. He's quiet for a minute, watching me. That your boyfriend I saw you with tonight? he asks.

My mouth goes dry. Where? I say.

It doesn't matter where, he says. His face is shadowed in the half-moon light, his jaw tenses. We look at each other. I've seen you with him lots of times, he tells me.

When I don't speak, Bo says, That's the judge's son.

I know who he is, I tell him.

He wipes his hand over his face and looks back at me. That your boyfriend? he asks again.

What would you say if he was?

He stares at me, then draws his eyes down the length of my body. He doesn't know what you saw, does he? he asks.

I breathe deep. He doesn't know, I say.

He keeps his eyes on mine and says, He's the one you been going to the body with?

I turn from him and start to peel a loose piece of paint beside my bed. Maybe, I say, but he doesn't know anything. Bo covers my hand with his and brings my arm down to the bed. Paint flutters to the pillow. He takes my chin in his fingers and brings it toward him. I'm not going to argue about some teenager who has a crush on you, he says, but I'll argue about the truth, Haley. Tell me straight, does he know?

Best I can with my chin still in his grip, I shake my head no.

I can tell he is trying to decide lie from truth. Finally he nods, releases his hold on me and takes a glance around the room. He pulls a cigarette and lighter out of his shirt pocket and starts to smoke. His shirt pocket's ripped and I think how men never fix anything. They just use it till it's wore out and then they buy new. It's women who are always fixing.

He smokes, takes his uncigaretted hand and touches my cheek. I watch his face and say nothing. With one finger, he brushes strands of hair off my forehead. It is the most tender he has ever been, and I can't stand it. I reach up and grab his arm as hard as I know how.

He doesn't flinch or move a muscle. Little lady, he says, are you tryin to hurt me? Because it ain't workin.

My grip looses.

You should have learned that by now, he says and smiles. That crooked front tooth gleams. His hand drops from my face. I lean back and watch him flick his ash on my windowsill. He's a do-gooder, he says.

His daddy's the do-gooder, I tell him.

He shrugs. Like daddy, like son. Those people are pampered pansies and the shit of it is, they're the ones makin decisions in the world. They don't know what the hell the stakes are. He shakes his head. And he can't know you, he says.

I lift myself up on my elbows. Why? I ask.

His cigarette is burned low and in a slice of light from the moon, I see the ash fall on my rug. He leans over me and mashes the cigarette out on my windowsill, then moves his face over mine. I don't want to talk about him, he says. I miss you, Haley Ellyson. His other hand goes under the sheet. He rubs my thighs. I been meanin to go out, he says while he touches me, and bury that body good so you won't know where it is anymore. He pushes his face against my neck. It's slicked with sweat. His hand holds my hip. I don't want that between us, he tells me. I want you, Jesus. A dribble of his sweat goes down his hairline. The burden of that dead man ain't yours to have in the first place, he says into my breastbone.

My hands grab his hair. You made it mine, I whisper. And I want you to tell me what all went on.

I ain't telling the family secrets, he says.

Bo you are the family secret.

You're the one came down the stairs that night. He looks up at me with his jaw tight and his eyes narrowed, there's a look to them like he might rise up and slap me. I didn't have nothing to do with that, he says. He licks three fingers and reaches them beneath the sheet, under my nightgown around the hem of my underwear. He starts to slick the folds slowly. A tingled numb feeling goes through me. I wanted to protect your daddy, he says. His fingers leave my folds and go up and rub my left nipple. Then he pulls himself up and kneels on my bed. He pushes himself down so his head is between my legs, his shoulders part my thighs.

On my daddy's land? I grip his scalp. He edges down, puts his mouth over my groin. A hot flush enters me.

The vibration of his voice murmurs into me. I didn't have anywhere to bury it.

How long you been livin in this town? I ask him. Heat rises inside me even though I wish it didn't. You didn't have anywhere else to put it?

His mouth is over my underwear. He sucks me through the cloth. Why don't you forget about that night? he whispers.

My mouth waters. I close my own eyes, a moan comes out. He says my name. I manage to tell him, I can't forget about it.

Oh Haley. He takes his hand from my breast and moves it beneath him. When he lifts his body up some, I see he's holding the swollen outline at the fly of his jeans. Try, he says. He squeezes his eyes shut and puts his hand under my panties.

My pelvis rises to his hand. In my mind I tell it not to.

I watch him fumble with his zipper. I try to still his arm on me, but it keeps on. I won't bother trying, I tell him, I can't.

He takes his penis from his fly. It is gorged and veined and it sticks out from his jeans. He grips it tight, I watch his hand move on himself. The hand on me stays rigid. I try to look away. I say, I need to know, you tell me or I'll tell somebody.

You tell on me, he groans, seizing himself, you tell on your daddy. His neck arches.

Then I lean up and reach for his hand. I grip Bo's forearm as hard as I can. He stops. No, I tell him, wait.

He stares down at my hand.

I can see a glistening piece of liquid on the end of his penis.

He closes his eyes. Fuck, girl, that ain't right to do to a man. He breathes in three times, then looses himself from me, sits at the edge of the bed and runs a hand through his hair.

He breathes deeply. I suppose you want me to tell you the whole goddamn story before you'll let me be with you, he says while he zips up. This your bribe?

Maybe it is, I say to his back. It isn't fair that I don't know it.

He shakes his head, looks at the ground. Life isn't fair, little lady. If life were fair I wouldn't be in this room right now. He turns his gaze to me, takes out another cigarette and lights it.

I straighten my nightgown back over my legs.

Bo turns and squints through the smoke at me. Last spring I made a pickup down south, bought a load of horses for what seemed like a goddamn steal. About two weeks into it, those horses weren't swallowing right and they were dragging and starting to shake. I had been in a hurry to make the sale. They were tested at the border, but the vet was either paid off or it was too early for whatever was wrong to show up. I don't know.

Bo picks something out of his teeth and looks at it. My feeling was somethin had happened on that land, rats or snakes had rotted there. They'd fallen to botulism, and the man we bought from found out it was corroded pasture and sold them to me to get rid of em. I tried to find him, but he ain't anywhere. Down there people disappear like that, Bo snaps his fingers. Anyway, there's not a thing you can do with a horse if they're sick like that without spending money on them. The farm was fixin to lose a heap of cash on them, and I hated to tell Feldman about it.

I was in late one night worryin about it and your daddy had just come around to see if I was goin down to Elsa's. Then like a miracle this Dodge Dually with a thirty-foot stock trailer in back rode up driven by that one-armed black boy from Louisiana, coked up and drunk on whiskey. Bo shakes his head. He said he heard we sold horses and he'd always wanted a horse farm. He had all this loose cash flyin around. That boy was offerin more than you would care to spit at and in a huge rush to get em. So I took him around back, showed him those horses. He hiked them into the trailer with his good arm faster than I could tell him not to without askin for a clean bill of health or anything else. I charged him around a third more than we'd have gotten if they were good. Your daddy and I pocketed the difference and I gave the rest to Feldman. We didn't know how he was goin to ride them anyway with one arm and we didn't know what kind of experience he had with horses, but he wanted them and he paid good money for them and a man in your daddy's shoes with a baby on the way wasn't gonna say no to money. And neither was I.

Bo puts his head in his hands and rubs his face up and down. His voice is muffled. That boy showed up at the stables two weeks to the day later. I was there late again. He came walking up out of the dark, like to scare the shit out of me. Bo looks up and puts his elbows on his knees. His hands are loose between his legs. He said he wanted his money back. Said we cheated him and if we didn't have the money, we should give him all new horses.

I told him no, that we couldn't do that. A sale's a sale. So he went to hollerin about how he was gonna have a bunch of dead horses on his land and not enough money to haul them off with. Said he'd sold his car and his truck and his trailer tryin to care for them and now he was flat broke. He'd hitched all the way up here and when he got back there again, they'd likely be dead.

I told him we weren't drivin eight hours to come get dead horses that he should have known were sick. We fought some and he got maddern rabies and Stony and your daddy were in the apartment and came down to see what in hell was goin on. Stony offered to call the law. So the nigger went off. Or I thought he went off. I went to Elsa's that night. Bo takes out a cigarette and lights it. He smokes quick. I came back to your house with your daddy a while after midnight. We went to take ourselves some beers out of the barn, come back to find that sonofabitch in your livin room. Pretty as a goddamn picture. He hit your daddy in the head with a lead pipe and I had my gun in my boot.

Bo flicks his ash on my rug and sets his jaw and says, He didn't have a vehicle. All's I can figure, he hid in the cab of my truck all night until I got there. Bo spits something out of his mouth onto the rug and kills his cigarette on the bottom of his boot.

I can tell he's done talking. I swallow. My tongue feels swollen. Finally I say, Did Daddy know they were bad-off when you sold them?

He purses his lips. I shoulda known better than to mess with that one-armed, low-life, drugged-out sonofabitch.

I feel sick rise inside me.

Did you tell Daddy something was wrong with those horses?

That nigger shoulda looked at them first. You study horses when you spend money on them, Haley, you know that. A man don't out and buy a bunch of horses in five minutes and haul them away without a thought to it. Your daddy didn't ask a single question either. If he wanted to know so bad he coulda—

I slap him hard against his shoulder blade. Shut up, I tell him. Don't you say a thing about my daddy.

He stands up quick, touches his shoulder and looks down at me. That's the last time you're going to hit me tonight, he says evenly.

Daddy wouldn't have done that. Let those horses rot there in Louisiana. He would have done the right thing no matter how much it cost. You should have told him.

Who has time and money to deal with some sick horses half starved by a nigger? asks Bo.

I swallow hard. Get out of my room, I tell him, get the hell out of here.

Bo turns his head to the side and looks at me. Don't you do that, Haley Ellyson. He points his finger at me and says, I'm one of the ones that raised you.

You didn't raise me, I tell him. Daddy raised me, and I raised myself.

He comes and kneels at the side of my bed, his voice is pleading all of the sudden. I'm the one taught you to ride, he says.

I look away from him. My head feels tight and there's a scream in me too big for my throat. Bo smashes his cigarette on the windowsill. It smolders and dies. Then he moves his hand to my chin and turns it toward him. Hey, his words come quick and quiet, look Haley, I don't mean you harm. Your daddy would have done exactly what I did that night in your livin room.

Then why didn't you tell him? I ask.

And leave two men carrying the burden of some good-for-nothin? It wasn't my fault you walked down those stairs when you did, but I'm glad of it. We saved your daddy from havin to carry it. It's not my fault I'm half crazy for you, either. All right? Listen, he says. He strokes the side of my face. I love you. I'm the one brought you to your first driver's lesson, remember? Let's don't talk about this stuff, it ain't important. Hmm? He moves the hair from my eyes.

I clench my jaw together.

I helped them stitch up your lip that time when your daddy was in Memphis and Dr. Parr came out to the farm. His lips go to my neck and my cheek. Don't tell me to get out, he says.

For the first time in my life, I am afraid of Bo Dickens. We need to stop this, I whisper desperately. I hate it, I tell him. It's making me insane—

But before I can finish, Bo says, No, Haley, I'm the one crazy, no good, in love with my best friend's daughter. Don't hate me, Jesus, just forget all this, it don't matter. Promise you'll forget it. Just—

His hand goes to his zipper. I hear it go down, his voice gets gruff. There ain't nothing wrong with you, he says. It's me, I want you so bad I like to kill myself for it.

My groin feels bruised where he touched it.

He grips his penis and leans his head back. I watch while his hand works up and down furiously. You got to believe me, I'm in for you, he says, wrecked without you. And then he is moaning in the way of a shot animal and his sperm is loose in my room.

When I look over, I see one drip of Bo Dickens leaking like a teardrop down my window.

20

FLETCHER

When I wake up, my dreams loose from me in slippery fragments and my mouth feels dry from the wine we drank at the highway bridge. Then I realize Haley is below my window whistling up to me. Every night I am wishing she would come, a small part of me stays awake in case she does.

I let her in through the back door and inch her up the stairs holding on to her hand. She climbs in my bed beside me. She smells of hot night.

Her voice shakes. You been sleepin? she asks me.

I nod.

She clings to me with an urgency I don't recognize. Her breath is jagged in my ear. I'm sorry, she tells me, I'm sorry I made you go all those times to that body. Do you forgive me?

I hold her and say, What's the matter, Haley? Hale? I try to look at her, but she ducks her head away. Why all that pleading in your voice? There doesn't need to be any sorry between us.

Yes but do you forgive me?

I tell her I do.

She says, Have you told a single soul?

No.

She holds me so tight around my waist I have to catch breath. Her hot tears come running down my chest. I rub her hair and don't ask her what or how come, just let her cry until sleep finds her and then I don't dare move her. In sleep she jerks some and lets out a small sound. I hold her and try to stay awake to keep bad dreams from her. Finally, though, that hungover sleep lays its heavy hand on me.

I dream we are in a school building and I am trying to pay attention in class. Haley is below my desk sucking on me and I can't do anything about my hands gripping the desktop and my throat making sounds. In the next instant my mother is there and we are seated around the den area in Haley's house. Haley asks her why she died, and my mother says, Oh I felt like dying. Dying isn't such a big deal.

I wake up with a start. Haley is turned away from me, curled around herself in sleep. The air conditioner hums. My digital says 4:02. I lean over Haley, watch her face, which is silent except for slight breath.

Suddenly I get it, and feel stupid that I never saw it before, she knows who did it. That body in the woods isn't something she just hunted on. I've come to know this in that gradual way, like you realize a season has come.

It seems like she's sleeping with that secret, clutching it to her as if she's afraid she'll betray it.

21

HALEY

Bo was in my house just five hours before and I am thinking this when I come home from Fletcher's through the sliders at 5 A.M.

Daddy is sitting in his easy chair.

The light is on beside him and yellows his face. We look at each other. I run a hand through my hair. He has a denim shirt on with the sleeves cut off, his neck muscles are tight with mad. You want to tell me where in hell you've been, comin in at five o'clock in the mornin? he asks me.

I swallow.

He stares at me long with his eyes narrowed, then grips the arms of his chair and says, I'd started to trust you, Haley, but I see I can't let my guard down at all. Now go to bed. I'll see you at seven.

At seven, I push my snooze button so many times I only have five minutes to dress. When I come out, Daddy has already started up his pickup. I go toward the Ford. He leans out and yells, Haley, you're ridin with me today.

I hoist myself to his passenger's seat and shut the door.

Daddy drives without speaking. He looks in his rearview and then back at the road. The street is empty. I lift a hand toward the radio to turn it on. He catches my wrist and I pull back, stare out the window at the golden light of morning, rising between the trees.

Who were you with?

Friends, I say. I look out at the black ribbon of Highway 12.
Which friends?

I sigh in. What is it you're getting at, Daddy? I can feel the tiredness in
my voice. Need for sleep aches my eyelids. I think of Bo doing what he
did at my bedside and a cold enters my belly.

I saw them out at the river yesterday, Haley, Daddy says. I saved Riley
from getting his ass kicked and saved that black girl from God only knows
what. They were baring all get-out for the world to see, having a go at it
in broad daylight, and I broke off some boys on the path who'd seen his
car parked and were aimin to find out where he was.

I clench my teeth together and say nothing, watching the kudzu going
by at fifty miles per hour.

You been goin out with them at night, Haley? Answer me or I'll pull
it out of you.

Those are my friends, Daddy.

Yeah, well they aren't the only people to be friends with in Houser
Banks and if friends do dumb things, then you stop hangin around them.
They've been told by Sheriff Hill. There's people ain't happy with it and I
think you ought to just stay away for now.

I am quiet. Daddy's got an old warped and beaten gun magazine on
the floor, and I read every word on the cover so as not to pay attention to
the silence between us.

Daddy brakes at Courthouse Square and sits looking at his hands on
the wheel. Then he turns right, toward the stable road. I can see we won't
be going to Elsa's this morning. Finally he says, You don't have a careful in
you. I'd leave you alone if I thought you wouldn't get yourself in a heap
of trouble. What is so great about Riley White that you need to be with
him and that girlfriend of his? I think Greel's son is fine, he seems like a
nice kid, and his daddy's a decent sort, but Riley isn't takin heed the way
he needs to.

I keep my eyes on a hornet bothering the front window. When we get
to the stable drive, some of the men are already at the top of the hill, getting out of their cabs. Mist rises over the Feldman field. Two horses are in
the front field, nuzzling each other's neck in midrun.

Billy saw you with your heads out the Roadrunner the other night on
Uni Park comin from East Neigh, Daddy says as he crests the hill. Don't
be dumb. That girl needs to leave it alone and so does Riley.

I am not dumb, I tell him. If it isn't one thing, it's another. You got the
mind to drag me off the backs of boys' pickups and now you are onto

telling me who I should be friends with, that the color of their skin could matter, and I don't believe in all that shit.

Daddy slows the truck and pulls over on the grass before we get to the parking area. He looks over at me. Don't sass me, Haley, I'm telling you it ain't safe. You think the people who want to kick them around some ain't serious? They won't be kind again, and I won't be there next time. You could be with them and who the hell knows what could happen.

Fuck those people, I say soft but firm. Fuck all your big-assed men friends think they know right from wrong.

His words come slow. What did you say?

I look over at him, and he is staring at me, his mouth is a thin white line. I can't look at him long and stare instead at the seat between us.

Don't use those words, Haley, he says. You can't just say forget it, you got to find out how dangerous some situations are and how to avoid getting hurt.

I lean my head back on my seat and say, Oh, you don't have dangerous friends, Daddy? Yeah, your friends are as safe as Betty Crocker.

He bangs his hands on the steering wheel. Haley Ellyson, goddamn it, I'm trying to be straight up with you. Trust me on this one. Those boys didn't have no business being out there looking for them, but it don't matter whose business it is. If Riley won't listen to reason, then you can at least stay away from him.

I don't want to stay away from him, I tell him. I start to open the door, but he grabs my arm. Daddy hasn't ever grabbed me so hard. My eyes water.

Close that door, Haley.

I see Stony walking to the field with two buckets of water off both arms. He's eyeing us. I don't close the door. I stare straight ahead at the shiny silver of the glove compartment's lock, cross my arms over my chest and look out.

He says, I raised you, and I kept a roof over your head and food on your table and you ain't gonna tell me about my life and not mind yours. Do you hear me?

Those folks up there are wonderin what you're doin stopped here, I say.

I don't give a damn what those folks up there are wonderin.

I think of the times Bo has ridden around in this cab drinking whiskey with Daddy, laughing and telling stories and all the time thinking of what it is like to get with me. You don't know the whole of it, I tell him.

You want to tell me some, then?

No.

Well, then, he says, pushing the gearshift into drive, you play by my rules. He starts up the road with my door still open. I lean over and shut it, and we come to the fence and park. He sits for a minute and looks over at me. I don't look back. I stare out over the front field and watch Daisy slop her nose in the water bucket. Seeing her makes me want to cry. I will myself not to until my head throbs from it.

Daddy's words come out in a rush, spilling forth like he can't stop them. You're just like your mamma, stubborn as a rock, not a careful in you. He shakes his head, starts to say something more and stops.

I stay perfectly still. My breath stops while I wait for him to take it back.

He doesn't. He reaches out and opens his door, pulls himself out of the cab and closes it with a slam. In the passenger's-side mirror I watch him raise a hand to the men who call to him. Bo isn't there.

My limbs are heavy and my eyes sting. I can't face Christina and Emmy and those others who are doing the brushing and the feeding, lifting saddles to ride. I am too sick inside about what happened with Bo last night and Daddy being so mad about the wrong thing. I can't go in there. I watch the men in the mirror. Two hounds circle them and then flop down in the dirt. The men open their gathering for Daddy and he stands with them, his back turned to me. My stomach twists and my temples go to beating with the words I want to shout and am not allowed to say. I push my body over to the driver's side and turn the key over, crank the truck and begin to back it out.

In the rearview mirror, Billy Towle points a cigaretted hand in my direction and Daddy turns to look, then starts running. He reaches the truck and holds on to the window while I drive. Jesus H. Christ, Haley Marie Ellyson, stop this truck. My foot is on the accelerator and it doesn't stop for him. He is running behind me, his hand grabbing at the tailgate. Then he is staggering and I am going down the hill as fast as I can, the dust billowing in back of me. In the rearview mirror, I see Daddy slam his coffee cup down on the ground and kick the dirt with anger.

22

FLETCHER

The courthouse sweats with heat. Pops turns again to the man seated at his left and asks, Mr. Murray, why do you need to go back to the house?

I got a TV set, a box spring and a mattress. I got some clothes in the closet and the blender's mine, he says.

The woman across from him stands up. He don't own that, she says. He don't own none of it.

Mrs. Murray, Pops says quietly, it is not your turn to speak. Please sit down.

She lowers herself into her chair.

Lakiesha Murray is twenty-two years old. Her husband James Junior is twenty-four. They come from East Neigh.

James Junior shrugs his shoulders and says, The woman wants y'all to believe they're hers. I say they're mine. Who you going to trust, Judge? She kick me out in the street without so much as the shirt on my back.

The man's suit is a few sizes too large. While he speaks, he jerks the material from his wrists in a motion like a broken machine.

It was my understanding she gave you three months to get out, Pops tells him. It's what you yourself stated when you first arrived.

Mr. Murray smiles sheepishly, one gold tooth in front gleams. Three months, yeah, he says, but then I got some things to take care of and it came all of a sudden. His eyebrows flick up and down while he speaks.

Judge, can I talk a minute? asks Lakiesha Murray.

My father sighs. In a tired way he says, What is it?

The woman's fingers are long and when she talks, they talk too, fluttering like birds wings. He don't own a goddamn thing, she says. Don't matter if he took six months to get out of that house, nothin in it is his. He don't own the TV or the bed or the blender or . . . nothing.

Pops turns and asks James if he owns these things.

James purses his lips, his eyebrows go crazy. No sir, not exactly, but I—

Mrs. Murray looks at Pops. I worked for four years to see him piss away liquor on my livin room couch and ain't nothin on God's earth belong to him. She points her finger at her husband. Why even that suit he's wearin is borrowed. She moves her hand from pointing to sleeking down the back side of her dress, then she sits. James looks down at his suit.

Pops laughs softly. He leans back in his chair. Well now, James Murray Junior, you borrow that suit?

Aah, James says, yes sir, mattera fact I did.

And do you or do you not own anything in the house where Mrs. Murray resides?

James puts out both hands the way a homeless man asking for a handout would. His palms are white next to his face. Well sir, he says, in a manner of speaking—

My father leans his torso forward, takes his glasses off and says to James, Yes or no?

James bows his head. No sir, he says. A cloud passes from the window and shadows lift in the room.

Thank you, my father says. He stacks the paperwork in front of him like a deck of cards. Is there anything else, Mr. Murray?

James inspects a thread coming off the suit's elbow. No sir, he says quietly.

Pops clears his throat. Mrs. Murray?

Her voice is barely a whisper. She says, No sir.

My father bangs his gavel. James Murray, by order of the court you must abide by the requests Lakiesha Dane Murray has spelled out. Pops goes over the rulings one by one. He takes off his glasses and says, I have no reason to believe that any property residing on 45 Sipsey Drive in East Neigh belongs to you. The papers will be in the mail Monday morning and you should sign them and have them back here, preferably hand delivered.

While he is talking, Lakiesha lets go the grip on the table and lays her hands in her lap. Her back curves, the shoulders bend forward slightly.

James Murray Junior unbuttons one jacket button of his blazer and wipes his arm across his forehead.

Back in his chambers, Pops asks me if I will go down and get the Smith versus Smith file in the storeroom, August 1985 divorce files, and bring it up for him.

Sure enough, I tell him, and go through his office door down the stairwell.

The cellar stairs smell like mold and the cement is cracked. I turn on a light to my right and one bulb shines on the cellar's hallway.

When I get in the file room, it takes my eyes a minute to adjust to the room's dim light. Stacks and stacks of fireproof files stand along the walls in rows.

I see the back of her wheelchair first and then Julian standing before her, his pants unbuttoned around his thighs. Her mouth is on his cock, pumping up and down. His eyes are half lidded and his jaw's slack. He looks once at me and then closes his eyes and lifts his face to the ceiling. Don't stop, he moans. His body shakes and his hands grip her head. I stand at the door and watch while he comes. She keeps her mouth on him. Then his body relaxes as if all his muscle is liquid, and he pulls away from her. I watch Robin wipe her mouth with her sleeve while Julian zips his fly with the hurried gesture of a man who's just pissed outside. He looks at me, his voice is gruff. You want to get the hell out of here?

Robin whips her head around and sees me. A horrible look of humiliation comes across her face.

I'm ashamed I've stood for as long as I have, paralyzed by the sight of them, and I shut the door quickly, ducking into the side bathroom, where there's a wide industrial sink, a urinal, two stalls and no toilet paper. I get in one stall and sit on the toilet seat trying to make my mind see nothing at all. But it is always her moving head and Julian's face.

The bathroom door opens. When I come out, Julian's bent over, spitting phlegm into the urinal. He looks at me in the grimy mirror facing him. I got a bad cold, he tells me. Always happens this time of year.

What in hell do you think you're doing with her? I say.

You think I don't touch her? he asks me. He wipes his forearm across his nose. She likes the smell of a basement when she gets it, he tells me. Makes her hot.

I look down at his big, empty hands. Then I am fast on him and have his head in the only wrestling move I ever knew. His feet shuffle beneath him. Sonofabitch, I say. I pull up tighter and he wheezes. When I slam him against the urinal, his legs buckle so I am holding his weight in my arms. You touch her again, I tell him, I'll make sure you're sent to the slammer on charges so tough it'll make your head swim, you understand me?

I throw him back and he lands sprawled out on the floor, his nostrils flaring. I stand above his huge form with my muscles ready. A cold, creeping fear crawls up my scalp. I glance at the door, then back at him. He rolls all the way over on his back, looks up at me and points his finger at my face. Between clenched teeth he says, Kid, if you weren't your daddy's son, you'd be a dead man.

I breathe in and watch him while he comes up to sitting. His eyes don't leave my own. They are mean eyes, the color of nickels. His face has turned a pale yellow with red splotches up and down his neck. He tries to steady his breath and says, That girl and I touch each other, little Greel, that's all there is to it. He puts his knees up and dangles his hands between them. He is a huge folded man, sitting like that. I can feel the sore spots where he struggled against me. He stares at the floor. You got a lot to learn, he says without looking up. One thing is, don't go juttin your skinny little honorable head into other people's business.

He blocks one nostril with his pointer finger and blows snot out the other one onto the dirty linoleum, then moves his eyes up and looks at me. The other thing is, you ain't gonna change nobody's world but your own. One strand of shiny mucus gleams on his top lip.

When I come out the front door of the courthouse, Robin is wheeling away on the sidewalk toward the street. I come up behind her. Robin, I say.

She keeps going.

I flatten my hair with my palm, tuck my shirt in and start after her. Somehow she knows it. Don't follow me, she yells back.

Listen, I call after her. Hey . . . I'm sorry. She keeps wheeling away as if she hasn't heard me. I stand there, feeling like an idiot. I don't know why I am trying, I can't think of a thing I would say to her, anyway. Except that I hope it isn't always like that for her. Some moldy basement room with someone like Julian.

When she gets to the street, she stops and turns to look for cars. Her eyes squint from the sun.

I jam my hands in my pockets and watch her cross to the other sidewalk. At the shop door, Rose comes out and waves to me. She pauses to see if I'll come toward them, but I shake my head, and they disappear inside.

23

HALEY

I stay with Gypsy through the following week after my fight with Daddy because Gwyneth says we both need some separate time. Gypsy has a pullout in her back den with a TV in front of it and real photos of old movie stars with their signatures that she got out of a Memphis bar when it closed up. She has two little dogs named Chip and Skippy, who bark at six in the morning to go out and sleep in beanbag chairs that rustle in the night. I miss my own pillow and my room and the box I look at before bed to help me sleep and Gwyneth's Crystal Gale record. I am homesick for Daddy, but more I am stubborn and cry myself to sleep wishing he could see my point of view and let me be.

On the phone Gwyneth says, Come on home during the weekend, honey, he's always more relaxed on the weekend, he'll be better then. You two love each other so bad you're about to rip your hair out for it.

I tell her I will be home after the fair Saturday night.

At the fair, men's hats line the fence waiting for them to come off the roundup ride drunked and dizzy. The controller's an Indian, he's got his blue-jeaned leg up on the platform. On his feet are green cowboy boots and his hair's back in a ponytail, silky and black as a piano key. He looks over at me without shame, chewing his gum slowly.

I smile at him. Hey, I say.

Missus, he says. He tips the brim of an imaginary hat.

Haley Ellyson, Crystal hisses, ain't you got no taste? She licks her candied apple with a bright red tongue.

It isn't him, I tell her, it's that kind of person who fascinates me.

I turn and watch the teacup ride slowing. Don't you ever wonder what it would be like to join the fair? I ask her.

Crystal shakes her head so the braids sway. I can't think of things like that, she says. I got to think practical. Like what will get me out of East Neigh, by how many hairs on my chinny-chin-chin will I be able to escape it.

And go where? I ask her. We pass babies in strollers and kids in baseball caps and women using deep voices to sell Polish and Italian sausages with peppers and onions for a buck twenty-five.

She shrugs. I don't know. Light shines off her candied apple when she turns it. Maybe I'd like to go up north to Chicago. Somewhere I could live as free as I want.

And sing? I ask.

Yeah. On the side I could work at a school, teach chorus and voice. I'd get up a band. We could play at cozy bars and blues clubs on the weekends.

Mmm, that sounds nice, I tell her. I'd come and watch you.

A skinny man with glasses thick as bottle bottoms shouts out at us, Quarter wins a game. He has about three teeth and hair so greasy you could slick a pig with it. Race your horse to the finish, he calls. First across the line gets the prize. Hey, come on up, pretty ladies. What about you, darlin? When I look up, he's watching Crystal. You want to race a horse? he asks her. More fun than a midget in your pants. He cackles gruesomely.

Crystal looks back at him with her eyes narrowed.

Ooh, hey pretty baby, he says, why don't you mount my horse?

At the chain-link fence next to the Ring-a-King, Crystal fishes around in her pocketbook for a pack of Virginias. She sets one between her teeth and lights it, then pats the smoke away with her hand. I take the cigarette from her and drag off it. We watch an Uncle Sam on stilts do circles in front of a group of sticky-faced kids.

They got some nerve, says Crystal, calling that white-haired, pink-faced, tacky old crony my uncle. She giggles.

I give Crystal her cigarette back and feel a hand on my shoulder. When I turn around, an ashen-faced man with rubbery skin breathes into my face. He smells like garbage down your sink and wears a dirty green uniform of someone who pumps oil into houses. There's a scared feeling in me like when an elevator stops for some time between floors.

He belches and leans closer. I need to tell you somethin, he says.

Sir, I tell him, you got the wrong girl. Me and my friend here were just leavin to find our boyfriends—

You listen to me, the man says. His neck hangs loose as a turkey gizzard. He works his whiskered mouth, I got a son who done kilt himself down by Oger's Brook. You know where Oger's Brook is?

Yes sir, I tell him.

The sonofabitches took me in say, That your son? It damn near looks like him, but I ain't sure. I made them show me near fifteen times. I tell them I weren't sure. My brother's first wife had to come and she said, Sure nough. You wanna know what else? A piece of spit hangs from his bottom lip.

What? I breathe through my mouth.

I got a daddy did the same thing, cut up his wrists with barbed wire. Wife did the same thing, lectrocuted herself with a hair dryer. I got to take in young uns not so much as toilet trained. Oncet the boy in Oger's Brook and two baby girls got theirselves pregnant.

A sunburnt man comes ambling out of nowhere with overalls on and bare feet. Under one arm he is holding a live baby lamb. His bicep is covered by a tattood sailboat. Hey Artie, he calls. His eyes look like two BBs punched into his face. You bothering this young lady? He pries Artie's hand from my shoulder and smiles at me with wide gray teeth. I do apologize, missy. You have to excuse this here Artie, my best cousin-in-law.

Still mumbling, Artie lets himself be turned around into the man's armpit. You come with me, the overalled man says. He looks back at me and winks. Artie spits. Part of it lands on his boot. He squats down and rubs it in so it shines the dirtied leather.

We watch them go. Putting out her cigarette on her sandal bottom, Crystal says, Some of the craziest people in this world.

Uh-huh, I say and shiver involuntarily.

It scares me so bad, says Crystal. That man, she gestures the way the men went, he was probably real regular before all that bad stuff happened. Crystal's voice is soft and has sweetness in it. That could happen to anyone, she says.

We start to walk between the trailers, stepping over utility cords. The grass is browned and already littered up with candy wrappers and ride tickets and rolled cardboard from cotton candy.

I told Pappa I didn't want to go back to Banks High this year, she says. What did he say? I ask her.

He was a little mad, but Pappa's real softhearted. It's Mamma who's the tough one and she was in Montgomery. Course Pappa tried to tell me why I should go, but Pappa'll listen if you ask him to. I told him best I could that to be with my own people would make me strong even if the book smarts weren't as good. He was real proud of me for saying that. His eyes got all wet. Crystal moves her braids back with her hand and steps over a trailer hitch. Those boys, Crystal nods her head around as if she were talking about all the men at the fair, they were botherin me before Riley started comin for me. Now they bother me in a different way, out of school. I want to get away from it.

We go out into a main aisle that has rides lining it. Beside the Tilt-a-Whirl Crystal stops. I turn so we are looking at each other. The bells and zaps and whistles of the rides come down around us.

Crystal says, I haven't told Riley this but I'm gonna tell my family about him. I hate the lyin. She looks at her sandal bottom, a bubble gum spot is pressed into it. She brushes her foot over the grass to get the gum out. I never lied to Mamma and Pappa before I met Riley. She looks past me and her eyes dart around the fair. I just decided, if Houser Banks isn't gonna welcome me, why not welcome Riley to East Neigh? She looks at me and her eyes are wide and hopeful. I'm gonna quit the Jitney when school starts so Hannaford and them can't come botherin me there. Mrs. Tiler said I could work this after-school program in East Neigh doing singin and art down in the Baptist church basement.

How do you think your parents will be about Riley? I ask her.

Crystal shrugs and watches a small boy selling giant lollipops. When she looks back at me, she is smiling. I think I been underestimatin them and Riley. She talks fast. I love him, they gotta understand. Anyway, girl, Riley is so damn likable, he could make friends with anybody. I think he gets on better with us than he does with his own. Those boys at Mamma Hatchey's accept him right in. He could charm himself into anybody's family, black, white, she laughs, purple. Crystal starts walking again and grabs my arm. I think it's a good plan, she says. Her fingers are warm on my elbow and her voice is singy-songy. Anyway, Haley, she says, I got to pee-pee. Do we have time to do that before we meet them?

The bathrooms are behind the slide, I tell her. I just saw them.

In the coming darkness, Crystal and I scurry under strung Christmas lights and American flags to find the Porta Pottis.

★   ★   ★

When we get to the Ferris wheel, Riley is bullshitting with the control man. Crystal starts to jog forward. You got any gold pieces? she calls back to me.

I hurry to catch up. Why?

Cause that's the only way Riley's gonna get what he wants.

Riley's standing on one foot and then the other, talking earnestly to the man who has a lazy hand on the control stick and isn't looking at Riley at all.

What's he after? I ask her.

That boy, says Crystal, slowing to a skip, wants us to ride lonesome on that thing, I bet. And he hasn't got enough money on him for a bribe.

Riley trades a pack of Camels and Fletcher's leather belt for us to ride by ourselves on the Ferris wheel.

We ride in back of them, and I watch Riley swinging their ride car in front of us. Crystal shrieks and grabs him by the neck. Fletcher puts his arm around me and points out Houser Banks and the flats of cotton and corn going toward Taylor. He shows me how the lights of the fair make a horseshoe. His hand is cool in mine. When I kiss his neck, he murmurs something into my hair.

What did you say? I look up at him.

He pushes a hair from my forehead. I said, I am in love with you.

I kiss him, long, on the neck and he holds my thigh. His head tips back. While the Ferris wheel swoops and circles and swings us through lights and merry-go-round music, the earth swims beneath us.

When the ride ends, we buy ice cream from a truck and boiled peanuts out of a machine and play eight ball pool and basketball. We ride the Sizzler and after it, Riley pays the Fool-the-Guesser $2 to guess Crystal's weight. Fool-the-Guesser is big around as he is tall and he pulls at his black mustache while he talks, bouncing up and down on his feet. Okay, batter up, batter up, batter up, weight within three pounds.

Cocaine addict, Riley whispers to me.

You're a strong girl, slender, well built, says the Guesser to Crystal. Let's see, I'm a gonna say one eleven. One eleven it is, step right up on the scale.

I don't want to get on no scale, Crystal says. She backs away and ducks her head, smiling at Riley.

Hop on the scale if you want to win a prize, says Fool-the-Guesser.

Squatting in front of her, Riley puts his arms around Crystal's thighs, picks her up while she squeals and places her on the scale. She giggles and parts her braids so she can see the numbers.

Well I'll be pickled in a barrel, says the Guesser. One twenty-one.

Crystal jumps into Riley's arms and says, I won!

People walking by stop and stare and the Guesser says, Where do you buy your shoes at? I shoulda made you take off them shoes.

For a prize, Crystal picks a stick that has a smiley-faced balloon on the end of it.

We ride the twister and the swings and then Crystal says no more rides or she will get sick.

In the fun house, the floors are tilted and turn around on us, the mirrors make us look eight feet tall and eight feet wide and we laugh at one another and at ourselves and Crystal gets stuck in the barreled hallway, so Riley has to go in there and drag her out.

Let's go in the tents, I tell them when we come out.

What you want to go in there for? asks Riley. They smell like pig shit and horse piss.

I grab Fletcher's hand. That's why I like them, I say.

Crystal links her arm with Riley's. Come on baby, she says, half the fun of a fair is the tents.

Riley's shoe toes drag on the ground. He looks at the tent, then around him. I'll stay out here, he says, and smoke a cigarette.

No you won't either. Crystal pulls him in by the wrist.

In the tents people sit around in lawn chairs wearing muddied rubber boots next to metal barrels full of manure and feed and hay. Freckled and sunburnt kids lie across coolers. The ones who take riding from me call, Hey Miss Ellyson. One of them leans into her mother and says, That there's my riding teacher.

I know it, her mamma says. She nods to me, looks right at Crystal and says, Haley how you doin?

Feed sells for twenty-five cents out of bubble-gum machines stacked with grain and we hand it to the llamas and camels and Scotch Highlands they've brought in from the zoo. Their tongues are warm and soft against my palm.

On account of Riley, we don't stay in the tents long, and when we come out, he insists he needs to play the rifle game. He makes us wait through six tries, killing the red star twice with one hundred bullets each out of a copper tube they won't let him save for a souvenir. The first win he gets a stuffed puppy for Crystal and the second one he chooses a red-

and-white striped chimney-pot hat for himself. Fletcher holds me around my waist with his chin to my head and I can feel him vibrating with laughter when Riley puts the hat on.

We get our picture taken at the old-time-photo booth. Fletcher and Riley duck behind a curtain set up for the purpose, and they come out in bullet vests with Jack Daniel's bottles in their hands and holsters slung around them and cowboy hats on their heads and chaps on their legs and rifles under their arms. They swagger and pretend to draw their guns and paint handlebar mustaches on each other while Crystal and I dress in shawls and feather caps and velvet garters and puffy bloomers and lace gowns. We curtsy. I lift my skirt so Fletcher can see my garter and Crystal hides behind an ivory-colored fan and sneaks looks at Riley.

The unsmiling man who runs the booth is bald as an egg and arranges us in the frame of the camera. Say, Cheese, he tells us. He's grim faced and surly.

While we are getting dressed, the photo develops. We each buy one and I stare at mine for a long time while we walk through the fair. Fletcher holds my elbow so I don't bump into anything. In the picture, the four of us look ageless and wild. Riley and Crystal are in the back. Riley has two fingers up behind Fletcher's head and Crystal has her head against Riley's shoulder. Fletcher is looking sidelong at me, and I am looking straight at the camera, with a daring smile, even though the man told us to keep our expressions deadpan.

We stand watching the crowd, waiting for the demolition derby to start in half an hour. I'm about wore out, says Riley. Let's go to the country tent and sit awhile, see if they'll sell us some beer.

The white flaps on the music tent are down on all four sides, so you can see only slivers of light at the seams. Riley leads the way and we duck in.

Onstage there's a woman in a cowboy hat wearing a glittery blue suit. She's singing twangy country. One man's on banjo and the other one has a harmonica. People sit around wooden spools drinking beer out of plastic cups and patting their denimed thighs to the music. Sing it on, Debbie, they yell to the lady.

Daddy is there.

It is too late to turn around. He's watching me and he isn't smiling. I look at the stage and steel myself for Daddy's being mad as hell seeing me there with Riley and Crystal. Out in public.

Well I'll be goddammed, Riley says, taking off his chimney-pot hat and leaning toward me, ain't that your daddy?

Behind me I feel Fletcher stiffen.

Riley says slow and low, He looks mad as shit.

T. Fingerling and Billy Towle are at his table. They sip their beers and look in our direction. Daddy pushes his chair away from the table and gets up slowly. Billy and T. watch him. Fletcher's hands are on my hips. He tries to take them away, but I stay them with my own hands and keep my eyes on the country singer. Daddy begins to walk toward me. I try to breathe steady. It comes rough-cut and irregular.

Riley whispers, He don't look happy.

Even when Daddy is standing in front of me, I don't look at him, I look around him at the stage.

You want to come outside? he asks me in a low voice.

I don't answer. The singer is singing with the banjo man, *We got married in a fever, hotter than a pepper sprout* . . .

Haley, Daddy says. His voice is half pleading and half angrier than brimstone.

Crystal shifts next to me. Fletcher's hands are perfectly still at my sides. People rock in their seats, clap their hands against their legs.

Daddy grabs my arm and says, Come with me.

I try to pull back, but he holds steady. When I look at him, his eyes are angry, his lips are a tight line.

Let go, I tell him, let go or I'll yell—

To hell you will, says Daddy.

You think I won't?

You won't young lady or I'll—

Get off me! I yell.

The heads of the people at the back of the tent turn, their feet slow their tapping. Daddy drops my arm fast. A guy unfolds himself from a table, and I see it is the overalled man who had been carrying that lamb awhile back and who saved me from Artie. The woman he is sitting with tugs at his elbow, but he gets loose of her. His walk is heavy and his arms hang from him like sanded weights. He stares down at Daddy and gestures toward me. Hey, he says to Daddy, you givin this little lady a hard time?

Daddy ignores him, his eyes narrow while he watches me.

A crimson color rises on the man's neck and fills his face.

Sir, I say, don't worry about— But before I can finish, the man pushes Daddy's right shoulder. Fletcher takes a step forward and holds me against his belly. Daddy turns to the man and I see his fists clench.

The man says, I *said,* you givin this little lady a hard time?

Mister— I say.

Daddy hits him in the face. The sound is like a saddle being slapped on the back of a horse. The man reels and before he has instinct to defend himself, Daddy hits him again, this time in the throat. The man falls against a table where two people jump up to get away. Their drinks spill and the man drops to the ground between two chairs with his hand to his throat, his eyes bulging. The woman he was sitting with pushes her chair over and runs to him. T. and Bill come on either side of Daddy who turns to go. Before he opens the tent flap he says to me, You see how you hurt a man?

Billy and T. follow him.

I stand like nothing happened. People turn to look at me and then look away, trying to pretend they aren't interested. The overalled man is struggling to get up. I'll kill that sonofabitch, he says in a wheezy voice.

There seems to be a little commotion out there, the singer tells us. It's too early for brawls to start, let's all get a happy drunk. She turns her back to the audience and drinks water from a glass on top of her amp.

Billy shoots his head back in the tent. Haley, for Christ's sake, you wanna come out here and apologize to your daddy? He looks at Fletcher, who holds my waist still.

In the most level voice I can manage, I say, You can tell him I choose my own friends, and if he wants to criticize, he might look to his own first.

Billy rubs his eyes with two fingers, shakes his head and leaves the tent.

With the help of his wife, the overalled man manages to get up, and he fights with her to get toward the tent flap. Leave it alone, Jimmy, she says, we can't go nowhere without you gettin yourself all skinned up. She takes him to the back where they're selling drinks. He gulps three plastic cups full of beer, brings his fist down on the plywood bar and says something I can't hear. I know it most likely has to do with how he'd like to finish Daddy off.

Fletcher keeps his hands clasped around my belly while we stand through a song. Twice the country singer blurs in front of me while I will myself not to cry.

Ellyson, darlin you gonna be all right? Riley asks me.

When I nod my head, I hear Crystal telling him to let me be for now.

Daddy doesn't come back in the tent and finally Fletcher leans into me and says, You want to leave?

I turn and then we are all four out into the fair again. Daddy isn't around. Corn husks and Coke cups and chicken sticks pile out the garbage buckets and the loudspeakers call out rides in whiny, staticky voices. Everyone's skin looks ghostlike under red and yellow and green lights.

We walk without direction past the giant yellow slide and the free circus and mini Indy and China Dragon. Game guys holler at us without conviction. Fletcher holds my hand.

Haley, girl, calls Riley, you say the word if you want to get on out of here.

We stand in front of the merry-go-round watching the horses go up and down with wild expressions on their faces, their tails in frozen movement.

Fletcher turns to me and says, You want me to go on one of those horses with you? We could ride double.

Yes, I tell him.

When the ride stops, we mount a purple one. It is statued in midgallop with its eyes rolled up in the sockets. We turn around and around under the sea of lights. The horse moves up and down, and I close my eyes. Fletcher places a hand between my shoulder blades and rubs back and forth. When the ride stops, I don't get off, and I hear Fletcher paying the man for another ride. This time I go by myself and pretend I am on Daisy. I put my body across it and my cheek against the cool of its neck and hold the ears.

It is past midnight when Riley drops me off at the Clarendon inlet. Walking toward our house, I see Bo's truck. I crouch down when I get to the front screen. The card table is set up and the boys and Daddy and Gwyn are sitting around it. Bo's chair is tipped. The toes of his boots are steadying his balance on the floor and one hand is gripping the table edge. He is singing *Jambalaya* out of tune.

Eddy's got the brim of his cowboy hat shadowing his eyes, so all's you see is the tip of his nose and his mouth. Dickens, I'm trying to concentrate, he says.

I was hopin to keep you from that, says Bo.

Daddy is sitting at the head of the table with a cigarette pinched between his thumb and forefinger, watching the cards. Gwyneth's sitting on Daddy's lap, twirling her hair around a finger. Hers and Daddy's are both soft, lonesome smiles. Daddy has one arm around her waist like she will break apart, cracked and fragile, if he looses his arm. He rides his knee back and forth so she sways.

McNeil O'Henry looks at his cards and makes a long *umm* sound, deciding.

O'Henry, Bo says, you sound like goddamn Elsa in heat for Christ's sake.

Eddy loses the smoke in his mouth to laughing, it comes out in one great cloud. He coughs. Billy Towle whacks Bo in the back of the head and tells him that's his woman he's speaking of and to watch his words.

I squat at the screen door watching. The night lies hot. Gwyneth's drink glass is beaded with moisture. Daddy and the men hold their beers by the bottle neck. They throw their cards on the table in the same way they put down money at Elsa's, carelessly and with some force and then looking long after it. They keep the unshown cards close to their faces.

Bo bangs down his chair and says, Whose turn, goddamnit?

I think it's yours, handsome, says Gwyneth. She takes Daddy's cigarette from him and pulls in one delicate drag.

Do a smoke ring, Daddy says. When she does one, he puts a finger through it.

Bo says, Aww Miss Gwyneth, when'm I gonna find a nice woman like you?

Bile rises in my throat.

McNeil O'Henry says, You have near as good a chance at gettin a woman good as Gwyneth as you would at turnin nigger.

Well I might then, says Bo.

Oh you boys, says Gwyneth, waving the smoke with one hand. Don't *say* that word.

Daddy pulls one strand of hair back from her face and kisses the side of her neck, closing his eyes when he does it.

Ahh, Dickens don't need to be married, says McNeil. Who needs a wife when your neighbor's got one?

Eddy says he's folding, slaps his cards facedown on the table and clasps his hands in back of his head.

I'll just find someone who doesn't love me, says Bo, looking at his hand, and buy her a house.

McNeil squooshes out a cigarette in the ashtray. If I smoke me another cigarette, he says, I'll turn into one. I can't quit em.

Billy Towle says, Y'all hear about the hurricane comin our way in a couple a days from the Virgins?

Eddy picks his teeth with a toothpick and hits the lip of his hat up. Aaah, it ain't comin here, that's just a weatherman's scare.

Bo sucks in his smoke. I wish it would, maybe I'd get me some building jobs if it hits real good.

Gwyneth studies her fingernails. Bo, she says, I can't keep up with mount of horrible things you say.

Only falls short a the horrible mount a things he does, Miss Gwyneth, says McNeil.

The room fills with smoke and their graveled voices. Heat makes their bodies leak moisture and puts hourglasses of sweat on their shirtfronts. For one moment I close my eyes and imagine being nine years old again, sitting on Daddy's lap and falling asleep to their jokes and their laughter, their smoke and beer smell and whiskey breath and Daddy's neck, the leather scent strong in its creases.

As if he can hear me thinking, Daddy looks at his watch and says to Gwyneth, Haley should be home soon.

Gwyneth runs a hand through his hair. She'll be all right, she says.

Eddy shakes his head and says, Surprised you don't have a goddamn leash on that girl.

Bo quiets, rocking back and forth in his chair, with his teeth jammed around his cigarette.

McNeil says, Hah! He bout does that. Might as well put a smoke alarm on her, things get too hot—

Shut up, McNeil, says Billy Towle. It ain't the night to go flappin your mouth.

They all go quiet. Daddy inhales smoke and looks at the men with his eyes narrowed. You know well as I do Southern men on a date aren't as gentlemanly as we pretend to be. I been keepin her from the likes of your type.

Gwyneth puts her elbow on the table, rests her chin on the hand of it. Amen, she says, ain't that the hard-earned truth?

Nah, says Billy Towle, you raised that girl right.

I'm foldin, says McNeil.

Bo rocks back and forth. I thought she was stayin at Gypsy's, he says.

Tonight she was gonna come home, Daddy tells him.

There is silence all around. I can hear the clock ticking and my own breathing, can feel the pain in the side of my thigh and left knee from squatting.

Finally Billy Towle says, You goddamn in or out, Dickens? All's us waitin on you.

Bo drops his cards in the middle. I'm out, he says. He gets up, picks his hat off the table and says, I gotta get on home to bed.

The whole table grunts and lifts their eyebrows. Eddy looks at his watch. Bo, chickenshit! It ain't half past twelve.

Bo's voice is gruff. I'm leavin, he says. It ain't like the old days, this tired body needs some rest.

Billy Towle says, Bo you just a sore loser.

McNeil is looking at Bo's hand. Ain't a sore loser, just stupid. Look at his hand.

Well, I'll be shittin worms, says Eddy. He got a straight flush.

Bo lifts his whole chair off the ground and places it away from the table, tips his hat to Gwyneth and starts walking toward the door. The men quiet behind him.

See ya, Bo, says Daddy.

I move as quiet as I can to the side of the house, flat against it so I can't be seen.

Bo comes out the door. His boots are worn at the heels, the jeans frayed around them. There's a tobacco bulge out one back pocket. I hear Gwyneth in the house say, Well I'll be.

Bo's footsteps are heavy and he swaggers when he goes down the porch steps. His hands hang slightly back from his body. When he gets in his truck, he sits for a few seconds, but I can't see what he is doing. Then he cranks it and wheels on out of there as fast as seems possible without burning the rubber on his tires.

When I come in the house, they all look up at me without saying a word.

Gwyneth rises. Oh sweetie, she says rushing toward me. She hugs me and kisses the top of my head. I look over her shoulder at Daddy.

Turnip, he says and nods slow. The men cough and smoke and look at their cards.

You okay darlin? Gwyneth asks. She bends over and holds the sides of my face with her hands and searches my eyes. Her fingers feel powdery. Come upstairs, she says. She turns to the table. Us ladies are gonna have some feminine time, she calls to them. Y'all go on with your men talk.

Daddy and I look once more at each other without smiling.

On the dresser are Gwyneth's silver comb and hairbrush, her earrings and perfume and makeup. She goes to the bathroom off Daddy's bedroom and comes back wearing a yellow robe. Her hair falls white around it.

Watching her all skinny without that baby in her belly makes me cry. They are silent tears, which she doesn't say a thing about. She picks up the silver-handled hairbrush from the dresser and says, Turn around, honey. She sits behind me on the bed and starts to brush my hair. Sighing, she says, Such beautiful hair you have, Hale. Does this feel good?

Mmm-hmm, I tell her. I sniffle.

When she gets to a tangle, she picks it up and goes through it careful. My scalp doesn't hurt from the tug or the pull, all I feel is the warm tingling of being touched.

We can hear the murmur of the men's voices downstairs.

Let's go to Gypsy's tomorrow, Gwyneth says. Gettin your hair washed and cut can make you feel all new again. There's nothing like a new do to wash away the Sunday blues. It's why she keeps it open on the Sabbath.

I close my eyes. All right, I tell her. Let's do that.

When I was a little girl, Gypsy used to do this for me whenever I'd get in a fight with Daddy, Gwyneth says. Daddy and I were always gettin into fights. Gypsy was closest to Mamma, but Daddy and I loved each other so much we about killed each other. He could make me so mad I'd cry till I was almost drowned. She strokes my hair all the way down my back. He was a bighearted gambling man, she says. Made and lost his money near a thousand times through, smoked Luckies like they were oxygen and died of cancer when I was just nineteen.

We are quiet and Gwyneth keeps brushing. Finally she says, Haley, you can't know the pain of loss till you lose your daddy. Watchin my daddy get sick and die made me almost lose my mind. He'd been the strongest man I'd ever known. Then there he was in that hospital bed skinny as an adolescent and blue in the face, all hooked up to tubes without so much strength as to get a breath of air. She stops brushing and pulls the hair out of the brush, leans over and puts it in the wastebasket next to the bed. Now, of course, I wish I could take back all those no-good, horrible things I said to him when we fought. I didn't mean any of it, in some way I was always fightin my own self. She pats my hair with her hand. I'm still foolish as I was then but now I don't have my daddy to go and blame. Every day I think of him.

I imagine Gwyneth's daddy, a big-bellied smiling man who thought she made the moon rise. My lids go heavy and finally I lie down on my side and she combs her fingers through my hair. My tears keep squeaking out, and she pushes my hair from my forehead.

I'm all confused, I tell her.

I know it baby doll, she says in a soft voice. Aren't we all just? Everything will change in a heartbeat. Rememberin that is the meaning to life.

I nod, slowly. The men's talking downstairs ceases and then begins again. Fletcher's face comes into my mind, his sweet face and smooth skin, the way his hand felt in mine while we walked the tents, the memory of his murmur on my hair. I make the summer over in my mind. It is just me and Fletcher, there isn't any hidden thing named Bo Dickens that I have to cover over and keep to myself. Fletcher and I are on that Ferris wheel riding up into a sky of clouds and sun. I imgaine that while I let myself fall to sleep.

When I wake up, it is near two by Daddy's digital. The men are still downstairs. I can hear them talking. Gwyneth isn't in sight. I get off Daddy's bed and pad down the hall. She's standing in my bathroom across from my room, putting toothpaste on her brush.

Hi, sweetie, she says. I didn't want to wake you so I used this sink instead of your daddy's. She bends down to brush, the water a slow drizzle before her.

Suddenly I hear someone at my window saying my name, Haaaleeey, dragging it out like a birdcall. Gwyneth takes her toothbrush out of her mouth and spits. When I hear the voice again, I know it is Bo. I stay where I am. Haaaleey. Gwyneth puts the toothbrush under the water and brushes her teeth with the clean bristles. Then he begins with the stones on my windowpane, a slight *ting-ting* on the glass. Some hit the screen softly. Gwyneth bares her teeth in the mirror. I listen to those *ping*s. She turns off the water.

Jesus, she says, you think I can get my teeth bleached? She looks at me. The yellow robe is opened to her cream white skin on her chest. I hear another *ping,* flat against the window. Gwyneth does not blink. She wipes her hands on the towel next to the sink. You think your daddy'd treat me to that?

He'd do anything for you, Miss Gwyneth, I tell her, quickly. There are two right in a row, *ping-ping.*

She laughs like those sparkles on the Fourth that last for only short minutes, then she comes out the doorway past me. G'night, Haley, she says. I'm going to get some beauty sleep. She walks down the hall, her robe wrapping around her ankles. When she gets to Daddy's doorway, she waves at me, one finger at a time. Careful of any Romeos out your window sweetheart, she says with a knowing smile. And I think how she must believe it's a high school boy out my window. In that moment, I want to run to Gwyn and tell her about Bo, only I don't know what she could do about it. So I just wave back. She shuts Daddy's door. Bo stops calling for a few seconds. I stand in the hall, knowing he is waiting.

I go into my dark room, close my door and lock it. I can't remember ever having locked my door. Even when Fletcher's in there with me I don't lock it. Kneeling on all fours, I crawl over to my window and peer over the sill at him. He is pacing the side yard like a caged animal.

When he turns to look, I duck even though I know he can't see in with my light off. Haley? he says. He whistles. When I look back down, he is lighting a cigarette. I crawl into my bed, hoping that Daddy and his friends won't leave the poker table before Bo leaves the house. There isn't any way for him to get by the downstairs table if he wants to get in my room. For a while I listen to the men downstairs and him out there waiting, muttering to himself, and then he must give up because I don't hear him anymore. A long time later when I have gone in and out of vague sleep, the men leave and the house darkens and Daddy's heavy footsteps go up the stairs to bed.

24

FLETCHER

I lie in bed waiting for Haley to whistle up to me, thinking of her on that merry-go-round when she went on her own the last time. Her horse was in midleap with its teeth bared and its eyes wild. While the ride went around, I caught looks of her. Her eyes were vacant looking, like someone came and tore life out of them, left her with just the tools for seeing.

Afterward, we drove around awhile, past the old highway bridge on little bitty side roads Riley knows about. It was quiet. We saw about three cars total the whole way back to Houser Banks. I wished we would just drive through Mississippi, come out on the other side of Arkansas and watch the sun rise somewhere in Texas. My arm around Haley's back ached, and I thought it would be fine if it would just go on fire with pain, I could handle that sacrifice. I wanted to tell Haley that to have her beside me, I could last through hunger and heat and thirst. Only I didn't know how to say any of those things to her, so I just kept quiet.

Riley had a bandanna tied around his head. A corner of it was loose and flapped in the wind. He kept looking in his rearview at me. He didn't wink like he has a habit of doing. Crystal leaned into him and watched the road.

I'm afraid, Haley finally said. Crystal turned to her and rested her chin on Riley's shoulder. What of? she asked.

Haley couldn't say. She told us that sometimes a fear comes up in her when she and her father aren't getting along.

Because who else do I have? she'd asked us. Riley watched her in the rearview. Mamma, she said, pulling her hair back from the wind, is just a girl like me, she can't even take care of her own self, and she is always sayin things and not doin them.

We were all quiet.

Haley told us in rushed words, When I get to thinking like this, then everything seems scary to me like the night is too dark and day is too bright and any river seems like water for drownin and any car feels like one that will wreck with me in it. After she said it, she leaned back on my arm and raised her head to look at the sky. We could see she didn't want to say another word about it.

Riley lit a smoke and Crystal turned the knob on the radio and sang along with Billie Holiday. I held on to Haley. Most of me wanted to take her fear away from her, get it into me so she didn't have to live with it. I had another messed-up thought at the same time, though. I half believed that without that fear Haley may not be hanging out with me. Maybe it's the fear that keeps her with me.

Tonight Haley doesn't come to my window. I sleep restless, half waiting. Between sleep and waking and bits of dreaming, the song Crystal sang to us after the Billie Holiday tape quieted shoots through my mind. She sang it low and sad, in a little girl's voice:

> *Peter Peter, pumpkin eater, had a wife but couldn't keep her.*
> *Bee baa oddi oddi bim baw, I can't see y'all, is all hid?*
> *One, two, I washed my shoe,*
> *Three, four, I knocked on the door,*
> *Five, six, I got some licks,*
> *Seven, eight, I made a mistake,*
> *Nine, ten, my eyes are open.*

25

HALEY

At Gypsy's shop with my hair just washed, newly cut and highlighted, I stand at the counter waiting on Fletcher to pick me up. They've pulled the drapes across the front window, so it's cool and dark in there. I can see the street through the slits on the venetian blinds covering the front door and I peek between them to watch for the Honda.

Joy's behind the receptionist's desk, painting her nails a bright pink color. Mamma, she says into the receiver, that's cause he used to drink like somethin droughted. He doesn't do that no more.

Ruly Heel and two other men sit along Spier's wall toothpicking their teeth and holding Coke can spitoons and newspapers. Spier's got an old yellow-jowled guy in his chair. He's bent over him, plucking out his ear hairs. I try not to watch because it makes me feel sick to my stomach.

One of the men waiting on his haircut gets up and starts to rub his back against the corner of the wall, getting the scratch out like a horse. Margie's got a bug in her today, he says, cause I wasn't coming in till half past three last night, and couldn't get Bruce to the ball field this mornin.

Well, I told him good, Joy says into the receiver. She keeps painting her nails. He can't be doin it again or I'll choke him silly.

Ruly Heel stands next to the scratching man, strikes a match on his boot and lights a cigar. I lost one hundred and seventy-five bucks and my brass belt buckle there, he says, and I was just tryin to win it back when I near lost my truck and my fishin boat. I'll not be doing that again, not if anyone and God the Father can help it. I'll drink at Eely's pub if necessary, he don't allow a card in the place.

The man still seated flips his newspaper down and says, That's a pussy bar if I ever knew one. When he sees me watching, he tips his hat and says, Sorry ma'am. I smile and look at Joy, who rearranges the paperweights on top of the desk and says, Mamma, I'm like a hound dog at him when he comes home. I could smell a woman a mile away and if he ever did that I'd just scoop up Jimmy and Elaine and take them somewheres else. No man is runnin his affairs behind a whore's door and then comin home to make my bed hot with his sweaty self.

Her mamma is most likely saying, Amen.

Gypsy! Spier calls out.

Behind the leopard-skin-print curtain in back, Gypsy's voice calls back, Hang on, I got a permanent needs rinsing.

The man smoking the cigar sits down, scuffs his boots once on the floor and squints up at the man against the wall corner. Did you hear they found a body? he asks.

My breath stops and my mouth goes dry. I stand rigid and will Joy to quit talking so I can listen.

The man at the corner of the wall raises his eyebrows. What body?

They found a body out near the river by Battle Creek.

In the river? asks Spier.

No. The man ashes his cigar on the bottom of his boot sole. Buried near it. Somebody hunted it up.

I find myself gripping the side of the receptionist counter so I won't fall.

Joy, honey, Gypsy says while she comes out from behind the curtain. Her voice sounds far away, as if she were in a tunnel. Her heels click on the floor. You gotta get off that phone, baby.

Sheriff's checking it out. Just happened half an hour ago. A friend of Jay Parker's lives right near there, how's I found out.

Haley, sugar. Gypsy passes me the bag for Gwyneth. She looks at my hand gripping the counter, then leans over and puts a palm on my cheek. You all right, baby doll?

I nod.

You're pale as an envelope, she says.

Her face goes blurry in front of me, and I close my eyes for a brief second. Bo, I think. Daddy. I open my eyes. I'm all right Miss Gypsy.

Well I'll be a bull's ass, says Spier. They identify it yet?

The man takes the cigar out of his mouth and inspects it. Nope, he says. I gather he was a black boy and gone some time now already.

Gypsy follows my gaze. Oh Haley, she whispers, my sister said you were boy crazy. Those there are old men, darlin. She waves her hand at them. Senior citizens. She glances down at the bag. Thanks for bringing this stuff back to her, I should have nabbed her when she dropped you.

That'll be all over the papers tomorrow, says the man who was scratching his back. He comes and sits.

They got suspects? one man asks.

Sure as hell they got suspects. Someone owns the land, that's a good start.

A horn blows outside. Gypsy sticks three fingers between the blinds and looks out the front window. Hey now, darlin, there's your boyfriend, Gypsy says. She lets the blinds drop and they swing against the door. You want to make that boy wait? She looks again at the men and back at me. I pull my eyes from Spier's side, tell my feet to move around to the door. You don't want that boy to have to hang on too long, Gypsy's saying. He's handsome, he might take off on you. I'll probably be over sometime later this week, to see how Gwyn's doin.

Behind me I hear Spier say, Whose land was it on anyway?

They got to find that out, says another man.

Gypsy leans over and opens the door, heat rushes at us. She fluffs my hair. Go on now sugar, knock that boy dead.

The door closes behind me.

Fletcher's got one hand on the wheel and the other one stretched out around the passenger's seat. He smiles at me when I climb in. Hey, he says, then he touches my hair. He's quiet for a minute. You look beautiful, he tells me.

I swallow. My voice is thin when I say, Do I look that different?

Fletcher leans back, squints his eyes and tilts his head. Uh-uh, he says, you're still Haley, new hair or old hair, and then he smiles slow.

I smile back but my lips quiver. I turn and look straight ahead and ask him, Where we going?

He pulls out and says, Riley told me to meet them in back of the Jitney at about, he looks at his watch, now, he says.

We ride in silence out to Highway 12.

I want to tell Fletcher about the body, but I want to tell Daddy first, or first I want to go to Bo's house. My mind reels between these things. Riding along in the Honda makes me feel trapped. My skin crawls as if the veins were on fire. I try to stay my eyes on the road. I am most of all worried about Daddy. I hate that we've fought and now he's gone for the day with Gwyn to see about cars in Memphis and won't be back, he said, till well past dark. I want to have some way to go to him. When I look down, I am rubbing my hands together in my lap.

Fletcher doesn't look at me when he says quietly, What's the matter?
Nothing.

Out of the side of my vision, I watch him nod. He puts a hand on my knee and says, You want to talk about it, you say the word, okay?
Yeah.

We park in front of the Jitney and Fletcher waits for me to get out my side. The Jitney closes at five on Sunday, and the parking lot's mostly empty, with a few people in red pinafores coming out to their cars after a long day. The sun melts around its hulking cement body.

My legs shake when I walk and Fletcher's hand feels dry and cool in mine. I want to say something so he doesn't worry about me, but I don't know what I would say. The night feels too hot and the sky is a bright glaring white. My mind is numb and blank. Bo's face stretches out of the blacktop. The woods on the night we did the burying and Daddy laid out on the couch like he was. We round the corner of the Jitney. Fletcher stops short.

Across the parking lot, I see Hannaford's bare back, his suspenders are tied around his middle. He's facing a green pickup, which is parked at an angle across from the Jitney's Dumpster. He looks fired-up red from the taillights.

Crystal's behind him, Fletcher says.

If I move to the right I can see she's sitting on the lowered tailgate with her legs hanging over the side. She's struggling to get free. Hannaford's holding her thighs and one of the Pierson brothers is sitting in back of her with his legs straddled on either side of her, clasping her from behind, his arms around her arms and her middle.

I start to run and almost holler out, but Fletcher grabs my arm. Hold up, he says. I stop. Fletcher doesn't let loose of my arm. I want to see what they're up to first, he says quietly.

A different Pierson brother is sitting on the wheel hub, smoking. Next to the other side of the truck Letchy's brother bounces a tennis ball hard against the concrete and catches it. Country music blares out the cab and both doors are open like a winged animal. Someone's feet are sticking out the passenger door, swinging to the music.

Hannaford is saying, I don't see why Riley gets to have all the fun.

The guy behind Crystal says, He ain't sharin either.

Letchy's brother holds the tennis ball and looks at them. Ain't nothin to share you can't get elsewhere. He makes like to pitch the ball at Hannaford, but it stays in his hand.

Where in hell is Riley? Fletcher asks me in a whisper.

Hannaford takes a flask out of the waist of his overalls and dips his head back to drink. The feet out the passenger door slam down on the pavement. A Broder boy comes around the truck. He points a finger in our direction. There's someone over there, he says loudly. Hannaford turns and looks at us.

Go, Fletcher says to me. I don't think you should be around here. Riley'll be comin in a matter of minutes. He starts forward with his shoulders squared.

But I wouldn't ever let Fletcher deal with them alone. It'll be all right, I tell him, I've known their younger brothers since I was itty-bitty, they aren't gonna do anything to us.

We walk toward them. The Broder boy moves his arm down.

I hear Crystal say something I can't hear.

Hannaford turns back to her, Did we ask you to talk, sweetheart?

Fear prickles at me. My bladder goes loose. Then Hannaford bends down and licks Crystal's thigh. He laughs, stands up straight and watches us come. That there's Ellyson and her brand-new boyfriend, he says when we get within a few feet. His words are slurred with drink.

Letchy's brother holds the ball steady and observes us with his chin up. What y'all doin, spyin on us? he asks.

We come to get Crystal, I say, trying to keep my voice steady. We stop about six feet from them. I want to rush forward cause I know Crystal must be scared out of her mind. But something in me thinks Fletcher is right, to be careful.

Where you been all day, Ellyson? asks Hannaford. His eyes are half lidded like they get when he's over his drunk limit. *We* been at Freely's Barbecue drinking up a storm, and missin you.

Who in hell is that guy? the Broder boy asks. He takes out a jackknife and starts cleaning his nails with the end of it, watching Fletcher.

Judge Greel's son, says Hannaford. Got his dick hard for Ellyson.

Behind Hannaford, I can make out the struggle of Crystal's legs. Hold steady, Pierson says, like I told you. Hannaford doesn't glance back at them, he keeps his eyes level with mine. Let her go, Han, I say, soft as I can.

Broder walks in front of Fletcher. He looks like a chest-flared rooster. Hannaford moves to stand directly in front of me. He watches my eyes.

I try to duck my head around him to see Crystal, but he blocks me when I do it. Y'all let her go, I say to him, c'mon.

Hannaford raises his hands over his head and says, I ain't doin nothing. Why don't you talk to Pierson? I bend down under his armpit to see Crystal and try to reach out. Her hands are smooshed together, sticking out from the grip of Pierson's arms. Pierson's head is floppy drunk, but his arms are holding tight. He's wearing her deli smock around his neck like a scarf.

Crystal's eyes are scared and she shakes her head, looking right into me. She mouths something I can't make out. In the half-light, I see streaks of tears on her cheeks. They're falling still. My stomach turns over. Hannaford moves in front of me, so I can't see her anymore.

I know I shouldn't but it comes out of me, Hannaford you're an evil, no-good sonofabitch. What are you trying to prove? I bang my hand against his chest, trying to move him, but he grabs my wrists and laughs. His grip is hard and my skin stings. In back of him Pierson says, Feed me some of what you got in your waist, Han, I'm the one who bought it.

Who'll hold my little girlfriend, then? Hannaford looks at me when he says it and stays my arms with his hands.

On the wheel hub, the other Pierson throws his still-lit smoke to the ground. Ah, this black un ain't no catch, he says. Just like gar, teeth are too big and nothing good to eat.

The Broder boy circles Fletcher once and then stands to the left of him. When Fletcher tries to move, he moves with him. Ain't your daddy the one put mine in the slammer for driving with a couple of beers in him? Broder asks.

Everyone knows Broder's daddy knocked down a kid on a sidewalk and almost killed her. He was put away for two years.

I ain't my daddy, says Fletcher.

There's something in the air that makes me more scared than I am normally. It tells me to stay my fighting a little. It's a feeling of a truck without brakes that needs a good uphill. I loose my wrists from Hannaford. My voice is as friendly as I can make it. His daddy got Letchy's daddy out of a misdemeanor, I say. I can feel the hope in me when I look to Letchy.

Broder lifts his chin at Letchy's brother. That true Johnny? Letchy's brother throws his tennis ball up, catches it around his back and shrugs.

My chest gets tight. I wonder where Riley is. It comes to me that they could have done something to Riley first and then come here. Lights go off around the top of the building. The Jitney is shutting down for the night.

Fletcher starts to walk around Broder to the side of the truck. I can tell by the slow way he moves and by Crystal's silence that we are all three thinking the same thing. Broder shadows Fletcher, who tries to ignore him. He says to the boy on the hubcap, What are y'all planning to do with a girl you got trapped there? Can't you get one that wants to go with you on her own volition?

A guy whose face I don't know leans over the driver's-side window and says, Who that?

Without keeping his eyes off Fletcher, Broder says, The Judge's son and he's using awful big words.

Through the cab window, I see a blond girl whip her head around. She's Liz Frizzy, ten years older than we are and lost on alcohol without a dime to her name. The closest thing to a whore Houser Banks knows about.

Fletcher nods to Letchy's brother. You guys gonna let the lady go? His tone is neutral, not pleading, just simple. I know he's forcing it to be like that.

Hannaford spits and rubs his shoe sole in it, and I almost dart around him, but he catches me on the waist. You think you're so smart, he says into my ear.

Fletcher makes a move toward the corner of the truck, but Broder shoves his body in front of him. Crystal you all right? Fletcher calls. He nods his chin to Hannaford. Come on, man, let her go, this ain't nowhere near a good time.

Riley's coming, Crystal says. Her voice is low. And terrified.

Hannaford puts his finger to his lips and turns around to face her. I thought I told you to shh.

Broder stands not a chin hair from Fletcher, sticks the knife blade between his two front teeth and makes like he's cleaning them. Who's gonna make us let her go? he asks.

With his arms still around my waist, Hannaford bends down and slobbers a whiskey-smelling kiss on my cheek. Now you want to talk to me, he says. After Greel's had his head up your ass all summer? He keeps his lips on my face. I bet that felt good, he says.

Fletcher makes a dash for the wheel hub and Hannaford jerks up. The Broder boy backpedals. I get around Hannaford and grab Crystal's hand, which is dangling out from the grip of the Pierson boy's arms. Her fingers are limp, cold and shaking.

I work to pry Pierson's hands loose, but Hannaford is wrapping his arm around my waist, putting his head over my shoulder, breathing hot liquor smell down my neck.

Just as I turn around to face him, I am blinded by headlights. The Roadrunner's motor cuts up the air, screeches across the blacktop and stops beside us. Riley jumps over the door. He comes toward the truck with quick, angry strides. But Hannaford gets in front of him. When Riley steps, Hannaford steps.

Broder's got a knife, I call out so Riley will know.

Broder's watching Fletcher out the side of his eye and keeping his face forward onto Riley. His knife is out from his side. Pierson shifts around, hugging Crystal tighter. His head's loose as a dead chicken's. His grip is still viselike. Let her go, I say to him. I try to scratch at his hands, but he bats me away, snarls and hauls her closer to him, edging his butt farther up the truck bed. Crystal doesn't say a word.

Riley glances quick at Fletcher. Broder, put down the goddamn knife, Riley says. Hannaford, he says, you got to the count of three.

With two fingers Hannaford pulls down the waist of his overalls and shows us a belt strapped around his belly. In the belt is a .45. His voice is thick with liquored saliva. You wanna make me, cousin?

I grip tight to Crystal's hand. Hannaford's about to say one more thing when Riley's on him, has him tripped and his face slapped down on the pavement.

Crystal's hand is snatched out from under me and when I look up, the Pierson boy's dragging her up the bed of the truck. The boy on the hubcap stands and jumps down to land on Fletcher. Broder lies on his belly like a snake, puts his knife to Fletcher's nose and says, Don't you move your sissy ass.

Haley, I hear Fletcher yell, get out of here. Riley's got an elbow grip around Hannaford's neck, and Hannaford's hands are struggling with that gun. Letchy's brother jumps the truck bed and bangs on the cabbie window three times, yelling for them to go.

The truck starts and the Pierson boy who's got Fletcher down scrambles up and grabs the moving truck's wheel hub to pull himself over the side. Broder follows him. The wheels spit gravel onto my calves and then

I am pushed to the side and have to catch myself from falling while Hannaford runs past, working to catch the tailgate. Riley chases after him. Hannaford grabs on to it before Riley can get to him and struggles around to face us while the truck moves away. He sits where Crystal was, with his legs hanging over. Split into the night air is a sound of something breaking and I look up to see Hannaford's gun firing into the sky, Riley making a run for him. Fletcher's legs are running as fast as you'd ever be able to, trying to jump the side of the truck. The Broder boy is standing over the side, his knife in the air, daring him.

And I realize I am yelling, calling Crystal's name, saying, Riley, get her!

Someone leans out and shuts the waving passenger door as the truck rams around the corner. A metal strip dangling off the truck bottom makes sparks against the cement. Then it's gone.

Riley's in the Roadrunner before we can catch him, screeching it into gear and peeling out after them, leaving Fletcher and me with kicked-up dirt, a couple of shopping carts and empty boxes of beer. The tennis ball rolls off down a rain sewer and Fletcher grabs my hand. We got to find them, he says.

26

FLETCHER

Haley says Sheriff Hill's been told before and he doesn't give a shit if anything bad happens to Riley White or Crystal Nash for being together. She says telling the sheriff will cause the wrong people to be right and end up making the situation worse. Mostly I'm worried on Crystal, she says. They'll scare her to death. She wrings her hands around in her lap when she says it. They aren't going to do anything to her, she tells me. They just like to pretend they're tough. In the car's faint light, her face looks drawn and sad, her lips are pale, the hair on her forehead matted and wet.

We stop at the pay phone outside of the Mobil station just down the street from the Jitney. Haley calls Riley's house to tell his brothers to be out looking. She explains who the boys were and the color of the truck, and that one should stay home in case he calls.

When she gets back in the car, she says, They'll leave Baby Judd home. I hope they find them before we do.

We drive long country roads out to places Haley knows about where they go for fires and keg parties, odd names like Dunk Rock and Chaffinch Hollow. There seem to be endless inlets and hunting camps. We get out of the car sometimes and walk the woods' scrappy paths with tools in our hands, hammers and jacks, each of us scared and hoping Crystal and Riley aren't in there, that they'll drive up in the Roadrunnner and Riley will yell out, Who y'all huntin up in there?

We stop at Letchy's house on Sunrise Circle. He clangs out the front door and stands leaning on his braces in boxer shorts and nothing else, his feet dragging behind him. Haley holds the door open for him while he tells us his parents are in Arkansas and his brother's been on a four-week drinking binge. He says he has a stomach flu and that the truck never came here. If I wasn't sick, he tells us, I'd help you look. They aren't gonna do nothing, though, they'll just scare em. Cat-and-mouse games.

Haley says she knows it and that we should go looking anyway.

Good luck, he says. He backs away into the dark hole of his front door while we head back to the car.

Haley directs me to the nondescript houses of the Broder and Pierson families, whole blocks filled with these names. There are useless cars in the yards and dogs chained up to porches. Mothers come to the screen and tell us in a cautious, untrusting voice that their boys aren't home. Sometimes the house lies in Sunday night emptiness. Other times no one comes to the door, but we can see a blue TV screen inside.

There isn't one green truck.

My eyes are tired from looking and I'm wound up tight worrying. My head starts to hurt and cars get pissed at how slow we're driving, honk their horns and swerve around us. I try to drive faster, but I don't know where I am going.

Finally we turn back and go out Highway 12 heading east. After twenty minutes, we are weaving in and out of the streets of East Neigh, past the Group Hope Missionary Baptist Home and Ma Rene's Home-Cooked Barbecue and tiny joints right up close to the side of the road with old hubcaps covering the outside walls. We drive back to the Jitney and out by the river dam, passing red cars that aren't convertibles and convertibles that aren't red cars.

Finally Haley says, We're not going to find them. She looks at me.

I watch her and nod.

She wipes her arm across her mouth. I need to go home Fletcher. I— take me home.

There isn't much of a shoulder, but I pull the car over and we sit there in silence. She rests her elbow on the window, runs a hand over her hair again and again.

I try to ask it gently, so as not to accuse. Why don't you want to go to the police? Why don't you ever want to ask for help?

Her eyebrows raise. She turns to look at me and shakes her head slowly. No, she says, you think they're all like your daddy. You got to trust me on this one, Fletcher. The law is good for some things but not for all things. They can make your problems worse sooner than later. Haley's words sound somehow forced, rehearsed. Anyway, you got to believe me, she says, I been livin in this town long enough to know those boys are just scarin around. You don't know them so you think they're gonna do something real terrible. They aren't. All those boys have is bark. Their bite isn't anything. Really.

A long minute goes by while I look out at the road. An armadillo crosses it, hunched and mechanical. I think of Hannaford's eyes when he kissed Haley, hazy, distracted, drunk eyes. And I think about the guy who circled me with a knife. Heat fills my neck and face. When I look down, my knuckles are clenched on the steering wheel. I can't figure out whether I want to do something to them because I hate them so bad for making me feel like a jelly-spined prep boy in front of Haley, or whether I am afraid for Crystal. I try to reason the two things out in my mind. The truth is, I don't know a thing about those guys and Haley's spent sixteen years with them, from crayons to this. I figure if anyone knows, she does.

I nod and loosen my grip on the steering wheel. Okay, I tell her. I'll take you home.

We ride in silence back to Houser Banks with the radio off and the occasional streetlight blaring down on us.

When I turn down her road, she says suddenly, No, Fletcher, just stop at the turnaround here, I don't want to drive up to my driveway.

She puts her hand on the door handle and I slow to a stop.

Haley, I say, you want to come to my house? They'll call there sooner or later. I know Riley will.

She looks down at the door handle. I can't, she says.

I wait for her to ask me to come to her house. She doesn't. Finally I say, You want me to walk you up the street?

I'll be all right.

A lump comes in my throat and it isn't anymore about Riley and Crystal. Something is wrong with Haley. Has been since I picked her up from Gypsy's, and I'm suddenly anxious, wondering if she has changed her mind about me, doesn't want to see me anymore because I'm leaving. In the half-light, I can see her new haircut. It makes her eyes look large. Listen Haley— I start to lean over, take her hand.

She interrupts me. Fletcher, she says, I'm sorry, I gotta go.

Okay, I tell her. I bend over and put my mouth on her mouth.

Her lips part to barely a give-back. Drawing away from me, she says,

I'm not good for kissing. My mouth is dry. She opens the door. Moist heat comes in. With one hand she picks up the bag from Gypsy's. Fletcher? she says.

Yeah, Hale? I wait.

She looks back at me. I don't know when I'll see you. I— There's some stuff. There's a lot of things. She looks right at me. I love you, she says. I love you like I haven't ever loved before. She leans over and puts her face on my shoulder and breathes, hot and hard, and then she is sliding over on the seat, getting out and closing the door behind her.

My heart slams against my chest and my palms sweat. Her words sound to me like something somebody says to you before they break your heart. She stands by the side of the road holding the bag and I circle the car around, roll down the window and tell her, I love you, too, Haley Ellyson. Nothing could make me stop.

She takes a hand from the bag and waves.

I tell myself to pull out and I manage to. In my rearview mirror, I watch Haley's face get red in my taillights and then she gets smaller and smaller and finally she disappears.

Pops is on the porch when I come home, standing with one arm wrapped around the column next to the stairs. When I park he puts both hands in his pockets and comes walking toward me. He's wearing denims and a blue tennis shirt. He isn't smiling and there isn't a drink in his hand. He watches his feet while he walks.

I get out and stand at the car. Hi, I say.

He stops and looks at me. The sky is a murky one with clouds coming and covering up a quarter moon and then uncovering it again. Time is it? he asks me.

I shrug. Eleven maybe.

He frowns a little and nods. You want to come inside, son?

Yes sir.

I walk a few feet in back of him. It looks as if each of his steps take concentration. I think of how Haley walks, like something pulls her along and she just does the motion.

I can't imagine what Pops is doing, why he wants me to come inside with him. In the space of time it takes to get to the porch, I think maybe he is going to start putting down rules. With only ten days left until I go up north, he's going to tell me he knows Haley sleeps here and doesn't like it. My face reddens at imagining him doing this. Or maybe he is going to tell me not to go up north. Stay home awhile, he'll say, we got a job for you at the courthouse. Even though I know that isn't half probable, my mind whacks itself back and forth between elation and doubt, between going to school like I should and being able to stay with Haley.

We come to the first porch step. Moths circle the light and Pops commences up the stairs. And then I believe he is going to speak of Riley. He's found out what happened to them. I get words formed in my mind to ask him this. The words are: Sir, has something happened to Riley White? But I can't say them and we cross the porch together in silence. He keeps the door open for me and I walk past him into the house. It's bright as hell in there with all the lights on.

Come to my study, he says.

I make my way across the living room floor. At the fireplace the room splits. To the right is the hall that leads to the master bedroom. To the left is the study, and I go in there and sit in the Tulane trustees chair in front of his desk, rub my hand over the wood curves of the arms.

Pops stands behind me, in the doorway. He doesn't come in. I look back at him. It reminds me of how he was when he told me about the cancer. Then he walks in, stands to the left of his desk, looks at his shoe and moves a tassel of the rug with it. He doesn't look up at me before he starts to talk. They have found a dead body here in Houser Banks, he says.

The space around my father's head outlines itself in black. I wait with my breath held.

He clears his throat. They'd like to keep it under wraps, it isn't something they want a whole lot of publicity about, yet. It may have criminal implications for some well-known people in this town. He looks up at me and I try as best I can to hold his stare, but I feel myself looking at anything else, his chin, his nose, the straight line of his mouth, which he opens to say, They found it on Ire Ellyson's property.

27

HALEY

I wait until Fletcher's car is out of sight, and then I run up to my driveway. It's dark and Gwyn's MG still isn't there. I get in the Ford, crank it and drive as fast as I know how to Bo Dickens's house, four miles from mine out a long deserted street by the old mill.

He's on the back porch, holding a beer, wearing an undershirt and jeans and barefoot. His dog starts to bark and come at me, but Bo grabs its collar. Easy, he says to it, then drags the dog to the door and throws it in. He comes back out, stands at the top step and smiles. He tips his beer at me. You gettin brave on me, little lady? His porch is littered with empties and a couple of rusted dog chains, a ripped-out car seat and the steering wheel of a tractor. T-shirts hang from the railing looking beat from weather.

He starts to come down the stairs. You're dead meat, I tell him before he can get to me. My voice sounds flat.

He stops, squints at me. The yard buzzes with tree frogs. I ain't dead meat, he says. There's a scare to his voice.

I back up three steps. You ain't? I ask him.

He shakes his head slowly. What is it you're tryin to say, Haley?

Looking directly into his eyes, I tell him, They found the body. It comes out awkward and shrill.

His left eye twitches and then he does something I didn't expect. He starts to laugh. He keeps his right hand across his heart like it hurts from laughing. His eyes tear up from it.

The laughing is uncontrolled and scary, it has no fun in it, and suddenly I am running around the side of the house to his driveway, where the Ford is parked and idling. His dog barks in the house, and I hear Bo behind me, serious now, yelling, Haley, stop, hey c'mere.

I jump the truck and recrank so it grinds, then pull out into the street and peel out while I watch Bo Dickens in my rearview mirror, trying to catch my truck's tailgate.

On the way home, I ride around corners so fast the truck comes half off its tires. When I park the truck at our house, I run up the porch steps, jam my key in the door, slam it behind me and relock it. My breath comes crazy and I am wet with sweat. Leaning against the door, I think I can feel the weight of Bo behind it. But there's only silence save my breathing and the sound of the clock in the kitchen. For stretched minutes, I stand with my hand on the knob. Finally my body slumps down from tired. I keep my fingers on the lock. My breathing quiets. For a long time I sit at the jamb listening to the silent house and the ticking of minutes.

That is where Daddy finds me, hours later, my backside fit into the corner of the wall and door frame. Elsa and Billy Towle and Gwyn are all there, too. Gwyn takes them to the back deck and Daddy kneels next to me. Turnip? he says.

I look into his eyes and then down at the scar on his neck, study his messy hair and the stubble growing in.

Daddy, I say, I need to tell you some things.

He puts his hands under my armpits and picks me up like he used to when I was a little girl, brings me to the den and lays me lengthwise across the couch. Then he sits next to me with his hands clasped together.

I talk about that night. The words pull themselves out without me thinking of how to say them and my voice sounds far away and not my own. Daddy doesn't ever interrupt. He listens, leaning forward and staring at a spot on the rug. His jaw stays tensed and tight and unmoving. He doesn't seem to blink at all. While we are sitting there, Sheriff Hill comes. Gwyn goes past us through the house to the door. I can hear her say, Okay, Sheriff, he'll be right out. Can you just give him a minute with his little girl? You can come out back if you like, have a cool drink. Daddy glances up once. Then he turns his eyes back to me and keeps them there.

After I finish speaking, Daddy stays perfectly still for some time, focusing on the couch cushion next to me. His forehead is creased and his face looks ruddy, like he's been riding awhile. The blue lights of the police car bounce off the den walls. Finally he says in a low voice, I am going through hell right now tryin to understand what made you think you didn't have to come to me with this. One of his eyes looks right into mine, the other is staring at a space on my cheek. His red cheeks are splotched with white.

My voice is from a stuck place in my throat and sounds thin. I thought it would be okay, I tell him, pleading. I thought everything would be all right.

Daddy points a finger violently at his chest. His voice is hard. It's me, Turnip. It's me you got to answer to, not the sheriff, not Bo Dickens, not your boyfriend, it's me. I could have helped out here. We could have done somethin before it came to this. He gestures at the lights on our den wall, which look eery and fatal, and suddenly the den comes in around me and the image of the day we buried Gwyn's baby, Bo Dickens's face in a dark tack room, the lump of the body and the fact that I didn't tell. I begin to ask myself why, at first just on the inside, and then I ask it out loud. I am sobbing, but no tears come. Daddy leans over me. He holds my head in his hands and brings it to his chest. He smells of Daddy, horse and leather, and he rocks me back and forth many times until my breath quiets some. Finally he says, You are a strong, willful girl, Turnip, thinkin you can hold all that. But we're gonna make it okay. He puts one arm around my back and one under my knees and picks me up. I place my hands around Daddy's neck and am again the girl I used to be, when I believed Daddy could fix everything.

The first time I saw it snow in Houser Banks, I held the white powder in my hands and said to Billy Towle when he drove up, Look what Daddy made it do.

Before he turns out the light to my room, Daddy watches me and shakes his head back and forth slowly. His mouth quivers in a kind of frown and he says, You can let it go, Haley. It's mine now. The light goes out and he closes the door to a sliver of yellow. I hear his footsteps go down the stairs and I lie there numb and worn out. My breath still sounds like a sob and I think over and over again of Daddy saying, *You're a strong, willful girl, Turnip.*

I must be real strong because Daddy doesn't know the whole of what I hold. I've left out the words about Bo's lips on me. I haven't told him anything about Bo wanting my body, or the way my breath went quick for him.

I saved Daddy from having to know all that.

28

FLETCHER

I can't sleep with want to get up and go to her. My bed feels hot and the covers bother my skin. I think of all those times Haley took me on that path. She was always sad afterward, crossing her arms over herself and getting real quiet.

For some reason I know she isn't going to be here tonight, and finally restless sleep comes. I dream Julian is on my mother's grave site during the burial. All the people are around mourning and crying and the priest is saying prayers. Julian rolls around on the new earth, laughing a horrible thick laugh. I am the only one who sees him. He stops rolling and looks up at me, flashes a flat piece of steel.

I wake up gradually, as if climbing out of water. Looking out my window, I wonder for the thousandth time whether or not she is awake and whether Pops would hear me leave if I went to her. The digital beside my bed reads 1:46.

I get up and put on a T-shirt and jeans and sneakers, come out my room quiet and close the door with a click. When I go down the back stairs, I think of how many times I brought Haley up them, and I'm crazy with wondering if something would happen to make her not come to me anymore. I go out the back doors onto the patio.

When I turn the corner to pass the front porch, Pops is standing there. He's smoking a pipe, which I haven't seen him do since Christmas, and rocking from heel to toe. He turns and sees me. His face doesn't show any surprise at all. Because I can't turn back, I start up walking again.

I'm going for a ride, I tell him, gesturing toward the Honda.

He nods, waves his hand and says, Okay.

When I get to her street, I park in the inlet and jog down the road listening for any human sound. There's a blue trailer neighboring Haley's house. Inside a dog barks three times. A lady's voice says, Shut up, Clover. The dog quiets.

At Haley's house, the lights are on in the downstairs and one upstairs. I crouch down and move from one tree to the next. Haley has only ever brought me here when there wasn't anyone around. My heart beats irregular. I find my way to her window, about twelve feet up and dark, and stand under it until I hear people talking around back, then I side up to the corner and watch from the slit between the clapboard and the drain gutter.

Spier's wife, Gypsy, is there. She's standing with her foot up on the railing, smoking a cigarette. I'm just sayin it don't seem right that it'd be here, she says.

The woman next to her says, Ah Gyps, he ain't a killer. I recognize it as the soft voice of the woman who picks up the phone sometimes when I call Haley. I know I am finally seeing Gwyneth Fox. She's as beautiful as Riley told me she would be, wearing a yellow shiny robe and smoking a cigarette. She grips the robe together at the throat. Her bones are slight and make her look fragile as a bird.

I'm not saying he is, says Gypsy, I'm just tellin you, you don't know what men do when they're not sayin sweet nothing to their women.

Gwyneth says, He didn't do it. The words are flat and believed.

Gypsy looks at her for a long time.

A man comes through the sliding door. She's asleep, he says. He sits in a lawn chair, leans back with his feet propped on the railing and lights a cigarette. I recognize him as Bill Towle from town.

Gwyneth turns back with her cigarette above her head. How many Valium you give her, Billy?

I gave her three.

For God's sake, says Gypsy, you're gonna kill the poor girl, she's too skinny for three.

Bill Towle takes the cigarette out of his mouth with a thumb and forefinger and says, Shit, Gyps, it's just Valium, for Christ's sake. She couldn't quit crying after that phone call.

I watch them while they smoke. They look into the night without any words.

Finally Gwyneth says, He's a good man.

Bill Towle looks up at her and nods. Yes he is, he says.

Gypsy puts her hand on Gwyneth's back. She rubs up and down until they all finish smoking. Without saying a word they go to the house. Bill Towle opens the sliding door for the women and they pass through, their arms around each other. Before he goes inside, he looks at the night like he is daring it to threaten him, and then follows the ladies in.

I go back and stand under Haley's darkened window for a long time, looking down at a dried bird skeleton and its scattered feathers in the grass. When I have waited for some minutes, I say the words *I love you, Haley Ellyson.* I want those words to go up and enter her screen and then sink into her body so that she sleeps better and maybe nothing could do her much harm, having those words inside her.

Then I jog back to my car, with the night's darkness crowding in around me.

I am in my bed looking up at the ceiling when the phone rings at eight thirty the next morning.

Hello? I say.

Yankee.

Riley, what happened to you? I stand in my boxers and T-shirt, pull the phone cord into my room and shut the door. We looked damn near everywhere for you, I tell him.

Yeah? Well you wouldn'ta found me. His voice is muffled like he has cotton in the sides of his mouth. You heard from Crystal? he asks me.

No, I say, quiet.

They took her, Judge, they fuckin took her. They beat the shit outta me. I woke up with my face in a goddamn gravel pit near Memphis and the Roadrunner sunk in a ditch. I been callin her house all mornin, but there isn't anyone there. I don't want to leave or call anyone else in case she calls here. His voice is frantic, coming at an unnatural speed so it's hard to hear him.

Then he tells me he could barely walk home. Calley Pearl was driving by all liquored up and out on probation. He helped get the Roadrunner back on the road.

My brothers were out till dawn, looking for me, Riley tells me. They're here now, pacing this house, wanting to kill the boys who did it, mad as hell I won't tell the particulars. But I'm not sayin a goddamn thing until I know she's safe.

Out the window the sun beats in a punishing way. A clock ticks in the hallway so I think I could rip it out of the wall for how constant it is. I say, Haley's asleep?

I haven't called her. Have her try to find out where Crystal is. Meet me at the river dam in two hours.

Haley's line rings and rings and finally Gwyneth answers. Good morning ma'am, this is Fletcher Greel, can I please talk to Haley?

Haley's sleepin, honey.

I know it ma'am, but this is a kind of emergency.

There is a long pause.

Sweetie, she's had a rough night. Is this a love emergency or a real emergency?

Her friend Riley's in trouble.

The phone drops and I hear Gwyneth say, Gypsy, go wake up Haley, she's got a phone call. Just do it, sugar, she can sleep later. She's got a best friend she'd never do without and seems he needs her.

Waiting for Haley to pick up that phone seems like a long, reckless eternity.

She says, I got it. Gwyneth clicks down.

Fletcher?

Haley, how you doin?

Haley begins to cry without stopping, trying to say something she can't get out. Finally she says, Don't leave me, Fletcher.

I wouldn't ever, Jesus, Haley. I close my eyes, my lids sting. Relief pours over me.

Then she says, You know how bad they did it to her?

Who? I ask.

Crystal called me last night. She had to sneak behind the night nurse to do it. She's in the hospital, Fletcher.

I stare at my thrown-back bedcovers while Haley tells me plain and clear what happened to Crystal. My mind goes numb. I find myself sitting on the floor of my bedroom, not saying a word.

Oh, Fletcher, someone's here, I gotta go, she says, I'll call you later. And then the phone goes dead. I sit there with it in my hand.

As soon as I hang up the phone, it rings again and Haley says, Fletcher don't ever tell what you saw in the woods. Promise me you won't say a thing.

Okay, I tell her, I won't.

Promise, she tells me.

I've promised before, I tell her, and I don't break them.

Riley has his back against the Roadrunner. His left eye's swelled to a slit and his mouth is swollen and warped like a fungus is growing there. He's got a cigarette in his hand. The end of it is long with ash waiting to drop.

How ya feelin, Riley? I ask.

He glances over at me. The left side of his face is beat so bad he looks deformed. I been a whole hell of a lot better'n this, Yankee.

The river rushes by and we listen to it.

He doesn't smoke, just leaves the cigarette hanging. Ash falls. Haley spoke to Crystal? he asks.

Yeah.

How'd she do that?

Crystal's in the hospital, Rile.

Riley flicks that ash. What the fuck did they do to her? His voice cracks. He wipes his forehead with the back of his palm.

I hesitate. She's going to be all right.

Aww come on . . . Riley's laugh is muffled and forced. I wince at it without meaning to. You think I'm stupid, Judge? Tell me how she is.

When I look up, Riley's watching me.

She's beat to hell, I tell him fast.

He stares straight ahead, then points his cigarette at me. I can hear a cry in his voice. You gotta straight shoot it with me, Judge, you tell me what they did.

I can't be the one to tell you Riley. She's gotta do it.

He flicks his cigarette and I watch it smolder against the dirt. Pacing back and forth in front of the car, he asks me three times how he can see her and is there a way and how can he, at least, talk to her. I say I don't know three times and then he leans against the car again and takes another smoke from his pocket. He puts it on the side of his mouth that isn't fat and lights it with his head tilted.

Maybe Haley can figure out a way to get a message to her if you want to talk to her, I say.

He shakes his head. Haley ain't figurin a goddamn thing unless her skin turns five times darker overnight. Now this happened, no white folks are gettin within five hundred yards of Crystal Nash.

I chew the side of my thumbnail and spit the dead skin away.

Quit eatin yourself, says Riley. You think they can do operations to reverse skin color? I could make myself a black man and love her in public till the cows come home. It is something Riley would usually say laughing, but today it sounds wrong and cruel.

He smokes and shift rocks with his feet. The day has turned overcast. Heat sits miserable and claustrophobic. I notice a coffee stain on my shirt.

You know what, Judge? It is the quietest I have ever heard Riley.

What's that? I ask him.

I'm gonna have to give her up. I'm gonna have to forget her. He looks in front of him at the trees surrounding us and not moving in the stilled air. He says, Now you tell me what happened to her. You tell me what they did. You have to do it, Judge. I gotta know.

I breathe in and out and wonder if the words will even come to me. I wonder if he can contain himself with the telling. If it was Haley and he wouldn't tell me, then I would drag it out of him. I would bare-fist him until he said uncle and mercy and until it spilled out onto the dirt so I could hold the truth of it and do with it what I had to.

You got to promise me one thing, though, Riley, I tell him.

What's that?

That whatever I tell you, you remember you aren't the cause of anyone being as messed up to her as they were.

Riley smokes. Finally he says, We aren't buddies so we can say bullshit into each other's ears.

Okay. I nod. Promises never been fair anyway. And then I say, quiet, They raped her.

29

HALEY

A handsome black man, broad across as the door frame, stands in front of Crystal's door. He's tight lipped with a gold cross around his neck. He says to me, You can't go by here.

Above him is a row of numbers. Six is blinking. Some patient has pressed that call button. I know this from when Gwyneth was in.

I am wanting to see Crystal a minute, I say, trying to make it firm so he knows I won't go away.

I know it, he says, I heard you at the nurse's station and I'm tellin you, we don't want you in there. He looks at me with his deep brown eyes and shakes his head no.

Patients in wheelchairs roll past us with their IV poles behind them.

I look down at his dirt-creased boots and stay still. Nausea makes my head hurt, and I'm so tired my body is weak just standing there. I think she'd want to see me, I start to say.

Now why don't you git along there—

I look up at him. He breathes through his nose and his nostrils flair. His lips barely move when he says, again, Git.

I say, level, Sir, I'm not an animal to git anywhere. I'm a friend of Crystal's, and I care what happened to her, and I want to say that to her, so she has a mind to get better.

He nods slow and turns his head slightly so he is glancing down his side at me. What reason you have to make you think she don't want to get better without you?

Someone in the room calls, Uncle Marcus, you comin in here? The voice sounds like Crystal's but it's higher.

Uncle Marcus throws over his shoulder, In a minute. His eyes stay narrowed at me.

A woman comes beside him with her hair in tiny braids and eyes a deeper black and larger than Crystal's. When she sees me, all the smile drains from her and her mouth gets tight.

Uncle Marcus turns to look at her and says softly, I'm takin care of this, you go back to care for our patient. She backs away, stays looking at me for some seconds, then turns and disappears around a curtain, where low voices resume. I strain to hear the sound of Crystal's. But I can't hear it.

Crossing his arms over his chest, Uncle Marcus sighs. He looks above my head at a spot somewhere behind me. How long you gonna make me stand here tellin you? he asks. His gaze comes back and rests on my eyes. I see a flicker of something gentle there.

I swallow. I'm sorry, I tell him. His chin lowers a little. I am sorry about what happened to her. I can't imagine it. I look at my bitten-down nails, filled with dirt from the stables. But I got a daddy, I tell him. I breathe in a chopped sigh that holds a waiting cry. And my daddy's got friends, and they're mean as the devil if somethin crosses them the wrong way.

When I look up at him, he is frowning and staring down at me hard. And listening.

Some of his friends aren't even nice to each other's kin, I say, quick, not figuring what words will come next. Sometimes they aren't even nice to each other, I tell him. Behind one another's backs they do whatever they please. They don't care whose harm it's to. They become animals and bein that way they could make you an animal too, just survivin. I think it's what got Crystal, that nastiness.

He looks me up and down and shakes his head slowly and says, I'm sorry for you, white girl . . . I'm sorry for us all.

I can see he isn't moving and won't budge until I leave, so I nod, raise a hand to wave at him and turn down the hall without looking back. I round the corner at the end of it.

The nurses at the front station glance at me. I go into a small closet with a telephone in it, and sit on the black seat. After I close the door, my forehead beads sweat. I put my face in my hands. I think of Crystal singing up onstage at the blues fest in July and I remember how she kissed Riley's fingers when she sat between his legs at Daddy's barn with a beer between her legs. I think of all those times Crystal and I were alone together in her room when I used to bring her notes from Riley right after they chased them from the Jitney. When I look up, my vision's blurry and I squeeze my eyes shut for some time before I open them again and stare at the phone. I want to pick it up and tell Crystal in a truthful way what I feel for her, that she is the strongest girl I know with a soul that can't quit. I want to say that I learned love from her and Riley and she isn't what they made her think she was last night. I know I could sit there for one long eternity, but I might never be able to say good-bye to her like I want to. I figure I will wait there for as long as I have to until I think it is safe to call the hospital's number and ask for her room. I'll just pray as hard as I can that it is Crystal who answers and not some person who doesn't understand.

30

FLETCHER

Riley's got his eyes closed and I'm in the driver's seat steering the Roadrunner past Old Willow Corner, down the dusty part east of the river where the water runs shallow and muddy. The fuzz floats around like mucus and the fish there are worse than seldom because the water's too hot to hold them.

Riley's got his elbow on the window and a cigarette burned almost to the quick. His hair's back in a ponytail, tangled up like wire, and he isn't speaking. We push fifty and he says, Go on a little faster, Judge, I could run this piece blindfolded on acid and no piggies would come out here.

So I push it up to seventy and the road seems to fall apart behind us. We about need the wipers to get the dusted grit off the front window.

He isn't telling me where we're going, and I need to go see about Haley soon as I can, but Riley's quiet is like a stamp of shut-up, so I don't say anything. The wind tears around the Roadrunner and pulls our hair every which way. We're driving with only a half-good muffler and still Riley's silence is louder than any of that. He flicks his cigarette out the window and runs his fingers down his ponytail as the car screeches past Max's Fish and Game. Finally when we're out into a stretch of farmland, Riley says, Slow down, I see a cop car up yonder. I ease my feet from the gas pedal. The engine quiets. We roll past the cop doing a mild fifty. Riley doesn't even look his way. We stay at fifty for a good ten miles before Riley breaks his silence. In a low voice he says, You got to get to her,

Judge, talk to her and ask her what she wants me to do about this. I won't do anything till you tell me what she says.

I nod my head, but Riley isn't looking at me. He's looking over at a field of blooming cotton. This can't be fixed, he says, as if he's talking to himself. Ain't none of it never gonna be fixed.

I would take a gamble that Riley White is crying, so I don't look at him again, I keep my eyes on the blacktop and the hot gray horizon in front of us and drive steady as I can until we come to the East Neigh intersection, where I roll to a stop. The Roadrunner grumbles beneath us.

Riley faces front and clears his throat. Take a left here, Yankee. He pats himself for another smoke.

I keep my foot on the brake. Clouds move in swollen hoards above us, dark and heavy with coming rain. My hand stays on the vibrating gearshift. Out of my side vision I see Riley shake a smooshed pack of Camels and fish out a bent one. He puts it in his mouth and pushes in the lighter. Then he leans on his elbow and looks out the car window again. Drive, Judge.

I run my hands over the steering wheel and take a breath in. I'm not havin you go to East Neigh today, Riley, it's like a suicide.

The lighter shoves out. Riley grabs it, inhales, puts it back and looks at the burning end of his cigarette. This pack's been damp, he says. Wrinkled as an old lady ain't it? He points it toward me. Dried-out, once-damp cigarette, says Riley, better'n none at all.

My jaw clenches and my legs shift from the heat of the vinyl.

C'mon, Judge, Riley says in almost a menacing tone, I'm not goin to her house, they're all at the hospital. I want to get my goddamn hair cut, is all, and I can't do it at Spier's shop, his voice rises, cause they'll all be privy to what happened. Those fools ain't bright enough to know who to blame, and I'm not gonna answer to anyone, especially bigots. Some of em my own flesh and blood. He kicks the dash in front of him and the glove pops open. I jump in my seat without wanting to and Riley moves forward to slam it shut. Then he leans back, shuts his eyes and breathes best he can, his cigarette smoking between two fingers. East Neigh, he says in a tight, controlled voice, they always been nice to me. Every guy at Mamma Hatchey's been welcomin and every black boy I ever worked with I got along with. I don't see why they wouldn't give me a decent haircut on a day like today.

I swallow and shake my head slowly. I go because it is Riley's car and Riley's the one beat up, and I can't say no. Putting my foot on the accelerator, I turn left down the hill past the garbage lot to the first streetlight in East Neigh, where baseball-capped black boys lean against the telephone poles with Coke bottles in their hands and rake their eyes over us. One sits on a metal milk crate and nods his head when we go buy. He's sucking a lollipop and his mouth goes into a loose frown when we pass.

Riley says to me, Keep going. He directs me through four blocks of houses until I know we are on Crystal's street because of the pink one on the corner. A man sits on the porch of the pink house with a huge square Band-Aid over one eye. You boys lost? he calls.

Riley shakes his head and tells me keep driving.

I watch the Band-Aided man look after us. My eyelids are sticky with sweat and my stomach spits wet and the insides of my elbows are damp. I don't know how much the people in this neighborhood talk to one another, but it couldn't be hard to know that the Nash girl was in a bright red convertible with a boy in a ponytail when she got hurt like she did.

As if he's listening in on my thoughts, Riley says, Just drive.

When we get to her house, his face sets like a stone wall. Around his eyes and lips a white color comes and the rest of his coloring goes a deep red. Once we pass it, his body looses itself, and he breathes out.

The barbershop sits next to the town hall. It's a one-floor brick building with two windows in the front and a cement block for a porch. An American flag with a tear in it hangs limply out front. We park and Riley climbs up to sit on the passenger windowsill for some seconds watching the street, then he hops down. I come out the driver's-side door and wait on him to lead in.

The prestorm air sits on us like a fat man. It's almost tough to move through. The red, white and blue of the barbershop sign goes around so slow in its circle, it looks broken. There's a black-painted sign on the door that reads *Praise the Lord for those who don't buy on credit. God loves a man who pays on time. Bless you for not asking. If you want your hair buzzed, you best be the man who works for his living.*

Riley stubs out his cigarette with his shoe toe on the cement and says, Here goes nothin.

Maybe this is a bad idea, I tell him.

He reaches for the door, holds the handle a second and without looking at me says, It was a bad idea a long time ago, Judge, but there ain't no turnin back now. He takes his hand back and rips a dirty elastic out of his hair. It looks silky as a woman's. He runs a hand through it, bunches it in his fingers and brings it around to his mouth, to kiss it. You can't wear yourself on the outside, Judge, they'll kill you for it. And that ain't how I aim to go.

Then he pulls the door open, steps in and nods to me that I should follow.

The floor of the shop is a dull mustard color. There are three barber chairs, but none are being used. The barber's got Scotch-taped glasses and white hair, his scissors are in the back pocket of his denims and he has an afro to beat a bird's nest. He flaps down his newspaper and stares at us.

Riley blinks rapidly and feels in his front pocket as if for change. I stand flat-footed with my heels burning in my shoes.

There's a guy leaning against the far wall eating a doughnut and two men playing dominoes off an old suitcase in the back of the room. They watch us as if we were walking dead. Ceiling fans beat out a fast rhythm, and no one moves.

Finally Riley says, Y'all cut white boys' hair, too?

Eyes flicker and feet change weight from one side to the other. Then there is laughter as if someone opened up a can of it and let loose. The room fills with it. The fat one eating a doughnut raises a hand and says, Welcome home, brother.

The barber says, Sit down boy, course we do, course we do. He points to one of the barber chairs. Then he nods to me and says, Sit where you want. There's doughnuts in the back and some coffee. Merry Christmas, he says and smiles wide.

Riley sits down and the man puts a smock around him. He pumps up the chair, but as he does it, a frown takes hold of his face. He picks Riley's hair up, looks at it uncertainly. You don't want to cut off this here head a hair, do you now mister? It's a mighty fine ornament and it must a takin a whole heap a time to grow.

Riley looks at himself in the mirror. For a minute I think he's going to change his mind. Instead he says, Let me just do this. He spins the chair around so he isn't facing himself anymore. Then he says, Don't take your time.

The barber shrugs, wipes his sheers on his denims and begins to cut. He doesn't bother to wet Riley's hair or comb it. He goes at it with the relish of a man just new to pruning sheers. I stand stunned at the doorway and the men stop their doughnut eating and domino playing to watch with me as Riley's hair drops to the floor in curved softness, revealing his long, pale neck. The more the man cuts, the more Riley's face starts to look thin and bloodless, exposed.

I wish I could tell the men to make him come to his senses, explain to them that this isn't at all what Riley looks like. I want to turn him around so he has to witness himself in this new, dull way. Maybe the barber'd be able to fix it somehow.

Only I have a feeling it wouldn't matter to Riley. That very little could matter. The barber keeps cutting his hair like my mother used to clip dill into her salads, carelessly and happily, without much forethought at all.

31

HALEY

The pig gets turned over an open fire. The skin bubbles and its mouth is forced open with a stick. Its hooves blacken. Every August, Houser Banks has an end-of-the-summer pig roast at the mayor's house. For as long as I can remember, I've watched the pure, flat, pink flank go to crusted brown meat. It's the last hot kickoff before school begins again.

I am standing on the edge of the yard in the shadows when Bo comes over the crest of the hill next to the mayor's house. He's wearing blue jeans, a black T-shirt and his straw cowboy hat. His eyes run over the kids and the picnic tables. He nods to people and they nod back, but no one comes up to him. Then he sees me. He stares at me. I make myself look back at the fire. Five children are holding hands, running in a circle next to the burning pig. Out of the corner of my eye, I watch him walking toward me. He's unshaved and his shoulders are hunched. When there are a few feet between us, he stomps his cigarette out and comes to stand beside me. Wiping his jaw with a shaking hand, he says, I want to talk to you.

Talk then, I tell him.

Away from here.

Bo, I say quietly, I don't have a thing to say to you.

He looks sideways at me. You told him, he says.

When I don't answer, Bo says, Haley look at me. I turn my eyes to him but I don't look for long. Didn't you? He touches my arm. I jerk it back. Listen to me, Haley, that man is angrier than hellfire, and I need to know what all you went and said. There's a choke to his voice. I'm not runnin from anyone buried, he says. I don't got a problem with that. But as for you and me, you need to come and talk to me so we can decide what's for the saying and what's not.

The flames of the fire are high now and the pig sizzles to burning.

I can decide what's for the saying, I tell him softly. I guess I don't need your help. Then I turn to Bo Dickens and look him full in the face. I watch his gray eyes and let myself look at his deep red mouth and the edges of his black curly hair going silver. I need you to get away from me, I tell him. I pick up one finger. I can give you to the count of three and then if you don't leave I'm going to holler so loud, the whole town'll come runnin.

Bo shakes his head. Don't you do this to me, little lady. He looks panicked and sick with himself.

I can feel my throat close up from something like fear. I raise my second finger. I've got to, I tell him.

Bo's nostrils flare. I loved you . . . he says. I—

But I pick up my third finger, take a breath in and open my mouth. Bo starts to back away. Three, I say quietly. And then he turns and I watch him go from the shadows into the light of the fire. He walks up the hill past the children and the mayor and Billy and Elsa without looking back.

As he climbs the hill, I think of what it was like the first time he came to me right after the burying, when the whole thing was most of all exciting. I didn't feel like a little girl anymore with Bo touching me, and I had a secret bigger than Daddy would ever know and that made me feel I could own the world.

I also remember a day a long time ago when I went into Elsa's basement. Daddy'd left his jacket there, and I went to pick it up. Elsa's was a place I wasn't allowed to go in much. It seemed always to be full of magic. That day all the overheads were on and the sun was streaming in the square, grime-streaked windows. It was that same room, but in the daylight it looked entirely different, sad and small. I could see how dirty it was and it smelled of touched money and sweat. The thought comes to me that this is what has happened with me and Bo. Someone has turned the lights on, and I am seeing all of him for the first time.

When he gets to the top of the hill, he turns and looks back at me. We don't smile. His jaw is rigid and his mouth is turned up slightly on one side. He turns and disappears down the other side.

I am still shaking a long time later when Fletcher and his daddy come walking down from the mayor's porch. The judge stops at the picnic table to talk with Mrs. Whitaker. Fletcher keeps walking. It doesn't take him two seconds to find me. He comes through the smoke without looking around. When he gets to me, he puts his hands around my waist and says hoarsely, Hey Haley.

People glance at us. I close my eyes and lean my head on his shoulder. His hair's still wet from his shower, and he smells starched and clean.

You okay? he asks.

I nod.

Your daddy okay?

I shrug. I bite the neck of his T-shirt collar so the tears stay away.

He strokes my back. They'll know the truth, Haley, whatever it is.

Over his shoulder I watch the people milling around. They've been stealing looks at me the evening through. What if— I start to say.

But Fletcher tells me there isn't any what if.

His father is watching us from that place on the hill. I have to get out of here, I tell Fletcher.

Let me come with you.

No, come to the barn tomorrow night at nine. I'll spend the night with you there. We can say good-bye right. Tonight I told Gwyn I would help her pack and stay at the house with her.

Fletcher studies me a long while. You goin somewhere? he asks.

I don't know, I tell him. I'm not sure what's happening. I grasp on to his neck tight as I can.

And then he kisses me. All right, he tells me, it's okay.

Johnny Cash sings *I Walk the Line* loud out the cassette player in the Ford. I drive fast as I can down Highway 12 all the way to the stables. The light is on in Stony's apartment. Di sticks her head out the upper window. Who's that? she asks.

It's Haley, I tell her.

Okay, girl, she says softly, Daisy's in her stall, where she'll always be.

Daisy smells of dust and lather. When I lay my cheek against her, she whinnies and stomps her feet with want for ride.

Be still, girl, I tell her.

She is.

I lean against her mane. Gwyn and I are goin away for a time, I tell her. Her ears prick back. Stony and Di will take good care of you, and I'll be back to get you. I promise. I love you so much, I don't know what all I'd have done without you.

Daisy stands perfectly still except for her eyes, which blink every once and again. I think of how happy I was when Daddy led her into my yard on my twelfth birthday. I close my eyes and try to remember every single time I've ridden her through the wood in cantor and gallop on days when there wasn't anyone else I wanted to be with in the whole world. I hold her muzzle in my hand and look into her eyes, staring at me like brown pools on either side of her head. I stroke her jaw.

Maybe Gwyn's baby was a kind of God, I tell her. She could see it all before it even happened and she opted out. I put my cheek next to Daisy's face. She saw what a mess it was and she just said, No thank you.

Daisy nuzzles at my neck, pushes her nose into me as if to comfort. Beautiful girl. I swallow and hold the tears back. Wait on me. And then I leave quickly, latching her stall behind me, jogging toward the end of the barn to the hung lead lines and the riding gear and the light switch, which I turn off so all goes dark. Before I close the big doors, I think I hear Daisy whinny. I run like wind to the Ford, which is idling out front.

Gywneth's at home packing her American Tourister suitcase, with a cigarette burning in the ashtray and her cream-colored slip on. Crystal Gale's singing *Don't It Make My Brown Eyes Blue* on the record player. I lie down on the bed next to the suitcase and watch her. She throws in chenille scarves and silk nightgowns and a black-and-white of Daddy as a boy.

Can I see that? I ask her.

She hands it to me and goes into the bathroom.

In the picture, Daddy is standing against a split rail fence with a cigarette in one hand. A horse is galloping in the distance. Daddy's squinting at the camera with a hint of smile to him. The back says 1967.

I count the years in my mind. When she comes out of the bathroom, I say to Gwyn, He was my age when this picture was taken.

She throws a black satin makeup bag on top of the clothes. He was one year older, she tells me.

I look at Daddy's unlined face. His curly blond hair is longer than I've ever seen it. I put the picture on top of Gwyneth's bag and lean back on the pillow. She comes around and opens the bedside drawer, pulls a sleep mask out and throws it in with everything else.

What's gonna happen to Daddy, Miss Gwyneth? I ask.

Gwyn stops and looks down at me. She comes and sits on the edge of the bed and wipes a hair off my forehead. Her eyes stare into my own, and I get the feeling she is seeing right straight inside of me. And likes what's there. I put my forearm over my eyes so as not to cry.

Honey, I'm goin to tell you something I probably shouldn't. You need to understand your daddy better than ever right now, so I believe it's okay. Before you were born, your daddy killed a man by accident in a bar on Beale Street in Memphis, hit him over the head with a full-up bottle of bourbon and didn't anyone know who'd done it except for your daddy himself. That man was a mean, no-good drunk who didn't have any business being in public. When all those cowboys got to smashin chairs and bottles and themselves like men will, he came at your daddy with a knife blade big enough to slit a man's heart. That man would have just as soon killed your daddy for a dime and not felt a pinch of guilt. But your daddy has regretted liftin that bourbon bottle every minute of his life. Gwyneth pulls my arm from my eyes. You understand me?

I watch her with my breath stopped in my chest. Her cheeks have color high on them and her lips look white. It doesn't matter what Bo says to try and save himself, she says, your daddy didn't kill that man down in your livin room. He decided long ago he would be an honest man, and I don't care which jury they pick, how many black men and how many white women, Ire Ellyson is too smart and true not to get pulled out of this thing.

I am out of words, but Gwyn doesn't need me to talk. Her eyes narrow some and she says, Bo Dickens is a no-good racist, women-hating pig with a mean streak longer than an L.A. highway. She puts her pointer finger on my chin and says, I know what he was to you, sweetheart. It isn't any of my business who you purse your lips to, but someday you might come to thinkin it's your fault. And I want to say right here and now while you have a mind to remember it, she says, leaning close to me, it's not your fault.

She sits up straight. Plain and simple as that, she says, brushing her hands across her lap, he used his manhood on a girl. Some men use women just to get power. She puts her hair behind her ear and tightens the diamond earring. It isn't important how, she says. They're just weak, is all. She looks down at me. You're the one with the power, and they need you for it. But baby, she says, shaking her elegant finger, you just take that power and you run from them.

I stare at her. She stares back, and her eyes get a little dreamy. Then she studies her nails, starts to push back her cuticles. In an altogether different voice she says, A jury is made up of people like you and me who aren't stupid and have a hard time getting fooled. If one gets fooled then the rest will sure set him right.

Miss Gwyneth, I say, Bo told me we were saving Daddy by not tellin him about the body. He told me no one would find it. I believed him. My voice comes out in a whisper. I shouldn't have believed him.

A small smile comes on Gwyn's face. You didn't have any other choice, she tells me. It's all you knew, baby doll.

I take a deep breath in and say, Does Daddy know?

About what Bo was to you?

I nod.

Gwyneth shakes her head. I don't think so, honey. She bends over and puts a cool kiss on my forehead. She says into my hairline, But your Auntie Gwyn was a girl once, too. Her breath is moist and warm on my head and she leaves her lips there for some time before she gets up and goes to her closet. I watch her pulling out clothes and throwing them in the direction of the suitcase.

Finally I say, Are they going to want me to testify?

She picks out her robe and folds it. You might have to come back and testify, honey, I don't know. What you know is hearsay. She turns from her closet and looks at me. You didn't see that man get killed, she asks quietly, did you?

I told Daddy the truth, I say. I heard a shot. Then I came downstairs and Daddy was passed out and that dead man was on the floor and Bo was standing there.

Gwyneth looks at me for a long time. One eye travels away from me. She looks at the floor and says, I heard a shot, too. But I just stayed put in bed.

She turns from me and goes back to the closet. Bo didn't frame your daddy, she says with her back turned, and he could have, he very well could have. She lifts a shoe box from the top shelf, and I see the strength of her calves when she stands on her tippy toes.

32

FLETCHER

I'm home by eight thirty, in time for work. I make my way up the back stairs, sit on my bed and stare at the room around me. The house is silent. Pops is at the courthouse. I lie down without taking my shoes off and think how I'm too tired to go to the courthouse even though I didn't go Monday, either, on account of Riley's haircutting. I believe Pops will understand. The sun's beating in through my window. The air-conditioning in the corner wafts out cool air. Haley and I didn't sleep at all, but when I close my eyes sleep doesn't come now, either. Instead, there's the image of her and of the barn that smelled of her and of the horses and the damp wood walls.

She was in the loft already, when I got there, leaning against a hay bale. I climbed the ladder and went to her and hugged her around the middle so my face was in her neck. She said, I can't ever remember not loving you. There was a sob in her throat, and she held my hair like it was the mane of a horse, wild beneath her. She whispered into it, I can't let go.

I told her not to.

For a long time we lay like that. She smelled of the jasmine oil I'd bought her from Rose's store for $22 an ounce. Rose had wrapped it in folds of black velvet and through the summer I watched Haley when she dipped it on the softest spots of her body.

Out the barn window, the night came deep blue and the trees were silhouetted skeletons of dark. She said that time of night when the sun first went down always made her sad. I told her I was sad all over with any time of day right now. I asked her if she would come with me if I decided not to go up north, could we go somewhere else for a time and make a life where all this wasn't happening? I told her I couldn't live without her, I wished I could, but I didn't think there was any way. I said I wanted to be with her in the same way you want something you could never have, to live in another age or to be born a different type of person, and that I believed if we left each other now, I would be hungry for her for the rest of my life. Death might be a little welcome for it.

She waited for a long time before she said, College will be wantin you. It'll be waitin on you and if you don't go now, then in years to come you'll wish you took it.

I told her it was the other way around, years from now I would be wishing I stayed with her.

She said she had to leave with Gwyneth. If she didn't, then it would somehow mean losing her daddy. But in all the world she would love only me.

I didn't speak because I felt an emptiness down in me where my organs live. Outside the sky went from a turquoise to a deep black.

Maybe love is smart, Haley said, maybe it will find us again. I could feel her crying. She pounded her fists dully against my chest and then the punches got harder and faster. Her rings hurt my skin. Later those spots would turn into tiny yellow bruises that I'd wish wouldn't ever go away so I could remember where she had touched me. Finally I gripped her wrists so her hands beat air, and I held her rigid body steady as I could. She was hard to hold, like an untamed, defending animal would be hard to hold. While she cried, she said, I wish, I wish, I wish, but they weren't the beginnings of anything she could finish, and she went limp against me. She said she wanted to say words to me, but they were words people had said to each other forever and she didn't want to say anything that anyone had ever heard before.

Then she said, It wasn't my daddy who killed that man.

I told her if she said it then it was true.

She told me she was afraid the truth of what happened wouldn't be replayed right in the ruined telling of it in a courtroom.

Who was it? I asked her. I kept my breath as still as I could while I waited for her to answer. Outside and far away, we heard cars coming and going on Highway 12, the sound reaching us and then falling back. She leaned her head farther into my chest, trailed her hand under my shirt and over my stomach. The hand felt moist and her breath came shaky.

And then she spoke of Bo Dickens.

She said how it had begun and how it had kept on. The times she had been with him and what it had felt like for her. She told me it had started to happen before she came to know me and she said it wouldn't have happened if she had known me all along. She explained that the secret of him and the murder were one thing to her. It was hard to separate them. She spoke in a pleading voice, telling me she didn't love him, she had come to hate him. She would lie in bed at night wishing he wouldn't come to her but then in a small space still waiting for it. She knew it was not good.

While she spoke, my body went cold, and I started to shake. I began to have a terrible thought that I had only half known Haley. I had been fooled into imagining she had let me in all the way. She had been thinking of herself and Bo at times when I was thinking of only her. Though I hadn't ever met this man, I imagined all the hell I'd like to place him in, how much I wanted to see him hurt and tortured and crying out sorrys for hours on end.

The feeling scared me.

She looked up and brushed my hair from my eyes while I stared at the ceiling rafters. Then she kissed my neck and buried her face there.

She said, I'm afraid what happened between me and Bo will make you hate me. I love you, she told me, and I didn't ever love him. You can't call it by the same name, what it was with him and what it is with you.

For a long time I didn't say anything. I closed my eyes and listened to the ringing in my ears and to Haley saying, Please Fletcher. Her voice seemed far away. My body was rigid beside hers, and as much as I tried to relax it, I could not.

Finally, though, I needed to be with Haley this last night. I told myself she had loved me as best she could. In the deepest part of me, I knew I had done nothing wrong in loving her.

I opened my eyes, kissed her head and left my mouth there until I could get my voice back. I am in love with you, I told her, and I won't ever stop. I said I didn't want Bo Dickens to have anything to do with what we were to each other and that nothing could stain what we had, but I couldn't be held responsible for what I would do if I ever had to stand in the same room with him. I hoped that wouldn't ever happen. I explained I was being as honest as I could, and I wasn't meaning to scare her any by saying it.

When she asked me if I really could forgive her, I turned to her and held her face in my hands and gently kissed her eyelids and her tears, her neck and the palms of her hands. I kissed her shoulders, the insides of her elbows, the back of her knees. I took off her sandals and rubbed and kissed the arches of her feet. Then I came up and lay beside her. I held her as tight as I could without hurting her while the birds flapped their wings in the rafters and mice ran the insides of the walls and stars went bright outside the barn window. When I did it, she said I love you so many times it began to sound familiar as my own name.

33

HALEY

Fletcher and I didn't sleep but a few hours in the barn and my body is exhausted, but around dawn I leave the barn so I can go visit Daddy.

He is leaning over the lime green counter in county, waiting for me when I come in. I sit across from him. We tell each other good morning like two strangers. Sheriff Hill stands in the corner with his arms folded in front of him, trying to give us space.

Daddy wipes thirsty white saliva off the sides of his mouth. Did you see Daisy? he asks me.

Yes.

He nods. Di will ride her, he says.

I bend down and put my face on the counter. Exhaling deeply, I feel the moist of my own breath. I think of what Gwyn said about Daddy and that man in the bar on Beale Street and it makes me more tired than I was.

Daddy places a palm on my head. It's warm. Turnip, we're gonna make this right, you'll see. You go with Gwyn now, I'll come find you in Salinas when it's all over. Hey, he says, pick your face up and look at me.

Daddy's jaw is shaved. There's a knick on his left cheek and the scar over his right eyelid looks darker today. The whites of his eyes are red.

Daddy, I'm sorry.

No, he says, I should have loved you better, I should have told you— His eyes fill up, he wipes the tears away as if he's angry at them. Listen

Haley, over my dead body will anything happen to you, and I ain't a man for dyin.

His chin trembles and for one horrible second I have the feeling that he will start to cry, really sob, and I won't be able to handle it. I want to say aloud, Don't let this happen now, please don't make me watch you.

Then suddenly Daddy does his best smile. It appears on the left side of his mouth. He reaches out and gathers my fingers in his. We hold on to each other's hands so tightly the knuckles go white and the fingertips turn red.

Our hearts beat there.

34

FLETCHER

The Friday before Labor Day, I go in the courthouse, upstairs to Pops's office. He is sitting at his desk with a pile of paperwork in front of him.

Hello there, he says.

Hi Pops. I came in to say good-bye to the girls in the office.

I'm glad, he tells me. He takes off his glasses and gestures to the door. Close that shut, will you, Fletcher?

I do this and come to sit in front of his desk.

The girls'll be glad to see you, he says. They loved having you here. Did you have the White boy take a look at the Honda?

It's all set to go, I tell him.

He nods. I got you a Triple A card, it's on the counter in the kitchen.

Thank you, I tell him, thanks a lot. I look at the calendar behind him. Three more yellow crosses are on it. He follows my gaze and shakes his head. Your old judge of a father'll be here when you come back, he says, smiling, if you ever want to.

I look down at my hands.

You were a hard worker, son. He sets his glasses on the desk in front of him. It wasn't an easy summer. I had the selfish want to see your face every minute to keep from going flat-out insane.

It takes me a long time to look up at him. When I do, he's smiling at me. He says, I didn't do it so you could follow in my footsteps, you know.

I'll tell you a secret, you can get damned tired of having to decide theory versus person. When the time comes, you'll have to choose whether or not you want a career like that. I used to think a boy with your sensitivity, brains and power of observation would be good for law, but I don't think anymore that anyone should be good for his career. Life's too short. A man's career should be good for him. I'm glad you are taking some time off. In some ways I wish I'd done that.

I nod, and watch the glint of his wedding ring.

He stands suddenly, and I stand with him.

You'll figure it out, though, he says, plenty of years ahead for that. He comes around the side of the desk and we hug awkwardly. He pats my back three times and looses from me. We stand there staring at the bookshelves.

She gone? he asks me.

Yes.

He nods. Well, she may have to come back to testify. He pats my shoulder. She'll be back. Not many people leave Houser Banks without returning. Wiping a hand over his jaw, he says, I know you loved her, son. I know love when I see it, this old man's not daft. I'm glad you got as much time with her this summer as you did, and I wish it could have been more. She woke you right up. That's what a good woman can do, wake you up. He goes back behind his desk and shuffles some papers around.

I watch him. I want to say more, to talk about Haley, but I don't know how to do it, so I say, I guess I better go downstairs.

He nods. I'll tell Robin you said good-bye. My schedule was clear, I have some paperwork to do, so I thought I'd give her the day off. Julian told me he wasn't feeling well, so he isn't here either. Pops takes off his glasses and rubs the lenses on his shirt. I guess they're probably spending the day together. He clears his throat. Will you be at the house tonight? I've asked Shelby to cook a nice meal this evening, your last night and all.

I'll be there, I tell him. I just have one last person to see this afternoon.

Pops smiles. Okay, he says, fine.

When I open the door, I turn around and look at him. His head is bent over his desk and he's scribbling something on a legal pad. Pops, I say.

He looks up.

Thanks a whole lot, I tell him, for everything.

No thanks required, he tells me, and for a minute my father looks young again. The lines disappear from his forehead and his eyes clear. I stay this image in my mind and head down that winding staircase toward the women in the front office.

Don't you bring Riley, Crystal had said on the phone. You know they'll do him harm if ever again—

I know it, I told her, I wouldn't do that.

Don't tell him till after you come, either, because he might be stubborn, if I know Riley, if he still—

He still does, I told her.

I meet her at three o'clock in a piece of park near the river where giant oaks have grown up in a cluster. We hide in the middle of them. She's sitting on a paint-peeled picnic table. Between the tree limbs, we can catch glimpses of the playground. I take the orange she's peeling out of her hand and say, Let me do that for you.

A leaf falls past us. She wipes her hands on her shorts and puts her fingers on her eyelids.

We are silent. The orange peel comes off in hunks and drops on the dirt.

She says, What are you gonna do now, Fletcher Greel?

I'm going cross-country in the Honda. I was trying to get Riley to come with me. But he says he can't leave. I'm gonna do some camping, check things out I haven't ever seen before. I don't want to go right to school, I say, and then I go quiet. There aren't any words to tell her how much I feel like I don't belong anywhere.

Crystal watches my hands on the orange and then she looks up at me. You gonna go find her?

I kick away the peels at my feet and tell her I might.

She is a girl like no other, says Crystal.

I tell her I know it.

They're sending me up north, she says, to skip senior year and go to college early. She bites her lip and watches the playground. Kids' screams come from there. Bored black women sit on the benches watching their children swing and slide.

I'm goin to live with my aunt in Brooklyn, Crystal tells me, and go to Brooklyn College. Her mouth twitches while she talks. Riley would have left me anyway, she says.

Riley would never have done that, I tell her.

I start to ask her when she's leaving, but she interrupts me. I dropped charges today, Fletcher. I can't go through with it. She searches my eyes, and I have a feeling she is looking for blame. I try to show her only understanding. It's what I feel.

I look down and peel the orange smooth, pick out the small white pieces so she can have it as clean as possible, then I pull apart a section and hand it to her.

She licks the sides of it and looks at it. You and Riley are two of a kind, she says, the way you take care of people. She starts to bite into the orange and then she stops and looks up at me. You tell me how that boy is, she says.

He's done apart, Crystal, I tell her. From the way my words come out, I know I've wanted to say this to someone for a while now, but there wasn't anyone to say it to. He wants to go after them and his brothers want in on it, I say. But he won't tell anybody anything without your say-so. He told me to tell you he'd do anything you want.

Crystal shakes her head. Her eyes are red and watery. They'll kill him, she says. She brushes some fallen leaves off the table and sits there. You should tell him to get out of here. There isn't any conviction to her words. Riley out of Houser Banks, Mississippi, she says quietly. Just a fish out of water.

A breeze kicks up and blows the ends of her braids.

Crystal looks at me with her head tilted. Aw Fletcher, she says, it's my people as much as yours. You think we don't beat each other? You think we're not out there rapin women? We are. We don't have anyplace to fix blame, except that— Crystal sets the piece of orange on the table. The juice of the part I am holding runs down my arm. Well, I heard this black comedian once, says Crystal. I watch her try to smile, but her eyes stay sad. She says, He was makin fun of those white folks out in the boonies who hate blacks so bad, they rob themselves of time, just mouthin and hollerin away about them niggers and how they'd be takin the whole country away in a garbage truck if someone let them. This comedian was sayin, Why don't those white boys complain about the cow in their yard? That cow has a hell of a lot more to do with their lives than the black man does.

Crystal picks up the orange slice again and bites into it. She chews slowly. That's how it is, she says. Whites got control over the whole of it and so they don't have any right to be pissin and moanin and takin all their hate out on our bloodshed. They shouldn't have a bit of desire in them to do what they did to me and Riley. Crystal raises her chin and looks at me. They just stomped me down, she says. You know what it feels like?

A wash of sick fills me and I think of Hannaford or any of those red-necks with common names who helped themselves to Crystal Nash's insides that night. Crystal Nash. *Our* Crystal Nash. And all the while she was probably worried about Riley, lying in an open dirt patch, beat by the head of a dull hammer kept in his own glove compartment to start up his boat motor whenever he fished.

No, I don't know what it feels like, I tell her.

Her pupils have gone to giant jewels and she swallows many times. Well, she says, my taste is gone, Fletcher. If you put a dinner in front of me, cooked by the best cook in the South, I'd say it tastes like cardboard, and when I sing, it comes out thin as breeze, and when I look at my body, it makes me cry. I still got bruises.

Crystal is dry eyed. I have a selfish want for her to cry so I could go to her. I'd like to hold her and demand the pain to me, bury it down somewhere inside and let it live there for as long as it needs to until she's free of it.

While we stand watching each other, I realize she isn't Crystal anymore, her skin isn't shining, and her hair is dulled. Her lips are a brown color instead of that corral she used to wear on them. She's lost weight and she stands in a hunched way. Wasn't it just two weeks ago we were at the fair, dancing in back of the rocking mobile ride while the Beatles sang *I Want to Hold Your Hand* out the back speaker? Riley twirled Crystal around and Haley stood behind me, holding my waist. That's true love, Haley had said. You think we have that, Mr. Greel? I'd nodded my head yes and was plenty grateful to Haley for being there, since it can be a painful feeling to see two people so in love and not have anyone for yourself.

Before this, Crystal's whole body used to smile. Now she's a trembling girl with sorrow deep in her. Even though it makes me sad as hell to see her like this, I keep looking at her. I take in everything there is to see of her. While we stare and she tries not to cry, I study her from forehead to toe. Because I know I will have to bring it back to Riley. He will want me to say what color her dress was and if she wore her hair the same way she always did. He will want to know just how she bit into the orange, how her hand shook when she moved her hair to the side. And Riley will be able to tell if I forget one small word of our conversation. He will know all those things not told, like you know a thing is missing from your bedroom after being gone awhile, even if you aren't sure what it is exactly. He will know these things because he loves her and because of the way Riley and I see through each other now, like brothers.

Crystal keeps her eyes on mine, then she gets off the picnic table and walks over to me. She stands not half a foot away, so close I can feel her breath and see how her eyelashes curve. Then she comes to me and falls into my chest. I put my arms around her, awkwardly at first, then tighter. Her arms are stronger than I thought they would be. I can feel the ribs through her dress. Her hands grasp my shirtfront like Haley's sometimes do, and I think she is crying, but when she speaks against my chest, it is a powerful voice full of will. Fletcher, she says, you get him to promise he won't fight violence with violence. I don't want it perpetuating, understand me? You got to make him swear on his love for me that he won't be jailbound because of some evil boys. They won't learn no matter who hurts them and what befalls em. You got to make him see that he needs to just leave it be. We are better than all that. Her voice trails off softly and she says, We are all just better than that.

Then Crystal starts to rock back and forth so slowly I barely notice she's doing it until my body is rocking with hers. I don't know how long I am there with her swaying back and forth to some silent music in her mind. All the while I wonder how Riley will take this news, what part of him will have to die in order for him to keep his word.

epilogue

FLETCHER

Pops told me the anniversary of my mother's death was one of the coldest days he'd seen in Mississippi's history. The wind blew fierce and leaves got pulled from the trees and flew all over our lawn. There wasn't a drop of rain, though.

We can only use one phone on the ranch. It's a pay phone out near the mess hall where the workers eat, and I had to try to concentrate hard on what Pops was saying because the men kept going by, tagging my hat and yelling, Hey Greel, come on in and eat, boy.

Pops said he hoped I didn't focus only on the sadness of her going. He explained death didn't have to be as scary now for a boy like me with a mamma already having gone through it. I put my head into the phone booth as far as I could and held my breath and squeezed my eyes shut so I wouldn't cry. I told Pops I was sorry I wasn't there with him. He said it was all right, that the easiest escape from grief was guilt, and I should try to rest easy when I went to sleep that night, not pile remorse over my bedcovers, or I'd get sick with no sleep, and a man hard-laboring horses like I was needed rest. Then we were quiet. Quite awhile later, it might have been a minute, it might have been five, he said, I'm proud of you, son. Real proud. Keep your chin up. Stay out of trouble unless you're bound to learn something from it. And then we hung up.

I wanted to talk to Riley after that, to hear the joke in his voice, the nicknamed way he had of talking. All last summer I'd prayed to the unfair

God who killed my mother that the summer of '87 wouldn't ever end. But it had ended. There wasn't anything left of it but the memories and I knew better than to push my luck with what was still living.

The day before I left I went to see Riley. He was still working the river dam. I needed to tell him what Crystal said and to ask him one more time if he would come with me.

Riley's hair had lost its goldenness in the cut and he looked suddenly too tall for himself. His left hipbone had been permanently splintered when he'd been beat up, and he walked with a limp so slight probably no one else but me noticed. In one hand he held a hard hat and in the other hand a cigarette. His legs shifted with the presence of me.

He'd listened carefully when I told him what Crystal had asked him to promise. He clamped his mouth shut and his eyes went to looking hard at nothing at all. Then he nodded. I could feel it was probably the toughest thing he had ever done. When he could finally speak, he said he would do anything she wanted. Anything. I should go back and tell her that.

He walked me to my car and I asked again, in the most casual way I knew how, if he wouldn't pack up his stuff and throw it in the back of my car that afternoon, start driving west with me. I told him we could take the Roadrunner if he wanted, and I'd pay for gas.

He smoked and looked back toward the river. He told me the Roadrunner probably wouldn't make it past Helena before it fell down on us. Then he told me he couldn't go. He had a hard time making eye contact with me when he said it. He just said, I can't, putting his arms out wide like he was encompassing all of what was around him. I can't leave here. It had a helpless sound to it.

He opened the Honda door for me, threw his cigarette on the ground and wiped his mouth with his sleeve. When I was settled in the driver's seat, he shut the door and leaned in the window. Hey Judge, he said, make sure you set that crazy world on fire.

There wasn't a joke to him.

I drove and camped for almost three weeks before I came to Montana. When I got out here and the forest fires were raging as if they'd never stop, I knew I had to stay on account of Riley's words to me. Most people were leaving because of those fires. I stuck around at a ranch that was badly in need of hands. They were surprised how fast I learned and said I had a natural affinity for it even though I'd only ever ridden in summer camp and that one ride with Haley.

I think of Riley a lot when I am leading trips of tourists through the four hundred acres that hold this ranch and these horses and cowboys. Everyone on the trips gets silent with reverence to the landscape. You take the noisest people and they get real quiet here. There isn't anything purposeful or worth saying in a place as grand as this one.

It took me a long time to understand what had really happened to him, why the flatness had come and why I couldn't ever bring myself to call him. He had gotten a piece torn out of him like when they rip out a piece of you they believe is riddled with cancer. But it wasn't any sickness. It was Crystal Nash. And maybe it was also the whole of the black community he loved so much. It was the thing that made him live and killed him, both. I imagine each night he laid his body lengthwise and thought of her before sleep found him, and it was his biggest respite, and the thing that left him feeling useless.

It must have taken a whole lot of courage to see those boys every day and not break his promise to her. It might have sapped him of most of his energy he used to have so much of. Riley loved Houser Banks. All he had ever wanted to do was make his own home bigger, widen it to include East Neigh and the souls of the people who lived there. He wanted harmony in that way unsung heroes want it. Most heroes are born of war.

Sometimes Crystal writes to me. She tells me she likes school. On Saturdays she teaches singing to kids in Washington Heights. I know she still thinks of Riley, that somewhere deep in her she is loyal to him. I can tell by the way she says things about her new life, almost like an apology. I only hope her memory of Riley isn't all mixed up in her mind with that terrible night and what happened to her. When we write, we don't speak of that night or that summer. It is too large for our pens and paper and the mail that carries it.

Montana has the biggest sky you could ever imagine, it goes on for miles. At sunset the horizon boils up and the earth looks like it is on fire. After dinner, I stand on the ridge and watch night come. I talk to my mother, tell her I like it here, that it is the wildest I've ever felt, riding a horse. I promise her I'll go to school when I've learned what I have to. And then I let myself think of Haley, of how I used to run my finger over the callused place between her thumb and pointer finger where she held horses' reins. Now my hands have that same callused part. Whenever Haley took her clothes off, I worked on memorizing the white pieces the sun hadn't ever gotten to. Now they are etched in my mind, solid as a real picture.

There isn't a time I saddle up that I don't think about Haley. She is to me the air I breathe, something I don't wallow in much anymore, but it keeps me with the living. She is also like a childhood you can't ever go back to.

Crystal told me she went out to California with Gwyneth. Her daddy met them there after he was acquitted. I haven't been there yet. I don't suppose I'll go. I believe the three of them must be trying to leave Houser Banks and that summer behind them as much as they can. I hope Gwyneth finally gets to have the baby she's been wanting.

I am pretty sure Haley is riding still, same as I am. They say the sky is just as big out there. Some say where it collides with the ocean, it goes on forever.

Acknowledgments

In gratitude, I would like to thank: Kasha Duffield Kingsbury, Jennifer Kingsbury Bogosian and Larry Kingsbury, who were there with me when it all began; Jan Frazier, for being the midwife of my writing; and all my fellow writers and cheerleaders in her groups; Jackie Vavra, Stacey Coleman Pope Sinclair, Tara Fleming and the WOTN; Angie, Kitty, Re, Janna, Liza, for the genius of their friendship; Patty Krasner, for being the lamplighter while we went spelunking through my soul; my muse, Peter Towle Jr., in whose arms this book was conceived; Ted and Elena Dodd and their creator's haven on Windmill Hill; Evie Lovett and Jeff Shumlin, for their friendship and undying generosity; Marshall and John, for the warmth and splendor of their hearth; Richard Epstein, who celebrated with me when the first draft was finally done; Ginger Williamson, for her eminent optimism; Ann Stokes and her dream of a Studio of Her Own; Drew McDowell, for his Missouri story; my SERVAS hosts for their kindness; Paige Adair and her family, for the moon pies and the view of wisteria out my Wetumpka window; Ole Miss, for the housing scholarship; Milly Moorhead, for her loveliness that first day in her gallery; Amos Harvey, my initiator in all things and the boy who shot at the street lamp to show me the moon; Johnny Little, fellow reader, lord of my summer abode, and partner in wild, necessary adventure; Lessie, Frank, Will and John Belk, on whose land I wrote this book and in whose presence I found readership and love; Scott Hooker, my first fishing partner; Ron Shapiro, Randy Yates, Jim Dees and Jamo, for the gift of their one-liners; JoAnn, Jere and, especially, Jeffrey Allen, for sharing their stories; Starla Barstow, Steve

Cheseborough and Caroline Bodley, for standing at the fringes with me and helping me see inside; Cynthia Shearer, in realizing it was just a matter of time; Robert Malone, for carving out a place in his heart and letting me rest there; Walter and Vivian, for the bounty around their long dining-room table; The Howorths and Square Books, for providing a pantheon of writers from whom to gain insight.

In mentorship, I would like to thank: Edie Meidav, for pointing me toward the yellow-brick road and envisaging for me what I could not; Larry Brown, for telling me to keep at it and showing me why it mattered; Robert Olmstead, for letting his writing be, finally, just for me in the letters that mile-marked my inspiration; Fred Leebron and Frank Conroy, in whose presence I took the first steps toward canning fantasy and engendering reality.

A huge thank you to Scribner and Gillian Blake, whose brilliance in editing polished these words, and to Rachel Sussman, for always seeming to be there.

I am exceptionally grateful to Alexis, Chuck, Liz and Kristin at Darhansoff, Verrill, Feldman. Especially to Leigh Feldman, whose over-joyed response and steadfast support tied a ribbon around my life. Special thanks goes to her son, Maxwell, for graciously waiting those extra hours to be born.